ALSO BY CLAYTON SMITH

Apocalypticon
Post-Apocalypticon
Broken World

Anomaly Flats
It Came From Anomaly Flats

Na Akua

Demon Zero
Scorched Earth
Shadow Realm

IF (Books 1 - 6)

Mabel Gray and the Wizard Who Swallowed the Sun

The Depths
Death and McCootie

Pants on Fire: A Collection of Lies

SLAUGHTERHOUSE RUN

Printed in the United States of America

First printing, 2024

ISBN 978-1-945747-10-6

Dapper Press

For Dave.

Thank you for giving your whole heart to these books and your real last name to one of its villains.

(Sorry I didn't ask permission for that last one.)

Don't get Slaughtered!

SLAUGHTERHOUSE RUN

CLAYTON SMITH

1.

Ben Fogelvee felt like shit.

He was in his fifth round of fever, and this one was on day eight. His face was hot, his head was on fire, and the rest of his body was cold as ice. His bones hurt from shivering and his stomach cramped from hours and hours of dry-heave retching, throwing up nothing but hot air and green bile. He hadn't eaten anything in the last few days except for a few strips of rabbit meat two nights before that he'd puked into his own lap because he was too tired to turn his head. His clothes were soaked with sweat. He was freezing. His skull was a sauna.

"Fucking kill me," he said out loud.

He looked around. He was alone in the train car.

"Hey!" he shouted toward the next car. "I said, 'kill me!'"

The door into the next car slid open. A girl peered out at him. She was tall and broad and might have passed for a grown adult, except her face was too round, her eyes were too wide, her curls were too blonde, and her cheeks were too pink. She wore glasses that had somehow managed to escape serious harm this far into the apocalypse, probably due to the sheer thickness of the lenses. She had once told Ben how old she thought she was, but he hadn't really been listening, because he never really listened to any of the Red Caps. Every time he got attached to one, they got a spear to the chest or their brains were eaten out by wolves or, in one particularly disappointing example, they accidentally tripped into a hungry badger's den and were never quite the same after. It was better not to get to know them, because if you got to know them, you were always the one who was asked to say a few words at their sad, embarrassing funerals. Ben hated making speeches.

He had the sense that the Red Cap staring out at him was fifteen, maybe, or sixteen at most. She seemed like a good kid. So Ben had remembered her name as a reward.

"Gabs. Kill me," he wheezed.

"For the eight hundredth time, it's Babs," she said, rolling her eyes. "And do you *actually* need something, or are you just looking for someone to swim in your swamp of self-pity?"

"It's not a swamp of self-pity!" Ben insisted, though to be honest, his body *did* feel pretty swampy. "It's a rock of resignation. Please join me on my rock of resignation and push me out of this speeding train."

Babs straightened the red cap on her head. It didn't fit quite right over her mop of curly hair. Sometimes she found things to clip it down with, but not today. "First of all, you're sitting at the steps. You're sitting *at* the steps. If you want off the train, you just have to lean a *super* little bit to your left."

"I have to be thrown," Ben glowered, "or else it's just sad."

"Secondly," Babs said, ignoring him, "the fog is so thick, Horace has us going, like, ten miles an hour, tops. You wouldn't die. You'd just get scraped up, and then you'd have one more thing to complain about."

"That's probably what he wants," called a voice behind Babs. Ben knew that voice. It was from the big dope, another young one, the boy with black hair and bad skin who looked like a cross between the X-Men's Blob and a Cabbage Patch doll.

"That's not what I want!" Ben shouted at the Cabbage Patch Blob over Babs' shoulder. "And you should treat the ill and infirm with kindness." He coughed violently into his arm. His sleeve came away covered in fresh green and yellow mucous. He held it up for Babs to see. "See?"

"I'll kill him," said the third Red Cap. She stared out at Ben from behind Babs and locked him in grip of her fire-black eyes. She pulled a Bowie knife from the sheath she wore at her hip. She put the point of the blade to her own chin and looked at Ben coldly. "A mercy killing."

Ben frowned. "Wait, no. Not you. You'd enjoy it too much."

"I'd enjoy it a lot," she confirmed.

Ben remembered her name. He remembered it because she was so scary. Even though she was just as young as the other two and five-feet-nothing, with bones as light and as hollow as a bird's, she was a terrifying creature. Her eyes were inkwells of darkness, and she very rarely blinked. Her skin was the color of moonbeams, and her hair was as raven-dark as her eyes. She spoke brutally with clipped and confident words. When they went out to hunt food, she was the one who would take down the animal.

Close-range weapons only. The knife was her favorite, but she was just as comfortable with a machete, a baton, a pair of brass knuckles. One time she'd brought down a mountain lion with just a length of fishing line. A grown-ass fucking *mountain lion*. She was fast as a hawk and as vicious as a bear. And the way she looked at him, he knew she could and would end his life as simply and cleanly as if he were any other animal. He'd never met anyone so casually soulless. Even Bloom, whom Ben considered to be pretty goddamn soulless, was at least a little showy about it. But not her.

Not Alice.

"Let's keep her and her knife away from me, okay, team?"

Babs snorted. "See? Told you it was self-pity." She slid the door shut, leaving Ben alone with his bad mood and fever once more.

"Stupid kids," he mumbled to himself. "No respect for their elders."

Ben looked around for Patrick. His fever-dream friend was appearing less and less often lately. Ben was starting to get the sense that even his own imagination was getting tired of his moping around. But what was he supposed to do about it? He was sick, he was *dying*—he was literally dying of the Green Flu—and no one cared enough about it to humor his every whim. *I'm going to come back and haunt them all*, Ben promised himself for the fifth time that day.

"If Patrick were here, he'd just make me angry," Ben decided aloud. "He'd make some joke about monkey soup and completely dismiss my suffering." He crossed his arms and closed his eyes. Being so obstinate for so many minutes straight had caused his head to throb even more, and he took some deep breaths and let himself feel the cool air of the Blue Ridge Mountains blow across his skin.

He should go easier on the Baby Caps, he knew. They didn't ask for this world any more than he did. They were kids. They were lonely. They were trying.

It wasn't their fault that Patrick was dead and that Ben was almost there too.

He just felt scared. Alone and scared.

"Ben!" Patrick shouted. "Beeeeen!"

Ben smiled. *Good timing, fever-brain.*

He opened his eyes. He expected Pat to be sitting across the coupler, or maybe poking his head out from the car behind him, the one that mostly served as Ben's private brooding space. But he wasn't. There was no one there.

Ben wrinkled his brow. "Pat?"

"Ben!" Patrick shouted again. "Ben, *stop!*"

3

Ben turned his head toward the voice. It was coming from outside the train. He struggled to crane his neck and peer over his shoulder, toward the rear of the train. Past the last car, maybe a hundred or so feet down the track, a shadowy figure with gangly arms and rubbery legs was running through the fog.

Ben frowned. "Patrick. Why are you off the train?" He'd never appeared so far away before. He was always right there. Right close. Sometimes too close. *Often* too close, in fact. Like the times he appeared when Ben was mid-evacuation. Patrick wasn't a hallucination that kept a distance. Ben slumped back against the cold metal wall, facing forward as the fog swirled by outside. He was no doctor, but he knew a significant change in hallucinatory behavior couldn't possibly be a good sign. "I'm near the end now," he said, really meaning it this time. "I can feel it. I can finally feel it."

"Ben!" shouted Patrick from behind the train. "Benny Boy! It's me!" His voice was strained and exhausted and desperate. That was different, too. He was normally a calm and collected hallucination.

"I hear you, I hear you," Ben said sadly. He stuck an arm out into the air and waved Patrick off. He coughed into his sleeve again. Blood and lime-green mucous spread across the cotton. "I barely even made it to the leaking part," he said miserably.

Though he guessed he should be grateful for that.

"Ben! Ben, it's me! Patrick! Ben, stop the train!"

Ben kicked out his foot and knocked against the next car. Babs reappeared and slid the door open. "What?"

"Get Horace, will you?"

"Why?"

"I need him to do last rites."

"Ben..." Babs said, rolling her eyes.

"No! Gabs. I'm serious."

"Babs."

"Whatever. No joke. It's happening. I can feel it. Get Horace. Please?"

"Can he even do last rites?" the Cabbage Patch Blob piped up from inside the car. "He's not a priest."

"He's a train captain," Ben pointed out. "He can marry people, so he can do last rites."

"I think that's boat captains," Cabbage Patch said.

"And you're not going to die," Babs assured him. "Not yet, anyway."

Ben leaned his head back and closed his eyes. He was so tired. "Tell them, Patrick," he mumbled.

"Ben! Beeeeeeen!"

Babs started. "What was that?"

"What was what?" Ben asked.

Babs stepped out into the coupling platform and cocked her head to listen.

"Benny Boy, stop!" called imaginary Patrick, sounding farther away than ever.

Babs stuck her head out of the train. "Did someone just call your name?"

Ben opened his eyes. He looked up at Babs. He blinked.

"What did you just say?"

"Please! Beeeeeeen!" Patrick was falling behind; the fog was swallowing him up.

"Someone's out there yelling your name," Babs said. "What the hell? Did we lose someone?"

Ben's eyes grew wide as hubcaps. He clamored to his feet. He gripped Babs on the shoulders and stared into her eyes. "Babs. Do *not* mess with me. Can you seriously hear that voice too?"

"Yes!" Babs said, exasperated. "I've been *saying* that I can hear that voice. I—" She stopped suddenly. She leaned forward and peered into the yellow-green cloud that was churning in the wake of the train. The fog blew away, and the figure emerged again, pumping its noodly arms and scrambling its awkward legs. "Do you *know* him?"

Ben whirled around and gaped at the form running through the mist. "Describe him to me."

"What?"

"Quick! Describe him to me!" Ben cried. "You see him, right? Who do you see?!"

"I don't know," Babs said, confused, squinting into the distance. "Tall-ish? Maybe a guy? Super skinny. Big head. I mean, *gigantic* head. God, how is he even running upright with a head that big?" she wondered.

Ben's heart stuttered. His legs melted, and he sank to his knees. His entire body flushed with chills, but not from the Green Fever.

He opened his mouth and screamed in a voice stronger than he'd heard from his own throat in years.

"PATRICK!"

"BEN!" Patrick screamed back, and now there was a strength in his voice, an iron that rose above the exhaustion, a joy that filled the world like a hot air balloon and rose and rose and rose until it pushed away the fog, and all they could see, at long last, after all these years, through life and death, from ends of the world and the depths of loss, unbelievably, was each other.

"Jesus!" Ben said through the tears he hadn't realized were now streaming down his cheeks. "Stop the train! Tell Horace to stop the train!"

"Ben, who *is* that?" Babs asked.

"Go tell Horace to stop the train!" he cried. "Please!" Babs nodded and ran through the door, heading toward the engine. Ben turned back to the flailing shadow running behind the train. "Patrick!" he screamed. "Patrick!"

"Ben! The train is so fast!" Patrick panted loudly.

"It's going slow!"

"It's fast for a person to run!" Patrick yelled.

"It's supposed to go faster than people!" Ben yelled back.

"I'm so tired!" Patrick cried.

"Hold on!" Ben threw a look down the train car and saw Babs disappear into the engine car. He popped back out and shouted, "Horace is going to stop the train!"

"Horace is still alive?!" Patrick shouted.

"I know, he's so small!" Ben shouted back.

"And has such a weird mustache, I didn't think—*yooof!*" He stepped into a gopher hole and bit the grass, hitting the earth hard and skidding across the loose gravel of the rail siding. "Owww…" he muttered into the ground. His bones were so tired. His legs were pudding. He decided not to get up just yet.

"Patrick!" Ben shrieked. Ben could feel the gentle lurch of the brakes gripping the wheels, and the train started to slow. Even so, it would take a while for the whole thing to come to a stop, and Patrick's crumpled body was slipping back into the Monkey fog. Soon he'd be hidden by the suffocating mist. "Absolutely not," Ben grumbled. He wiped his hands on his jeans and lined himself up to jump. He took some deep breaths. "We're going slow," he reminded himself. "We're going slow. We're going slow." But from up on the platform, even eight miles an hour seemed like a lightning pace.

Ben frowned. He glanced at Patrick. He was almost fully gone now.

"Ah, fuck it," Ben spat. He jumped.

His foot slipped on the metal and he flailed off the platform. His legs kicked up behind him and he slammed into the gravel siding chin-first. He skidded down the embankment, his flat body spinning across the rocks and grass like a starfish Frisbee. "Oww," he groaned.

He propped himself up on his elbows. He could just make out the shape of Patrick doing the same, far down the tracks. Ben struggled up onto his feet. Patrick did too. Ben's muscles were still aching with flu, and his legs didn't respond as well as he would have liked. He staggered forward, trying to keep his balance. Patrick's legs weren't any better, having run down the better part of the mountain, trying to catch the train. He wobbled in a wavy line as he stamped through the fog, toward Ben. But after a few steps, they both hit a rhythm, and then they were jogging, and then they were running. They collided into each other. Ben wrapped his arms around Patrick's ribs; Patrick held Ben like tendon grips bone.

"How the fuck are you here?" Ben asked, shaking with sobs.

Patrick laughed, streaming tears onto Ben's shoulder. "That…is a *real* long story."

"You were dead."

"I thought *you* were dead."

"I was fine."

"I was not."

"You died. At Disney World."

"I *almost* died at Disney World."

"You let me think you were dead."

"I thought I basically was."

"Jesus, Pat. I could kill you right now."

"I know, Ben. I know." He squeezed harder. "I could kill you too."

They stood like that for a few more moments, or maybe thirty seconds, or maybe five minutes, or maybe an hour, neither of them could tell. Finally, Patrick said, "Should I let you go now so we can be normal?"

"No," Ben said. "You should not."

Patrick smiled. "Okay."

2.

"Hey, Ben. Who's your weird friend?"

The train had ground to a stop a quarter mile down the tracks, and eventually Patrick and Ben had made it back on board. Ever since he'd climbed up into the old rust-routed, blood-stained Amtrak, Patrick had been shuffling around like a confused ghost, acting strangely. He touched a metal shelving unit and shuddered with a sigh of relief. He found an old lock box, one that looked familiar, and he touched his fingers to his chest, feeling the warmth of that lock box in his heart. He saw the grimy carpet and he knelt down onto it and stroked it lovingly, as if it were a long-lost pet.

"He's not my weird friend," Ben said uncertainly. "He's my normal friend."

The whole crew watched as Patrick walked up to the door of the long-defunct toilet. He rested his forehead against the nameplate that said "RESTROOM" and placed his palms flat against the dirty door. He burst into tears.

The crew turned back to Ben. They raised their eyebrows. "*That's* Patrick? *The* Patrick? The 'apocalypticon'?" Babs asked.

"He's…fine," Ben muttered. "Okay? Shut up. He's fine. Now, listen. Get out. Give us space," Ben grumbled at the Baby Caps. He herded them toward the door to the next car. "Go play your Tamagotchis or whatever."

"What's a Tamagotchi?" Cabbage Patch asked, confused.

"Some old person thing," Alice said.

"Out!" Ben shouted. The Baby Caps shuffled reluctantly out of the car, leaving Ben and Patrick alone with the conductors.

"Thanks for having me aboard, Horace," Patrick said, dabbing his eyes with his shirt. "I love what you've done with the place."

Horace beamed with pride. "Thank you! We've made some upgrades in the last few years. The cars are easier to uncouple. Simpler mechanisms there. That was Rogers' doing. That's Assistant Conductor Rogers over there—sorry…bad at introductions."

The man in the corner of the car raised his hand in greeting. "Heard a lot about you," he said. "You were strictly imaginary until just now. Sort of unsettling to learn you're real."

"Well, I knew the last Assistant Conductor on this train, so sort of unsettling for me to learn that position still exists!" Patrick said happily. "Please don't try to kill me."

"Rogers is a pacifist," Horace assured him. "Good mind for the train. He'll be a great replacement when I'm gone."

"Oh, stop—you'll never be gone," Rogers and Ben said in unison, in an exhausted voice that made it clear this had long been part of a strange routine for the crew.

Horace twitched his mustache to show that he was pleased. "As you can see, we've removed about three-quarters of the seats in every car," he continued. "Gives us space for some bunks and just some general room to stretch our legs. We also keep the weapons in the car nearest the engine now. Keeping them in the back of the train had been Bloom's idea…" He drifted off uncomfortably. He cleared his throat. "Keep 'em away from me, I guess. Keep 'em for himself."

The other men exchanged awkward glances. "Hey," Patrick said, clearing his throat. "Bloom, and everything he did? That wasn't your fault. I mean, look, people who are bald just naturally command fear and re-spect. That's Lex Luthor, that's Michael Chiklis, I mean. Come on. Patrick Stewart? Please. Bald people just operate on a higher plane than we do, and that's okay. I hope to ascend to that plane myself one day soon," he added, massaging his receding scalp.

Rogers grimaced, and Ben coughed like he might actually be chok-ing on Patrick's words, but Horace seemed to take great comfort in what he said, because he nodded sagely and whispered, "Thank you for saying that, Patrick. You're right. You've always been right."

"Oh, come on," Ben groaned.

"No, no," Patrick said, shushing Ben with his hands. "Let him express this."

Horace took a deep, self-assuring breath. Then he nodded and got back to work. "Anyway, the train is in the best shape of its life. We actually took your hydraulic ramrod, Patrick, and made it stronger, lighter, and sharper."

"Gross!" Patrick cried gleefully.

"We also run lighter now, as you can see." Horace gestured toward the back of the train. "Five cars now instead of the seven, sometimes eight we used to pull."

"It's a lean, mean, slow-chugging machine," Patrick said admirably, patting the overhead luggage rail. It was sticky. He didn't like that.

"That is part of it," Horace nodded. "Though, also…cargo isn't what it used to be." He sighed sadly.

"How can that be?" Patrick asked. "The world's as over as it ever was, right? People need *stuff*." He scratched his chin. "Right?"

"Sure," Rogers nodded. "It's not the 'stuff' that's the problem. It's the tracks. Seems like every few months, some lunatic fringe blows up another line of track somewhere. Whole Northwest is cut off to us now, after Iowa. Can't get to New York, either. God knows what'll happen to those folks out there, now we can't reach them. As for us, our delivery map has shrunk. And what we do have is pretty low-value, ever since the Fogelvee incident."

"Hey!" Ben shouted.

"Sorry," Rogers said, raising his hands innocently. "It's just what they call it. The Fogelvee incident."

"Stop saying it!" Ben cried.

"Someone please *immediately* tell me, what is the Fogelvee incident?" Patrick asked, rubbing his hands together and practically salivating.

"It's not my incident!" Ben insisted.

"This thing about a year ago," Rogers said, ignoring Ben. "We had some high-dollar cargo. Taking it out west. The train was ambushed in the desert. They took the cargo, and Ben went after it. To his great credit," Rogers added quickly, watching Ben's face turn crimson. "But after a week or so, we got Ben back, and turns out, he bungled the whole thing, and the cargo was lost."

"I didn't bungle it!" Ben cried. "I fought a giant! And a tiger! And, like, eight thousand zombies!"

"They're not zombies," Patrick whispered.

"Shut *up!*" Ben said.

"Anyway, it's not Ben's fault, it's just what happened," Horace said, trying to keep the peace.

"I agree," nodded Rogers. "Ben was not to blame. He was the only one of us who went off after the cargo. Far as I'm concerned, he's something of a hero."

Ben took a deep breath. "Thank you," he said.

"We did later learn that the reason he went out after the robbers wasn't even *for* the cargo, but still—"

"Oh, fuck right off!" Ben yelled. His lungs tightened, and he coughed into his fist. The phlegm was thick, and his chest worked so hard that he fell to his knees during the fit. He choked up a glob of red and green mucous into his hand. When he saw the flash of color, he dropped his hand to his side, hiding it from the others. But Patrick saw it.

He drew in a sharp breath. "Oh, Benny Boy…" he said, sinking down to a crouch next to his friend. "No…"

Ben glowered at everyone. "I'm fine," he insisted. Then he coughed for three minutes straight and wound up on his side, curled into a fetal position with dribbles of blood and Monkey pus stringing down his lips.

Patrick was down on his knees, trying to find ways to hold his hands around Ben's convulsing body that they might be able to be helpful in some way. "Not you, Ben," he said quietly, new tears welling up in his eyes. "You got the Green Flu?"

"No," Ben said, coughing into a fit.

"Yes," Rogers said, crossing his arms. "And you should know…it's bad."

3.

"Okay, so how bad is it?"

Patrick and Ben were back in the train car that was basically considered "Ben's," because it contained his cot and his blankets and his notebooks and things, though to be fair, it also held the canned food, the dried meat, and a few boxes of someday-useful things, like bottle openers and tweezers and rusty old cans of compressed air. Horace and Rogers had gone back up to the engine, to get the train moving again, and Ben had given Patrick a short tour of the train he already knew, which didn't take long, but which also took all of the energy Ben had left, and he felt like he had to lie down.

"It's fine," Ben sighed, sinking into his bunk. "I've actually never been stronger." He reached under his bed and pulled out a small box. He opened it and held it out to Patrick. "Here. Before I forget."

"I love that you got me a present, but we're still going to have a heart-to-heart," Patrick warned him. He peered into the box. Sitting inside was a child's watch with a purple plastic band. The cracked plastic jewel had taken on a smoky yellowish hue with time, which made it difficult to make out the Disney princess in the flowing yellow gown beneath. Difficult, but not impossible.

"I found it with some other stuff you left at Fort Doom. I figured I'd keep it."

Patrick lifted Izzy's watch carefully out of the box. A tear drop fell and splattered across the purple band. "Thank you, Ben," he whispered, his voice hoarse. He fixed the watch around his wrist with the help of the familiar handmade hole. He smiled sadly down at the last and long-lost piece of his daughter. He hugged Ben hard. "Thank you."

The Baby Caps entered the bunk. Without even trying, they took command of the car in the way that truant officers might have taken control of a shopping mall arcade about twenty years earlier "Bad time?" Alice asked dryly.

"No, perfect time," Patrick said, pulling away and wiping his eyes. "I was just about to yell at Ben, and you can help me."

"Love to."

"How bad is the flu? *Really?*"

"I'm fine," Ben insisted.

"He's essentially dead," Babs corrected him. "He literally told us to kill him not three minutes before you showed up. Literally. Asked us to do it."

"I was up for it," Alice chimed in. She tapped her fingers along the handle of her knife. "I'll still do it, if you want."

"Okay, Jim Jones, calm down," Patrick said. "There'll be plenty of time to kill Ben later."

Alice wrinkled her nose. "Who's Jim Jones?"

"Geez, what are schools teaching these days?" Patrick asked.

"He was a cult leader," Babs said helpfully.

Alice nodded. "I could lead a cult," she decided.

"You most certainly could *not* lead a cult," Patrick said, "because the first thing you need in order to be a cult leader is charisma. Don't take this the wrong way, I know we've just met, but you have the charisma of a sock."

"Hey," she frowned.

"But you *do* have the whole cold-blooded killer thing going on," Patrick quickly added, trying to make her feel better. "You're a Jim Jones without all the fun."

"His cult was fun?" the big Baby Cap asked.

"You know what? I'm losing the thread here," Patrick admitted. "Talking to people with absolutely zero pop culture knowledge is exhausting."

"Oh, yeah," Babs said, rolling her eyes. "*We're* the exhausting ones."

"It can't be easy to hear," Patrick said gently. He patted her arm. "But I still like you, Gabs."

"It's Babs," she hissed through clenched teeth.

Patrick threw Ben a confused look. "I thought you said it was Gabs."

"I keep forgetting," Ben shrugged weakly. He lay back on his pillow and shivered. He closed his eyes and began to drift.

Patrick frowned. "Okay. Babs. Like the bunny."

"Bunny?" she asked.

Patrick skipped right over that particular bit of confusion. His heart would give out and his soul would leave his body forever if he had to explain *Tiny Toons*. "And what's your name, Jim?"

"Alice," she said flatly.

"Alice." Patrick closed his eyes. "Babs like the bunny, and Alice, full of malice. Babs like the bunny, and Alice, full of malice." He opened his eyes. Everyone was staring at him. "Mnemonic devices. I'm terrible with names." He turned to the final Baby Cap. "What about you, Baby Huey? What's your name?"

The young man's face turned red. He looked down at his shoes. "Uh… Lex," he said.

"Your parents named you after a Superman villain?" Patrick asked. "That's Bizarro." Patrick beamed around the train car. "Get it? No? Jesus Christ, I need to talk to an adult. Ben, did you—?" But Ben had fallen asleep. He was snoring softly, dribbling neon-yellow saliva onto his cot.

"It's actually…" Lex started. His voice cracked, and he cleared his throat. "Um. It's actually…I'm actually named for the watch."

Patrick raised an eyebrow. "Excuse me?"

"There was a watch company. Rolex?"

Patrick scoffed. "I'm sorry, your parents named you after a premium watch brand?"

"His parents were rich," Babs explained.

"Yeah, I'm getting the vibe," Patrick said. "Boy, Lex. I have so many questions, but we do not have the time. Listen. Little Red Caps. How far gone is Ben, really? How far down the symptoms hole are we talking?"

They exchanged uneasy glances. Babs, who was the clear leader of the trio, was wordlessly elected to answer. She sighed. "It's bad, like I said. He really did ask me to kill him right before we found you."

"*I* found *you*, but please continue."

"It's going slower than I've seen it in others. He's had the cough for maybe a few months? So I guess it could be worse, but…he's had a bad fever for a few days now, and just yesterday, I saw he had Monkey blood dripping out his ear."

"Monkey blood?" Patrick asked.

"That's what we call it. The yellow-green stuff."

"Got it," Patrick nodded slowly. "So he's leaking."

"Yeah," she said. "Just started."

Patrick sighed. He sat down on one of the few seats still bolted to the floor of the train car. "Soon it'll be coming out his pores."

Alice nodded. "Then he goes pop."

"Alice!" Lex gasped.

"What? That's what happens," she insisted.

"It's fine," Patrick assured him. "It's sure not inaccurate." He turned back to Ben. It may have been the strange way the light filtered through the Amtrak windows, or it may have been Patrick's imagination completely, but Ben's skin seemed to have just the faintest hint of a pale green hue. Even by conservative estimates, it wouldn't be long now. The leaking was really the beginning of the end. Once the Monkey blood started dripping from the orifices, you were basically dropped down a death well. Ben's deterioration would pick up speed every day now. He'd be dead in two weeks. Maybe less.

Patrick realized his face was wet. He wiped his eyes and turned back to the Baby Caps. "We have to try to save him. I know a scientist, in Asheville. She's been working on…I don't know, 'duster science' for years now. She hasn't figured out a cure, but maybe if we go there, maybe if we can help, get her more ingredients or more equipment or—I don't know, *something*, maybe if we go there, she can figure out a way. We have to save him. I spent the last few years thinking he was dead, and now that I've found him alive, I'm not letting him die again. We have to go to Asheville. I know it's crazy, I know it's a longshot, I know no one's been able to make a cure, but—"

"I know where to find a cure," Babs said.

Patrick blinked. "What?"

"We all do," Lex replied. "We all know where to find the cure."

Patrick opened his mouth, then closed it, then opened it again, then closed it again. He waved his hands in the air. "Wait. Stop. You know where to find a cure? To the Monkey Flu?!"

"Yeah," Alice said. "It's in Ohio."

Patrick's face felt like it was going to drop right off his skull and run away without him. "What do you *mean* you know where to find the cure?! What is he still doing here?! Why is he still dying if you know where to get the cure?! And how in happy hell do the Little Rascals know where to find a cure?!"

Babs shrugged. "Ben told us."

"Ben—" Patrick started. He fell back in his seat. He gasped. He launched back upright. He shook his head. "*Ben told you?* I'm sorry, *this* Ben?! *This Ben* told *you* where to find the cure?! *Benjamin Agatha Fogelvee* has known about a cure for so long that he had time to tell *you* all that he knew about the cure?! The one who is literally and quickly now *dying from the fever* is the person with the most knowledge of how to *stop* the fever?!"

"His middle name is Agatha?" Lex asked.

"Of course not!" Patrick exploded. "What is going on?! Why are you not there right now, pumping him full of anti-fever?!"

"I don't know," Babs said helplessly. "He said he didn't want it."

Patrick thought his skull was going to blow to pieces. He could picture it happening. He could picture his head literally exploding, with the shrapnel of his brain moving at such incredible velocity that globs of his gray matter would take out every single person in the train car. "You guys! You don't wait for him to tell you he feels comfortable with the option of not popping to death. You bring him to Ohio, and you jam the cure into his body, and you deal with how cranky he is forever after that!"

"Whoa," Lex said, raising his hands and stepping away. "Dude. His body, his choice."

"That's an incredibly broad interpretation of that very important mantra," Patrick shouted.

"Hey. Look. We tried," Babs said, moving over to sit next to Patrick. "You have no idea. We seriously tried. Ben is old and cranky and he complains a lot and he has a lot of weird opinions about some show called *Frasier*, but we love him. He's the one who brought us onto this train. Like, he saved us. From all of that wild shit out there. Okay? We love Ben. We had your same reaction. We tried so hard to get him to go to Ohio and get the shot. But, man? I'm telling you. He does not want to live."

Patrick leaned back in his seat. He covered his eyes with one hand, using his fingers to massage his temples. "This is a lot of new information to take in," he said. "It might help if we can wake Ben up so I can punch him in the face."

"Don't punch face," Ben moaned, sitting up drowsily. He wiped sleep from his eyes and rubbed his jaw against his sleeve, trying to dry the tracks of drool. "Why the punch? What's the punch?" He smacked his lips together, then recoiled from the moistness of his own mouth.

"The punch is because there's a cure to the fever," Patrick glowered. "You could be cured; you could have been cured a long time ago. And you're choosing to not go get cured."

Ben considered this. He sniffled. He shook his head to welcome in some oxygen. "Tell Horace," he instructed the Baby Caps. "Ohio. I need to go get cured."

The Baby Caps stared at each other, confused. "Uhhh..." Lex said. "Just...like that?"

"Don't you want to die?" Alice asked, a little hopeful.

"We're all going to die," Ben said, sitting all the way up. He pointed at Patrick. "But I will be absolutely damned if I die before this idiot does."

Patrick beamed proudly and clapped his hands with joy. "I just saved your life!" he crowed.

"Your ability to induce spite has mortal value," Ben agreed. "Now please go tell Horace to turn the train north and leave me alone to vomit in peace."

Patrick ushered the Baby Caps out of the car. Ben waited until they were well out of earshot. Then he leaned over and hurled green poison into an old plastic Wegman's bag.

4.

"We can't just change course because someone's dying in the back!" Horace hollered. "I've got a schedule to keep! I'm a railway man!"

Patrick didn't have the first idea how to adequately respond to that. "Horace...I respect you a lot...but, like...the world is insane. You know that, right? The world is actually insane. I genuinely think it's interesting that you're aiming to be the UPS of the apocalypse, but Ben's life against toilet wand refills is not really a choice at all."

"Patrick, I hear you. I do. But our cargo isn't toilet wands," Horace said, fidgeting with his mustache. "It's guns. It's food. It's papers and messages of incredible importance."

"Our current inventory list includes rubber bands and GAK," Assistant Conductor Rogers confirmed.

"Dammit, Rogers, don't undermine your conductor!" Horace said, hopping up and down.

"I'm just saying, I think this load can wait."

Horace's face darkened. He pulled his blue cap down over his ears in some strange show of aggression. "Well, of course it can wait!" he exploded. "I was going to get to the point where I made a big gesture of turning the train, but now that's gone, isn't it, Rogers?"

Rogers made a casting-off gesture with his hand. "Whatever gets you to the right decision," he sighed.

Horace turned to Patrick, annoyed. He straightened his vest and pulled at the ends of his mustache. "Yes, we'll go to Ohio," he said curtly. Patrick could tell that the little conductor felt the absolute deflation of the wind having been set loose from his sails. "This whole shipment was paid in advance, so I'll just say we were held up at gunpoint or something."

"Happy to point a gun at anyone's face if it helps the lie!" Patrick chirped.

"Probably not necessary," Horace said, stroking his mustache. "Go back and settle in. We'll head north at the next switch point. It'll take a day or two to get where we're going."

"That's perfect," Patrick nodded. "Ben and I have a few things we need to discuss before we get there."

5.

"So? How've you been since the House of Mouse?"

Ben glared over the top of his water bottle. The vomiting hadn't stopped, and now that he was leaking, too, he was losing fluids at an alarming rate. He finished his drink and swallowed as angrily as he could. "You mean since you faked your own death so you could get rid of me for a few years? Pretty bad, Pat. I guess I'd say I've been pretty bad."

Patrick sighed. He sat down on the foot of Ben's cot, with his back propped against the wall. "That's not what happened," he said.

"Well?" Ben made a *go ahead, then* motion with the bottle.

"I did pretend to be dead," Patrick began. "That part is true."

"Clearly."

"But only because I was absolutely positive I was *going* to die. I mean, I was stabbed with a *sword*. Look at this thing." He lifted up his shirt and showed Ben the pale scar on his belly. "I was dead as houses, as they say in England."

"No one says that anywhere."

"I pretended to be dead pre-death because I knew you wouldn't leave me there otherwise. The Red Caps were coming, and I didn't want them to kill you, too. There was no sense in both of us dying."

"Except neither of us died," Ben pointed out.

"What a mitzvah!" Patrick beamed. Ben glared at him. Patrick cleared his throat and continued. "After you left, I managed to drag myself up to Cinderella's castle. Which hurt a lot, by the way. I sat up there in the window and I read Izzy's letter. I ate the last pudding cup…and I just sort of waited for all the blood to run out. But then the Red Caps got there, and they saved my life."

"Wait. *Bloom's* Red Caps saved *your* life?"

"Yeah. Wild, right?"

"Why did they do that?"

"I don't know. Some sort of penance thing," Patrick said. "That's what they said, anyway. Turns out, they're just...I don't know...scared. To be on their own."

Ben shook his head in disbelief. "But they tried so hard to kill you," he pointed out.

"Yeah, well, they came back around to it after a while. But we were together for a long time. Maybe a year?"

Ben spat his water across the room. "You spent a whole *year* with Bloom's Red Caps?"

Patrick shrugged. "The sword wound was seriously infected. I was pretty delirious for a couple months. By the time I came out of it, they'd dragged me up to North Carolina. I spent the next year trying to get back to Fort Doom. They just sort of decided to come with me."

"Wow," Ben said. He coughed into his arm. "What happened? Why didn't you make it back?"

Patrick looked down at his hands. His fingers suddenly became very busy picking at the callouses on his hand. "Well, that's sort of something we need to talk about," he said quietly. He swallowed down the lump in his throat. "I, uh..."

Ben sat up, alert. "Why are you speechless? You're never speechless. You're freaking me out."

Patrick's mouth was dry. He made grabby hands for the water bottle. "Bemme," he croaked. Ben passed him the water, and after a few gulps, Patrick handed it back. His hand was shaking. "It's just that...well...I *did* make it back. To Fort Doom."

"So you saw what Spiver did. He burned it to the ground," Ben said. A darkness flashed across his eyes. He gritted his teeth. He had gotten pretty good over the years at stuffing down the sounds of their screams. Of Sarah's screams. But now, it all came back. He could feel the heat of the flames, the pressure of the smoke filling his lungs. He could hear the crackling of his friends' skin.

"No," Patrick said, shaking his head. He tried to look Ben head on, but he couldn't lift his head high enough. "Not Spiver."

Ben's eyebrows knitted low over his eyes. The water bottle squeaked as his grip tightened. "Go on."

"There was…there was a man we met on the way back. Roman Marwood. Have you ever heard that name?"

"No," Ben said, his mouth tight. "Should I have?"

"I don't know. It seemed like he was a pretty big deal around the Gulf. He was smart. He was into science. He had a big compound in Mississippi, a working farm. It was like a whole little society. He brought us there, and it was—it was great. But he showed me the science he was working on. And that…that was bad."

"Bad how?"

"He said he was working on a way to turn dusters back into regular humans."

"A cure."

"Sure. Yes. But it wasn't working. And he showed me…he was using migrants to test it."

"Migrants?"

"Including women and children. He turned them into dusters so he could try out his serum. He tortured them, and then they died."

"How do you even turn people into dusters? Just cram Monkey dust down their throats?"

Patrick shook his head. "Some sort of concentrated vapor. Which he knew how to make, because he's the one who developed the dust in the first place."

Ben's eyes grew wide. "Hold up. This guy was Jamaican?"

"No," Patrick shook his head, "No. He was a finance bro. Funded a lot of shitty projects. Some of them were weapons development. He helped create the dust, then he sold it to the Jamaicans."

"Jesus," Ben said, leaning back against the train wall. "You met *the* guy responsible for all of this?"

"One of them, yeah. I got pretty furious when I found out."

Ben scoffed. "Yeah, I imagine you did. I hope you pushed him off a cliff."

"I smashed a kerosene lantern into his face and set him on fire."

Ben blinked. "Oh." He considered this news. "I was sort of joking about the cliff thing."

"Yeah. Well." Patrick went back to picking at his palms.

Ben cleared his throat. "What does this have to do with Fort Doom?"

Patrick pushed off his shoes and drew his legs up onto the cot. He pulled his knees under his chin, huddling his thin bones close to his chest. "After I burned him, Roman tried to feed me to some dusters. I escaped, thanks to my—thanks to a…friend. I escaped from the farm. I ran out through the corn fields, and I didn't stop until I got to Mobile."

"And I was already gone?" Ben asked. He was trying to sound hopeful, but the edges of his voice were heavy with the dread that belied the churning in his stomach.

Patrick heard it, clear as breaking glass. He shook his head. "No," he whispered. His throat was dry again. "Roman had turned the Red Caps. He sent them after me, and they caught up. Right at the end. Roman's orders were to kill everyone inside Fort Doom. Burn it to the ground and make me watch." He turned his sad, watering eyes to ben. "So they did."

Ben sat rigid as a steel poker. His eyes stared straight ahead, into nothing, unblinking.

"They made me watch from the roof of a building nearby," Patrick continued quietly. "I watched Fort Doom burn with my friends inside. I saw it all. I *heard* it all." Ben flinched when Patrick said that, but he was otherwise still. "When it was over…they were supposed to kill me, too. But they didn't. Figured they owed me a favor, I guess. They knocked me out. By the time I came to, there was nothing left. Just ashes and bones."

The sun was easing toward the horizon in the world beyond the train. The light switches forgotten, the two men sat quietly in the gathering darkness. Neither of them moved. Neither of them spoke. Not until the sunlight had drawn away, and all they could see of each other was shadows.

"They did it because of you," Ben said. His voice was hoarse and flat.

Patrick swallowed. "Yeah."

Ben nodded slowly. Another several moments of silence passed. Full darkness was on them now, and they sat in that darkness like bones in a mine.

"I'm going to need some time," Ben finally said.

Patrick exhaled sadly. "Okay." He unfolded his stiff legs and felt his way toward the door. He turned back to Ben. He wanted to say something, say *anything*, some last word that might help ease the awful truth. But he couldn't think of what that could be, so instead he just slid open the door and left Ben to the darkness, alone.

6.

"Wow. How did *that* go?" Babs asked.

Patrick started. "Were you eavesdropping?"

"Only for, like, half of it," she insisted.

"It was most of it," Lex corrected her.

"We heard the whole thing," Alice said.

"Wow, great," Patrick muttered. He slipped past them and strode toward the next door. "I always love hanging with Red Caps."

"I'm sorry, we didn't mean—!" Babs started. But Patrick passed out of the car and slid the door shut behind him, cutting her off.

He stepped into the dining car, which had four tables with booth seats. Beyond the tables was a snack counter, and Assistant Conductor Rogers was behind it, rifling through the paltry stash of food. He nodded at Patrick as he came in. He held up a bag of well-past-the-best-by-date Takis. "Hungry?"

"For inedible sodium? Absolutely." He held up his hands, and Rogers tossed him the bag before grabbing one for himself.

"Mind if I join you?" he asked Patrick, coming out from behind the counter and gesturing to a table.

"Sure, if you like people who are very poor company for company."

They sat and tore into their bags. The heady smell of spices felt like it took the hair out of Patrick's nostrils. He'd been eating mostly mealy fruit and spoiled vegetables for the last couple years, and his body wasn't used to interacting with flavors. "These things are absolutely toxic," he said happily.

"There are water bottles in the tub in the corner," Rogers said, nodding at a black Rubbermaid bin by the door. "Help yourself."

Patrick trotted over and grabbed two bottles. He set them on the table and slid back into the booth. "You all are rich in hydration here," he said admirably.

"Had a client a while back, couldn't pay the whole fee so he set up a rainwater catching and filtration system on the train. Hell of a value." They toasted with their bottles as the dark night flashed by outside the windows.

"You and Horace take shifts driving the train?"

"Mm," Rogers nodded. "We try to run as close to 24/7 as we can. These days, it seems like any time we stop, we get hit. After a certain point, you'd sort of thing people would get *less* desperate, the longer this all goes on. That they'd all figure out how to make something of the world. But..." he trailed off.

"The world is more broken than we thought," Patrick said.

Rogers raised his bottle. "I'll drink to that."

Patrick glanced at the train car around them. "You've managed to keep electricity going. That's pretty impressive," he said.

"This is our home," Rogers said simply. "We try to take care of it."

The train rocked gently on the tracks. The rhythmic clacking of the wheels and the sway of the car was comforting. Patrick gradually felt the tension begin to melt from his shoulders. He sank back into the hard plastic booth. His heartbeat and his breath were returning to normal. The hardest part of finding Ben was over.

"We've heard a lot about you. Sort of feels like I already know you, a little," Rogers said.

"Well, this is embarrassing. I haven't heard a thing about you."

Rogers bobbed his head thoughtfully. He crunched on a Taki. "I'm glad you're here. I mean, I'm certainly glad you're alive, of course. We all thought you were dead. But I'm glad you're *here*. You'll be good for Ben. He deserves some good."

Patrick snorted softly. "Yeah. Well." He spun the water bottle on the table, fidgeting with the plastic ridges. "We'll see, I guess."

"Mm. The Red Caps mentioned something about a difficult conversation."

"What is this, a train or a high school locker room?"

"Word spreads fast," Rogers agreed. "Not so surprising, is it? We are all we have."

Patrick slumped in his seat. "Yeah. I guess that's right."

"Listen. I don't know what you said in there. But I know Ben fairly well. I feel like I know you, at least a bit, given how much he talks about you. Can I share with you a little about me?"

"Please," Patrick said, gesturing with one hand. "Restore my hope in Assistant Conductors."

"I grew up on a farm in Illinois. My father was abusive."

"I'm sorry—" Patrick started, but Rogers waved him away.

"Just bear with me. As soon as we were old enough, my sister and I ran away. She went back; I didn't. He put her in the hospital for leaving. She never healed quite right. I never saw either of them again.

"I spent a lot of time on my own. Years. Didn't know what to do or who I was. Got angry, lashed out a lot. They say hurt people hurt people, and that was certainly true in my case. I did a lot of damage to a lot of folks. Then the bombs fell, and it felt like some sort of punishment. For me, for all the bad people doing bad things. I retreated even further into my resentment. Became an even worse version of myself, somehow. Like I was trying to show the world that I was more brutal than it was."

Patrick shifted uncomfortably in his seat. "Not really doing a whole lot to repair the reputation of Assistant Conductors," he said.

Rogers snorted a laugh. "Well, that's how it was for a while. Thought about killing myself plenty of times, but never quite saw the point in it. One day I did something stupid. I ran into a campsite with a bat and started swinging. Figured I'd lay them all flat, then run off with whatever they had on hand. Except those folks were really on their guard. They heard me coming, and they were ready. Used my own bat to beat me within an inch of my life. They didn't kill me, but I was unconscious for, I don't know, days, I think. When I came to, it was dark night, a pitch black night, and I crawled away into it, because that's all I could do. I should have died out there. But when the sun came up the next morning, I found myself near some railway. And lo and behold, there was a train coming down the track. Horace and Ben found me out there, bleeding to death in the desert. They took me in. Ben nursed me back to health. Acted grumpy about it, but he took care of my wounds and made sure I was eating. Once I was well enough to leave, he suggested maybe I should stay. Horace had been without an AC for some time. Ben squared it with Horace, and, well, here I am."

"That's a hell of a story," Patrick said.

Rogers nodded. "See…Ben saved me. Him and Horace. In more ways than one. If they hadn't come along when they did, if they hadn't been who they are, I'd have died out there in that dirt, a pointless end to a useless life. These last few years, I've had a purpose. I've done good things.

I'm learning what it means to be a person who cares about other people. I don't know what guilt you're carrying, or how it affected Ben...but I can tell you, whatever it is, it's one small part of a much bigger story. If the past hadn't gone exactly like it did, I wouldn't be here today. And I'm not the only one Ben has helped. Dozens of people. Maybe hundreds at this point. Their lives made better, even saved, because of the path your history sent him down. And that path brought you back around. You understand? Don't be hard on yourself for how things went. How things went is the reason for so much goodness. We're all on a journey much bigger than we can see."

Patrick fiddled with the water bottle. He felt a lump rising in his throat. "That doesn't make any of it much easier," he said quietly.

"It's not supposed to be easy," Rogers countered. "It's just supposed to be. And so it is."

Rogers finished his water. He crumpled up the empty bag of Takis and pitched it in the trash box. "Well. About time for my shift. Nice talking with you, Patrick."

Patrick looked out the window at the mountains passing in the darkness. The world rushed by, following its own path, indifferent to the guilt and regret that filled the little train that was crawling through its valley. But it was also a world that existed in its own, beautiful present because of the myriad awful cataclysms that had brought them each to this point.

"Yeah," Patrick said, leaning his head against the glass. "Nice talking with you, too."

7.

Ben emerged from his car in the dark hour before sunrise. He had slept a little, though not well. His fever didn't seem quite so bad, so that was something. But his bones still hurt, and he still had to take a few moments to dry heave into his used-up Wegman's bag, the smell of which prolonged the gagging by a good ten-count at least. He was nauseous and sore, but it was time to get out of bed.

There was too much shit to do.

"Wake up," he said, passing through the Baby Caps' car and pulling their ratty blankets off of them. "Early training."

"Training?" Lex asked through a yawn. "Since when do we train?"

"Since today," Ben said. "Be ready in five." He flipped the light switch on his way out, blasting the car with a bright fluorescent wash. The three Baby Caps groaned in pain, and Ben smirked as he passed to the dining car.

Inside, he found Patrick and Horace, fast asleep at different tables. "Everyone who wants to stay the fuck alive, wake up," he shouted.

Patrick and Horace snorted awake. "You are a very aggressive alarm clock," Patrick groaned.

"Too bad," Ben said. "We have to fight the Source of Mercy today, and we're probably all gonna die."

Patrick cleared the sleep out of his eyes. "It's not even sunshine yet," he complained. "What's a Source of Mercy?"

"He's the one who has the cure. And he's got an army of jacked-up mutants, so we need a plan. Horace, do we have any C-4?"

"Of course we don't have any C-4," Horace yawned. "You know the rule, no explosives on the train."

"That's a terrible rule," Ben grumbled. "We're attacked almost every day—it's insane that we don't have any explosives."

"That's precisely *why* we don't have explosives. They get accidentally detonated in a raid-fight, we're all done for!"

"It's actually *very* difficult to detonate C-4 accidentally," Patrick pointed out.

"This is what I'm saying," Ben said. "I didn't know that was true, because I'm not a nerdy virgin, but it supports my argument."

"Hey. I have had relations with women," Patrick frowned.

"Allegedly," Ben replied.

"My sperm has made seed! You know this!"

"We don't know she was yours. I never saw the blood work, you virgin nerd."

"I don't like dying Ben so much. He's very angry."

"My fury is my strength," Ben agreed.

"Hey, speaking of your fury…" Patrick began.

But Ben held up a hand to stop him. "I'm not mad at you. I don't have the first idea how to even begin to process what you told me. But it wasn't your fault. If I ever meet this Roman guy, I'm going to blow his goddamn head off with an axe—"

"Not really how axes work," Patrick pointed out.

"—but you, I'm not mad at. I'm glad you're alive and here. Now shut up and find me a bomb."

"We don't have any bombs!" Horace insisted.

"I have some bombs," Alice said, strolling into the car.

"You had better not, young lady!" Horace shouted.

"Of course I do. Just cherry bombs right now, though."

"'Right now'?" Horace grimaced.

"I'm working on pipe bombs."

Horace pulled at the edges of his mustache. "Do not work on pipe bombs!" he cried.

Alice shrugged. "Okay, we'll just protect ourselves with pool noodles."

"Hey, that feels like a personal attack," Ben frowned. "Those are just for practice."

"How do you even make a pipe bomb?" Patrick wondered.

"I scavenge black powder from fireworks. Takes a while to get enough, but I'm almost there."

"You have black powder on the train?!" Horace shrieked. Alice looked at him with pity in her eyes. "Ben! Control your Red Caps!"

"I hate to say it, Horace, but this is actually great news. This is what we need."

"She's putting the whole train in jeopardy!"

"Oh, so *this*...is...Jeopardy," Patrick said. He beamed at the rest of the crew. They stared at him, confused. His face fell. "No? No Johnny Gilbert fans?" He sighed. "That would have killed at my grandma's hospice center."

"I want that girl and her explosives off my—"

But before Horace could finish his sentence, something cracked against the dining car window from the outside. Patrick turned and pressed his face to the glass. The sun still hadn't risen, but the darkness was turning a watery gray, bright enough to see shapes moving outside the train. Then a flickering tongue of fire appeared outside the window. It grew larger and larger as it hurtled toward the train. Patrick fell backward when the Molotov cocktail smashed against the train wall and exploded in a kerosene fireball. "I think we're under attack!" he cried.

"Great analysis," Ben muttered. "Horace, get to the engine and—"

"I know, I know, make sure Rogers keeps us moving."

"I was gonna say make sure they haven't picked him off. But yeah, also keep the train moving." Horace hurried through Business Class and shouldered his way toward the engine. Ben turned to Patrick. "When's the last time you fought for your life?" he asked.

"I don't know. What's today? Tuesday? Feels like a Tuesday." Another cocktail smashed against the window. This one cracked the outer pane as it exploded. "Been, like, two days."

"Great. There's a hatchet under that table."

"There is?!" Patrick exclaimed. He felt underneath the table and found a smooth wooden handle secured to the underside with duct tape. "How fun!" He ripped it away and drew out the hatchet. It was old and a little rusty, but it would work. "I feel like a serial killer pilgrim," he said, delighted.

"Great. Get ready to serial kill anyone who boards the train. I have to—"

He was cut off by Alice entering the room, holding a cherry bomb. "I need a match," she said.

Patrick felt his pockets for a lighter, nearly cutting off his own arm with the hatchet in the process. "Empty," he said.

"Here." Ben popped open a hatch in the wall and pulled out a medical supplies kit. Inside was a mostly-empty box of Diamond matches. "Only a few left. Make them count."

"I only need one," she said pointedly. She slipped a match out of the box and struck it on the side. Thet match popped to life. Alice held it to the fuse of the cherry bomb, and it started to spark.

"Outside, Alice! Outside!" Ben snapped.

Alice rolled her eyes. "I know how long a fuse lasts, Mom." She turned and carried the cherry bomb out into the passageway between the cars. The attackers outside were on horseback, still hurling rocks and Molotovs at the train. One stone slammed against the inside of the passageway, less than a foot from where Alice was standing. She didn't flinch. She watched the fuse until it was down far enough, then she flicked the cherry bomb out into the air. They heard one of the riders say, "What the—?" and then the bomb exploded, blowing a significant percentage of his face to a bloody mist. The rider screamed and screamed. They heard him hit the ground when he fell off his horse. The other riders shouted in confusion and alarm. They all pulled back, and the Horace Express chugged on ahead, leaving the raiders behind.

Alice poked her head back inside the dining car. "That's why we need explosives," she said.

"Hey, preaching to the choir," Ben said. His chest caught hold of something, and he dissolved into a coughing fit. "How much black powder do you have?" he managed to choke out when he was finished.

"Decent amount."

"Good," he said, wiping his eyes. "We're going to need it."

"How much of it?" she asked.

"All of it," Ben said, gritting his teeth. "And a hell of a lot more, besides."

8.

"Okay. This is going to go badly."

"Is this supposed to be a pep talk?" Babs frowned.

"No. It's a 'don't get dead' talk. And it probably won't work," Ben said.

"Good to know," she sighed.

"Hey. You guys are the ones who wanted me to get cured. This is how I get cured."

Alice raised her hand. "I never cared if you got cured or not."

Ben gritted his teeth. "Yes, Alice, thank you."

"I'll mark that in your record," Patrick assured her.

They were standing in the Baby Caps' car. The sun had just risen, and the world was coming into a foggy sort of focus. The mountains of West Virginia had given way to the ruined neighborhoods of southern Ohio, visible from the train only when the wind whipped a tunnel through the mist. "We're stopping at the next station," Ben explained, "so there's not much time. Listen. The place we're going is a cult. A massive, thriving cult. Their leader is a lunatic who calls himself The Source of Mercy, and he makes his followers swallow hot stones and smash their own ankles to shit. He calls them The Peaceful Ones, and they are not fucking around. We can't fight these people. The Peaceful One I met is a woman named Alma who's basically a Mickey Rourke She-Hulk."

"It shouldn't, but that description somehow makes perfect sense to me," Patrick said.

"Because I'm a goddamn poet," Ben said, or at least tried to say, but his lungs were starting to give out, and he ended up in a wheezing fit that sent him doubling over. He collapsed down onto one knee, clutching at his chest. Patrick jumped up and helped Ben back to his feet. Ben let himself be lifted up by the elbow. He used his free arm to wipe his mouth. Bright green streaks came away from his lips. "Specifically, I'm a struggling poet," Ben said weakly.

Patrick frowned. He pulled an oily handkerchief from his back pocket and used it to wipe Ben's jaw. A lime green trickle had dribbled down from his ear canal.

"Thanks," Ben said, swatting him away. He stared hard at the floor, avoiding everyone's looks of pity. "Okay. So. I don't know how many there are, but even Alma just by herself could literally destroy all of us. And for the Source to have the power he has over her…well, he's likely to have some serious tricks up his sleeve. We can't go in heavy."

"So we lob some bombs from outside and blow them up?" Alice asked eagerly.

Ben shook his head. "I'm not sure Alma even *can* be blown up, to be honest. It'd be like firing musket balls at a mountain. But we have a plan. Patrick, can you tell them the plan?" Ben's face had gone flour-white, and it was obvious he was having trouble standing. His arms shook as he lowered himself to a seat on Lex's cot. Based on Lex's facial expression, he was clearly uncomfortable with the idea of Ben leaking green on his blanket, but he managed to keep his complaints to himself.

"Yes indeed, Captain Benny-Boy," Patrick said with a clumsy salute. Ben didn't see it; he had already closed his eyes. Patrick turned to the Baby Caps. "Okay, so no fighting. No weapons. No hand stuff."

"Hand stuff?" Babs asked.

"Yeah. You know. Punches and slaps."

"That's not what—" she began. Then, upon a moment of reflection, she said, "You know what? Never mind."

"Think of this as a diplomatic mission," Patrick continued. "We're visiting dignitaries. We're kind, we're charming, and we just want to ask for a little bit of their Zelda potion. We will be absolutely suffocated by danger on all sides, but we have to act like we're not."

"I think I'm going to be sick," Lex said.

"Oh, you can use Ben's barf bag!" Patrick said brightly. It was a comment that didn't seem to help Lex's general state of wellness.

"I think we should blow them up," Alice said dully.

"And I respect that instinct, I do," Patrick nodded. "But blowing them up is A, morally challenging, and B, not strategically smart, for the reason Ben laid out, and also, because if we explode them, we probably explode the cure."

Alice crossed her arms. "Then why did Ben tell me to get my bombs?" she asked, eyes narrowed.

"Ah! Great question. Because that's our back-up distraction." Patrick looked frantically around the train car. "Does anyone have a whiteboard? I feel like this would all go better with a whiteboard. Oh well. Okay. So. The rest of us go in, all smiles and glad-handing. But Alice, you're going to post up outside whatever compound they have with your Bob-ombs. If everything goes well, we won't need you. But if things get ugly, we'll send you the signal, and then you blow up as much shit outside the wall as you can."

Alice frowned. "Shouldn't I blow up shit *inside* the wall?"

"No, see, that's the whole thing. You're not an attack, you're a distraction. Once you start blowing shit up *outside*, the people *inside* will suddenly become preoccupied with what's *outside*. And that should give us some time to do a snatch-and-grab. Remember—we do not want to attack them head on. We will not survive. So sayeth Ben, and so sayeth we all."

"I'll make do," Alice decided. "What's the signal?"

"Probably, 'Ahhhhh!' Or maybe, 'Alice!' We'll figure it out. Now, for the rest of us, something to keep in mind: We don't know what we'll be running up against. We don't know the compound, we don't know the layout, we don't know anything. Ben's intel says this Alma Hulk brought the cure back to the Source so he could replicate it for the cult, so we can expect there to be some sort of sciency area. That's probably where we'll find the cure. So if things go badly, and if Alice has to bomb stuff, then our job is to scatter and try to find this thing. Look for science equipment. Okay?" The Baby Caps nodded. Patrick nodded back. "Okay. Good. Otherwise, just be charming, and we'll be okay."

"How do we do that?" Lex frowned. He looked down at his hands as if he'd never seen them before. He held them up and shrugged.

"The fact that you seem to think that charm lives in your hands is incredibly concerning," Patrick assured him. "But no time to go down *that* particular rabbit hole, looks like we're here!"

Indeed, the train was skidding to a stop at a station that was wild and overrun with weeds and roots. The faded signs on the fence said MAYS-VILLE, KY.

"Don't worry about the fact that we're not in Ohio," Patrick said. "I'm sure this is fine." He looked down at Ben, who had fallen asleep. "Okay, who wants to wake the princess? He's the only one with street cred in this place."

9.

They shuffled out onto the cracked concrete platform of the Maysville station, everyone except Horace. "I'll be ready for a quick escape," he said, "but this isn't no Miata. It'll take some time to get up to speed. Just remember that."

"A Miata?" Patrick said, his lips curling in distaste. "Who are you, Malibu Barbie?"

Horace frowned at him. "I'm going to ignore that remark, because I'm glad you're alive, and also because I'm half-certain you'll be dead again soon." He climbed back aboard the train and gave a half-hearted wave. "Nice knowing you," he said, before disappearing back into the engine.

"He has a hurtful sort of candor about him, doesn't he?" Patrick observed.

"You have no idea," Rogers said.

The station was nestled on a short bluff alongside the Ohio River. Across the chalky brown water loomed the hills of southern Ohio. A little way east of the station stood a suspension bridge that connected the two states, and it appeared to be mostly intact. The air was quiet. The station was overgrown, but abandoned. The nearby streets seemed pretty clear of cars, and there wasn't a single sound aside from the occasional chirp of a bird.

The whole place was dead.

"Are you sure this is right?" Patrick asked Ben.

"Honestly? Alma never told me, I just heard it was here from other people we met along the rail."

Patrick clapped his hand against his forehead. "I'm sorry, we're here because of a *rumor?*"

"I don't think it's a rumor," Babs said. She pointed at the small, brick station house sitting alongside the tracks. Someone had spray-painted huge letters that took up the whole broad side of the building: SEEK MERCY, it said across the top. And below that, FIND PEACE. On the side of the station house was a simple arrow that pointed across the river.

"That does feel a bit like a bread crumb," Patrick agreed. He turned and peered across the river. It was difficult to tell from where they stood, and the Monkey fog blowing down the river didn't help, but he thought he could just make out the shapes of a civilization in the Ohio hills—tents, maybe, and small clearings, which would have been good for fires. Sitting in the foreground was an old theatre building with a scrollwork façade and a classic marquee stretching out over a ticket booth on the sidewalk. "I guess that's it."

"All right, grab a weapon and let's get this over with," Ben grumbled.

"A weapon?" Lex asked. "I thought you said we weren't going to fight them."

"I said we're going to be polite, I didn't say we're going to be stupid." He climbed back onto the train and shuffled to the weapons closet. He picked up a three-pound hammer, but his arm felt so weak, it was hard to hold it steady. Annoyed, he dropped the hammer and picked up a switch-blade instead. "Fucking fever," he growled.

Everyone took a weapon from the closet. Alice chose her usual knives, and she also had a coffee tin full of cherry bombs and black powder. Babs grabbed a lead pipe, and Lex picked up the three-pound hammer easily, giving it a few swings. Ben glowered at him, but Lex didn't notice. Rogers selected a baseball bat.

Patrick was the last to approach the closet. He gasped when he saw what was inside. In addition to the nightsticks, brass knuckles, steel batons, knives, bricks, and stakes, there were five handsome machetes leaning against the wall. Tears sprang to his eyes. He'd lost his lost machete more than a year earlier, when he'd been awoken from his brush pile by a pair of women with an angry dog. He had bolted up, grabbed his bag, and lit out, but the machete must have fallen out.

He loved that machete. He'd found it in the back of a FedEx truck on his way back to Mobile, and it had been the closest thing he'd had to a friend since he lost Ben. He hadn't quite gotten over that loss. But here, he had nearly half a dozen beautiful machetes, oiled and mostly clean, with rubber grips. Absolutely gorgeous.

"This is the best Christmas on record," he said through his tears. He chose a particularly ostentatious machete, one with a curved blade and a bright yellow grip. "I will call you Bleakachu," he decided in a reverent whisper. Then he jogged over to his bunk and dug through his bag. He pulled out a spray bottle full of water. He strapped the machete to his waist and he hooked the water bottle into his pocket. "Ready," he said.

"What's the spray bottle for?" Babs asked.

"Never know when you'll meet a bad cat!" Patrick beamed, hopping off the train.

"Hey, Ben," Babs whispered.

"What?"

"Your friend *is* weird."

Ben sighed. "Yeah," he said. "I know."

10.

They set off across the bridge and crossed into Ohio. "I haven't been to this state since I was a kid," Patrick said, taking in the ruined buildings, the overgrown radio tower, the craters in the street. "Looks like the apocalypse hasn't changed it much."

The air was still as they stepped off the bridge. Nothing moved. Nothing rustled. No animals stirred. No birds chirped. "Seem a little quiet to you?" Rogers asked. "A little too quiet?"

"I don't know," Ben said. All he could hear was the pounding in his own head.

"It is a little strange," Patrick agreed. "You expect a thriving cult to be a little more thriving."

Rogers nodded. "Careful, everyone. Something's not right."

They crept closer to the old theatre. The letters on the marquee had once spelled SOURCE OF MERCY, though several of the letters had long since fallen away.

"Gave himself top billing," Patrick said admirably. "Nice."

"Guess this is the place," Ben mumbled. He locked eyes with Alice and bobbed his head toward the side of the theatre. Alice broke off from the pack, slipping silently around the corner of the building, keeping her head low and disappearing into the shadows. "All right. Let's go."

The crew approached the theater. Lex instinctively reached for his hammer, but Patrick laid a hand on his arm and shook his head. "Diplomatic mission," he reminded the Baby Cap.

"This suddenly feels like a very dumb plan," said Babs.

"Diplomacy isn't dumb," Patrick insisted. "It just never works. Let's go!" He approached one of the doors and pulled the handle. The door opened easily but noisily. The squeal of the hinges cut through the air like a saw blade, and everybody winced. Patrick peered inside. The lobby was dark and it smelled like mold. "Okay," he said, propping open the door. "Ladies first."

"Gee, thanks," Babs said dryly.

"I'll go," said Rogers. He stepped through the doorway and into the darkened building.

The others followed close behind. The carpet was spongy in spots, threadbare in others. The room smelled like standing water and rot. A little light filtered in through the doors and a small set of windows off to the right. The concessions counter lay directly ahead of them. It was littered with wrappers and other debris, notebook paper and rags and empty bottles and dead leaves. A set of five movie poster frames clung to the wall on the left, though most of them were broken open with their original posters missing. The only one that remained was a promo poster for *Abraham Lincoln: Vampire Hunter*. It said, "Coming Soon."

"Was anyone else expecting something a little more—I don't know—churchy?" Patrick whispered.

"You make do with what you can find," Rogers replied.

"I guess so. But still. Sexy Lincoln is a wild first impression for a cult of mercy. More like the cult of *have* mercy. You know what I'm saying?" he said, nudging Ben. "*Full House.*"

Ben ignored him. He leaned into the first of two auditorium rooms. It was pitch black inside. He clicked on a small flashlight and swept it across the room. "Empty," he said.

Rogers entered the auditorium and moved carefully down the steps, toward the screen. Using a flashlight of his own, he examined the front of the house. There he found a grimy generator that was hooked up to an old-fashioned overhead projector. He lifted up one end of the generator. Fuel sloshed around inside. He set it back down, then plucked a transparency from the top of the projector glass. He held it up and shined his flashlight through it. A handwritten list blazed to life on the movie screen.

"The Thirteen Mercies," Rogers read. "1. The Hundred Apologies. 2. The Beggar's Foot. 3. The Penitent Path." He turned to Ben. "What is this?"

"The steps to becoming a Peaceful One," Ben said, his jaw set. "We're in the right place."

"Why is it so empty?" Babs asked.

Ben gave her a look. "I'm not so sure it is."

"How come everyone has a flashlight except me?" Patrick cursed under his breath. He was having trouble finding his way down the steps. He smashed his knee into the back of one of the seats and hollered in pain. He leapt back, slamming into a metal railing that ran down the center of the aisle. He pinwheeled his arms and fell backward into something that was mostly solid, but with some squishy give. Ben and Rogers moved their flashlight beams over to Patrick. He had landed in the lap of a decomposing body.

"Oh God!" Patrick shouted. He scrambled off the cadaver, spinning around and sprinting down the row of chairs. He tripped over the foot of another body and fell forward. This time he landed face-first in the sticky, rotten cheek of another corpse. "I am going to throw up!" he shrieked.

Ben panned his flashlight up into the auditorium. From this angle, he could clearly see that they were not alone in the theater. There were two dozen dead bodies slumped over in their chairs. Most of them had huge, gaping holes in their torsos. Dried gore crusted the seats around them. Their organs had swollen and burst through their deteriorating bones. The bodies had all been exploded from the inside.

That was the final stage of the Green Flu. They had all succumbed to the sickness.

"You said it was empty!" Patrick cried, scooting away from the bodies and out into the side aisle.

Ben shrugged. "Looked like it from up there. I can't help it if they're not taller."

"Oh my God, I *taste* him," Patrick said, gagging. "I'm going to cut my own lips off and burn them with fire." He turned and threw up onto the carpet. He grabbed his spray bottle and furiously squirted water onto his tongue.

Rogers cautiously inspected one of the corpses. "This was the fever," he confirmed.

"I thought they had the cure," Babs said.

Ben frowned. "They did. They do." He shook his head. "I don't know. Something's wrong." He could feel the green run-off oozing from the corner of his left eye. He smeared it away with his shirt and tried not to look at the bodies before him. His heart was pounding, and he was on the verge of hyperventilation.

"I need sandpaper," Patrick wailed from the side of the room. "To scrub my whole face right off."

"Let's go," Ben said. He used the railing in the center of the aisle to pull himself back up the stairs. He tried not to look at the burst and bloated corpses.

The rest of the crew followed him back out into the hallway. "What now?" Lex asked.

Ben pointed his flashlight down the far end of the hall. "We keep going."

They gave the second auditorium just a cursory glance with their flashlights and kept moving. It was empty, or at least there was no one in there alive and moving. There was a pair of restrooms near the end of the hall. The men and women signs had been removed; they had been replaced by handwritten signs that read "purge" and "satiate," respectively. "Anyone want to go in there?" Rogers asked.

"No," was the resounding response.

At the far end of the hallway were two doors. One had a broken EXIT sign still fixed in place above the frame. The other looked like it led to an administrative area of some sort. The sign on the exit door read Garden of Grace. The sign on the office door read Pruning Room.

Rogers didn't even have to ask. "Garden of Grace," he said, pushing open the door.

Even though the fog was heavy, the light outside was still bright enough after the darkness of the theater that they all had to shield their eyes. They cautiously stepped outside and found themselves in a grassy yard at the back of the building. A hand-laid stone path led from the theater door back into a wooded hill a few dozen yards away.

"We're not going in there, are we?" Lex asked.

Patrick slapped him on the shoulder. Lex screamed. "If there's a cure, we have to find it. Hopefully we'll find it there and we won't have to go into the Pruning Room."

"Or the Satiate room," Babs blenched. "Blech."

They walked along the stone path and entered the woods. Ben was itching to take his knife from his pocket, and it was a struggle to plunge into the forest empty-handed. The stench didn't help. The wind carried the fetid smell of rotting meat. Lex gagged and nearly choked on his own bile. They were a few yards away from the edge of the woods when they saw the first bodies.

"Oh my God," Babs breathed. "They're all dead."

Dozens of corpses dotted the forest floor. They had been laid at the bases of some of the smaller trees. There didn't appear to be a pattern to their placements; they laid scattered across the ground like seeds. There were bodies as far as they could see through the thick trees, and probably further. Patrick did a quick count and stopped at thirty. There were at least twice as many as that, just on one side of the trail.

It wasn't true that they were all dead, though. Quite a few of them were still alive...if only just barely. Their raspy moans of pain were hardly audible over the sound of rustling leaves. The live ones writhed slowly in pain, like human vines coiling and uncoiling in the wind. It was a scene straight out of a folk horror movie. Which reminded Ben that they'd left Alice at the theater. "We should go get Alice," he whispered.

"I've been here," Alice said loudly. The others screamed and jumped.

"Jesus, Alice!" Babs cried.

"What? I saw you guys leave the building, I figured the plan had changed."

"The plan did *not* become 'scare the shit out of your own people,'" Patrick gasped, clutching his chest.

"Fun bonus, though," Alice decided. She wrinkled her nose. "Smells awful over here." She handed the tin of explosives to Lex and crept closer to one of the living bodies. It was a man whose skin was covered in green slime. His belly was distended; his whole torso strained against the dirty tunic he wore. His eyes were closed, and he was gasping for air. "Whoa. These people are literally on Death's doorstep."

The man's eyes flew open. Everyone except Alice jumped, again. "It is the remaking," he hissed. Greenish-yellow spit bubbled up on his lips as he spoke. Monkey juice spilled from the corners of both eyes. "We will die and be remade as trees. Our seeds will spread. We will cover the land with our mercy. Then we will uproot and reclaim the earth from humanity." There was a sound like a couch cushion ripping apart at its seams, and the man's belly burst open. Blood and green fluid soaked through his tunic, which became lumpy with loose organs and entrails. He closed his eyes and was gone.

The crew was horrified. They stared at the newly dead body for several long moments. Patrick placed his hand on Ben's shoulder. "Ben…" he began.

But Ben shrugged him off. "I'm fine," he said, wiping the green fluid that trickled from his ears. "Let's go."

11.

They pushed further into the woods. Some of the trees had faces carved into them, rough-cut sculptures with knobby features and hollow eyes. These were the trees around which were wrapped the desiccated bodies of cult members who had been dead long enough that there wasn't much left to rot. The faces in the wood were like some sort of death mask signifying the soul that would come to inhabit the tree.

The deeper they walked into the woods, the thicker the ground became littered with dead and dying cultists. The crew did their best to keep their eyes straight ahead on the path, but it was difficult not to look at the sour and festering death that surrounded them. Especially when one of their own was so close to that same fate.

"Ben, you don't have to keep going," Patrick said, fighting to hold his vomit down in his throat. "We can check it out and bring you back the cure."

"If it exists," Babs said. She instantly looked horrified. She clapped her hands over her mouth. "I did *not* mean for that to be out loud," she gasped.

Ben pushed past them all and continued on without a word.

After a few dozen yards, they came to a clearing on the side of a small mountain. The gently sloping hill formed a natural amphitheater. Simple felled logs served as benches, and there were about thirty of them lined up in two rows. Bodies were draped across the logs. Some were alive. Most were dead. The ground was slick and saturated with green slime.

At the bottom of the hill, nestled in a hollow, sat a wooden platform stage. It was small, maybe ten feet by five feet. In the center stood an antique armchair styled to look like a throne. The curved arms of wooden scrollwork had been painted gold, though the paint had long since started to flake, and it was marred in spots by yellow-green stains. Purple velvet cushions had been tied to the seat and to the backrest. These too had seen better days; stuffing leaked from popped seams, and they were likewise discolored and soggy.

Sitting in the throne was a pale man in his late fifties or early sixties. He had gray hair with white streaks that fell around his shoulders in wet, matted tangles. A scraggly beard hung down to his chest. He wore a discolored white tunic beneath a dingy purple robe, which he held around himself like a blanket. His legs and his feet were bare and filthy with mud, blood and Monkey juice. Even from a distance, they could tell there was something wrong with his eyes. It was like jaundice, but the whites had gone pale green instead of yellow. The discoloring made his crystal-blue eyes seem to glow, and when he saw the visitors, the corners of those eyes wrinkled in a smile, and he gestured for them to come closer.

"New acolytes. Please, come. Approach the Source, that you may feel its mercy." His voice was weak, but it was warm, like bread from the oven.

Ben shuffled down the mountainside, watching his own steps closely. He hadn't been this active in weeks, and it was taking a toll on him. He wanted to lie down between the logs like the Peaceful Ones around him. He was tired. He wanted to sleep. Maybe he wanted to be a tree. He could see the appeal, at least.

He felt a hand grip his arm gently. "Come on," said Patrick. "I'll help you."

This time Ben let himself be helped. He shifted his weight into Patrick's hand, and together they approached the Source of Mercy.

"I know you," the Source said, gazing at Ben with curiosity. "I have seen you in a vision."

"I bet," Ben said. He felt dizzy. "Look, we're here because—"

But the older man raised his hand for silence. "I know why you are here," he said. He looked up at the rest of the crew and welcomed them all down to the stage with a kind gesture. "I know why you are *all* here. You are here to find mercy."

"Not exactly," Rogers said.

But the Source only smiled. "Not mercy from me, perhaps. No, now that I see you closely, you've not the look of acolytes after all. But you desire mercy all the same. Mercy from the sickness. Mercy from..." He gestured at the legion of corpses. "...from all of this."

"We were told you had a cure," Patrick said, glancing around uneasily.

"And so I do," the Source said. He reached into his robe pocket and pulled out a small glass file. It had a few milliliters of orange fluid resting in the bottom.

"Where's the rest of it?" Patrick asked.

The Source tilted his head and looked upon Patrick with amusement. "Intravenous," he said.

"No, I mean…sorry, okay," Patrick sputtered, waving his hands to clear the words out of the air, "that was a stupid way to say it. What I mean is, we were under the impression that you were replicating the cure. In a lab. And now, as I say that out loud, and look at your confused face, and remember that we just walked through eight thousand dead bodies, I'm realizing we have been *grossly* misinformed, and maybe we should show ourselves out." He looked around for a quick exit route, but there were only bodies, logs, and a mountain with a fairly steep grade. So instead he eased slowly to his left and hid himself behind Lex, then closed his eyes and pretended to be invisible.

"We are far too primitive for a scientific lab of such sophistication, I'm afraid. This sample wasn't meant for replication. It was meant for the perpetuation of Mercy."

Rogers narrowed his eyes. "You mean it was meant for you." He inclined his head toward the bodies on the ground. "Not for them."

"Of course not for them. They have already received the blessing of mercy, or else they were found wanting, or else they were on the merciful path before falling ill. These are ends that are expected and welcomed among the faithful. They will now transition to the forest and become one with the trees, that upon the Day of Merciful Bounties they will uproot and reclaim the Earth. Their deaths are a blessing. Their sacrifice is a mercy to the generations to come. I exist to usher what legions I may save into that warm future. They are free from pain and sorrow; I persist in a combination of grief and light, a heady tonic that waters the roots of the faithful."

"How is this guy somehow *more* insane than the Post-Alignment Brotherhood?" Patrick asked, amazed.

"You are so full of shit," Ben glowered. "Mercy? I met one of your Peaceful Ones. You mutilated her. *Mutilated her.* Inside and out. You're a fucking beast from hell, and your final cruelty on these dumb fucks was to let them die while you took the cure." His heart was pounding and skipping beats. His stomach was churning. He wasn't finished, but the bile rose in his throat, and instead of speaking more, he turned and vomited green stomach tissue into the dirt.

The Source leaned back in his throne. He stroked his filthy beard. "True mercy requires repentance," he said. "I don't require my children to undertake any one of the Thirteen Mercies. Those who do, do so because they desire charity and forgiveness. They are entitled to that. And they choose to earn it. So I respect that choice and, yes, I allowed myself to be the one to be cured. Which would be its own precious burden, wouldn't it?"

"A true leader doesn't let his people die so that he might live," Rogers said, though his voice was even and his demeanor was calm.

The Source appeared completely unburdened by this claim. "No?" he asked. He seemed genuinely intrigued. "Are not the believers the wick? Should I not then be the flame?"

"That's not how *my* Sunday School did it," Patrick said.

"Indeed," said the Source, his blue eyes twinkling. "And where is that faith now?"

"About thirty-seven mental blocks deep," Patrick replied.

"Exactly so. Yet here, the faith is strong." The Source relaxed back into his chair. He wriggled his shoulders in order to fit them comfortably against the cushion. He closed his eyes in a show of calm repose. "But to your additional point," he continued, "I have taken no cure."

The Red Caps exchanged confused glances. "What do you mean?" Patrick asked. "The vial is, like, empty."

"Oh yes. I welcomed the serum into my blood. As you can see, I'm as infected as any of my flock, and the intent *was* to cure myself, certainly. But the serum didn't work. To call it a cure would be…disingenuous."

"Bullshit," Ben snarled. "You're sitting there on a dipshit throne while everyone else here is too dead to sit up. You seem fine to me."

The Source nodded thoughtfully. "Mm. Do I," he said. He pulled open his robe and revealed his pale belly poking through beneath his tunic. It was swollen, and a green stain had spread across the cotton. The skin that was pulled tight over his ribcage was also slick with the green pus that was leaking through his pores. "I'm as done for as any of them, I'm afraid." He closed his robe and resettled into his throne. "Some of us just take longer than others. Wouldn't you agree?"

Ben seethed with anger. Or maybe it was frustration. Or maybe helplessness—he couldn't tell. And he didn't care. It wasn't possible that the Source of Mercy was a dead end. It wasn't fair. It wasn't true. "Liar!" he shouted. "Alma took the cure! I watched her do it. Covered in zombie bites. She took the cure and was fine! It *is* a cure. It works. And you're a liar."

"Ah. Alma." The Source smiled sadly. "Yes. Now I remember why you've been in my visions." He leaned forward once more. He rested his elbows on the armrests and tented his fingers beneath his chin. "But tell me, bulldog. Where is Alma now?"

The hairs on the back of Ben's neck prickled to life. He was so focused on not focusing on the bodies scattered around the compound, he had forgotten to look for her. He had always pictured her strong. Powerful. Calculating. Alive. He hadn't given himself a breath to consider that maybe… maybe…

Ben shook his head. "No," he said, his lips set into a firm line. "No." He backed away from the stage, his legs faltering. He climbed up the mountain slope backward, determined not to let the Source of Mercy see him turn tail, but suddenly desperate to run out, to be away, to go back to the train, to go back in time, to exist in a world where none of *this* was real, and the cult was a force of unimaginable power that he'd never dare to face instead of the reality, which was that the cult of mercy was a lonely and laughable pile of death. Ben hitched his way back up the mountain, darting his eyes this way, that way, looking for the path, looking out for logs, looking at the bodies, looking like a fool. It was at the top of the ridge, when he was worn out and panting, that his eyes caught a flash of tangled blonde hair clotted with thick brown mud.

He stopped. He focused. He felt his stomach drop.

Alma lay between the last two logs. Her frame was so broad that both shoulders rested atop the logs while the flat of her back pressed down into the wet earth between them. Her skin was the color of mint cream, and the green blood in her veins pressed up against the flesh like tendrils of sinister seaweed. Monkey juice spilled out from her eyes, her nose, her ears, and her mouth, marking her face with emerald streaks of slime.

Tears filled Ben's eyes. They spilled onto his cheeks. "Oh, fuck," he whispered, his mouth full of green saliva. "Alma. Not you."

Alma opened her eyes and took a sharp inhale of breath. Ben stumbled backward out of surprise. Her eyes searched across the sky in vain, then she tilted her head up and saw Ben recoiling on a log, one hand out for balance, the other held up for protection. Their eyes met. Ben lowered his arms. His eyes were wide and wet.

Alma cracked her dry lips apart. "You," she rasped from her scarred throat.

She didn't have the strength to hold her head up any longer. She let it fall back. It hit the earth with a *thud*. Her chest rose and fell with great, heaving breaths.

Ben found his legs and pushed himself up off the log. He moved cautiously over toward Alma, almost as scared as he was sad. This was the hulking creature who had chased him across the desert, had sent him off a cliff, had held a gun to his temple and had left him to die, strapped to Bergamot's table. He could feel the iron in her fingers and the cold chill that frosted his veins when she pressed him down, bored death in her eyes. He'd never met a human being as cold and casual and capable as Alma. He hadn't thought someone as brutally uncaring and effortlessly powerful could even exist. She terrified him, back then in the desert, and here, too, weak and fading as she was. But she had also spared his life. She had also left him a gun. She had also saved him from a drugged-out rape, in the ghost town of Scudder's Point. They were not friends. They did not care about each other. They owed each other nothing. And seeing her there, lying in the mud, coated in green slime and dirt and sweat and fear, Ben burst into tears.

He stumbled forward, onto his knees, and he picked up Alma's giant hand and held it with both of his. "Not like this," he said through split-open eyes and a cascade of tears. "Come on. No. Alma. This isn't how you go. This isn't how you go." Spittle dripped down from his lips. It pooled on her shoulder.

She lifted her free hand and set it on her chest, covering her ham hock heart. "Wrong," she wheezed. She looked up at Ben. She gripped his hand. She pushed it back. She pressed his palm against his belly. "Go," she rattled. She punched his hand in a manner that was meant to be playful, but the force of her drove his palm into his own stomach, knocking the wind out of him. "Live," she said.

Alma settled her head back into the mud. She exhaled a breath that sound like a baby's rattle. Then her sternum exploded, and a geyser of green liquid and froth fell across her open, ruined chest, and she was gone.

12.

"A dedicated soldier," the Source of Mercy called up from his platform. "Would you be so kind as to place her against a tree?"

Ben stared down with all the fury his failing body could muster. "This is your mess," he seethed. "You clean it up."

The Source sighed. "Ah, well." He closed his eyes again and let his body go limp.

"Let me ask you something," Rogers said as the rest of the crew stalked quietly up the amphitheater. "Out of curiosity. Your whole cult looks pretty wiped out, all together. Not great odds that the fever just happened to catch up to them all at the same time. Some sort of suicide pact?"

"No. Nothing so tawdry as that. We were all helped along, weren't we? The fever can spread many ways. For us, it was our little friends." He perked up his ears. A smile spread slowly across his face. "Speak of the devils. Here they come now."

Chit-chit! Chit-chit!

Squeee!

Rogers slowly lifted his eyes at the sound, up to the canopy of branches that covered the forest like a hale and suffocating web. The leaves at the ends of the branches fluttered. The sounds of *chit-shit-squeee* came closer, grew louder, increased in mass. The branches started to shake. Rogers gripped his baseball bat with both hands and squeezed. "Guys," he said over his shoulder, up at the rest of the crew at the top of the hill. "Go!"

A scurry of squirrels exploded from the treetops of the forest. They scampered furiously across the branches, chittering and squealing and foaming at the mouth. There were fifty of them at least—ratty, battered squirrels, their fur matted down against their flesh, tiny bones poking through their pelts, their teeth dripping with foam and slime. They moved with unfathomable quickness, sprinting like racehorses along the limbs, furious and hungry and desperate for flesh.

"Dusters!" Rogers screamed. "Run!"

Babs screamed. Lex sank into a dark place and had a hard time moving. Alice grabbed his arm and yanked him down the path, pulling him toward the edge of the forest. Rogers sprinted up the mountain, desperate to catch up, desperate to outrun the oncoming horde of zombie squirrels. Ben stumbled backward from Alma's corpse. His brain refused to fire. He heard the *chit-chit-chitter*. He saw the Red Caps running. None of it made sense. His head was a fog. His ears rang. His skin felt loose and wet. Rogers grabbed him by the wrist as he puffed up the hill. "Come on!" Rogers shouted, and he pulled Ben behind him, yanking him out from the logs and practically dragging him up toward the sun.

Only Patrick remained in place, shielding his eyes with one hand, looking at the onslaught of squirrels like a Midwestern dad examining the sprinklers. "Here they come," he said, with all the energy of Alan Arkin in a low-stakes scene in *Edward Scissorhands*. The squirrels leapt from their branches and bombed the forest floor, screeching their war cry of *chit-chit-squeee!* The crew sprinted and dragged and coaxed and screamed, but Patrick just looked up at the squirrels, admiring their glorious trajectories as they sailed down into the woods, hell-bent on ripping him and his friends to bits.

Patrick pulled the spray bottle from his pocket. He pulled the trigger a few times, sent some puffs of mist into the air. The diving squirrels dove with their claws open and their teeth bared. But once they hit the sprayed mist, they ratcheted themselves out of formation. They used their forepaws to claw the burning scent out of their little nostrils. They all hit the ground different than they'd approached it, burning and angry and scared instead of hungry and confident and strong. The squirrels hit the earth, then they spun around in start-and-stop circles, losing themselves completely and as they desperately pawed the scent of the spray from their olfactory nerves. They scooted around on the forest floor, confused and frantic.

The Red Caps watched, stunned, as Patrick moved between them, easing away from the woods like they were at a party where the lights had just gone on.

"You said that was for cats," Babs said, throwing up her hands in frustration.

"Sometimes it is!" Patrick explained. "It's also good for foxes. Kind of good for bears, sometimes. Super good for squirrels." He holstered the spray bottle in his right pocket. He was immensely pleased with himself. He looked around at the Baby Caps. He worked to turn his smile into a frown. "What? Do you all not have Zom-Be-Gone?" he asked.

No one knew what to say. But Ben knew what to do. He ignored Patrick completely and staggered across the bridge. He had seen enough. He was feeling enough. His fever was raging. He was tired.

Down on the stage below, the Source of Mercy watched them go. He smiled and shook his head in disbelief. "Duster repellant! What a wonder."

Then his stomach exploded, and he joined his Peaceful Ones in the vast plain of death.

13.

The return to the train was silent and solemn. No one uttered a sound.

"I don't want to talk about it," Ben snapped, heaving himself up into the train. He landed on his belly. "Everyone leave me the fuck alone."

Patrick grimaced at the rest of the crew. He did a silent motion that said, *I'll take care of this.* He climbed up the Amtrak steps. He reached down and rubbed Ben's back a little. "Hey. Buddy. You need some soup?"

"Fuck. Off."

Patrick lowered himself onto the platform and sat cross-legged next to Ben's limp, sad body. "Listen. Ben. I don't know how to process what's happening to you right now. Which I know means that if I am the Mercury of not being able to understand the sun, you must be about eight Plutos past Pluto. I can't even fathom how much you can't process it."

"Pluto's not even a planet anymore," Ben said sadly into the floor.

"That only proves my point more. Look. I know I'm sort of a 'nonsense optimism' guy. Generally speaking. But I mean to take this thing for what it is. I don't know a single person who's survived the Monkey Flu. I've never even *heard* of someone surviving it. And I once heard two separate strangers, eight weeks apart, tell me they heard the moon had split in half and turned out to be an alien egg. One of them said it with a full moon clearly visible in the sky."

"They sound like a blast," Ben said dryly.

"One of them had been alone—and I mean, *alone*—in the Sonoran for, like, two years. He chewed on leaves from plants I couldn't spell with a whole-world dictionary and ten years of free time. So I don't know. The point is, the flu is real, and I understand that. The cure is fake. Now we have to understand that. You're the one going through it, so you get to decide how it goes down. But in the gaps between the steps you're envisioning right now…I'm going to do the best I can to fill them with a meaningful Patrick-Benicus experience. We're already both intimately familiar with the regrets we have when one of us dies while we're apart. If you're going to die now, I'm going to use every ounce of my energy to close that gap of regret so tight, the worms of 'What If' can't squeeze through."

Ben tried to listen, but it was hard. The cold metal floor, which felt so nice against his skin, was heating up in response to the warmth of his cursed body. He pushed himself into a roll and landed on his back. Horace had just started the train back up, and a sweet autumn breeze was slowly stirring to life outside the slow-moving car. That breeze draped his skin in a thin sheet of ice drops, and his skin unclenched and welcomed in the coolness. "Patrick," he said through dry, cracking lips, trying like hell not to think about his body withering to dust against a carved-up tree. "I don't know what the hell you're talking about."

"Neither do I, Benny Boy," Patrick confided, patting Ben's shoulder. "Neither do I."

Ben swallowed. It scraped down his throat like sandpaper. "Do me a favor," he said. "Don't let the Baby Caps see."

Patrick nodded. He squeezed Ben's arm. "They really like you," he said.

"They don't know anything about the world."

Patrick snorted. "Ben, they grew up in this world. They know it in ways you and I can't even begin to imagine."

Ben sighed. "No," he said. "They don't know about *our* world. They would have been good there."

Patrick sighed. "Yeah. They would have been great at D&D, wouldn't they?"

"Really great," Ben agreed.

Patrick smiled. "But you know what? They're going to be good in this world. I can already tell. Hell, this world practically *is* D&D. And every one of them is a dungeon master."

"Except Lex," Ben said.

"Lex is a Tortle," Patrick sighed.

Ben nodded. "Definitely a Tortle."

"If they had to roll an eighteen to find you a cure, those kids would make it happen."

"They'd go to the ends of the earth to find the other doctor, no doubt," Ben said.

That gave Patrick pause. He looked down at Ben. "Say what?"

Ben sighed. "Long story," he said, waving it away. The hot fuzz of fever sleep was creeping into his skull. He struggled to turn back onto his hands and knees, and he started crawling back toward his bunk.

"What other doctor?" Patrick asked.

"I don't know. Tomorrow," Ben said. He used the bathroom door to pull himself up to his feet. He wobbled and had to crouch low to keep his balance.

"Ben, what other doctor?" Patrick demanded.

Ben groaned, exasperated. "In the desert. I don't know, Pat. The guy who made this fake cure worked with someone else who left, who maybe made a different version. Maybe hers works. Maybe she's dead. I don't fucking know. All he said was she went 'west.' There's a lot of west."

"Hold the goddamn phone," Patrick cried. "You didn't tell me there was a cure, now it turns out you didn't tell me there are *two* cures?!"

"There's probably *no* cures," Ben replied. His tongue felt thick in his mouth. His words were slurring. He had to lie down.

"Ben! Stop!" Patrick caught him up from under his arms and helped pull him upright. He turned Ben around so he could look him in the eyes when he shook him. "Was there anything else? Any other clue? A name, a town, a hair color, Christ's sake, a birthmark? Anything?!"

"No," Ben yelled. He swatted Patrick away. He stumbled back into his car and tipped himself toward his bed. "Just a name," he slurred as he tumbled onto his mattress.

"I literally just—!" Patrick began, but then realized he didn't have the precious seconds it would take to be appropriately pedantic. "What was it?"

"I don't remember," Ben said, drifting off to sleep. "Dr. Dust Head."

Patrick screwed up his mouth. "Dr. Dust Head? Dr. Dust He—?" Something snagged in his brain. "Wait. Dust Head…Dusthead. Dust—oh, shit." Patrick's eyes bulged so far his retinas nearly detached. "Ben! Do you mean Dr. Gustheed? Is the name Susannah Gustheed?!"

Ben coughed. More Monkey goo came up. He spat it into his Wegman's bag. "Gustheed. Yeah." Then he completely lost consciousness.

Patrick stood there, gaping. His brain spun and slid and clacked and clanged, trying to fit all the impossible pieces together.

Gustheed. The cure. Ben.

Philbin.

"Oh my God," Patrick breathed. The last few years of his wandering life collapsed in on themselves, and suddenly he was back in North Carolina, with Roman's crew, in a house surrounded by zombies.

Like an ice block taking a bullet, Patrick shattered back into action. He sprinted through the train, blasting his way into the engine. "Asheville!" he yelled at a bewildered Horace. "*Now!*"

14.

Patrick rubbed his hands together eagerly. "Which one of these buttons makes the train jump to hyperspace?"

Horace grabbed Patrick's wrist and squeezed. "Ow," Patrick whimpered.

"Patrick. I'm glad you're back with us in one piece. But if you touch a single thing in this car, I will—and I mean this—remove that hand from your body and feed it to a zombie. Understood?"

Patrick nodded. "Yes, though you'd never be able to cut off these hands," he said, proudly displaying his wrists. "I'm a Milk Generation kid. I have incredible bone strength."

"We'll see," Horace replied.

Patrick sighed. "No, we won't," he frowned. "Because I'm not going to touch anything."

"Good man."

"But can *you* push the button that makes us jump to hyperspace? We are running out of time."

"You're not going to want to hear this, but we're currently going as fast as we can."

"No way," Patrick shook his head. "Ben is dying back there. We need this train to go the speed of my anxiety at least, and right now my brain is John Henry-ing the hell out of this race."

"John Henry lost that race," Rogers informed him.

"What, really? Is that true?"

"Yep."

"Wow." Patrick patted his chest as if looking for a misplaced pair of glasses. "Did I mis-internalize the great American tall tales?"

"Sort of seems like it," Rogers shrugged.

Horace straightened his blue cap. It didn't fit quite right anymore, now that he'd let his hair get a little longer than usual. He hated when his hair grew out, but he'd been so busy running the train all over hell and creation he hadn't had time to give himself a proper shearing. Now his quickly-graying tufts of hair kept popping that hat up on his head. "Listen, Patrick. I know we're running against the clock here. We want to save Ben as much as anyone. But I am telling you, the tracks are dangerous. There hasn't been a lick of maintenance done since M-Day. Half the Amtrak line is about ready to shake itself apart. We're going as fast as we can without derailing."

"He's right," Rogers added.

"Stop giving context!" Patrick cried. He mopped his hands down his face. "Arrgh. Okay. Fine. At this speed, how much longer 'til Asheville?"

Horace took a deep breath. He glanced at Rogers. Rogers shook his head as if to say, *I'm no gonna tell him.* "Well," said Horace. "That's the other thing. The train doesn't actually go to Asheville."

Patrick gaped at him. "The train doesn't—? Horace, I don't care that it's off the planned route, we have to go to Asheville!"

"He means it literally," Rogers said. "Asheville doesn't have an Amtrak line."

"How is that possible?!" Patrick exploded. "Asheville was a charming metropolis! A goddamn charming metropolis!"

"The nearest the station we can get to Asheville is probably Spartanburg. That's about seventy-five miles," Horace estimated.

"Seventy-five miles? Seventy-five *post-apocalyptic* miles?!"

"If we jump to the CSX line, we can get as close as Marion," Rogers suggested.

"How close is Marion?"

"About thirty miles."

"Oh my God, thirty miles now is like eight million miles in the Before Times." Patrick sat down on an old crate and buried his head in his hands. "19th-century American capitalism has really fucked us on this one," he said. "How is it possible there are no train tracks in Asheville, North Carolina?"

The conductors exchanged uneasy looks. Patrick clocked it. "What?" he asked.

"Well," Rogers said slowly, "there *are* some tracks that run through Asheville."

"Okay. Great. What's the issue?"

"It's…complicated," Horace replied.

"It's not complicated," Patrick insisted. "We're a train on a track. This track connects to that track. We switch our train from this track to that track. The mechanics are actually very simple."

"The mechanics aren't the problem," Rogers said. "Or, I should say… the mechanics *are* the problem, but not the mechanics you mean."

"Let's pretend like I don't have a Ph.D. in train nerd…can someone please explain the issue in English?"

Horace groaned. "The track that goes through Asheville is part of the Norfolk Southern Railroad. The Norfolk Southern mechanics union was always a little…um…"

"Over-eager," Rogers said helpfully.

"Over-eager," Horace nodded. "Once the bombs dropped, they seized up those tracks pretty fiercely. They don't let any other trains on those tracks. And they *definitely* don't let Amtrak on."

Patrick rolled his eyes. "My best friend is dying three cars back, he is literally *dying*, I don't care about bullshit train dork politics. We'll pay them with…whatever. We'll give them some weapons or half our food or, like, one of the Baby Caps. This isn't complex, this is a transaction."

Rogers shook his head. "They won't be bought."

"Everyone can be bought!" Patrick insisted. "Didn't you ever see *The Sopranos?*"

"No," Horace said.

"Well, see, this is the whole problem. Tony Soprano would get on that rail, and so will we."

Rogers frowned. "Patrick, please, I'm telling you. We won't get on the track. We should go to the CSX and cover the thirty miles. We won't get on the Norfolk Southern, and we'll lose more time trying."

Patrick crossed his arms. "We have no idea what's out there. Thirty miles on foot might take a week. Hell, it might take six months. I say this from experience."

"It's not going to happen," Horace said.

Patrick turned to the conductor. His eyes blazed blue with fire. "Horace. Get me to the Norfolk Southern. I'll make it happen."

"You don't know what you're asking," Horace insisted. "They're not going to let us on."

"Oh, they'll let us on," Patrick said. "I don't know if you've heard, but I am the apocalypticon. I can be very persuasive.

15.

"Please, please, *please?*" Patrick begged, knitting his fingers together and holding them up to his chin.

The man with NSR spray painted onto the front of his overalls considered this while he chewed on a stick from a birch tree. "No," he decided.

"Come on! We have a sick man here!"

The Norfolk Southern man shrugged. "He might get our rails sick."

"You can't get rails sick, are you hearing yourself?" Patrick cried.

The man spat a glob of phlegm onto the siding. "Can't be too careful," he said.

They had made good time to the junction. During the ride down, Patrick had been so distracted by Ben's general decline and by the questions of the Baby Caps, who wanted to know a lot of specifics about his life as a sad and lonely wanderer the last few years, that he hadn't had time to think up a good plan for getting the train onto the Norfolk Southern's tracks after all. The lack of mental preparedness annoyed him. A lot. "If I don't have a plan, I have nothing!" he had screamed to himself while locked in one of the train's bathrooms. He had hoped that screaming it out loud would release some of the pressure.

He had been wrong. It had not released the pressure. In fact, it had made the pressure worse. He was so mad that he fumbled the lock on the door and couldn't get it to open. By the time he emerged from the bathroom by jamming back the lock and slamming the door off its track and bellowing like an absolute ghoul, he still hadn't come up with a plan.

And not long after that, Horace had come back through the car and announced, "Norfolk junction in five minutes!"

"No!" Patrick yelled. He slammed his fist into the wall and then immediately screamed, "Ow!"

Horace just lowered his head and exhaled a long sigh. "This was your call, son. The next steps are in your hands."

Which was how he ended up begging, "Please, please, *please*" to an NSR mechanic who had driven a dump truck across the tracks so it blocked the train and told them they were not allowed to ride his rail.

"You actually *can* be too careful," Patrick told him, trying to come across as relaxed. "Sometimes, a railway will turn people away, and then, like two years later, they'll learn that that person got bitten by a duster and became the Railway Wrecker. The angry Bigfoot of train stuff. Then you have to carry that horrible knowledge and guilt all your days. You know?" Patrick then drew his mouth into a sad pout and nodded slowly, as if sympathizing. "You do know," he decided. "Yes. We are brothers in knowing."

The NSR mechanic chomped his birch and crossed his arms and said, "No, weirdo. You're not getting on my tracks."

"Why?" Patrick cried. "We have an emergency here, a verifiable emergency! You're train people; they're train people. You should help us! Why won't you help us?"

"Because you Amtrak people drink babies' blood so you'll live forever," the mechanic said easily, and with total confidence. He sounded almost bored when he said it.

Patrick threw both hands into the air, and his whole face puckered in a blatant show of disbelief. "What?" he shouted. "We don't drink babies' blood! Why would we?! Baby blood is the weakest of all blood! It hasn't been run through any gauntlets! It's weak blood! It's lie-down blood! What are you even talking about?! Of *course* Amtrakers don't drink babies' blood. Where would they even find babies calm enough to lie down and be chill while they drained all their blood?!"

The mechanic chewed more of his birch root. He considered Patrick's words for a good, long while. Eventually, he pulled the twig from his teeth and said, "Y'all use abortion magic."

"What even *is* abortion magic?!" Patrick exploded. "What could abortion magic possibly *be?!*"

The Norfolk Southern mechanic shrugged his shoulders in a lazy kind of way. "I don't know. Death-baby blood-magic. Don't want no part of it."

Patrick reached for the nearest seat cushion and yanked it over so it covered his face when he screamed as hard as he could into the cheap polyester. Once he'd emptied his feelings into the cushion, he flipped it back over his shoulder and tried to resume a reasonable pose. "Listen, loony. We have a man on board who will die if we don't get him the care he needs. He will die soon. *Very* soon."

The mechanic tilted one eyebrow and chomped on his twig. "We all gonna die pretty soon," he said.

Patrick was so mad. He didn't know if he'd ever been madder than he was right then. He gripped the dipshit's whole face with his two hands and brought it close his own face. "Listen to me, you backwoods, low-country, fish-fucking ass hat. We're not turning this train around. We are using your tracks. You have eight seconds to say yes, or else I'm going to eat your heart out of your throat and smash your dumb, dead legs through your own face."

"I'll allow you the opportunity to let go of my face," the man said. "Then, 'cause you was disrespectful, I'm gonna make you watch while I throw your friends into the zombie cage, one by one."

Patrick let go of the man's head. "Zombie cage?"

"It's where we keep the zombie," a second NSR dummy piped up from over by the rail switch.

"You don't have to explain it, Neil, it's right there in the name," the first man said, annoyed.

"Well excuuuuuse me, *Bill*, but he *asked* like he were wantin' clarification!" Neil snapped back.

"I'm sensing some tension here," Patrick announced. "I did understand that the zombie cage was a cage for keeping a zombie. Sorry, Neil. It was more of a surprise reaction."

Neil frowned. Bill smirked and said, "Yeah, I bet it was a surprise. Didn't think you'd come all the way down here just to get your men ate up by a duster, didja?"

"No, I'm surprised you would be stupid enough to threaten us with something so dumb. You want to throw this crew into the zombie cage? *This* crew? Into the *zombie* cage? Puh!" Patrick crossed his arms. "Knock yourself out. Throw 'em in, see how many seconds it takes until you don't have a zombie anymore."

"They're actually not even zombies," Neil chided quietly, kicking at a rock.

"Thank you, Neil!" Patrick cried. "I've been saying that for *years*. I've just given up, but I'm glad there are men out here like you, fighting the good fight." He raised a fist in solidarity. Neil grumped at him and stormed off. Patrick shrugged. He turned back to Bill. "Anyway, what were we saying?"

Bill drew a butcher knife from a leather sheath on his hip. "You was just about to pick one of your crew to get eaten up."

"Oh, right. I don't know, man, pick any of them! Go ahead! Any one of them will have that zombie on the floor in three seconds. Right, gang?" Patrick turned to the rest of the team. Ben was asleep in his bunk, and Rogers was laying low in the engine car so they'd still have a conductor if the NSR crew did something awful to Horace. Horace, for his part, had turned the color of wet flour, and it was extremely clear that his biggest regret in life was letting Patrick handle negotiations with the Norfolk Southerners. The Baby Caps were lined up behind Horace, and they looked absolutely horrified. Well, Babs and Lex looked horrified. Alice looked pissed off. "See? They're ready!" Patrick said.

Bill smiled a wicked grin. "Oh, this is gonna be fun," he decided. "Boys, get the cage ready!" he shouted over his shoulder. "Fresh meat comin' in!" A few of the mechanics ran off around the back side of a few train cars that were sitting on the side rail. A few more formed up behind Bill followed him onto Horace's train. Bill shoved Patrick into the wall. "This one watches," he ordered.

"That didn't hurt me—I'm from the Milk Generation."

Bill ignored him. He gazed at the rest of the team, relishing the opportunity to choose which one Patrick would watch die first. Finally, he pointed to Lex. "You," he said. "Come with me."

Lex's mouth fell open. "M-m-me?" he stammered.

"Yeah, you, Winnie the Pooh. You're first."

Alice stepped between Bill and Lex. "Let me go first."

Bill smirked. "Nah. You go last, darlin'. After you've gone a few rounds with the boys."

The mechanics behind Bill snickered at that. Alice's eyes flashed dangerously. "I can't wait to cut your dick off," she said.

"You'll get your chance," he promised. "Come on, Fat Albert, time to go."

"Patrick?" Lex pleaded. Tears had welled up in his eyes, and he was visibly trembling.

Patrick, in contrast, was calm, relaxed, and practically beaming. "You're going to do great, Lex! I predict a total K.O. Thirty seconds, tops. Give us a second, will you, Lex?" Patrick put his arm around Bill's shoulder and pulled him aside. "Listen. I think this is going great. What do you say we make it interesting?"

Bill raised an eyebrow suspiciously. "I'm listenin'."

"Let's say we give the kid a weapon. You know, just so he's got a fair shot. Lock him in the cage, then throw in a bat or a hammer or something. Make it a real fight. *Mano y mano*. Let Lex and the zombie duke it out. If the kid loses, okay, the zombie gets a free meal. A big, big free meal. But if the kid wins, you let us on the track, and we go on our merry way."

Bill drew away from Patrick. A broad smile broke out across his face, and he roared with laughter.

Patrick laughed, too. "We're having so much fun!" he said.

Bill wiped tears from his eyes. "Brother, if your kid can survive that zombie, I'll brand the Amtrak logo on my ass and send you off myself."

Patrick put out his hand. "Deal?"

They shook on it.

Bill motioned at the men behind him, and they moved in and grabbed Lex by the arms. The poor Baby Cap was now in full blubbering mode, tears streaming down his round cheeks. Babs and Alice watched in horror as the mechanics dragged him to the door. "Patrick! Do something!" Babs cried.

Patrick held up a hand for the mechanics to pause. "Quick pep talk?" he asked. Bill nodded. "Okay, Lex. I want you to breathe. You got this. Okay? You have *got* this. You've got this, but you have to breathe, or else you'll die of asphyxiation. And I need you alive, because a lot is riding on you being alive. Breathe, Lex. Are you listening to me?"

"Patrick," Lex sobbed.

"Lex, your face is red. You look hot. You know what you need? You need a spritz." Patrick grabbed his spray bottle from the ledge and covered Lex in a fine, cool mist. "Ah! There you go. Now you're ready." He patted Lex on the shoulder, then he nodded to the mechanics. "Carry on."

"No!" Lex cried. "Patrick, please!" The mechanics dragged him down the steps and off the train. They led him out into the night, to the dark place behind the freight cars.

"Come on," Bill said, slapping Patrick on the back. "Let's see how it goes for him!"

Patrick turned to the astonished Baby Caps. He held up both hands and showed them his crossed fingers. "Here we go!" he said.

He jumped off the train and went to see the zombie.

16.

"Wow, that is a *big* zombie," Patrick said admiringly.

The duster in the cage was well over six feet tall. Even with the various tears in his skin and some chunks taken out of his flesh, he was still well-defined, with swollen muscles and a thick neck. Each of his legs was the size of a barrel. He was, in fact, a very big zombie.

"Angry, too," Bill grinned. "We ain't fed him a few days. Glad you boys came 'round when you did."

Lex had gone to a dark place. He was probably in shock. His eyes were covered with a hazy film, and he had stopped struggling against his captors. He moved now like an automaton whose battery was about to run out. Patrick tried to catch his eyes, to give him one last reassuring look, but Lex only stared dully into space.

Which was probably for the best, because Patrick had a feeling his looks weren't putting the poor Baby Cap at ease anyway.

Horace and the other Baby Caps had reluctantly followed them to the clearing beside the tracks. Babs and Horace were practically hyperventilating. Even Alice looked like she was going to be sick.

"Wanna say any parting words?" Bill asked.

"Give him hell, Lex! And make it quick." He held up and tapped his princess watch. "We're in a rush."

One of the mechanics brought over a ladder and placed it against the cage. The duster swiped at it, but this wasn't the mechanic's first time climbing the cage, and he'd angled it in such a way that kept the ladder out of reach. The mechanic scrambled up and balanced on the bars at the top of the cage. He pulled open the hatch. The zombie jumped for him, but tall as he was, and strong as his legs were, the cage was too high for him to swipe the top.

The men holding Lex shoved him toward the ladder. He was on full autopilot now. He climbed dutifully and quietly upward, rung after rung at a slow but steady pace. The duster watched him hungrily from inside the cage. But he didn't approach the ladder and didn't try to swipe at the boy's legs.

Bill bristled. It was small, almost indiscernible…but for just a moment, a shadow of concern flickered across his face.

"So, we gettin' the boy a bat, or what?" Patrick asked, rubbing his hands together.

Bill frowned. "Uh. Yeah. Yeah, right. Hey! Marv!" He snapped his fingers at an older mechanic on the edge of the crowd, leaning on a bat for support. "Toss it in."

"Oh…" Marv said, disappointed. He had been enjoying his rest. But he hobbled up to the cage and tossed the bat through the bars.

The zombie didn't even register its arrival. It was hyper-focused on the Baby Cap balancing across the top of his cage.

The mechanic holding open the hatch snorted. "Better suck it in, fat-so. You get stuck on the way down, you're gonna get eaten legs first." Lex didn't respond. He didn't blink. He barely breathed. He just lowered himself, slowly and mechanically, onto the edge of the hatch. He went limp and let himself fall through, like pudding.

"Oh, this is going to hurt," Patrick winced.

Lex hit the bottom of the cage hard. The air rushed out of his lungs like a huge bellows being jammed together. The duster watched the Baby Cap fall with a furious and scared look in its eyes. Now that Lex was on the ground, the duster moved to strike, but it immediately recoiled, as if something hard had hit it in the face. Lex was dazed. He looked up and didn't seem to understand what he was seeing. His head rolled over to the side, and he saw the bat lying there, within reach. He picked it up and swung it clumsily from his spot on the floor of the cage. The duster snarled and snapped its teeth, but it didn't come any closer.

Bill gritted his teeth. "What the fuck is happening?" he grumbled. The mechanics, who just moments before had been whooping and hollering and ready for a show, had all fallen totally silent.

Lex seemed to come back to himself a bit. He used the bat to push himself up to his feet. The zombie stalked the edges of the cage like an agitated tiger, but it wouldn't move close. Lex took a practice swing with the bat. He wasn't particularly athletic, and never had been, so the swing was gentle and flimsy. He was still trembling, but now he licked his lips and cocked the bat on his shoulder, ready to try again. He took a step toward the zombie. The monster yelped with fear, turned, and ran. But it was already at the edge of the cage, and it slammed its own head into one of the bars. It reeled backward, dazed. Lex raised the bat to strike, but he didn't have to; the zombie was desperate to get away from him, and it charged the bars again. It lowered its head and tried to drive through the iron grating, and every time it struck the cage, the sickening sound of its skull cracking filled the air. *CRUNCH! CRUNCH! CRUNCH! CRUNCH!* Over and over again, the crunching and cracking of its brain plates, until the sound wasn't a *CRUNCH* anymore, but a low, wet *THUNK...THUNK... THUNK.*

Eventually, the zombie stumbled, swaying like a drunken boxer, its head mashed in and misshapen. Greenish pink chunks oozed from the cracks in its skull and dribbled down its head. The zombie lunched one last time, face-first into the bars, then slid down the iron and fell to the floor, dead.

Bill's jaw hung open. "How the fuck—?" he asked, completely bewildered.

"Looks like a K.O. to me," Patrick said. He slapped Bill on the back. "Get those pants down, will you? Imma go heat up an Amtrak pin, then we gotta go."

17.

"Hey. Lex. You did really great, kid."

They were rumbling down the Norfolk Southern track, just a couple of hours from Asheville. The Baby Caps were gathered in their car, with Lex sitting on his bunk with his knees pulled up to his chin. He hadn't really stopped crying since they left the junction, but the tears were slowing down now. Patrick knelt next to the cot and frowned up at the kid.

"I'm sorry I couldn't tell you the plan. It all came together so fast, and they were standing right there, I couldn't let them know we were about to cheat our way through a zombie fight."

Lex rocked a bit on his haunches. "I—I knew," he said, his voice faltering. "I knew it worked on the squirrels. I just—I didn't know what would happen."

"I know," Patrick said.

"I was really scared," Lex whispered.

"We were *all* fucking scared," Babs said, hugging Lex close. She shot daggers at Patrick. "That was really fucking scary."

"Listen. Lex. Babs. I wasn't scared. Because I know this stuff. I've worked with it for years. I knew without a sliver of a doubt that it would work. Otherwise I wouldn't have dared try it." He gripped Lex's hand. It felt clammy and cold. "We were in more danger of the mechanics than we were the duster. I would not have let them take you if it wasn't safe. I don't expect you to believe that."

"We don't," Babs snapped.

Patrick took a breath. "Okay," he said. "I know. Just...I value you. All of you. I aim to protect you. I will always do everything I can to protect you."

"We don't need your protection," Alice said.

"Maybe not," Patrick agreed. "More likely, I'll need yours. I am in this with you. We're in it together. And we are going to find that goddamn cure for Ben."

"Why Asheville?" Rogers asked. He had materialized out of nowhere, melting forward quietly from the back of the car. "What's out there?"

"A scientist. The one who developed the Zom-Be-Gone, actually. We met a few years ago, and I've gone back a few times since then for refills. She's a good person. And she knows Susannah Gustheed intimately. If Gustheed has a cure, like Ben says, then Dr. Philbin is our best chance of finding her."

Rogers raised an eyebrow. "Philbin?"

"Don't get me started," Patrick said. "And she doesn't know where Gustheed is. So it's still a long shot. But maybe she and Ben can put their pieces together and figure out a good place to look. We have to try."

Rogers nodded. "Yeah. And we will."

"You shouldn't have let them take Lex," Babs said angrily. She squeezed her friend tighter. "Anyone but Lex."

Patrick sighed. He stood up from the floor. His knees cracked and his spine ached. "It didn't work out that way," he said. He sounded tired.

"Like he hasn't dealt with enough since M-Day. Are you happy?" Babs demanded, glaring.

Patrick turned his eyes on her, dark circles like bruises beneath his lids. "No, Babs," he said. "I am not."

18.

They pulled into Asheville a few hours before sunrise. Exhaustion wore their skins like split and fraying suits. Lex was still huddled on his cot, staring into space, not falling asleep but not keeping fully awake, either. Babs kept dozing off, then jerking awake, wanting to be there for Lex. Alice stood in the corner of their car, facing the wall and resting her head against the metal, letting the strange coolness of the steel plating calm her mind. Horace refused to let Rogers take over, said it was his responsibility to maneuver the train through enemy territory, though since they left the mechanics, there had been nothing but smooth riding. The Norfolk Southern tracks were less traveled than the Amtrak rails, and therefore in much better shape. Horace was so tired he almost missed the Asheville station. He engaged the brakes just in time; the engine car squealed to a halt beyond the station platform, but the rest of the train presented more or less easy exits.

Patrick and Rogers had spent their time sitting quietly in the dining car, Patrick using his thumb to trace the scar in his other palm, Rogers tapping a pen against his tabletop, lost deeply in thought and more or less oblivious to the world.

Ben had roused himself, in the musty quiet of his own car, but his fever was hotter than ever, and his left arm had begun to leak goo from its pores. He kept wiping it every minute or two, but the slow flow was constant. The oozing would spread. Soon his whole body would be leaking. The clock was ticking.

No one knew how many minutes were left on the timer.

"Asheville!" Horace called from the engine car. His voice was hoarse and tired, and no one heard him. But they were able to read the chipped and weathered signs on the station platform. A jolt shocked through the crew. Everyone stood up. The feeling tingled back to life in their fingers, their toes, and their brains.

"How far's this doctor?" Rogers asked Patrick.

"Not totally sure about my bearings, but I think actually not far at all. If we are where I think we are, we can be there in less than an hour."

Rogers bobbed his head. "Good news. Grab your spray bottle and let's go."

They gathered their weapons, and Patrick poked his head into the Baby Caps' car. "Anyone want to come with?" he asked. Alice was already strapping throwing knives to her thigh. So she was a gimme.

Babs rubbed her eyes. She'd been rubbing them all night, and now they were puffy and irritated. "Yeah," she decided. "Let's do it."

Patrick gave her a relieved if cautious smile. "Good."

"I want to come," Lex said, suddenly looking up and uncurling his legs.

Babs wrinkled the corners of her mouth. "Yeah? You sure?"

"You're not just winding us up?" Patrick asked.

Lex nodded. "I got us down here. I want to see it through."

Patrick clapped his hands together and rubbed his palms. "All right! Five is a good number. In my experience, this area's generally pretty safe, if there are no psychopaths with paddle wheel boats around. We should be good with five."

"Six."

They all turned toward the rear door. Ben stood there looking like absolute death. His shirt hung loosely on his shoulders. His skin was pale green, and his left arm was streaked with vibrant green remnants of the goo seeping out of his pores. His eyes were bloodshot, and the whites had begun their transition to sickly mint. Green fluid trickled down his cheeks, leaking from his ears. His cough had never sounded worse. It was wet and heavy and full.

"Not six," Patrick said. "We have no space for a Jenna von Oÿ."

"A who?" Alice asked, frowning.

Patrick ignored her. "You're on bed rest. Doctor's orders."

"You're not a doctor," Ben replied.

"I'm a mechanical engineer, which is basically a doctor."

"Name one bone."

Patrick hesitated. "Head bone," he guessed.

"Exactly. I'm coming with you."

Babs stepped forward and placed a gentle hand on Ben's shoulder. "Ben...I say this with love and respect, but you have never looked older or worse."

"And I'm probably never gonna look younger or better," he said, his voice heavy with exhaustion. "I'm at the end of my life, and somehow the only good thing going in that life is that this idiot is back from the dead." He lifted a finger at Patrick. "I lost track of you once. Not again."

Patrick placed a hand on his heart. "Ben. That's very sweet. I love you too. But you can barely stand. How are you going to make this walk?"

"I'll carry him," Lex said, stepping forward.

Patrick straightened up with surprise. "Like a baby?" he asked.

"He can ride on my back," Lex said. "It won't be hard. He's small."

"I'm above-average height," Ben insisted.

"Sure you are, big guy." Patrick patted him gently on the head. His hand came away slick with a trace coating of green juices. Patrick's face soured. "Ew. He's messy."

"Hold on." Babs hauled a cardboard box out from beneath her cot and rummaged through her things. She presented a large blue and white beach towel. It was stained and a little shredded at the ends. She tossed it around Lex's shoulders. "There. Now Ben can leak."

"Great," he said miserably.

Rogers and Babs carefully lifted Ben up onto Lex's back. His arms fell like noodles around the Baby Caps' neck. "Should we tie him on?" Patrick asked.

They decided that was probably a good idea.

Rogers found a bungee cord in the engine room, and they used it to secure Ben to Lex's back. Lex stood up tall and wriggled his shoulders a little. He shrugged. "That'll work."

"You look like a turtle with a Ben shell," Alice pointed out.

Patrick beamed. "Aw, you *are* a Tortle!" he said.

They gathered up their weapons and their flashlights. Alice handed everyone red, deflated balloons. Everyone took one and knew exactly what to do with it, except Patrick, who had no idea what the hell he was supposed to do with a rubber balloon.

"We put them over the flashlights," Rogers explained. "Doesn't let through as much brightness as you'd like, but it makes the light red."

"And harder for other people to see," Patrick said. "Aha." He tapped his temple. "Very smart."

"It was Babs' idea," Rogers said.

"Red cellophane is better, but we haven't had any for a while," Babs added, pushing her glasses up her nose.

"Oh! I have presents for you all, too!" Patrick said, remembering. He dug through his bag, digging out an eyedropper, a roll of twine, and a small vial that was maybe one-quarter full of purple liquid. "Wrists," he instructed. He cuts lengths of twine and tied them around each Red Cap's wrist. Then he used the dropper to distribute two drops of the purple liquid onto each person's bracelet. "There! Now you're zombie-proof."

"You know, you could have done this for all of us two days ago," Babs said.

"I know," Patrick replied, shaking his head dramatically. "Where *is* my head these days? Oh well! Better late than never, right? Let's ride!" He gave himself an extra drop of Zom-Be-Gone, right onto his watch strap, then leapt out of the train and into the darkness. "Come on, Tortle!" he shouted. "Tick-tock!"

"I guess we're going," Rogers said.

Ben lifted his hand and pointed at the doorway. "Forward, Tortle."

They all eased down into the platform and set out into the pre-dawn Carolina morning.

A few minutes later, Horace popped his head through the engine room door and into the empty train. "Hey. Guys?" He looked around. He frowned. "Hello?"

19.

"Should we have told Horace we were leaving?" Lex asked.

Patrick shook his head. "Nah. I'm sure he'll be fine."

Navigation was a challenge in the deep darkness of the night, with only muted red lanterns to illuminate the steps ahead. But Patrick had a pretty good sense of where they were headed, and he was reasonably confident they were moving in the right direction. "I think those are the woods we cut through to get to Philbin's place," he said, pointing at a long stretch of dark and scraggly trees in the distance. "Her subdivision should be right on the other side."

It was nice that things were going so smoothly for a change.

They cut their way across the overgrown lawns and looked for a trail leading through the forest. Alice found a trampled path, which they decided was probably the best they could hope for. They crept over the trail of broken brush. What little light the moon gave through the Monkey fog was swallowed up by the quilt of branches that wove itself together overhead. "Don't let the *Blair Witch* vibe freak you out," Patrick said, sounding pretty freaked out about the *Blair Witch* vibe. "There are houses at the other end."

"What's a Blair Witch?" Babs asked.

Patrick slapped his hand to his forehead. "God forgive this lost generation," he begged.

"Uh, my generation was born into *this*," Babs said, indicating the world around them. "Your generation is the one that got lost, old guy."

"Old guy?!" Patrick cried. "Lost?! You would feel *such* regret for saying that—*existential* regret—if you knew about Green Day's *Dookie*."

The Baby Caps exchanged glances. Babs said, "Man…I have never heard anyone sound older than you sounded just now."

"Wow. 'Welcome to Paradise' was right," he said sadly.

"That means nothing to me."

"Because you chumps gotta take the longview!"

"Is that another Green Day reference?" she asked.

"No, you basket case. God, it's like pulling teeth with you burnouts."

Lex raised his hand. "What's a Green Day?" he asked.

"I don't like what's happening here," Babs decided. "Please stop being so old."

"Don't worry, Pat," Ben said tiredly, his whole body slumped onto Lex's back. "They'll come around."

Somehow, despite the darkness and the stretching fingers of branches above, they were surprised to find that the woods felt more comforting than the open suburban sprawl. At least in the forest, they were hidden; God knew what might be hiding out there in the trees, but creeping through open asphalt and open grass was somehow worse. The woods made them feel protected. The woods made them feel safe.

Alice grabbed Patrick by the arm and yanked him back "Stop!" she hissed.

Patrick yelped in surprise. He slipped on a pile of leaves and landed hard on his seat. "Ow! Butt root," he moaned, rubbing his ass and cursing the tree root he'd fallen on.

"Quiet," Alice instructed. The whole crew instinctively froze. If Alice was saying it, it meant something.

"What's wrong?" Babs asked.

Alice didn't respond. Instead, she crouched down in the leaves and let her fingers cautiously trace the path ahead. They quickly came into contact with a set of sharp, steel teeth spiking up from the ground.

"Oh, shit," Babs gasped. "Is that a bear trap?"

Alice pointed down along the path. "Lots of bear traps."

Now that their attention was focused, the rest of the crew could just make out the tips of other bear trap teeth rising secretly from the bed of leaves that covered the track.

"Okay, so how do we feel about going a different way?" Patrick asked the group.

A man screamed at their left. He exploded out from the brush and charged with a machete held up over his shoulder, ready to swing. Alice dove forward and lifted the bear trap from its place in the dirt. She flicked it with a hard snap of her wrist, and the steel trap came down on the attacker's head. The jaws snapped, and the metal teeth sank deep into his skull, catching his mouth in front right where his lips split and driving into the back of the man's scalp. He screamed. His limbs trembled, the nerves animating his good-as-dead limbs. He fell back onto the forest floor. He fell onto another trap, and that one snapped onto his shoulder, ripping a huge chunk of muscle and tissue away from his bone socket.

He wasn't alive long enough to feel it much.

The crew held their breath. The air was still. After several long moments, Rogers asked, "Think he was alone?"

"Well," Patrick said, wetting his lips, which had gone totally dry with fear. "If there are more, they don't seem particularly interested in…meeting Alice." He held the back of his hand to his mouth and tried not to throw up.

"That was *brutal*," Lex told Alice, his voice a mixture of fear and awe.

She scowled. "Just did to him what he tried to do to us," she said.

"I can't see," Ben complained. "I want to see!" Lex turned so Ben could get a better view of the body. "Oh, I don't want to see that," he decided.

They decided not to try to navigate the bear trap minefield until it was light out. Even trying to go around was risky, since they couldn't be sure how far the traps had been spread. For all they knew, they'd lucked their way past several already. They could be surrounded. So instead, they hunkered down for about an hour, tense and ready for another attack. But no second attack came. Eventually, the first hints of sunshine began to rise over the mountains to the east. When there was enough light to see pretty clearly, they gathered themselves up and made ready to continue. Patrick sprayed more Zom-Be-Gone into the woods behind them—not that it would have helped with bear trap attackers, but it was nice to take some sort of protective action, even if that action wasn't at all protective.

"Who feels good about moving off the path?" he asked, raising his hand. "Anyone else feel comfortable chancing the brush?"

Everyone agreed. The path less traveled seemed like the safer choice.

They cut through the scraggly growth, sometimes literally, swinging machetes when the branches got too thick, stamping down bushes when the way forward was rough. After twenty minutes of tromping through overgrown forest, they finally broke out into a clearing, with small houses dotting a cul-de-sac that Patrick knew very well.

"Ah!" he said, his eyes lighting up. "We're here!"

He led them toward a mid-size ranch with pale blue siding that was tucked back into the further recesses of the circle. The house was still in bad shape; the windows were still boarded, the siding was still slipping, and the gutters still hung off the roof at awkward angles. It was all just as Patrick remembered it. Except for one thing.

The yard was completely free of dusters.

Each time Patrick had visited the house, the dusters were a constant. They had been crucial to Philbin's work, so she kept them corralled in front of her house. But now they were gone. The unnatural order of things had shifted.

"This isn't good," Patrick decided. "There should be zombies."

Rogers gave him a strange look. "It's bad because there *aren't* zombies?" he asked.

Patrick didn't respond. He walked cautiously to the mailbox, every nerve sparking to attention. He pulled the mailbox lid down. He put his mouth to the opening. "Hello?" he said. The Baby Caps exchanged worried glances. None of them had expected Patrick to start talking to mailboxes. "Dr. Philbin? Hello?" he said.

There was no response. The walkie was inside, but the speaker didn't crackle.

The line was dead.

20.

"Hey, Lurch, unbuckle me, will you? I'm all sweaty," Ben said.

Lex unhooked the bungee cord, and Ben slid off his back like a slug sliding off a leaf, slowly, leaving a sticky trail in his wake.

Ben walked over to the mailbox, which Patrick was smacking with his hand as if it were an old TV set that wasn't getting reception. "I have questions about what you're doing, but I'm too tired to ask them," Ben said miserably. "Are we going inside or what?"

Patrick frowned. "I guess so. But I got a bad feeling about this, Benny Boy." He bent down and lifted the manhole cover off the storm sewer. He swung his legs over the side and started to climb down.

"What in God's absolute nightmare are you doing?" Ben demanded.

Patrick blinked. He looked down into the sewer. He looked back up at Ben. "This is how you get in," he said, as if it were the most obvious thing.

"Into the house?" Ben asked.

"Yeah."

"*That* house?" Ben said, pointing at Dr. Philbin's house.

"Yeah, *that* house."

"You know that house has a door."

"Oh, yes, well, it does, but Philbin doesn't like it when people use the front door. We use the sewer." He climbed down another rung.

"Look, you weirdo, there's no one here. I'm not crawling through an old sewer to get into an empty house. I'm using the door." He turned and shuffled up the walk.

"You don't know she's not here!" Patrick called after him. "It could be a test! To see who uses the sewer and who uses the door! If this ends up being some kind of test she devised in secret because she knows she can only trust people who enter through the sewer, you're going to be sorry!"

Ben ignored him. He shuffled up to the front door and turned the handle. It was unlocked. The door creaked open.

Ben poked his head inside. There was not a single sign of life.

Patrick watched with interest. "Okay, maybe it's not a test," he decided. He hopped out of the storm drain and jogged up the walk. "Wait up!"

The rest of the crew stayed back in the cul-de-sac, watching the street and the woods for threats. Patrick popped his head in over top of Ben's. "I've always wanted to be a *Scooby-Doo* cartoon," Patrick whispered.

They entered the house, Patrick with the trusty machete Bleakachu in hand, Ben finding it difficult to walk but trying not to show it. The house was dark. Patrick pulled the balloon off his flashlight and clicked it on. As far as he could tell, things looked pretty much the same now as they had every other time he'd visited. The rooms were sparsely outfitted and tidy, if not clean. There were no signs of life, though in Patrick's experience, Philbin had never been a "signs of life" person anyway. He crept through the house, his grip tight on the machete. Ben moved more slowly and decided to go through the kitchen cabinets instead of following Patrick down the hall. After a few minutes, Ben had found nothing of interest, and Patrick returned to the main room. "Nothing," he said.

"Is there a basement?"

"Where do you think the sewer tunnel goes?"

They made their way down the basement steps. Philbin's generator wasn't running, and it was the first time Patrick had been down there in darkness. A chill ran up his spine. He swept the flashlight back and forth across the subterranean space, his eyes alert, Bleakachu ready.

But just like the main floor, the basement was empty.

Also like main floor, this space hadn't been ransacked. Everything was pretty much how it had always been. "Doesn't look like she was attacked," Patrick said, peering around the room. "Seems like she just sort of…left. And took all the zombies with her."

They did a deeper exploration of the house, with Patrick taking the lead and Ben stopping every few minutes to lean against a wall and catch his breath. His shoes had begun squishing when he walked, a clear sign of Monkey juice leaking out through his feet.

There was a test tube rack near a centrifuge in the back that still held six vials of a familiar purple liquid. Patrick plucked them out of their slots and slipped them into his backpack. "She didn't take the Zom-Be-Gone. Or at least not all of it. She must have been in a hurry."

They didn't find anything else of particular interest in the basement. They went back upstairs, and Patrick had to lend Ben his arm so that he could make the climb. They headed toward the door and on a whim, Patrick popped open the kitchen trash can and looked inside. Sitting on top of a pile of empty tin cans and cardboard food packaging lay a half-folded piece of paper. Patrick reached in and drew out the note. He spread it open on the kitchen counter.

"Ben," he breathed. He looked up, his eyes huge. "Look."

Ben shuffled around the counter so he could see the paper. It was a small sheet, ripped neatly from a notepad, the kind once found sitting next to a phone in a hotel room. The print was sharp and deliberate, and this is what it said:

Re −
I did it. It works.
Come see.
                    -Susy

Patrick's hands began to tremble. His eyes glowed like moons. "Susy is Susannah Gustheed. It *must* be. She was working on a cure. 'It works.'"

"Great," Ben groaned. "We still don't know where the hell she is."

Patrick's face broke into a huge grin. "Oh, yes we do," he said. He tapped the logo at the top of the stationery. It was a red, white, and blue ocean liner sitting atop a set of aqua blue waves. Beneath the image in a small and tidy font were two lines of text:

THE QUEEN MARY
LONG BEACH, CALIFORNIA

"Long Beach?" Ben read.
Patrick grinned. "Buckle up, Benny Boy. We're going on spring break."

21.

They called in the Red Caps and did a full sweep of Philbin's house, packing up anything that might be useful—beakers, lighters, a small stash of food, a cache of batteries, a bunch of scientific equipment that none of them could name. "Isn't she going to be mad that we took this stuff when she comes back?" Lex asked.

"She's not coming back," Patrick said.

They hauled a few boxes out the front door. At the end of the driveway, Patrick opened the mailbox and yanked out the walkie-talkie that was fixed to the inside. He tossed it in his box, along with its mate, which he'd found lying on the floor near the couch.

They also grabbed a few of the bear traps from the woods, just for fun.

Back at the train, Horace was putting out fires. Literally.

"Couldn't leave me just one person to help watch the train!" he shouted as the others came running up. "Let's all just go on an adventure—ol' Horace has it under control!"

There was a pool of blazing oil beneath the engine. Horace had a push broom and was trying to spread the oil thin enough that it would burn out, but the bristles of the broom kept catching fire, and he had to stamp them out with his boots every time they lit. Babs and Alice ran inside and grabbed a bunch of blankets. The whole team went to work smothering the fire, and after five minutes and only a few singed hands, the fire was out and the blankets were ruined.

"What happened?" Rogers asked.

"Some black-eyed daughter of Satan ran up out of nowhere and lobbed an oil bomb at my head!" Horace cried. "Her aim was off by about ten good feet, thank God. Could have really burned up the engine, though!"

Patrick looked around, scratching his head. The tracks were surrounded by thick brush, and aside from the path they'd tramped down themselves on their way in and out of Asheville, the rest of the overgrowth was tall and undisturbed. "Where'd she go?" he asked.

"I don't know! Ran up, threw the bomb, ran away!"

"Are you sure you didn't just accidentally catch the train on fire?"

"What?!" Horace exploded.

"I'm just asking if the train had an oil leak and you accidentally caught it on fire and tried to blame it on an imaginary terrorist," Patrick said innocently.

"Of course not! What a thing to accuse a man of!"

"If I look under that engine, am I going to see a hole in the oil line, Horace?" Patrick asked.

"Well, there's probably a hole there *now*! This train ain't had proper maintenance in almost a decade, she's probably riddled with holes down there!"

"And this oil bomber...?"

"She was real!" Horace cried.

"Mm-hmm, mm-hmm," Patrick said, tenting his fingers together thoughtfully. "And is the oil bomb woman in the station with us now?"

Horace's face darkened to a deep shade of purple. His whole body trembled. He was so worked up, he forgot how to form words. He just sputtered like a cartoon character, flecks of spit raining out from between his clenched lips.

"I'll check the engine," Rogers said, pushing up his sleeves, "see if she did any real damage. I'll let you tell Horace the plan," he told Patrick. "But you might want to take a few steps back. He looks ready to pop, and this might just about do it."

"Why?" Horace finally managed to holler through his stifling anger. "What's this *plan*?"

"Oh! It's good news! We know where to find the cure," Patrick said brightly. "Long Beach!"

Horace was suddenly still. He pulled his hat back down on his head so that it nearly covered his eyes. "Long Beach...California?" he asked, in a voice that balanced on the edge of a knife.

"Uhh..." This simmering glower was not the reaction Patrick had expected. "Yes?"

Horace's eyes blazed. He turned back to the train. He stomped up the steps. "We are *not* taking this train to California!" he yelled. He stormed into the dining car and slammed the door behind him.

Patrick was confused. "He got a thing against coastal elites?"

"No," said Rogers. Then he reconsidered. "Well, yes. But it's not the destination. It's the journey."

"Yes, I've heard that before," Patrick nodded.

"What's wrong with *this* journey?" Ben asked, easing himself down to a seat on the platform.

"What's wrong is, all the other tracks are blown, and there's only one track to California left," said Rogers, crawling beneath the train. "You want to get to Long Beach? We take the Slaughterhouse Run."

22.

"Okay, exceptionally cool name aside, what is the Slaughterhouse Run?" Patrick asked.

Horace crossed his arms and gave Patrick his most obstinate look. "The Slaughterhouse Run is a death trap."

"You're not making me less interested," Patrick said, rubbing his hands together.

"It's a stretch of railway that runs right through the ninth circle of hell. The whole line is clogged up with murderers and rapists and thieves. Been that way for years now. Gangs and gypsy terrorists, boarding or derailing every train that goes through. Slittin' the throats of Red Caps for fun. Flaying Blue Caps like me alive, then hanging them from trees like trophies. All the way from New Orleans to Los Angeles, two thousand miles of death traps. There's not a single conductor who's made the run since the butchers set up shop along that rail. We run that line, we're all dead. No other possibility. That answer your question?"

Patrick frowned. "I don't think we're supposed to use the word 'gypsy' anymore."

Horace sighed. He sat down at one of the tables. "Look, Patrick. I know you want to save your friend. I want him saved, too. Ben's become like a son to me these last four or five years. I'd do anything to help that boy. But if we try the Slaughterhouse Run, he'll die anyway, and so will the rest of us."

"That's not a very can-do attitude," Patrick pointed out.

"I'm not putting every person on my train at risk to make an ill-fated attempt to save one."

"You guys know I'm here, right?" Ben said weakly from the floor of the dining car. "I'm lying down, but I'm here."

Horace frowned. "Sorry, Ben. It's not personal."

Ben gave him a thumbs up.

"Horace, I understand your concerns. I do. I mean, as neither a Red Cap nor a Blue Cap, it sounds like I actually might do pretty well in this situation, but I don't want to have to watch them flay you alive. It takes hours to do that, and my attention span is—look, none of us wants anything bad to happen. But bad things are always going to keep happening. If it's not lunatics in Los Angeles, it'll be nutbags in Nashville or mercenaries in Madison or pirates in Pittsburgh or killers in…hmm…does this train go to Kalamazoo?"

"Stop being alliterative," Ben said.

"No, never," Patrick replied. "My point is, death is coming for us sooner or later. It's here for Ben *now*. We can stop it."

"If it's coming for all of us sooner or later, why not just let him get it over with sooner on his own?"

"Still right here," Ben said.

"Because none of us have to get it over with sooner! We can all die way more slowly, together!"

"You're talking in circles, son."

"Horace, we can do this!" Patrick cried, slapping his palms on the table. "I feel it in my bones!"

"You don't even know what we're up against."

"Sure, killers and gypsies and all that! I got it!"

"But you don't know *how*," Horace insisted. "We can't plan to make it because we don't know *how* they'll try to murder us down there. Not *really*. None of us does."

"Well. I do." Rogers stepped onto the train, wiping his oily hands on an old and grease-stained handkerchief. "Some of it, anyway."

"Oh, well that is convenient," Patrick beamed.

"So then you know firsthand how bad it is," Horace countered.

"You're a real glass half empty kind of guy, Horace," Patrick frowned.

Rogers tucked his handkerchief into his back pocket and walked over to the tables. He almost stepped on Ben but stopped his foot at the last second. "Oh. Sorry. Didn't see you." He stepped over Ben's green and sweaty body and took a seat at the table across the aisle from Patrick and Horace.

"You and everyone else," Ben mumbled.

"We're good to go, by the way. The oil line is in bad shape, but—"

"Was it Horace?" Patrick interrupted excitedly.

Rogers raised an eyebrow. "Inconclusive," he said. Patrick's excitement melted away. "Got it patched up for now, should last us a while, until we can get our hands on some scrap pieces to swap." He sat crosswise on the booth seat, propping his back against the train wall and letting his feet dangle over the edge of the bench. "I used to run with some of the guys who ended up on the Run," he said. "Hell, I even spent a few weeks helping one of those gangs dig in near the tracks until I realized they were the kind of men to kill any outsiders once the work we were doing was done."

Horace slapped his hand on the table. "See? This is the kind of man we're talking about here!"

"They're dangerous. Probably run into the most dangerous men— and women—we've ever seen if we try to make the Run."

"Thank you," said Horace.

"But Patrick's right," Rogers continued. Horace nearly choked with surprise. "They're not boogeymen. They're not the stuff of legends. They're human. They make a lot of mistakes, and they can be killed just as easily as we can."

Patrick squirmed a little in his seat. "Okay, well, I wasn't necessarily angling for us to *kill* anyone…"

Rogers ignored him. "I'm not saying it's a good idea. But I'm saying it *is*, theoretically, possible to make the Slaughterhouse Run."

"Then why hasn't anyone done it yet?" Horace demanded.

"Fear looms large. How many people you think even tried? A dozen? Less?"

"Fewer," Ben corrected from the floor.

"Ben's a writer," Patrick explained proudly. "He wrote my life story." He slapped his leg and shouted, "Oh *yeah!* I *knew* I was forgetting to tell you something, Ben! You know how I found you? Someone had a copy of the book you wrote about me! I *knew* you were writing a book about me, you son of a bitch! I used to say it all the time! I *knew* it!"

"I didn't do that until after you were dead," Ben insisted. "Don't make me wish for you to die again."

Patrick folded his arms and smugly sat back in his seat. "I knew you were writing a book about me," he said again.

"Can we focus, here?" Horace asked.

"I'm honestly not sure," Patrick whispered.

Rogers cleared his throat. "What I'm saying is, it's dangerous, yes. Extremely dangerous. But it's possible to survive it. I have some idea what's waiting for us out there. We've heard a lot of campfire tales about the other traps, maybe they're real, maybe they're just based on a kernel of truth.

We can use that. We've got the best conductor on the Amtrak line, hell, probably on any line. We've got an engineer, right? Who was good enough to design the ramrod plow, seems like he's probably good for another few tricks up his sleeve."

"I only wear short sleeves," Patrick said proudly.

"Not helping," Ben said.

Rogers continued: "We've also got three young Caps back there who were forged in the death of this world. They're not learning how to adapt to the ruin; they went full native in the ruin. Even that kid, Lex. Good man, soft heart, but there's steel in him."

"Ben also brings things to the table," Patrick announced loudly, making a big gesture down toward his prostrate friend. He gave Ben an exaggerated wink. Ben flipped him off.

"We've got about a day's ride before we hit New Orleans. That's a fair amount of time to make a plan and get to work."

"We are, everyone one of us, going to die on this mission," Horace insisted. But his voice was less certain now. There were audible cracks in his resolve.

"Listen, Horace. We can make it," Patrick said. "And if we do die… then we die for family."

Horace took a few breaths. He looked away from Patrick. He looked down at Ben.

So did Rogers.

So did Patrick.

"What?" Ben grumped. "Stop looking at me, I barely know you people."

Horace sighed. He looked back up at Patrick. "Maggie and I have been together for over a decade, Patrick." Patrick looked at Rogers. *Maggie?* he mouthed. Rogers gestured to the train. "I don't intend to lose her. Definitely not to the Slaughterhouse."

"I don't think you'll have to," Patrick said, patting Horace's hands. "I already have some ideas."

"It's not always good when he says that," Ben moaned from the floor.

Horace frowned so hard his mustache drooped. "It's going to have to be good this time," he said. He let loose a mighty sigh as he pushed himself to his feet. "Come up with it fast. I'll get us moving toward New Orleans."

23.

"My favorite thing about me," Patrick said happily as the train pulled out of the Asheville station, "is that no one ever learns not to listen to me."

"I learned not to listen to you a long time ago," Ben said.

Patrick shook his head. "No you didn't. You've never once not listened to me. And you should know better than that best of all."

Ben pressed his hands against his head. "My fever is too hot for your syntax."

"That's okay." Patrick pressed himself up from the table and stretched until his spine cracked. He leaned over and patted Ben on the knee. "I'm gonna go get started on Slaughterhouse prep. You just keep laying there on the disgusting floor of a sad, mobile cafeteria."

"Lying," Ben corrected him.

"I'm not. This is the most depressing food hall I've ever seen." He stepped out of the dining car and headed toward the back of the train. He needed to take a full inventory so he knew what they were working with. He tipped his imaginary hat to the Baby Caps as he trundled through their car, but Babs leapt out in front of him and blocked his path, her curly hair bouncing with excitement.

"Are we seriously doing the Slaughterhouse Run?" she asked.

"Oh. Uh...well. Yeah. It...yeah. We are." Patrick swallowed. He looked at the little Caps. "We should have asked you first. Shit. I'm sorry. Look, if you all have—"

"*Woooo!*" Babs cried, throwing her hands up in celebration. Patrick took a step back. He glanced at the other Baby Caps. Lex was clapping to himself, and even Alice let her lips curl into a small smirk.

"Wait. You…? You're good with it? Even though it's death and horror and everything?"

Babs clapped her hands to his shoulders. "Patrick! You don't understand!" she beamed. "We have been *dying* to take on the Slaughterhouse."

"O…kayyyy," Patrick said warily. "I'm glad that we're all on the same page with next steps. Just…to be clear, you're all just *actively excited* about the opportunity to probably get butchered alive? Horace made a big thing about throat being slit and skin being flayed, so I just want to be sure."

"Everyone treats us like kids," Alice said. "They don't take us seriously."

"I take you *very* seriously. Especially you. I saw what you did with that bear trap. I take you very, very seriously, Malice."

"Alice."

"It was a joke, please do not harm me," he whimpered.

"Thinking about it."

"This is so exciting," Babs interjected. She clapped her hands together and bounced on the balls of her feet. "Let us help."

"If you don't let us help, I will kill you," Alice said, sounding bored.

"Hey. No. Listen. Yes. I need all the help I can get. You're hired. Okay?" He tilted his head toward Lex. "How about you, you big lug? Are you into this whole thing?"

Lex looked at him with soft, sad eyes. "I'm not water," he said quietly. "Everyone thinks I'm water. But I'm not water."

Babs hugged Lex around the waist. "Lex is wood."

Patrick nodded. "This feels like some sort of new-generation slang that I fully support. Okay. Well, this is a relief. The first thing I need help with is doing a full inventory of the train. Everything we have, whether it's obviously a weapon or obviously not at all a weapon. We're going to have to get creative, and fast. Knowing what we have to work with is critical."

"I have some pipe bombs," Alice said. "I told Horace I didn't. But I do."

"Excellent," Patrick said, scribbling in his notebook. "That's excellent. And helpful. I'll start in the caboose, can you all take an inventory of this car?"

"On it, chief!"

Patrick soured. "Don't call me chief. Feels too appropriated. I'm also only in charge by default. I'm the least qualified person on this train to be in charge." He waved them off and disappeared into the next car.

"I think I'm starting to get the whole 'apocalypticon' thing," Babs decided. Alice and Lex nodded their agreement.

They set to work, following Patrick's instructions. If they were going to tackle the Slaughterhouse, the whole train would have to follow one lead.

It was becoming pretty clear which voice they'd bet their lives on.

24.

"Horace? Real quick. Weird question," Patrick said, staring up at the ceiling instead of making eye contact. "What percentage can I fuck up this train?"

"Son, if you put one scratch on my train, I will carry you hogtied off this train and drop you on an angry scorpion," said Horace.

"Hmm," Patrick said, tapping a pencil against his teeth. "I was hoping the answer would be at least eighteen percent. Can you meet me at eighteen percent?"

Horace closed his eyes and rubbed his nose. "Patrick. Can you just tell me what you want to do so I can tell you how mad I'm going to be when you go ahead and do it anyway?"

"I love that we understand each other," Patrick said. "I want to cut holes in the top of the train so we can pop up and shoot stuff."

"We don't have anything that shoots."

"Well, you haven't seen Alice's workshop, clearly," Patrick said, feigning disgust. "I'll tell you, that girl has some pretty post-modern ideas about weaponry, and I am *very* terrified to watch them work. But mostly, 'shoot stuff' is kind of a catch-all term. Shoot stuff, throw stuff at people, escape from stuff people throw in here…it's a pretty wide umbrella."

Horace pinched the bridge of his nose. "Patrick, how are you even going to cut holes in the top of the train?"

"Cutting torch."

"We don't have a cutting torch."

"Listen, Horace I'm not kidding; that Alice girl is deranged, and you have *got* to start regulating what she brings onto this train, it is *not* safe." He gave Horace a formal salute, then he turned on his heels and marched out the door. "Glad we could settle on eighteen percent. Plus or minus ten."

"Don't do anything that's not absolutely necessary!" Horace shouted after him.

"Can't hear you, bye!"

Patrick whistled on his way back to the storage car. The Baby Caps were in there, on his orders, organizing things into three piles: Useful, Not Very Useful, and Not Very Useful but Potentially Fun to Throw at Someone. "Great news, everyone, Horace doesn't care if we fuck up the train!"

"I find that hard to believe," Babs said. "So what's the plan?"

Patrick rubbed his chin. "We start with the hatches," he decided. "Each car gets one in the ceiling. Two would be better, but I don't think we'll have time. Cut them in three-by-three squares. Be careful; they'll be heavy. Each one will need hinges and a latch. We'll take apart some storage compartments for those pieces. None of it will look pretty, but it should work. I'll draw it up for you. Alice, I assume you know how to use that oxy-acetylene torch?"

"Yeah. I've only used it on people, but I guess it works the same on metal."

"Horrifying. Absolutely horrifying. Hatches first, and we'll need to make sure we can reach them easily. Molotovs and oil bombs next. You all work on those things, that should keep you pretty busy."

"What're you going to do?"

"I'm going to figure out how to blow up the train."

25.

"Does Horace know you want to blow up his train?"

"I don't *want* to blow up the train," Patrick corrected Ben. "I just think we need to be *ready* to blow up the train."

"Why? This is our home. You don't blow up your own home."

"You do if it's raided by mercenaries. If we get boarded, I need to be able to blow the cars, individually or all at once. Uncouple them so we can leave them behind while we make a thrilling escape in the engine car."

"Oh." Ben lay his head back down on the floor.

Patrick looked down at him and clucked his tongue. "Why don't you lie down in your bed? I can help move you."

But Ben shook his head. "Too goopy," he said sadly. His skin was leaking a lot more Monkey juice now. A *lot* more. His condition was worsening quickly. Patrick was no expert, but based on other folks he'd seen succumb to the disease, Ben didn't have much time left. Maybe three days. *Maybe*. "I don't like how my mattress squishes when I'm in it now. The sound makes me want to throw up."

"I think it's the Monkey Flu that's making you want to throw up."

"That too," Ben agreed. "How are you going to do it?"

"Blow the train cars? Still sort of tinkering with that one. Alice straight up lied about not having pipe bombs, which is helpful. If nothing else, we can strap one to each coupler and blow it to hell. It would be spectacularly fun!"

"But?"

"But they work on fuses, and I'd like a solution that's a little more instantaneous. Plus, I'd rather hold onto the pipe bombs. You never know when you're going to need to hammer-throw an explosive at a raider. So those are a back-up plan."

"What's the front-up plan?"

"The front-up plan is probably this." He held up a small matchbox.

Ben squinted at the box. "You're going to try to melt the coupler with a match?"

"Fun idea! But no. This is not a matchbox."

"It is a matchbox."

"It is not a matchbox."

"I'm too tired for this."

"So I'll pretend you said, 'Then what is it?' And I'll say, 'It's a proto-type.'"

Ben held up a finger and spun it in a circle, encouraging Patrick to continue.

"Okay! 'A prototype of what, Patrick?' Great question, Ben! It's a pro-totype of a hyper-portable explosive packet. Here, catch." He tossed it at Ben. It landed on his chest with a soft *whump*, then bounced off onto the floor. Ben didn't flinch. Patrick frowned. "It would have been more fun if you'd panicked."

"Too dead to panic."

Patrick picked the matchbox off the floor. "I think I'm starting to pre-fer you alive." He shook the matchbox. It rattled like it was filled with sand. "Black powder," he explained, though Ben hadn't asked. "I just need to figure out how to ignite it. I'm thinking about putting little shards of steel and stone inside. Then, in theory, if you smashed it with a sledgehammer, there's a pretty good chance the metal would spark, and the whole thing would go boom. But there's no guarantee one strike would do it, and even so, if you hit it with a hammer, there's a chance you might take your hand off. I'm not sure the range on this much powder."

"This is boring," Ben informed him.

"I know, but you're too sick to stop me from explaining my brilliance in excruciating detail," Patrick said, delighted. "Think of it as source material for your next book about me." Ben grumbled something Patrick couldn't make out. He decided to ignore it. "Anyway, I think what I'll do is stick one of these to each coupler, then work out some sort of longish range torch mechanism that we can light, then bring down like a flaming oar on the boom box from farther away."

"Boom box?" Ben asked.

"Yeah. That's what I'm calling it."

"That's not what a boom box is."

Patrick held up the matchbox full of explosive powder. "A boom box is *exactly* what this is. Your problem is with the eighties. You'll have to take it up with them."

Ben frowned. "Is that enough to blow the coupler?"

"Aw, you *were* paying attention!" Patrick cheered. "Uncertain. I can't really test it without damaging the train prematurely. I don't want to break anything until it's time to break stuff. So I think I'll cut through the coupler pins, about a third of the way through each. It'll weaken them, so hopefully this little blast breaks them the rest of the way."

"Weakened couplers. Sounds great."

Patrick frowned. "Yeah, it *does* make them riskier for all the times we *don't* want them to break free. Which is statistically one hundred percent of the time until we want them to break free. So that's tricky. Especially because Horace is going to have to do the thing he wants to do least of all."

"Bathe?"

"Close. He's going to have to make this train go very, *very* fast."

"He doesn't like to do that."

"I know. I just said that."

"When are you going to tell him?"

"Not yet," Patrick said. "Let him live in his sweet pillowy blanket of ignorance for a few more hours. I still have to saw through the coupler pins and sabotage his train first."

"You also need to come look at these trap doors," Babs said, popping her head into the car. "Alice got one cut away okay, but I don't think the hinges are going to work."

"See?" Patrick said, nudging Ben with his foot. "Busy, busy, busy. I'll be back, try not to explode all over the floor."

"I hate you."

"I know, pookie. I know."

26.

"Okay, I see the problem. The design is horribly flawed," Patrick decided, examining the Baby Caps' work.

"It's your design," Alice pointed out.

"Well, not everything can be ready right off the drawing board," Patrick replied, tossing the hinges over his shoulder. The square hole above was pretty clean. "Now it's just a skylight," Patrick decided. "Even better, in some ways. Much easier to access."

"It's bad if it rains," Lex pointed out.

"Not ideal against rain, no," Patrick agreed. "Or if we get boarded from the roof. But ah, *c'est la vie.*" He held up the three-by-three square of train-roof metal and examined it carefully. "See if you can find some sort of strap to attach to these guys. We can use them as shields." He tossed it onto a nearby chair. "And don't forget to stabilize something beneath it so we can climb up and down easily. Nice work, Alice. You are scarily exact with that torch."

"The train is even better than a person," she said, flashing a wicked grin. "The train doesn't move when you cut it."

"Okay!" Patrick said. "Keep up the gruesome work. One other thing while I have you all here. We're going to be taking the Run fast. Understand me? *Fast.* That means there won't always be much time to communicate clearly before we're descended on by furious lunatics. We need some shorthand."

"Like 'Code Blue'?" Lex asked.

"A lot like that, yes," Patrick nodded. "But easier to understand. Like... Code Stuff."

"Code Stuff?" Babs asked uncertainly.

"Yes, Code Stuff. That means, grab all your stuff—only the things you *need*—and get them to the engine car, because we're decoupling."

"Okay. Got it. What else?" Babs asked.

"'Fire' is going to mean actual fire. Like, if an actual fire breaks out on the train, you say, 'fire.' So firing a weapon at someone has to be different. If you want to give that instruction, you say, 'shoot.' Okay?"

"What if we screw something up and want to say, 'Oh, shoot'? Won't that be confusing?" Lex asked.

"The word for that sort of thing is 'fuck,'" Patrick said.

Lex nodded. "Oh. Okay. Right. Got it."

"Directions will also be hard. It's going to be an absolute frenzy. No one's going to know which way is up, and we'll all be facing different lefts and rights. The front of the train is the front, and the back of the train is the back. From there, we go nautical. The right-hand side—looking at front—is starboard. The left-hand side—again, as far as the train is concerned—is port."

"Those words mean nothing," Alice said.

"They mean something very specific, actually," Patrick said. "It's too late to have you start reading *Moby Dick*, but just go with me on this. Starboard and port. Any questions?"

The Baby Caps shook their heads.

"Good. Lex, come with me for a second?"

Lex followed Patrick out into the space between the cars. "What's up?"

"I need your big arms," Patrick said. The train was trundling slowly through an old forest. The dead and dry limbs of trees stretched out and scraped against the train. "Think you can grab a few of the longer branches and break them off without losing a limb?" Patrick cracked a smile. "Get it?"

Lex frowned. "Maybe."

"Maybe you get it, or maybe you can do it without a severe maiming?"

"The second one."

"That's the spirit! See if you can get four. But I can't stress this enough: Do not let your arm get ripped off. And do not fall off the train."

"I don't think I like this plan."

"Everyone always says that to me," Patrick said, waving away the criticism, "but a lot of them live to apologize. You'll be fine! You got this. Just dial in." He slapped Lex on the back, then ducked back inside the train.

He checked in with Rogers, whose assignment was to separate and organize two stores of cooking oil, one for the train and one for weapons. He had split the reserve stores fairly evenly, maybe 60/40 in favor of fuel oil. "I assume the faster we go, the more fuel we burn?" Patrick asked.

"You got it," Rogers said.

"Okay. Take about half of what you set aside for weapons and put it in the fuel pile."

Rogers raised an eyebrow. "Horace isn't going to like that."

"No, he is not." Patrick turned and headed back through the train, examining everyone's work and trying not to step on Ben.

The whole plan was coming together. The train was becoming something new. Something powerful.

For the very first time, he was starting to think that they actually really did have a chance of surviving.

27.

The sun was still high enough several hours later that Patrick realized that the landscape outside the train was starting to look familiar. He gazed intently out the window, recognizing the land but not quite sure why. It was like waking up from a dream; the harder he tried to pin down a memory, the further away that memory slipped.

Until the train rolled through an Amtrak station and he saw the signs that said LAUREL.

Memory jolted through him. His spine stiffened. "Oh," he said. "Shit."

"What?" Ben asked.

Patrick picked up Bleakachu. He squeezed the grip so hard it squeaked. "I know where we are."

"Where?"

Patrick swallowed hard. "The farm."

Ben frowned. "Which farm?"

"Roman Marwood's farm." He stood up and walked out to the gangway.

Ben struggled after him. By the time he reached the end of the car, he was out of breath. "That's the guy who did all this?"

Patrick nodded. The train rumbled slowly across the countryside. In the distance, Patrick could see the silhouette of the old Victorian where Roman had left him to die. Next to it, the storage units where the man and his demons slept. In the middle distance were the crop fields. They were choked with weeds, overgrown and strangled. Old, broken cornstalks stuck out of the dirt like jagged teeth. The soybean field was brown and bedraggled beneath a forest of switchgrass and black-eyed Susans. The fields were empty. The yards were empty. The farm was abandoned.

"Must have moved on," Ben observed, looking out over Patrick's shoulder. "Looks pretty dead."

"I don't know why he would have," Patrick said softly. Something must have happened to force them out. Maybe a blight hit the crops. Maybe they were raided and overpowered. A small piece of him wanted to hope that maybe Carla had raised a rebellion against Roman and thrown him in the duster house. But he couldn't bring himself to actually believe that it might be true.

He couldn't bring himself to think that she might have been allowed to live.

"I hope he's dead," he said, his voice even. "And I hope it was bad."

Ben considered his friend. "I don't think I've ever heard you talk like that before."

Patrick snorted. "Never felt it before. He was the architect of all of this. The whole world destroyed. Izzy and Annie gone. Everybody gone. The things we've done since that day...the people we've had to be..." Patrick fell quiet. He wiped the tears from his eyes with the back of his hand. "He's the root of all of this evil, and I hope he's dead."

They stood there in silence, watching the farm fade out of view. When the tip of the Victorian disappeared over the horizon, Ben clapped his hand on Patrick's shoulder. "Come on. We've got work to do."

Patrick took one last, long look in the direction of the farm. "Yeah. Okay," he said.

He turned and helped Ben hobble back inside.

28.

"About ten miles to New Orleans," Horace announced, stifling a yawn.

"Have you slept?" Patrick asked him.

"No."

Patrick planted his hands on his hips. "Horace, I told you to sleep. I told everyone to make sure to sleep. We're going to be awake for a long, long time."

"Unless we die early," Ben offered.

"Unless we die early," Patrick nodded, "correct. Then we get to have *lots* of sleep."

"I'm fine," Horace said. "How's the train?"

"It's fine. Don't go back there."

Horace sighed. "Patrick. How is my train?"

"She's an absolute treasure! You're going to love it. I promise. Don't go back there."

Horace gritted his teeth. "Fine. Rogers said you wanted to talk to me."

"I do, yes. Please, have a seat," he said, gesturing to a row of passenger seats.

"I'm find standing."

"You'll want to sit," Ben said.

Horace glared at them both. He crossed his arms. He decided to sit.

"Okay. What's the top speed you're comfortable with on this train?"

"I like to keep it around thirty-five," Horace said warily. "Why?"

"Okay. Now think about the craziest, most out of his mind conductor trying to set a land speed record through the Slaughterhouse Run. Just so fast, everyone must think he's got an absolute death wish. How fast would that conductor go?"

Horace snorted. "I'd say forty-five miles an hour. Why?"

"Horace, I need you to go eighty."

"Eighty!" he exploded, jumping up from his seat. "Maggie can't even *go* eighty!"

"How fast can she go?"

"Thirty-five!" he yelled.

"Seventy-five," Ben said.

"You be quiet! How do you even know that?" Horace fumed.

Ben shared a small smile. "I pay attention."

"I am *not* running my train seventy-five miles an hour through the Slaughterhouse Run, that is *suicide!*"

"It's actually suicide *not* to," Patrick said. "Listen. You're telling me that every train that's tried the Slaughterhouse Run has maxed out around forty or forty-five, right? And not a single one of them has made it. You know why? Because the traps that are set along that 2,000 miles of track are all set for trains maxing out at forty or forty-five miles an hour. They're not built for a train going seventy-five. We'll be coming through almost twice as fast as they're expecting. We shoot that run at blazing speed, we'll knock every single one of those gangs back onto their heels. They'll have to scramble to adjust. If we can force them do that, we just might make it through."

"That rail hasn't been serviced in almost a decade! And in fact, it's been all manner of mucked with, so it's worse than failing, it's actively damaged! It won't support a train going that fast! If we go seventy-five, we'll jump track, and then we'll all die!"

"We don't know the track can't handle it. Maybe you're right, and it can't. But we don't *know* that. What we do know is, there's 2,000 miles worth of bloodthirsty maniacs out there waiting to slit the throats of the next group of Caps on a forty-five mile an hour train. If we go seventy-five, we might die. If we go forty-five, we *will* die."

Horace's cheeks swelled out so far on both sides that it looked like he was holding a watermelon in his mouth. His skin was glowing scarlet. Ben had never seen him so mad, and he had seen Horace *mad*.

But he also knew Horace was a logical person at his core. He had a short fuse. He had strange ideas about power dynamics. And he had *really* strange ideas about the relationship that could exist between a man and a train. But he was also a man of reason. He was more or less an adult in a world that had left responsible grown-ups behind. So Ben wasn't surprised to watch his face slowly fade back down to an irritated shade of purple while as he paced around the car in great, stomping kicks that eventually became gentler, stalking steps. "This train…" he said, his back turned to Patrick and Ben. "This train is all I have. She's all I've *had*. We're what's kept each other together. Do you understand that?" He took some deep breaths. He rested his shoulder against the luggage rack.

"I think we do," Patrick said gently.

Horace sniffed. "No, you don't," he said.

"I chased a band of marauders across a desert and faced bad people and a zombie horde and an Incredible Hulk and a tiger because I didn't want to lose my notebook," Ben said.

"I dragged my best friend on a suicide mission through the Midwest and Deep South so I could eat a pudding cup at the top of a princess castle," Patrick threw in. He walked over and rested his hand on Horace's shoulder. "Horace. We do know what it's like. To need a thing that not a single other person in this broken fucking world gives a single shit about, just so you can wake up the next day and be miserable but alive until the sun goes down again. We all grab onto something. My pudding cup saved me. Ben's adoration of my story saved him."

"Hey, wait…"

"Your train has saved you. And it'll save you as long as it's here. But listen to me." He pulled Horace's shoulder and forced him to turn around. He placed both hands on both of Horace's shoulders now and lowered himself to look directly into the conductor's eyes. "This train is not who you are. This train is what you've *built*. This train is a testament to your will. But this train is a thing that will rust in the end, and you are a man who survives."

Horace's eyes were wet. He didn't cry, because he wasn't the type, but his emotions were swirling in his chest. "Patrick," he said, very quietly. "What happens if we derail the train?"

"Then those of us who survive it get up and fight like hell. Because those are the people we are. Not for a train. Not for some pudding. Not for a notebook, and not for a queen among buffalos named Ponch."

"Who?" Horace asked.

"We do it for our people," Patrick said, ignoring him. "We do it for each other. We do it for the idea that humans were *human* before the world was ripped away from us." Patrick glanced around the car. "We do it for our family."

"The real train is the friends we made along the way," Ben offered weakly.

"He has a fever," Patrick reminded Horace. "But the core of that message is sweet."

Horace looked down at Ben. His skin was practically radiating green. He was slick with the Monkey juice oozing from his pores, and he wasn't really trying to stop the flow from his nose or his ears or the corner of his eyes anymore. It was all flowing too fast. Lying on the floor was now his preferred way of being present in any given car. He could get up and move between them without a whole lot of help, sort of, but he was too weak to stand, and too unsteady to sit. He needed to get to Long Beach. The boy was on the front walk of Death's doorstep.

"I don't know what I'll do if we jump track," Horace said, his voice helpless.

"None of us knows what to do if we jump track," Patrick replied. "Hopefully we won't. If we do…well, what aspect of the years since M-Day *hasn't* been a horrifying adventure of discovery?"

Horace looked down at the floor. He shook his head. "No, I don't like it," he said. He looked up at Patrick. "Excuse me." He turned his back and huffed toward the door.

"Where are you going?" Patrick asked, suddenly in a panic. They'd be eaten alive if they cruised at Horace's speed. "Wait, Horace!"

Horace stopped at the doorway. "I don't like it," he repeated. "But I'm going to the engine to tell my assistant conductor to open the throttle. We need to fire it up if we're gonna hit speed by New Orleans."

Patrick exhaled, relieved. "Thank you," he breathed. He handed Horace one of the walkies he'd swiped from Philbin's house. "And take this. Keep it on. I'll call you if the train shakes apart."

29.

The sky was dark and the world was whizzing by fast when they rounded the bayou into the New Orleans station.

"Not so fast," Horace warned. "Not yet. We can't run her through NOLA Union at full speed; we've got a hard connection to make."

"How fast do you want to take it?" Rogers asked.

"Twenty."

"How fast do you think we *could* take it?"

Horace gave Rogers a look. "Twenty."

"Right," Rogers agreed, nodding. "But how fast *could* we take it?"

Horace grimaced. "I don't know. Maybe thirty-five."

Rogers nodded. "Maybe I'll cheat toward that, then." He eased into the brakes, and the train began to slow. They rumbled into the tracks beneath the station. "How do we get onto the Run from here?"

"You know what the Slaughterhouse Run was called before M-Day? The Sunset Limited. Doesn't that sound nice? The Sunset Limited."

"Horace."

Horace sighed deeply. "We hang a flag." He nodded toward an old cardboard box stuffed beneath the console."

"Which one?" Rogers asked.

"The black one."

Rogers raised an eyebrow. "We've never hung the black flag before."

"We've never jumped to a death track before."

"They'll switch us when they see the flag?"

"If they don't, they'll be doing us a favor."

"Okay." Rogers rummaged through the box of cotton flags, most of which had been cut from old bedsheets or stitched together from a few extra-large shirts. He found the black one down at the bottom. He pulled it out, shook it off, and then dropped the window on the starboard side. He reached out and hooked the flag on the metal barbs outside the window.

Horace pulled at his mustache. "I never thought I'd see the day where I'd hang the black flag," he said sadly.

"If we can get Ben cured, you'll be proud you made the call."

"And if we all end up dead and split open and strewn across Texas?" Horace asked.

"You'll have only a flash of a very small instant to regret making the call," Rogers said.

"Then I'll be out of my misery," Horace replied miserably.

They were coming in fast to the station, or at least faster than Horace would have liked. He held his tongue, though he couldn't help but grip the side wall handle so hard that his palm squeaked. A line worker a few dozen yards ahead waved an old oil lantern to signal a slowdown. Horace clicked on one of the working flashlights and popped his arm out the window, illuminating the black flag. The signalman seemed confused. He wove his lantern around in a wide circle: *Are you sure?* Horace flicked the flashlight on and off three times while keeping it pointed it at the flag: *Yes, we are insane, please switch the track.*

The signalman put down his lantern. He pulled the switch, and the track connection locked into place. Maggie hit the junction with a groan, but she held tight to the rails, speed and all.

Just like that, they were onto the Slaughterhouse Run.

Rogers caught a look at the signalman outside the window as they passed. The signalman took off his cap and held it to his heart in solemn acknowledgement of their imminent deaths.

30.

"We're picking up speed," Patrick surmised, looking out the window. He turned to the rest of the group. "We're out of the station and officially on the Slaughterhouse Run. Everyone feeling good?"

"I guess?" said Babs.

"Not really," admitted Lex.

"Urgh," moaned Ben.

"Yes," said Alice.

Patrick moved to a window and peered out into the darkness. The cloak of night had drawn down tight over the city. He could only just barely make out the shapes of tombs clinging to the earth in the distance.

"Is that a cemetery?" Lex asked, putting his hands to the glass and squinting out the window.

"Yep."

"Why is it all above ground?"

"We're basically at the water table here. If you dig down to bury the bodies, they just float back up. So you have to bury them above ground."

Lex gulped. "I don't like that."

"I never really minded it until now," Patrick admitted. "But I *could* do with a little less eerie shit at present. Given everything."

"Jeez, how big is this cemetery?" Babs asked. Several minutes in, and the tombs were still flashing by on either side of the train.

"Yeah…" Patrick said curiously, rubbing his jaw. "And why are we going right through the middle of it?" He climbed up the shelving rack that the Baby Caps had bolted into place beneath the new hole in the roof. He climbed up to the top shelf and poked his head through the hole. Visibility wasn't great, between the darkness and the dust, but even so…his stomach filled with dread as he looked ahead down the tracks and saw tombs lined up on either side as far as he could see, until they were swallowed up by the fog. "We're not going through a graveyard," he decided. "The graveyard has come to the train."

The tombs were all new, erected sometime in the last few years. They were more like cairns than tombs—sepulchers of dry-set stones and chunks of dried cement, some with old rebar twisting out from the sides, giving the tombs the eerie appearance of Medusa heads in the moonlight. Rising graves built of found materials that were scrapped from the ruined world.

"Why would they do that?" Babs asked, trying to keep the tremble out of her voice. "Why would they build a—a *graveyard* along the train line?"

"Maybe as a warning." Patrick shrugged. "Maybe as a welcome."

"Maybe both," Ben groaned.

Patrick nodded. "Maybe both."

Flickering lights appeared in the distance. The train was really picking up speed now; Horace was true to his word, giving the old Amtrak all it could handle. Soon they'd be at top speed, and now the fog was spinning around them, sucked into the vacuum of wind crashing against the engine. Through the twisting whorls, the uneven dance of firelight blazed into view. The fires multiplied as they got closer. First there were two, one on either side of the tracks. Then four, then six, then eight, then more, all spaced evenly down the tracks like dismal spotlights illuminating a runway.

"They're turning on the lights," Patrick said quietly. This was it. There was no turning back. He had led them straight into the Slaughterhouse Run.

He climbed down from the porthole. "It's happening. Right now. Everyone get ready."

"Defense until we know what we're up against," Ben reminded them. He pushed himself to a seat and struggled with one of the square metal shields. "Offense when we know how to fight back."

"And when we do, offense *hard*," Patrick added.

Soon they reached the fires. The flames flashed past the windows in an evenly spaced sequence that made it feel like the train was shooting through a theme park tunnel, like any second the track would drop and they'd go into a freefall to the bottom of the earth.

Small objects struck the train. Metallic pings and wooden clatters sounded against the exterior walls, a disconcerting hailstorm in the night. Patrick popped back up through the porthole and peered into the darkness.

"What is it?" Babs asked from below.

"Sticks and stones," Patrick replied. "Literally." He looked down at Babs. "They're pelting us with sticks and stones."

The Baby Caps exchanged confused looks. "Why?"

"I don't know. Maybe it's—ow!" A rock smacked Patrick in the forehead, knocking him out of the porthole. He slipped from the shelf and crashed to the floor. The Baby Caps moved to help him, but he waved them off, more annoyed than hurt. "Maybe it's some kind of fear tactic," he said. He touched his forehead, looking for blood, but his fingers came away clean. "Anyway, I probably wouldn't go up there."

Ben rolled onto his side and tilted his head so he could better hear the world outside. The clattering rose to a crescendo, battering the sides of the train with an ever-present noise that clouded his thoughts and ground at his teeth.

Then, abruptly, it stopped. But that didn't mean it was silent; another noise, off in the distance, rose to take its place. It was a whirring churn of metal on hot, melting metal, low and mad and stuck and viscous. Ben shook his head. He wasn't thinking straight. He wasn't hearing right. The *sound* of it wasn't right.

Until suddenly it was.

Ben gasped for air.

He knew that sound. He knew what it meant for them.

"An alarm," he wheezed, his voice wavering. His head felt like a furnace, and he could swear the train car was floating. "They're ringing the bell," he whispered. "To call the giants home."

Patrick frowned down at his friend. "Ringing the bell to call the giants home?" he asked.

"He talks like that sometimes. When the fever's bad," Lex explained.

But then they heard it too: a whining, growling sound in the distance, rising up from the bayous all of a sudden and getting louder, fast.

Alice's ears perked up. She knew that sound. She'd run with some motorheads for a few months when she was younger, and there was no mistaking the sound she now heard getting nearer and nearer the train. "Four-wheelers," she said.

Headlights blazed to life outside the windows. A pack of five souped-up ATVs was approaching the train from the south and closing in fast. Swamp water from the bayou sprayed up in huge arcs from their angry, spinning tires, small droplets of brackish water drifting away in the air, lit up by the taillights like sprays of blood. Each vehicle had one driver and one rider. Each rider was cradling something in their hands that the Caps couldn't make out in the darkness.

"Bad," Ben murmured, sinking back down onto the floor. "Bad, bad, bad…"

"Weapons!" Patrick shouted. "Shoot!"

Alice smiled. She'd been itching for that order.

She slipped the crossbow off her shoulder and scurried up to the porthole. She pulled a bolt from her quiver and locked it into place. She had wrapped an oil-soaked length of cotton around each of her arrows earlier in the day, and now she clicked a lighter and set fire to the edge of the bolt in the chamber. She took careful aim at the nearest quad. She slowed her breath. She pulled the trigger.

The fiery bolt slashed through the night and pierced the fuel tank. The four-wheeler exploded. One of the tires blew straight out and smashed into the head of another quad driver. He jerked the handle too hard and rolled the four-wheeler. The passenger's neck snapped as the full weight of the ATV smashed down on his spine.

"Two down!" Patrick yelled.

The other quads were closing in. Alice nocked another bolt in her crossbow while Patrick, Babs, and Lex ran to cover the entrances. Patrick raced through the door and skidded to a stop between cars just as one of the four-wheelers zoomed up next to the steps. Patrick dove back into the safety of the car as the passenger hurled its bundle into the train. The thing hit the train floor with a *WHUMP*. Then it scrabbled to its feet, its long claws scraping on the metal like nails on a chalkboard. It stepped slowly into the car, waving its head from side to side, snapping its jaws with hunger.

"Holy shit," Babs whispered, shaking so hard her glasses slipped off. "It's a fucking crocodile."

"It's an alligator," Patrick murmured, his body freezing with fear. "Everyone. Climb. Now."

Nobody moved. The gator swept its eyes across the room. Its nails clacked on the linoleum floor as it took a step forward.

"Climb!" Patrick said again, screaming this time. "Now!"

Broken out of their paralysis, Lex and Babs leapt up onto the shelving unit. "It's not going to hold us all!" Alice cried from the top. But they didn't stop; they scrambled up, and the unit began to sway. One of the bolts holding it to the floor popped. The metal frame groaned.

Patrick rushed forward, grabbed Ben by the wrists, and hauled him back. The gator darted forward, snapping at Ben's foot, missing by only inches. The monster's tail thrashed, smacking between the storage cabinet wall and the latrine door. "Ben, get up! Come on!" Patrick screamed, yanking him further back. The gator lunged again. Patrick couldn't believe how fast it moved. It was on them in a flash. He reached out and grabbed the first thing he could: a wadded up blanket soaked in cooking oil. He stuffed it into the gator's mouth, his hand so close to getting bitten off that the monster's teeth grazed the skin on the back of his fingers. The gator retched and flung its head from side to side, loosening the blanket bundle and trying to fling it out of its mouth.

Alice aimed down with her crossbow and pulled the trigger, but Babs and Lex were still scrambling up the shelves, and the whole thing was shaking. The arrow went wide and stuck in the wall to Patrick's left, missing his head by only a few inches. The gator hurled the blanket away and scrabbled onto Ben's legs, its mouth opening wide. Patrick grabbed the bolt and yanked it out of the wall. He jammed the arrow sideways through the gator's head. It went straight in through one eye and came out an inch behind the other with a sickening *squelch*.

The gator stopped moving.

The train car was quiet.

"Holy shit," Alice breathed.

Something hit the roof right next to her head. A second alligator struggled for purchase on the slick, metal top of the speeding train. It flailed with its claws and slashed Alice across the face, just beneath the cheek. She cried out in pain. Strips of flesh fell away from her bone and hung down from the deep, bloody cuts. She lost her balance and fell to the floor, landing hard on top of the dead alligator inside. The gator on the roof scrambled after her, but it slipped on the metal and tumbled over the edge of the speeding train.

"Oh my God, Alice!" Babs jumped down from the shelf and knelt next to her friend. "Jesus, are you okay?"

Alice's eyes blazed. "I'm going to kill those motherfuckers," she spat. She pushed herself up off the dead alligator and ripped the bolt from its head. She held it in her left hand, dripping blood and reptile gore. "I'll catch up," she snarled.

Patrick furrowed his brow. "Catch up?" he said. "What do you—?"

Alice stepped past him and out onto the gangway. Another quad was ramping up the siding toward them. The passenger held her gator, using some tool to squeeze its snout shut with one hand while gripping it around the belly with her other arm. The driver angled toward the train. The passenger stood up in her seat and started to hurl the gator. Alice growled and leapt off the train. She dove at the passenger. She slammed her shoulder into her so hard that she tumbled off the back of the quad, still holding the gator. The tool around the animal's snout slipped off, and they heard the sickening snap-and-chomp sound of the gator crunching through flesh, and the passenger's screams as she was eaten alive. Alice nearly rolled off the bumper, but she hooked her arm through the rear rack and dragged behind the four-wheeler instead. The driver tried to shake her loose, but she held on tight. He turned away from the train and peeled off into the bayou. Water drenched her, threatening to drown her. She flung herself back up toward the seat and drove the arrow into the cushion, using it as a handhold to pull herself back up. Soaking wet and angry, she straddled the seat behind the driver, wrenched the bolt back out of the cushion, and drove it into his neck. He spasmed, then slumped over and fell off the quad. Alice snatched up the handlebars. She leapt into the front seat and took control of the ATV. She fired the throttle and sped across the bayou, back toward the train.

The last two quads were running right alongside the tracks. Alice ramped up the siding and knocked into the rear quad, sending it skidding through the loose gravel. The driver fought for control and righted the vehicle. Alice pulled a knife from her hip and stabbed it into the passenger's upper arm. The man screamed and dropped the alligator. Alice wrenched the knife back out and then lunged forward, stabbing it into the driver's back, right beneath the shoulder blade. The woman lost control of the quad. She jerked the handles right and slammed into the side of the train, tipped the ATV, and got caught beneath the tracks. The train lurched as it crushed her, but it stayed on the tracks.

Alice peeled away, giving her death a wide berth. The last four-wheeler, the one up ahead on the siding, had pulled alongside the train. It matched speed and hovered next to one of the gangways between cars. The driver held steady while the passenger stood and hurled the gator toward the train. Patrick stood back in the opening, holding a sledgehammer like a golf club. The gator flew through the air. Patrick swung as hard as he could. The sledge caught the gator underneath the chin and knocked it back. The creature flipped and landed on its side. Patrick stumbled forward and used the sledgehammer like a push broom to shove the alligator out of the train.

The ATV's passenger kicked her leg over the seat, lining up to the train, and leapt toward it. Patrick raised the sledge, but she was quick, and she knocked him down with a shoulder to the chest. She jumped on top of him, straddling his ribs with her knees. She pulled out a knife and stabbed it down at his chest. Suddenly, Lex charged out of the train car and rammed the woman at full speed, crushing her into the metal wall. She cracked her head, hard. Her eyes rolled up into her skull and she went limp, her unconscious body falling to the floor.

Patrick yanked the knife out of her hand. Then he and Lex lifted the woman and tossed her out into the night.

Alice drove her four-wheeler up next to the train. The other quad was nowhere in sight. She stood up, her hands working to level the handlebars, and then she jumped at the train. Lex caught her arm and hauled her in. The ATV spun out and flipped over in the field, sinking halfway down into the bayou.

Alice's face was streaked with blood, but she was smiling.

Patrick raised an eyebrow. "All good?"

"I lost my knife," she said.

"Here. Have a new one."

"Thanks." She took the knife and slipped it into her sheath.

"Your face looks awful," Lex pointed out.

"*Your* face looks awful," she countered.

Patrick ushered them back into the train car. "First aid's on the shelf, patch yourself up. Quickly. We might not have much time before we get hit again."

A few minutes later, Horace's voice crackled through the walkie-talkie: "Get topside. We have a problem."

31.

Patrick sighed. "I hate being so right all the time," he said.

He clamored up the bookshelf, forgetting that it had been partially ripped out of the floor. The whole stack swayed, and he threw his weight forward, clinging to the metal shelves. "Five points to anyone who can fix this while I'm up here," he moaned.

He pushed his way to the ceiling and poked his head out of the hole. It took a few moments for his eyes to adjust to the darkness outside. As they did, the form of a train station slowly melted into view through the shadows. The train's headlights shone through the fog and cast a diffuse glow over the platform ahead. It was filled with sword-wielding shadow people.

"Shit."

There were about forty of them crowding the platform. From this distance, in this darkness, they were mostly shapeless, just heads floating above bodies, but the clean lines of the blades were sharp against the glow. The weapons were held low, but with a tension that was obvious even through the gloom. The amorphous mob shifted with the fog. They were anxious. They were ready.

They were waiting.

The train would be at the station in less than thirty seconds. Patrick leapt down from the shelves. "Oil bombs! One at every starboard door. Light and throw the second we hit the station," he ordered. The Baby Caps scattered, splitting themselves up wordlessly, grabbing their weapons and taking up the posts. Patrick jammed his thumb against the button on his walkie. "Kill the lights! Now!"

"It's pitch black outside!"

"I know! We're lit up like a goddamn Christmas tree. Might as well have flashing lights over every doorway saying ENTER HERE. Shut them down!"

"I won't be able to see the track," Horace insisted.

"The train is on rails! Turn off the lights!"

The track split into two. They were almost to the station.

The train lights flickered off, plunging them into darkness.

A round of curses rose from the raiders on the platform. The train barreled on, hidden by the night. It blasted into the station. Patrick grabbed an oil bomb and lit it up. Outside on the platform, a hot flash of orange exploded. People screamed. A second explosion. More screams. More confusion. Patrick recoiled as he rolled past the two fireballs. Someone lunged at him. He hurled the glass jar. It burst against the man's chest and the engine oil inside caught instantly, fully consuming him, sending flames curling back among the mob. A fourth burst of fire, this time from his right. Screaming. Wailing. The sound of worn cotton clothing and dry skin catching fire. The whole platform was one long sea of burning bodies, twisting and crackling into corpses.

Then they were clear. The platform slid by, and just like that, they were free, out of the station and on to the next, leaving a bonfire of bones in the Louisiana night.

32.

"Does anyone want to talk about it?" Patrick asked.

The Baby Caps looked at him, confused. "Talk about what?"

"The fact that we've killed a pretty decent number of people in the last hour or so?"

"Not really," Babs said with an uneasy shrug. "I mean, it's called the Slaughterhouse Run."

"We weren't expecting to make friends," Lex added.

"I know, I know," Patrick said, shaking his head, "it's just, that's a lot to process, and I'm here if anyone needs to—you know—process. It."

Alice raised an eyebrow. "Do *you* need to process it?"

Patrick scoffed. "No. I'm an adult."

Alice rolled her eyes. "You were forty years old before you saw your first dead body."

"Hey!" Patrick cried. "First of all, I wasn't even forty when M-Day happened! I don't even know if I'm forty now!"

"You're way over forty now," Ben said.

"Shut up! And second of all, going several decades without ever killing someone doesn't make you weak, it makes you blessed! Hashtag blessed!"

"What's a hashtag?" Babs asked.

Patrick threw up his hands in frustration. "Ugh! The youth!"

"Sometimes you have to kill people so they don't kill you," Lex said gently. "That's how it works."

Patrick frowned. "I know. But it's not how it worked when I was your age. I would have been horrified. Honestly, I'm horrified *now*. So I just want to make sure you're all okay."

Babs shrugged. "Different worlds."

"Yeah. I know." Patrick stuffed his hands into his pockets and trudged out of the car. He made his way to the head of the train, where he found both Horace and Rogers at the control panel, peering through the windshield, both on high alert. "What's up?" Patrick shouted. Both men jumped. Horace screamed.

"You're probably pleased with yourself," Horace grumped, fixing his cap.

"Just trying to ease the tension."

"Trying to give me *hyper*tension, more like."

"A little scare now and then is good for you," Patrick insisted. "The ghost of my grandma tells me that all the time."

"Did you need something?" Rogers asked.

"Nah," Patrick shrugged. "Just had to get away from the kids for a few minutes. They're scary."

"How so?"

"Oh, the usual. They're all bright-eyed and cotton-tailed. Totally on board with human slaughter. Normal kid stuff."

"They're native to the shitshow," Rogers agreed. "It's pretty unsettling."

"But they're good to have in our corner," Horace said.

"I'd be scared as hell if they weren't. You should have seen Alice singlehandedly take out Quad Team Six. Thrilling and horrifying."

"It's their world," Rogers said. "We belong to sometime different."

"Indeed we do." The train cars clacked as they bumped over a break in the track. The car swayed and Patrick reached out a hand to steady himself. "That normal?" he asked.

"Just a junction," Horace said.

"Very normal," Rogers added.

"Great." Patrick stared out the windshield. The first hints of dawn were beginning to crack through the fog behind them. The world was taking on the off-grey wash of morning. "How we lookin'?"

"Quiet right now. But won't be for long." Rogers nodded at a faded metal sign propped up at an awkward angle in the grass between the train tracks and the interstate. It said, WELCOME TO THE LONE STAR STATE.

"I hate Texas," Horace said.

"Everyone does," Patrick assured him. "Everyone hates Texas."

33.

"I hate Texas," Ben said.

"I know. That's what I told Horace."

"Look at it. It's flat and stupid." The Texas landscape flashed by, and it was mostly weed-choked grassland and bone-dry creek beds. It was very flat, and it was very stupid.

The sun was fully up now. Patrick had instructed the Baby Caps to get some sleep. Babs and Lex curled up together on one of the cots, but Alice declined to follow orders and instead changed her bandages, then set to work sharpening her blades.

"How you feeling, Benny Boy?"

"Bad."

"You look pretty good."

"Fuck off."

"Green suits you! You look like the Incredible Hulk. But weak, and sad."

"The Hulk was always sad."

"I think he was always angry."

"He was angry because he was sad."

"Yeah. I guess that's true."

They heard the bullet hit the train half a second before they heard the blast of the gun. Patrick dropped to the floor. "Was that a gunshot?!" More bullets pinged off the outside of the train. First it sounded like drizzle on a tin roof, but soon it was a full-on hailstorm. Windows cracked. Bullets zipped through the car. Babs and Lex jolted out of the cot, and Alice pulled them down to the floor. "How the hell do these people still have ammunition?!"

"This is Texas," Ben said miserably. "Bullets over brains."

"Cover me!" Patrick yelled.

"With what?" Alice asked. But Patrick was already on the move. He dove over to the windows and peeked his head up over the ledge, peering out at the field beyond. It was empty. There was no sign of life anywhere,- just a rundown barn on the horizon, and a couple of half-dead farmhouses. But the bullets were still flying.

"Where the hell…?" he murmured.

Then he saw wisps of white smoke curling out from the windows of the barn. There were more shots being fired from the windows of the farmhouses. There must have been two dozen people shooting at the train, but they were two hundred yards away and staying put. They were apparently not keen on actually taking the train. They just kept firing away from their windows. Patrick screwed up his mouth in confusion. "Are they…are they taking *pot shots* at us?"

"What does that mean?" Lex asked.

"It means we're target practice," Alice said.

"*Literal* target practice," Patrick emphasized, astonished. "They're wasting all that ammo for fun?!"

"Bullets over brains," Ben repeated.

Patrick sighed. He turned his back on the window and sank down to the floor. "Go back to bed," he told the Baby Caps while shots pinged through the car. "We'll wake you when it's real."

34.

"I'm not saying this hasn't been dangerous," Patrick said, careful to set expectations. "And I really don't want to jinx anything. But do you get the sense that this is all a little overblown?"

"What's overblown?" Ben asked, resting his head against the window.

"The legendary Slaughterhouse Run. I thought it would be more…I don't know…insane."

Ben raised an eyebrow. "What do you mean?"

"I mean it's bad, we *have* already killed *several* people, and I didn't want to say anything back there to the Baby Caps, but they were right, I *do* need to process that."

"We know."

"But the way everyone talks about the Slaughterhouse Run…I don't know. I thought it'd be a little…crazier."

"You don't think using alligators as throwing knives is crazy?"

"Sure," Patrick said, waving his hands through the air, "but that's like baseline post-apocalyptic crazy."

"And you want crazier."

"I don't *want* crazier, I just *expected* crazier."

Ben looked out at the Texas landscape. "It's been, like, four hours," he pointed out.

"Yeah. I guess you're right," Patrick frowned. "I just sort of thought we'd already come across someone who is completely and utterly un-hinged."

***

Dewey was making pretty good progress on the sacrificial killing field. It looked a lot like the drawing he'd gotten from the demon Ulcerrot.

He pulled out the old Denny's placemat just to double check his work. There it was, in green crayon—the whole field drawn out like a map. The skeleton crosses looked just like they did in the picture. The first few had been clumsy, but after twenty or so, Dewey was really in the rhythm. The Killin' Pit was maybe a little smaller than it should have been, but the Goat Man had made up for that! He'd built the Goat Man about twice as tall as it looked in the drawing. He thought Ulcerrot would like that. All in all, the sacrificial killing field was looking good. The only thing Dewey was a little nervous about were the candles. He had a hard time finding enough, so he had improvised. He'd made do with some flashlights, a few flares, and five of those glow-in-the-dark necklaces that actually got pretty bright if you left them out all day. It wasn't perfect, but it was pretty close, and all together, the Pentagram of Light still looked pretty badass. He'd taken care to really mix in the candles among all the artificial lights, and the effect was actually pretty spooky. Way spookier than just candles.

He really didn't think Ulcerrot would mind. Ulcerrot was a worm demon, which, as Dewey understood it, was one of the lesser demon classifications. He figured most of the pomp and circumstance of the Goat Man, the skeleton crosses, all of that was more show than go, as his mother used to say. As long as he got people into the Killin' Pit, that was what was important, and Dewey didn't think it really mattered if the Pentagram of Light has some hot pink necklaces as all the star points.

He checked the drawing. The only thing left to do was draw the runes in blood on a boulder. The runes were all on the other side of the placemat. There were a lot of them, but Dewey wasn't worried. Ulcerrot's messenger still had yet to appear to signal the approach of the sacrificial riders, so he still had some time. What he did *not* have was a boulder. There were some rocks, but they were all pretty small. Ulcerrot had been very clear on this point: the runes had to be painted on a boulder large enough that they could be seen clearly from the train tracks. It was important, because the runes were what set the whole thing in motion.

Dewey looked around. He scratched his head. There were no boulders. He wasn't sure what to do.

A crow cawed overhead. Dewey looked up. The huge, black bird was sitting atop an old billboard. The image was faded, but Dewey could still see the faint outlines of the Rocky Mountains plastered on the board.

Printed over the mountain range in big, bold letters were the words VISIT BOULDER.

Dewey laughed. His demon had a very good sense of humor.

***

"I haven't had any hallucinations since you got here," Ben said.

They were resting in Ben's car. Ben had his head pressed against the window, using the glass to cool the fire in his cheeks. Green ooze dribbled freely down his cheeks and jaw. Patrick was sitting on the other end of the cot, trying not to fall asleep. Babs and Lex were still napping in the next car, and Alice had gone to the dining car to find something to eat. "All this murder has made my hungry," she had announced.

Patrick rubbed his eyes, trying to ward off sleep. "That's good," he yawned. "Maybe you're getting better."

"Yeah, I feel awesome."

"Or maybe your brain is so cooked that it doesn't know how to make things up anymore."

"I was sort of thinking that," Ben admitted, watching the Texas landscape slip by. "I was thinking it might be a good sign to hallucinate. So maybe I'm glad that it's back."

Patrick looked at home, confused. "What's back?"

"My hallucinations."

"You just said you haven't had any."

"I know. I was using it as a way to tell you that I hadn't had any until just now," he wheezed. "But you didn't let me finish."

"You took a long pause after you said you hadn't had any," Patrick pointed out.

"I know. My lungs are bad now. It takes time."

"So I'm back? You see both me *and* hallucination me?" Patrick whipped his head around, looking for a second Patrick. "Which one looks stronger? Who would win in a fight? Please say it's me. I don't want to be the weakest Patrick."

But Ben shook his head. "Not you," he said. "Skeletons."

Patrick blinked. "You're seeing skeletons?"

Ben nodded. "A whole, big army of them. Marching toward the train."

Patrick turned and looked out the window. "Holy shit!" he gasped. "I'm hallucinating too!"

"You see them?" Ben asked, confused.

Alice rolled open the door and ducked her head in. "Hey. You guys see the skeletons?"

They all pressed their faces to the window. The field outside the train was covered by human skeletons sticking out of the earth like tombstones. Patrick grabbed a pair of binoculars and zoomed in for a closer look. Each of the skeletons was in the shape of a cross. The leg bones were planted in the earth, sticking straight up so the feet dangled from the top. The arm bones had been lashed to the center, forming the cross. One hand drooped down from either end. The rib cage was draped across the arms to form a sort of shield around the center, and the skull was planted on top of the feet, the mouth carefully hooked through the toe bones.

"Well, I don't like this," Patrick decided.

There were hundreds of skeletons. They stretched toward the horizon, at least a football field deep. The only break in the rows of crosses was a big hole that had been dug in the center of the field, maybe twenty feet across. Other than that, it was skeletons all the way down.

"Are those all skeletons?" Ben asked.

Patrick moved the binoculars over the field. "Yes. But some of them are fake."

"How do you know?"

"They still have tags that say 'Spirit Halloween.' But I'll tell ya, I think most of them are genuine human skeletons."

"Are you sure?"

Patrick blenched. "A lot of them still have human tissue attached." He held the binoculars out to Ben. "Wanna see?"

Ben pushed the glasses away. "I'll throw up," he said, looking greener than usual.

"Wow, that'd be different," Patrick said sarcastically.

"Shut up."

Here in Ben's car, they'd secured an actual ladder to the square hole cut into the ceiling. Alice scurried up the ladder to get a better look. "Whoa. Okay. Two things," she said, holding up two fingers. "Number one: the skeletons continue as far up the tracks as I can see. There are literally thousands of them."

"Bad," Ben said, shaking his head. "Bad, bad, bad."

"Number two: there's a man dressed like a goat."

Patrick blinked. "What?"

"There's a man," she repeated. "Dressed like a goat."

"I mean, I heard you. I just don't understand what you mean."

"I mean there's a goat man in the middle of the field. Coming up now. Look."

The creature came into view through the side windows. It wasn't actually a man, at least not a real one. It was essentially a scarecrow, but a *big* scarecrow, probably thirty feet tall. It wore a long, patchwork robe of dark, sewed-together sheets. Its arms stuck straight out to the sides, and it didn't have any hands. But it did have the head of a goat.

"I think it's real goat," Alice decided.

"Not possible," Patrick said, shaking his head. "It's way too big."

"I think it's several real goat heads, cut apart and tied together. With stuffing inside. Like a soccer ball. To make one giant goat head."

Patrick's stomach lurched. "Ben," he said, making a grabby hand. "Bemme barf bag."

"Get your own barf bag," Ben said indignantly, clutching the Wegman's bag to his chest. "This one's taken." He opened it up and hurled into it. Then he pulled his head away and made a disgusted face. "I really need to clean this thing out."

The Goat Man was far enough away that despite the train's speed, it moved slowly past the windows. They stared at it quietly, as if it were a puzzle they could unlock, if they only concentrated hard enough.

Babs entered the train car. "Hey, you guys see the goat?!"

"We see the goat," Patrick confirmed.

"I don't get it," she said, stretching. "Is this, like, a play?"

Patrick lifted his hands in the air, looking dazed. "I'll be honest…I have no idea what this is."

"It doesn't look, like, dangerous, right?" Babs asked.

"It's a goat head on a stick," Alice replied. "It's lame."

"It is confusing," Patrick said.

"Hey, you guys see the goat?" Rogers asked, poking his head in the car.

"Yes, yes, we see the goat!" Patrick cried.

"Pretty weird."

"We were just talking about how weird it is," Babs said.

"It's like they're doing some kind of weird immersive theater experiment out here."

"That's what Babs said," Alice told him.

Lex entered the car too, rubbing the sleep out of his eyes. "Hey. You guys see the—"

"Yes, we see the goat!" Patrick exploded.

Lex shrugged. "It's weird, right?"

"I'm not worried about the goat," Patrick said, jumping to his feet. He began to pace around the car, cutting a winding path around all the Red Caps. "I'm worried about the people who *built* the goat and surrounded it with eight thousand human skeleton art projects."

"Must be a good-sized group of folks," Rogers said.

"A good-sized group of folks who are absolutely out of their minds," Patrick added. "Anything up front?"

"Not yet. Just skeletons and Goat Man."

Patrick sighed. "Okay. Everyone stay sharp. Lex, watch the starboard. Ben, you good to watch port?" Ben raised his thumb. "Great. Babs, Alice, you and I get the upper decks," he said, pointing to the porthole. "Report anything. *Anything*. Got it?" Everyone nodded. "Rogers, keep us posted from the engine."

"Will do," he said, disappearing back to the front of the train.

Patrick gritted his teeth. "Whoever did this, they are *very* unwell. And they probably have ten times our number."

***

Dewey had never climbed a billboard before. It was hard. The ladder was half rusted through, and the rungs were all slippery from the fog. Still, he wasn't one to complain. Ulcerrot would protect him. Ulcerrot gave him strength.

He hauled himself up to the metal grating that served as the ledge for the billboard. He wished he had some whitewash so he could cover up the advertisement. That would *really* make the runes stand out. But he didn't, and he figured no one could actually read runes regardless anyway, so it probably didn't matter if they could see them clearly. It was probably just important that they saw them at all. Just get it in front of their eyes, then the rune could do its magic and start the ceremonial progression.

The crow was still there. It cawed again. It was really loud up close. And really big, too. Dewey didn't like that the bird kept squawking at him. It felt like he was being micromanaged. He hadn't cut his manager's heart out with a steak knife way back when at the Walmart and burned it as an offering to Ulcerrot with a BIC Flex Wand in the break room because he liked to be micromanaged, and he sure as shit hadn't done it to be micro-managed by a *bird* later on down the road, after M-Day and all that. "Shut up, bird," he said sourly.

Caw! said the crow.

Dewey glared at it. "You know, I gotta use blood for this next part! Maybe I'll use yours!" He broke off a rusty corner of the grating and hurled it at the bird. He missed by three feet. "Stupid wind!" he yelled.

The bird looked at him. It bobbed its head. *Caw!*

Dewey decided to ignore the crow. *Back to Plan A.* He knelt down next to the broken bit of grating and sliced his finger on the edge. A scarlet pool of blood oozed to the surface and trickled down his hand. He smoothed out the Denny's placemat and looked over the runes one more time, just to make sure he had them in the right order. Then he got to work, drawing on the dirty old billboard in uneven streaks of his own blood.

The crow watched him bleed and said, *caw!*

***

"Anything?" Ben called up to Patrick.

"No," Patrick said from the porthole, studying the horizon through the binoculars. "It's just bones and molded plastic as far as the eye can— wait…maybe something…"

"What is it?"

"Hmm." Patrick leaned forward and dialed the binoculars in to their highest setting. "Nah. Never mind. Just a billboard."

"Maybe they only do the scary stuff at nighttime," Lex offered.

"Yeah, I clocked that too," Patrick told him. "It'd be a hell of a lot scarier in the dark. Set some bonfires, maybe light up a pentagram. Oh, look!" he said, delighted, pointing out into the field. "Candles set up in a pentagram!"

"Are they lit?" Ben asked.

"Doesn't look like it. Hard to tell in the daylight, but I don't think so. Those glow in the dark necklaces sure aren't glowing."

"Glow in the dark necklaces?"

"Yeah," Patrick nodded. "I have to say, I don't think we're dealing with particularly sane people."

***

Dewey sneezed. His hand jerked, and the blood streak went wild. He stood back and looked at the rune he'd just messed up. "Close enough," he decided.

The crow hopped over to his end of the billboard. *Hurry up!* it said. The crow had been speaking English for about an hour now. Dewey thought it was sort of surprising.

"Relax, I'm almost done," he said.

You have gathered and set bones for nigh on a decade in preparation for this moment. You have slaughtered and mutilated goats. You have dug a comparatively small pit. You have dedicated your existence to the pleasure of Ulcerrot. He has asked of you this one task—to capture for him the last train on the Slaughterhouse Run.

"You sure are really well read into this stuff," Dewey said, sounding annoyed. He'd always sort of hoped this whole project was private be-

125

tween him and Ulcerrot. He didn't like the idea of some bird being told about it, too.

The Path of Ulcerrot is a trap that, when completed, will only be tried once. If it is incomplete or ill-made, the last train of the run will go free.

"I know, I know! Why are you telling me this like I don't know this? I know this!" Boy, that bird was *really* irritating.

Because you have not yet finished your runes. And the train is almost here.

Dewey perked up at that. This was new information. "Like…how almost here is almost here?"

Like, two minutes, the crow said.

Dewey blinked. "Aw, hell."

He sliced open a finger on his left hand and started drawing runes in double time, one with each hand. They were *way* sloppy, and not at all even, but they looked enough like the ones on the Denny's placemat that Dewey figured they would work. It would be okay. "I'm almost done, I'm almost done!" he said.

Hurry! said the crow.

"Stop breathing down my neck!" Dewey screamed. "Everything is under control!"

Did you fuck this up? the crow asked. *Dewey, did you fuck this up?!*

"No, I didn't fuck this up!"

Recite the plan to me, Dewey, because I think you have fucked this up.

"I didn't fuck anything up! I've been working on this since M-Day, I think I know the plan! The train arrives. The passengers see the runes on the boulder. The runes put them under a spell. They see the skeletons. The spell makes them think the skeletons are dancing the Devil's Dervish. The Devil's Dervish itself is a second spell, which will cause them to see the Goat Man as a fiery-eyed, cloven-foot ifrit. The ifrit's fires will hypnotize them so that they leave the train, walk to the Killin' Pit, lie down in the earth, and slit their own throats with their own weapons so that Ulcerrot may drink from the deaths of the last train of the Slaughterhouse Run."

Yes, that is all correct, the crow bobbed its head. *The order is important. The runes set off a domino effect of cursed magic. The riders must see the runes first.*

"I know, I know! There!" he said, putting the finishing touch on the last marking. "They're done! Happy?"

I am not happy, the crow informed him. *Neither is Ulcerrot.*

Dewey frowned. "Why not?"

Because, Dewey…you have set up the killing field backward.

Dewey peered back down the tracks. From his privileged vantage point, he watched the Amtrak train enter the skeleton graveyard. He watched it pass the Killin' Pit, then the Goat Man. The train carried straight on through, past the rest of the skeletons, before rumbling right beneath the billboard and leaving Ulcerrot's killing fields behind.

"Oh," said Dewey. "Shit."

He hadn't thought about the fact that the train might be coming from the east.

Good luck with your severe dementia! the crow cawed as it flapped its wings and flew away.

Dewey sat down, and he began to cry.

***

"Is that a guy up there?" Ben asked, staring up at the billboard as they approached.

"Sure is."

"I can't read it. What'd he write up there?"

"It's kind of hard to make out..." Patrick said, focusing the binoculars.

"I can read it," Alice shouted from the porthole one car back. "It says, 'Denny's Grand Slam, $12.99 plus tax.'"

Patrick blinked. "Huh," he said. He gave the man an awkward wave as they zoomed past. "Poor guy," he said with a frown. "I hope the goat cult doesn't get him."

35.

"This all feels a lot less threatening in the daylight, doesn't it?" Patrick yawned. "Not just the bone goat field, I mean. All of it."

"I'm not sure taking on a hail of actual bullets for three minutes straight really qualifies as 'not threatening,'" Ben said.

"But the daytime makes them feel quaint, right?" He pried a bullet loose from the train wall and popped it into his palm. "Happy bullet!" He gestured outside. "Happy fog! Happy trees! Happy Goat Man!"

"I think you need some sleep, Bob Ross."

"That probably wouldn't go amiss," Patrick agreed. "I just…I don't know. Part of me feels like, if I close my eyes, if I fall asleep, I'll miss it."

"Miss what?"

"I don't know. *It*," he said, spinning the princess watch around on his wrist. "The thing that's going to end our run. Derail the train. Keep us from the cure." He nodded in the direction of the car where the Red Caps were reorganizing their stores. "The thing that's going to get those kids killed. I didn't see Roman coming. He was right in front of my face, and I didn't see him. Then he tried to kill me, he tried to kill you, and he murdered everyone at Fort Doom."

Ben squirmed in his seat. "It's not your fault," he said.

"But if I hadn't closed my eyes to it, they'd all still be alive." He turned to look at his friend. "Sarah would still be alive."

Ben didn't meet his stare. "I've been trying to find a way to tell you."

Patrick raised an eyebrow. "Tell me what?"

"Sarah." Ben's voice was as thin as paper and dry as an autumn leaf. "We were…" He cleared his throat, trying to dislodge the knot of pain that cinched his chest tight. "She was pregnant."

The train seemed to fall away beneath Patrick's bones. He was falling into a void of dust and quiet. "What?" he managed to croak.

Ben nodded. His eyes twitched. Green tears spilled from the corners. "She was pretty far along. Seven or eight months."

"Ben…"

"I wanted you to know, but not because I want you to feel guilty. Because you should know. And because I don't blame you. It's not your fault." At last, he raised his eyes and met Patrick's. "They're not dead because of you. They're dead because of him. It's not your job to stop all the bad shit from happening."

Patrick dug his forefinger and his thumb into his eyes, holding them shut, rubbing the lids. "It *is*, though. It's the only job I have left."

"Your job was to come back. And you did. Whatever you missed wasn't yours to see. It was his to hide. I hope that motherfucker is dead, and I hope he screamed in slow fucking agony while it happened. But you can't see what's in another man's heart."

Patrick shook his head. "But I can see what they do. I can watch for it coming. I can still save them."

"You're not the only one watching anymore," Ben said. "You did your job. You found us. You found your goddamn family, Pat, and we *all* keep watch now. Together."

Patrick let the tears roll down his cheeks. He shuddered a sob as a tension rod in his spine loosened, and he crumpled up next to Ben, pressing their shoulders together on the floor of the train. "I'm so sorry, Ben. For your loss."

Ben nodded slowly. "Yeah." He coughed. "Me too."

"Did you have a name?"

Ben sighed. "If it was a boy, we were going to name him Patrick."

"Oh, fuck." A water balloon burst behind Patrick's eyes. Tears flooded down, threatening to drown them both. "I don't know why I asked that. I don't want to know that."

"If it was a girl—"

"Don't say it," Patrick pleaded. "I can't hear it."

Ben shoved him with his shoulder. "You know there was no other choice but Isabel."

Patrick burst into heaving sobs. He buried his face in his hands and wept. "Goddammit, Ben," he managed to whisper.

"Some people would consider it an honor," Ben said.

Patrick shook his head. He wiped the snot from his nose. "That's the whole problem," he choked. "I don't deserve that honor."

Ben snorted. "Pat. Man. Look where you are. Look what you've made happen. Years—*years*—of this dumb fucking world, and here you are." He coughed and wretched up a small glob of green into his sleeve. "Sorry," he mumbled. "Anyway, go to sleep. We'll watch for you."

"You've tricked me with emotions, and now I'm tired," Patrick frowned, drying his eyes.

"Good. Go to sleep."

"Well. Maybe I'll close my eyes for a second," he replied. He stretched his arms, and his back popped in three places. He lowered himself onto a makeshift nest of towels and rags, pretty much every scrap of fabric they hadn't yet soaked in oil. "Thank you, Benny Boy. We're gonna get you that cure."

"You'd better."

"Thanks for keeping watch. Wake me up when we're being murdered."

The rhythmic churn of the wheels on the tracks lulled Patrick down into a soft, warm place. He closed his eyes. He took a deep breath. He felt someone poking his shoulder. "Wake up," said Alice.

"I just closed my eyes," he groaned.

"You've been asleep for an hour. Wake up. We've got riders."

Patrick opened his eyes. The disorientation was suffocating, like a layer of cotton wrapped around his brain. When he'd laid down, he and Ben were alone in the car. Now, one second later, Babs was up the ladder, Alice was strapping knives to her waist, Lex was running through the bunk on his way back to the storage car, and Ben was nowhere to be seen.

He sat up and rubbed his eyes. "Okay. Okay. How close?"

"Very," Babs said.

"Okay," Patrick repeated. He stumbled up from his nest and grabbed the first weapons he saw—a baseball bat and a fistful of pipe bombs. He staggered out the door, shaking the sleep from his brain and trying not to drop the bombs. He found Ben in the gangway between the last two cars, watching the riders closing in.

"Hold my bat, I have to throw a pipe bomb," Patrick said.

"Hold on," Ben replied, holding up a hand. "I think I know these guys."

Patrick stepped around Ben and poked his head out between the cars. There were five men on horseback, riding up fast. Patrick found this annoying, because he didn't know much about horses, but he knew they weren't as fast as trains. Horace must be slowing a little. "Babs!" Patrick hollered into the train.

"Yeah?"

"My hands are full, can you go ask Horace why we're going slower than horses? You have my permission to punch him in the mustache."

"Roger."

Patrick returned to his spot at the edge of the gangway. "Okay, sorry. You were saying. You know these guys?" Patrick squinted at the approaching riders. He rubbed his eyes with the back of his hand and nearly put his own eye out with a length of pipe. He wasn't sure if he was still asleep. "Wait. What am I looking at?"

"I think these guys are with the Injun Express."

The men on horseback all wore beads around their necks and crude leather loincloths around their waists. They had clothes on beneath that cultural garb, real clothes, tattered dress pants and button-downs. They all wore feathers tied around their heads. Most of them had just two or three feathers, but the rider in front had a full chief's headdress that fell to the small of his back.

"Boy, every single thing about this is *incredibly* offensive," Patrick decided.

"They're messengers," Ben sighed. "Horribly, horribly offensive messengers."

"Lo!" the chief messenger said as he drew near on his horse. "Can we come on board for a pow-wow?"

Patrick leaned over to Ben. "You have a lighter handy? I *really* want to blow this guy up."

"I know. Just...hold on." Ben held onto the train handle with both hands to keep himself standing upright. "What do you want? Go away."

"We're being chased by white men!" the chief cried.

"You *are* white men," Patrick said.

"The Bringanote tribe of the Injun Express does not see color," the chief said, sounding a little offended.

"You just said you were—! You know what, forget it. I'm getting a lighter." Patrick disappeared back inside the train.

"Can you help us?" the chief begged. "Please!"

"We fear for our women and children!" added another member of the tribe.

"I don't see any women *or* children," Ben said.

The messenger looked around at the group. "Oh, no!" he wailed loudly. "They got our women and children!"

"Boy, I do not have the energy for this," Ben said. He motioned them over. "If you can jump without killing yourself, you can board."

"Give me your hand!" the chief pleaded.

"No," Ben said. He went back inside the train car, too.

The Baby Caps were waiting while Patrick kicked at boxes, looking for a lighter. "If you put down the pipe bombs, you could actually use your hands to look," Babs said.

"You don't look with *hands*, Baby Cap. You look with eyes. Where did you go to school?" He continued to kick at various boxes.

"Who are those guys?" Lex asked, pointing at the messengers with his chin. They could see a couple of them out the window, psyching themselves up to make the jump to the train.

"It's the Jabroni Express," Patrick said. "I'm going to blow one up."

"They're mailmen," Ben clarified. "Dumb, racist mailmen. I've met a few, they're okay. Aside from the racism. They said they're being chased by people who want them dead."

"I could see that," Babs said.

"Maybe we can use them as human shields," Patrick suggested.

"I'm gonna do it!" shouted the chief from outside. "I am! I'm gonna do it!"

"Any updates on that train speed, Babs?" Patrick asked.

"Horace said there's a curve coming up. He's going—"

"As fast as he can—yeah, yeah, I got it." The walkie-talkie clipped to Patrick's waist crackled to life. "What's going on back there?" Rogers asked. Patrick looked at the walkie. He looked at his full hands. He looked back at the walkie. He sighed. He set down the bat and the bombs, and he picked up the radio. "Some idiots Ben knows are coming on board. We're going to use them as shields."

"Are you sure he knows them?" Rogers crackled.

Patrick looked at Ben. Ben shrugged. "No."

"Describe them."

"I don't know, Rogers, they're all dressed in Kevin Costner cosplay. They think we're going to a *Dances with Wolves* convention."

"What else?"

"It's a bunch of idiotic white guys with dress shirts."

The walkie was silent for a few seconds. "What color dress shirts?"

Seriously? Patrick mouthed to the others. He held the radio up to his lips. "Blue ones. With white collars."

"Do *not* let them on the train," Rogers crackled, his voice suddenly urgent.

"Okay, fashion police. I don't like it either, but—"

The door slid open and Rogers burst through. "Don't let them on!" he yelled. "That's not the Injun Express!"

Ben frowned. "It's not?"

"No! They're—" Rogers froze in his tracks. He was staring over their shoulders. The crew turned around.

All five of the riders had boarded the moving train. They stood there in the gangway, grinning in at the Red Caps. "Hello, my dudes," said the chief, pulling off his headdress and tossing it off the train. He flashed them a huge, toothy smile. "Thank you for allowing us to share in the resource of this train. That was a true show of critical altruism." The man put his hand on his heart and patted it. "This is what our community is all about."

"What is happening?" Babs asked.

"Opportunity is happening," the man said. He stepped inside and wrapped his arm around Bab's shoulders. "I don't know where you were going before, but my dude, this train is now on the track…to opportunity."

"Oh, no," Patrick groaned. "Don't tell me we just got boarded by day traders."

"Worse," Rogers grimaced. "Necro bros."

36.

"What is a 'necro bro'?" Patrick asked as if his mouth were full of sour milk.

"That is a pejorative term, my dude!" the lead bro said, looking hurt.

"You just rode up wearing a Native American headdress and called yourself 'injuns,'" Patrick reminded him.

"That was a *disguise*," the man said, rolling his eyes. "And now, the prestige!" he added grandly. "Necro bro is insensitive. We prefer necrocurrency enthusiasts."

"Absolutely not," Patrick said, shaking his head vigorously. "This is a FinTech-free train. Get out. Go." He shooed at them.

"That is not a very warm welcome," the leader observed.

"That's because you're not welcome here, Todd. I assume your name is Todd?"

"*I'm* Todd," said one of the guys in the back, raising his hand.

"I'm also Todd," said a second.

"How many of you are named Todd?" Patrick demanded. Three of them raised their hands, though the leader wasn't one of them.

"More offensive stereotypes," he said sadly, "thinking only guys named Todd can lead in the necrocurrency industry." He *tsk-tsk-tsk*ed. "My name is Blake. These guys are Todds. That one is Tommy. Say hi, Tommy."

"Hi, Tommy," said Tommy. The Todds laughed, and they all high-fived.

"You're a grown man, you can't go by 'Tommy'!" Patrick exploded.

Blake lifted his arm from Babs' shoulders and laid it heavily across Patrick's shoulders, leading him away, up toward the front of the car. "Listen, bro. I get it. You're skeptical. You're obsessed with fiat. You probably don't even own any hemo tokens. Bro. I get it. You're not ready for this world. And that's okay. You don't need to be ready for this world. But this world is ready for you." He drew his hand across the air, as if revealing a powerful vision for Patrick. All Patrick saw were five douchebags with admittedly well-toned arms.

"Listen, I don't know what the fuck you're talking about, and seeing as how money hasn't existed for eight years, I'll be honest with you, I could not possibly care less. You have eight seconds to get off my train before I sic our children on you."

"Sorry, no can do-ski, brewski!" Blake shoved Patrick and sent him smashing into the side wall.

"Ow…" Patrick said meekly as he crumpled to the ground.

"Ladies and neanderthals, listen up!" Blake called, clapping his hands for attention. "This won't take long! We have no issue with you all. We're just here on a necrocurrency mining sesh. Everyone cooperate, and we'll be on our way in no time."

"Can someone please translate what this asshole is saying?" Alice demanded.

"He wants to peel off our flesh and use it for money," Rogers said.

"*And* your bones," Blake added. "We're not only talking flesh notes here. We mine bone coin too."

"In what sick universe is human flesh *money*?" Babs demanded.

"It's sort of a thing for people operating at a…higher level," Blake admitted. "The onboarding is intense, and you wouldn't really get it."

"Hey, incels," Patrick said wearily, pulling himself up from the floor, "if you want money-bones, I have great news for you. If you go like twenty miles that way, you'll find one thousand acres of bones. Riches beyond your imagination. Go get them. Go away."

Blake beamed. "Yeah, bro, nice call! I like the way you think. We saw that field, sent the interns to go gather up the b-lot. That's what we call free bones. Cha-ching!" he laughed. He turned and really noticed Ben for the first time. He had fallen asleep on his cot in the midst of all the chaos. Blake squinted down at him. "Hey, who's this little leprechaun? He got the sickness?"

"Yes. Riddled with it. As you can see, it's all up in his skin cells. Bad flesh. Probably not worth much on the ketamine maniac market. Leave him alone," Patrick said.

"Hey man, there's always a market for green notes," he shrugged. "We'll take it." He pulled out a hunting knife and moved toward Ben. Patrick leapt between them, but Blake knocked him away easily.

"Oh, fuck this," Alice said. She grabbed a metal bat and swung it at Blake's ribcage. He turned just in time and caught the blow on his powerful abs. It knocked him back a step, but he didn't even double over. "Oh-ho-ho shit!" he said, amused and probably a little turned on. "I'm saving you for last!" He motioned toward one of the Todds. At the signal, the Todd pulled a TASER gun from his waist and fired a pair of hooked bolts into Alice's chest. She seized up, her eyes rolled up in her head, and she fell to the floor, unconscious.

Lex exploded across the room. He rammed his shoulder into the Todd with the TASER, knocking him back into the gangway. Todd screamed and went bouncing off the train. Lex turned, his lips bared, a growl in his throat. He ran at the next Todd, but Tommy pulled a billiard ball from his pocket and beamed it at Lex's forehead. It hit with a loud *THOCK!* and Lex hit the floor so hard that the train shook. Rogers reached for a machete, but the last Todd leapt at him like a cat, drawing a knife and pressing it against his throat.

Babs was out of reach of any weapons. She was still working out what to do.

Blake looked around the room. "We cool? Everyone got that out of their system? Yeah?" No one replied. Blake took that as a yes. "Baller. Let's mine." He picked up Ben's hand and sliced into his forearm.

Ben opened his eyes. He looked at the man running a knife through his flesh. "Hey…" he said, confused. He watched the mixture of blood and green slime spill from his arm as if the whole situation belonged to someone else. "Stop that?" he said, more of a guess than a demand.

Suddenly, a Todd that was standing near a window became visibly irritated. "Blake!" he shouted.

"Dude!" Blake shouted back, annoyed. "I'm mining!"

"I know, man, but we got trouble!" He pointed up toward the ceiling. "It's the Squirrels!"

Blake stopped. He closed his eyes and exhaled. "Goddammit," he sighed. He pulled his knife out of Ben's muscle tissue. "Put some ice on that. Keep it cool for me. I'm coming back for it."

Babs ran over to Ben and held a rag against his wound. It was bleeding pretty heavily, but Blake hadn't hit any arteries or anything. "We can get you stitched up," she promised Ben.

"Why doesn't it hurt?" he asked, dazed.

"What is *happening*?" Patrick asked from the floor. He'd hit his head when he landed, and the whole train was spinning. "What are the Squirrels?"

THUNK.

Something landed on the roof.

THUNK. THUNK-THUNK.

Everyone looked up. A face appeared in the porthole. It was a woman with dark complexion, a thin face, high cheek bones, and small, mousy ears. Her curly hair was wild, but short, sticking out on all sides in tumbling curlicues as the wind whipped it around her face. Her brown eyes were sharp, with a certain mischievous light. "Hi," she said cheerily. "I love this train. Can I have it?" She swung around and let her legs dangle down into the car. She slipped through and landed lightly on the floor. She was wearing a black and purple wingsuit. "Come on down, ladies!" she called back up through the porthole. "This train's only got high levels of *in*security."

"Is that supposed to be some kind of insult?" Blake asked. He asked it in a way that made Patrick pretty confident he actually didn't know if it was supposed to be or not.

Three other women dropped in behind the first, all of them wearing wingsuits.

"Fly away, little Squirrels—this is *our* train," Blake spat.

"We're mining!" a Todd added helpfully.

"You're morons," the lead Squirrel said. "Now go away, the grownups need to talk." She turned to the rest of the crew. She looked them over one by one before finally settling on Rogers. "You're in charge?" she asked.

"No, ma'am," Rogers said.

He nodded down at Patrick, who was still on the floor, his t-shirt wrenched up over his belly, one leg twisted up in a blanket. Patrick wiggled his fingers at her. "Hello."

The woman's face fell. "Okay, maybe 'grown-ups' is too strong a term." She squatted down next to Patrick. "Hi, little fella. Listen. Your train is still running. Despite everything. So that means it's probably got some useful mechanics. We're going to take those. We do not care if you live or die. You sit there, let us do our thing, and we'll be on our way. Try to stop us, and my friend Melanie over there will boil your brain inside of your skull with the microwave X-ray gun she developed. Okay?"

Patrick looked at the one called Melanie suspiciously. "You do not have a microwave X-ray gun," he said.

Melanie held up her microwave X-ray gun. It looked like a handheld steampunk Gatling gun. She aimed it at Tommy and pulled the trigger. Nothing happened—no sounds, no lights, no sparks, no shots. Nothing happened at all, except for the fact that Tommy started to scream, and then he began to claw furiously at his own head, and then something inside his skull went POP and he fell down dead in the gangway.

"Holy shit!" Blake yelped. "Did you just kill Tommy?!"

"The brains don't usually boil that fast," Melanie said, almost by way of apology. "His must have been *really* small and stupid."

Blake growled. He lunged at her. She tried to fire off another shot, but he was fast, and he knocked the gun out of her hands. It smashed against the wall, and a few very important-looking pieces broke off. "Hey!" Melanie yelled. "That was *mine!*" She flicked her foot and a blade sprang out from the toe of her boot. She kicked Blake in the kneecap, sinking the blade in a good two inches. Blake howled in pain. He punched Melanie in the face, and she fell back against the seats. Blake turned to the lead Squirrel and started swinging. She held up her left arm, and his fist smashed into the steel gauntlet she wore beneath the wingsuit. The bones of his hand cracked and broke against the metal plate. He stepped back, howling louder. The Squirrel back-armed him across the cheek, breaking his nose and sending him stumbling backward.

"Stop!" Patrick yelled. He leapt into the space between the Squirrels and the necro bros. He held out his hands, and everyone froze. "Listen! Everybody! We've got injured people in here and some really important equipment that's no good to anyone if it gets broken. Obviously, you all have some issues to work through before you strip our train for bone pennies or whatever the fuck. You are free to kill each other as hard as you want to, but *please*, can we not do it in here? We have a whole car made just for this purpose, right back that way," he said, pointing to the last car in the train. "That's our dojo. Fighting is what that car is for."

Babs and Alice exchanged looks. *Dojo?* Babs mouthed. Alice shrugged.

"Can we *please* take this fight back there? You guys sort your shit, then we'll deal with whoever comes out. Okay?" He looked pointedly at Blake. He was in bad shape; his bloody face was already swelling, his hand dangled uselessly from his wrist, and his left leg wasn't going to support his weight much longer. The Squirrel he'd punched out wasn't faring much better. She had hit her head hard enough to leave a dent in the interior wall, and she was out cold, probably with a severe concussion.

"Fine," Blake said. He turned and limped toward the back car. The two remaining Todds followed him.

"I don't like being interrupted mid-fight," the lead Squirrel glowered. "I take back our offer. Once we kill them, we're going to kill you, too."

"Okay, great," Patrick said, ushering them all to the rear car. "We'll all be in here, preparing for the sweet release of death." He shuttled them into the car, which was more or less empty. "Lots of fighting space in here," he said, pleased. "Best of luck to you all."

He closed the door. The fighting started immediately, and the screams were so loud that no one inside heard the click of the padlock Patrick slipped into place.

"You know that won't hold them," Rogers said.

"I don't need to hold them. I just need a minute. Help me bring Lex inside." They grabbed the young man's ankles and dragged him in from the gangway. Then Patrick pulled the makeshift torch off the wall, the torch he'd constructed by tying an oil-soaked towel to the end of one of the branches Lex had pulled off the dead trees back up in the Blue Ridge. "Anyone got a lighter?"

Alice clicked hers to life. Patrick dipped the rag into the flame, and the whole thing caught fire with a small *WHOOSH!*

"Okay, stand back. I haven't tested this yet." He smashed the burning end of the torch down on the couplers. The matchboxes exploded, and the damaged coupler pins blew into pieces. The car uncoupled from the train and immediately began to lose speed.

There was a real blood bath happening inside. The windows were coated with red and gray gore. It was pretty thick on the glass—otherwise, the people inside might have seen Patrick smiling and waving as the rest of the train pulled away, leaving them stranded together on the Texas plain.

37.

"One car gone, four to go."

"I wish you wouldn't talk about my train like that," Horace frowned. "I don't like losing a car. It feels like losing a child."

"I take it you never had children," Patrick said.

"I had this train. How's Ben?"

"Babs patched him up. She stitched his wrist with some fishing line. I think he'll be okay. The wound is pretty bad, but he's not really using his arms anyway, so he should be okay, if he can live long enough to let it heal."

Horace grimaced. "I'm going as fast as I can," he reminded Patrick.

"I need you to go faster."

"I am going *much* faster than I feel comfortable with already."

"I know. But we need to go even faster."

Horace chewed on his mustache. "I hate this," he decided, frustrated.

"I know," Patrick said again. He caught some motion outside the windshield. He walked over and pressed his nose against the glass. "Oh, God," he murmured, squinting out into the wasteland. "What in the fresh, unholy hell?"

***

"Okay, everyone, we've got a Code Mad Max Mutant!" Patrick shouted, clapping his hands for attention. "Who's got ideas?"

The Baby Caps blinked at him. "What?"

"I literally cannot describe it any better than I already did," Patrick said, throwing up his hands. "We've got a Mad Max mutant situation, and we need ideas!" He pointed out the window. The periphery was limited, but slowly the train caught up to the scene on the horizon, and the Baby Caps recoiled in horror.

There was a whole motorcade of madmen charging them across the field. They rode all sorts of unhinged apocalyptic vehicles: motorcycles with war spikes sticking out from the wheel spokes; dune buggies with orange flames belching from their exhaust stacks; four-wheelers with pneumatic dart guns mounted to the handlebars; and even a few Toyota 4x4's with human skulls strung across their grills and obscene words painted on their fenders in blood. The raiders drove like a flock of birds in a V-formation, each of them tethered by heavy chain on the backs of their rigs to one huge iron-bar cage on wheels. Inside the cage was a hulk of a man with bulging muscles that were wrapped snake-line with veins. He was completely hairless, at least as far as they could tell, which was pretty far, since he wore only a short loincloth that didn't do its one job very well at all. His skin was pale and wet, as if he'd just been hauled out of a cave for the first time in a decade. Red tattoos covered his pearl-white skin. His left hand was missing, and in its place some psychopath had grafted an old sledgehammer head onto the stump. Half a dozen knives were stuck into his right leg; the handles stood up from the skin, marking his thigh like a post-apocalyptic cactus.

"What the absolute shit?" Babs breathed.

Lex squinted at the entourage. "What am I looking at?" he asked. There was a huge knot on his forehead where he'd been knocked out with the billiard ball, and his vision was swimming in and out of focus.

"Patrick pretty much summed it up," Rogers said. "Mad Max mutant squad."

Ben sat up weakly on his cot. He had to wipe the green ooze from his eyes so he could see. He held up a pair of binoculars and peered out at the oncoming horde. He immediately turned back away from the window, dropped the binoculars, and curled into a ball. "Nope," he said, and he promptly fell asleep.

"What do we do?" Lex asked.

"I don't know," Patrick confessed. "We hit them hard. With everything we've got. And we do *not* let King Kratos onto the train. That'll be their plan—drop him off and let him clean house."

"And he will," Rogers said.

Patrick nodded once. "If he gets on board, we're done—us, the train, probably the tracks. Maybe the earth for twenty feet down. It's over. Understand?" The Baby Caps nodded. "We do not let him onto this train."

Lex took a deep breath. His lungs shuddered and his heart was pounding. "We might not have much choice," he whispered.

The raiders were closing in fast. The Baby Caps split up and ran through the train, gathering whatever weapons they could get their hands on. While Patrick was collecting pipe bombs, Alice grabbed her crossbow and took up a spot near an exterior door. She pushed it open just wide enough to let the bolt slip through and give herself a big enough field of vision. When the raiders were about fifty yards out, she shot a bolt at the man in the cage. It sailed between the bars and lodged in his chest.

He didn't even flinch. A small stream of blood poured out from the wound, and the monster didn't even notice.

"Aim for the riders!" she yelled.

The next arrow hit one of the dune buggy drivers in the shoulder. He yelled in pain, but he kept rolling. She fired again, aiming for the gas tank this time. She missed, but the bolt hit a tire, and the buggy spun out of control. The raider leapt out of the buggy, wounded shoulder and all, and snatched a pin out of his hitch, freeing the chain and detaching from the cage before the stalled buggy could drag it down.

"They're trained," Alice called out over her shoulder.

"What does that mean?" Babs asked.

"It means they're going to be a real pain in the ass to kill," Alice said through gritted teeth.

Patrick appeared one door further down. He threw it open all the way and stood ready with a pipe bomb in one hand and a lighter in the other. He didn't know how far he could throw one of these bombs and he didn't want to chance wasting one, so he forced himself to wait on trembling legs as they barreled closer and closer. He saw Alice's bolts flying. She was a hell of a shot, but the raiders weren't falling like they should. Then the albino's eyes locked with Patrick's. His guts turned to water.

It was like looking into the face of Death itself.

"I do not like this, Sam I Am," he whispered to himself. He lit the bomb and hurled it at the cage.

The timing was perfect. The pipe exploded as soon as it touched iron. There was a loud roar and a brilliant flash. The creature in the cage threw up his arms to protect his eyes from the bright light…but that was all the damage it did. At least, that's all the damage it did to *him*. But the bomb had also managed to blow open the cage's lock. Now the door swung open, hanging by a solitary hinge. Patrick had just done a small favor for the raiders.

"Oh, come on," he sighed.

***

"Did Patrick just blow open the goddamn door?!" Babs cried.

"My head *really* hurts," Lex moaned. "I think I need to lie down."

Babs threw him a look. "Lex. Man. If you can keep it together for, like, ten minutes, we could *really* use your help."

"I know...I know..." Lex said, closing his eyes.

Babs cursed under her breath. Shit was about to go bad.

"They're not stopping!" Alice yelled from the vestibule. She'd fired more than half a dozen bolts at the raiders, and she'd only taken out two vehicles. They were still coming, some of them with her arrows sticking out from their limbs.

Babs spied Alice's favorite knife lying on the floor in her car. She picked it up and ran out to the gangway. "Here," she said, flipping her the knife.

"Thanks. What's your plan?"

"I—I—" Babs stammered. She shook her head. She shrugged.

"Babs. Do not freeze up on me. That thing is going to be here in three seconds. Grab some shit. Fight like hell. Got it?" Babs nodded. Alice gave her a little shove, and she was off, running up through the forward cars, searching for a weapon that felt right for the moment.

Which was when her eyes fell upon the bear traps.

"Oh," she said, blinking. "That'll work."

She picked one up and carefully pried it open as Patrick coming running through. "The riders will likely peel off when they drop the Sloth," he said. He glanced at Babs. "Don't lose an arm in that thing."

"Thanks."

"Alice! Stop shooting, he's already here. Close range and bombs. We take him out fast, or he takes the train. Go!"

Babs and Patrick were in the Baby Caps' car; Rogers was one car back with an unconscious Ben and a semi-lucid Lex. Patrick grabbed the walkie. "Horace, whatever happens back here, do not stop this train," he said. "If it goes bad, I'll try to get Ben to the engine. You guys decouple and you get him to the Queen Mary." Horace crackled back some sort of reply, but Patrick didn't hear it. He tossed the walkie onto a nearby seat just as the entourage pulled up alongside the train.

"Give it everything!" Patrick yelled. "Now!"

143

Babs scrambled up the bookshelf and popped up through the port-hole. She held the bear trap by its chain, swinging it over her head like a lasso. "Come on, Babs...come on," she whispered. She focused on the monster, who was leaning out of his cage. She felt the rhythm of the bear trap, took aim, and let it fly.

The trap connected with the hulking figure dead on. The metal teeth snapped down on his arm, sinking the sharp metal points two or three inches into his bicep. Babs whooped with victory, but the sound died in her throat as she watched the monster reach up with his other hand and pry the trap off his arm. He broke the pulled-back steel as easily as if it were made of matchsticks. The springs popped, and the pieces of the broken trap fell to the ground.

"Well, goddamn," she grunted.

The drivers were well-rehearsed. They disengaged their chains and broke off from the pack in in a complex and elegant ballet. Soon only the Toyotas were hauling the cage, and they pulled it right up alongside the door. Alice had found her case of throwing knives; she hurled them, one right after the other, at the enormous, red-tattooed man. They sank into his flesh, *thoomp-thoomp-thoomp-thoomp*, deep into his shoulder and fore-arm, but he didn't flinch. He gripped the edges of the cage's doorway and launched himself out with a ground-shaking roar.

"This is how we die," Ben whispered in his sleep.

The creature slammed into the side of the train. He hit right at the door where Alice was standing. The two cars on either side slammed down, then bounced up, skipping the rails for a half a breath before crashing back down again, the steel wheels skittering back onto the tracks. Alice stumbled backward and dove into Ben's car, narrowly missing the huge white hand that swiped at her. The monster was too broad to fit through the doorway onto the train. He bellowed with frustration, an ear-shattering roar that exploded across the prairie. He planted his right foot in the gangway and gripped the door frame with his right hand. Then he took his sledgeham-mer hand and started wailing on the top of the train, beating the absolute shit out of the steel, crunching it inward as if it were no stronger than tinfoil. The contraction of the Baby Caps' train car forced two of the win-dows to explode. Shards of tempered glass pelted Patrick and Babs. They covered their faces with their arms, arms that came away slick with blood where they'd been nicked.

"What do we do?!" Babs shrieked.

"I'm working on it!" Patrick lied.

"Decouple!" Rogers shouted over at them.

"No good!" Patrick shouted back. "He's got both cars and we can't risk moving Ben past him!"

"What do you want to do?" Rogers hollered.

"I'm working on it!" Patrick lied louder.

Over in the next car, Alice grabbed an oil bomb. She pulled the rag out of the neck of the bottle and quickly tied it around the blade of a machete. She set the rag on fire with a lighter, then she slipped out into the vestibule with her flaming sword and her bottle of oil. The monster's head loomed over the top of the train, and he was focused on the roof, still hammering away with his sledge. Alice ran forward and smashed the bottle over his shoulder. In one quick motion, she shoved the jagged points of the broken bottle neck into his chest, then she plunged the flaming sword into his stomach. The fire lit on the oil and roared up his torso. The monster became engulfed in flames from ribcage to jaw. His white skin crackled under the fire, and he screamed in pain. He punched at Alice with a fist the size of a basketball. She danced out of the way, but the blow caught her on the hip. It only grazed her, but the force was enough to send her flying across the gangway and slamming into the far set of doors. She fell to the floor, the wind knocked out of her lungs.

The monster reached in to grab her, but Rogers leapt out of the car, driving a crowbar down into the creature's arm. It didn't do much damage, but the hulking thing was blinded by the flames on its chest, and he couldn't see into the train. He pulled his hand back and gripped one of the butcher knives that was lodged in his thigh. He drew it out, flipped it around, and drove it blindly into the gangway. Rogers had turned his back to help Alice to her feet, and he didn't see the knife coming. He was far enough out of reach that the monster couldn't do much damage, but as he swiped the blade around wildly, the tip shredded the back of Rogers' shirt and drew blood from shallow channels in his flesh. Rogers grunted back the pain as he lifted Alice. He tried to back her into the train car, but the flames were burning out now, and the monster could see through the smoke curling up from his own charred skin. He pulled a hunting knife from his leg and flung it at Rogers. It caught the conductor in the back of the arm, piercing straight through his triceps and slicing straight out the other side.

Rogers fell backward into the car holding Alice. They were still half-out into the vestibule. The creature pulled a third knife and hurled it at them. Lex dove into the gangway holding one of the steel train-roof shields. The blade clattered off the shield. Another knife, and another, and another. The monster moved quickly and furiously, wrenching knives from his leg and his shoulder, flinging them at Lex, who blocked them all with the shield.

The monster bellowed. Lex was still seeing double, and his brain felt fuzzy. He was having a hard time standing straight. He was having a hard time thinking straight. But he sensed weakness. He gritted his teeth and charged forward, shield-first. He rammed the monster with the steel plate, slamming it into the burn wounds on his chest. The monster slipped and reeled back. He tilted away from the train, wheeling his arms for balance. Then he caught purchase with his sledgehammer hand through one of the broken windows and wrenched himself back onto the platform. He crouched down in front of Lex, a murderous fury in his eyes. He drove his head forward, straight into the steel square. It dented so hard that it cracked down the middle. Lex fumbled the pieces, and they fell away, sliding across the floor and off the train.

"Oh, great," Lex moaned.

The monster backhanded him and sent him careening off the interior walls. Lex just barely managed to pull himself back into Ben's car before losing consciousness again.

"Did you see that?!" Babs yelled. "It just broke that shield with its *head*! What *is* that thing?!"

"Skull harder than steel," Patrick murmured. "It really *is* a mutant."

The train was shaking. The creature was smashing in the walls. Now he was trying to rip the doorway open wide enough for his hulking frame to fit. He had both feet planted on the metal floor and was thrashing his shoulders, muscling the walls open wider.

The mutant had boarded the train.

Patrick patted his pockets frantically and cursed when he found them empty. "Babs! I need to get to the other car!"

"Yeah, good luck," she snorted.

"Can you distract him?"

Babs' mouth fell open. "With *what?!*"

"I don't know—a Molotov? Fire kind of worked."

"I mean, I guess. What are you gonna do?"

"I just need to get past him. See if you can draw him back."

Babs pushed her glasses up her nose. "I want a raise if we survive this," she decided. She snatched up the last Molotov in the train car. She lit the rag, then leaned out the broken window. "Hey, you weird asshole!" she shouted. "Get burnt!"

Patrick screwed up his mouth. "'Get burnt'?"

"I don't know!" Babs yelled, exasperated. She hurled the bottle at the mutant. It broke across his left arm and flames spread all the way down to his sledgehammer hand. He reared back and roared, slamming the top of the train with his burning arm.

"Nice work!" Patrick called as he sprinted through the door. "Watch out for the sledgehander!"

Babs blinked. "The what?"

The monster slammed its sledgehammer hand through the open window frame. It bashed into Babs' elbow, snapping it in half with gut-wrenching crack. The force of the blow knocked her against the far side of the train. She hit the window so hard that she broke it, sending spiderweb cracks through the glass plate. She fell to the floor behind Alice's cot, wedged there between the metal frame and the hard plastic wall covering.

Hot waves of nauseating pain crashed over her like lava and brought her down into the darkness.

***

Patrick dove through the open door into the next car.

"I hope this means you have a plan," Rogers said.

Patrick didn't respond. He started searching the train car frantically. He turned over cushions and shook out blankets. He upended bags and kicked over boxes. "Come on, come on," he said, his brain too frantic to remember where he'd stashed the bag.

"What are you looking for?" Rogers asked. "I can—"

"A-ha!" Patrick cried triumphantly. He held up a vial of Zom-Be-Gone.

Rogers frowned. "You don't think—?"

"I watched a lot of *X-Men* growing up, I know a mutant when I see one," he replied. "I don't know how they did it, but that thing's part duster." He peeked out into the vestibule. The monster was still thrashing, but the fire on its arm was dying. Patrick pulled the stopper. He moved out into the gangway, but Rogers grabbed his arm.

"What if you're wrong?" he said.

"Then I'm just as dead now as I would be in four minutes." He shook Rogers off and stepped into the gangway. "Hey!" he hollered at the mutant. "Catch!"

He hurled the vial at the creature's head. The monster was confused by the sight of such a tiny projectile coming his way. He stared at it curiously as it flew through the air. He watched with interest as it thumped against his chest, spilling most of its contents down his powerful belly. He poked at the purple liquid with a finger. He brought it to his nose and sniffed.

"Is it working?" Rogers asked.

The monster sniffed again. He frowned at the liquid. He popped his finger into his mouth and sucked it dry.

"Um," said Patrick.

Suddenly, the beast froze. His eyes began to water. He opened his mouth and reared his head back.

"Oh, gross, he's going to sneeze," Patrick grimaced.

A crossbow bolt whizzed through the air. It flew into the mutant's open mouth and sank deep into his soft palate, the iron point stabbing through to his brain. The monster's head fell slowly back. His arms lifted from the train, and he crashed backward onto the gravel siding, dead.

Patrick wheeled around, stunned. Alice lay on the floor behind him, nocking another arrow in the crossbow, just in case. "Nice shot," he squeaked.

"Thanks for the opening," she replied.

38.

Patrick stumbled into the engine car. "Horace, please tell me we're almost there."

Horace tugged at his mustache. "Patrick, we're not even out of Texas yet."

Patrick doubled over and put his hands on his knees. "How is that possible?" he said, shaking his head.

"How's it going back there?"

"Really great," Patrick replied, nodding enthusiastically. "Don't go back there."

"You keep saying that. Do I need to go back there?"

"I wouldn't."

Horace frowned. "What's the status report?"

"On the train or on the people?"

"Both."

"Oh," said Patrick. "Bad." Horace crossed his arms and stared at him over the top of his spectacles. Patrick sighed. "Car three is kind of—I don't know the right word…tin-canned?"

"Tin-canned?"

"Yeah. It's pretty crunched up. Car four is better, but it's got some dents in the side. The dining car is basically untouched, so that's something. And the rest of the raiders high-tailed when they saw Solomon Grundy take a dive. That was nice."

"And the crew?"

Patrick looked down and ticked off the list on his fingers. "Two concussions, maybe three. Babs has a broken elbow. Like, *broken* broken. Alice's face is cut up pretty badly. Rogers has slash wounds all over his back, but they're not very deep. Also, a knife wound in his arm, and that one *is* deep. Lex is sort of one big bruise, with the biggest bruise being up here," he said, pointing to his forehead. "Ben's got a flap of muscle tissue hanging off his arm, but we bandaged it up, and for some reason he doesn't seem to be able to feel it, which I take as a *tremendously* bad sign for his health."

Horace shook his head slowly. "We're not even out of Texas yet," he said again quietly. He looked up at Patrick. "How about you?"

"I'm one of the concussions. And I have this," he said, holding up his arms so Horace could see the cuts from the shattered window glass. "Babs has a matching set, but hers have taken a backseat to the broken elbow."

"We never should have done this," Horace said, his voice hoarse. "They're just kids."

Patrick gave a sad shrug. "It doesn't matter now. We're in it. The only way out is through."

Horace turned and focused on the tracks. The silence hung between them like a pendulum. They stood like that for several long minutes, watching the prairie slip past the train, eyes twitching at the horizon. "What'd you come up here for?" Horace finally asked.

"A few of them have some really dangerous swelling going on. We need ice."

"We're in Texas," Horace snorted.

"Believe me, I am oh-so-well aware," Patrick said. "How far south do the Rockies come? Are we going to hit mountains at all?"

"We'll hit mountains," Horace nodded. "Not mile-high snow caps. But high desert."

"Will there be snow?"

The conductor shrugged. "Sometimes. It's gettin' on in the season now, there might be snow if we're lucky. If I see it, we'll stop for some."

Patrick wiped his hands down his face. Sometimes, that old exhaustion that lived inside his bones liked to seep out and spread into his blood. "We don't have time to stop," he said.

"You just said—"

"I said we need ice. If you see snow, give me a buzz. I'll figure out the rest." He sank backward out of the engine car, running his hand along the wall for support. "How long, you think?"

"I don't know," Horace said. "To the mountains? Maybe five hours."

"All right," Patrick nodded. "Okay." He drifted away and left Horace alone with his helplessness and quiet.

39.

Ben finally woke about thirty minutes after they'd killed the mutant.

He raised up on his elbows and looked around the train. There was the train…there were Patrick and the Red Caps…there was most of their stuff…but something was off. He couldn't put a finger on it, but something was different. "What'd I miss?" he croaked.

"A lot," Patrick said, joining him on the bunk. He leaned forward and propped his elbows on his knees, and he sank his chin into his hands. "You missed a lot, Benny Boy."

The pieces started to fall together for Ben. Babs was there, sitting in a chair, but her arm was in a sling that Rogers was tying around her neck. It looked like it had been made from an old t-shirt. Lex was on the floor, and Alice was running a wet rag over his forehead. Rogers' shirt was covered in blood. Come to think of it, *everyone's* shirts were covered in blood. Ben looked up. The ceiling was crunched in.

"Jesus," he said. "Was that Kratos?"

"The God of War is real, and he is *very* angry," Patrick confirmed.

"Was," Alice corrected him.

"Right," Patrick nodded. "Was."

"Jesus," Ben said again. "I thought I was dreaming that."

Rogers finished setting the sling. He helped Babs position her arm inside the cotton shift. She inhaled sharply through her teeth. "Sorry," Rogers frowned. "It's going to hurt like that for a long time. We'll try to find a doctor when we get to L.A."

"Hey. No one died," Babs said, her head drooping. "That's something." Her glasses had been smashed in the brawl and one of her lenses was cracked. She didn't have the first idea how to find a replacement.

"Don't tell anyone, but I have some moonshine stashed in the engine," Rogers said. "I'll get you some for the pain. Okay?" Babs nodded, and Rogers went off to find his flask.

"We should have chased those sons of bitches down and broken every bone in their bodies for what they did to our people," Alice seethed.

Patrick cast her a sad glance. "It's better we stay and help the injured," he said.

"For all we know, that mutant was their slave," she spat. "They deserve to die."

"Hey," Patrick said softly, trying to sand off her edges. She glared up at him. He held his hands up in a sign of truce. "They *will* die. Just like all of us. And even if it takes a long time for that to happen…well, sometimes life is more punishment than death."

Alice held his eyes for a few more seconds. Then she looked down, back toward Lex. She pressed the wet rag against the knot on his skull.

Patrick stood up and crossed the car. He grabbed a bottle of water and brought it over to where Lex lay. He knelt down and dribbled some water into his mouth. Lex shifted and licked his lips, which had become dry and cracked and crusted with blood.

"I'm sorry I got you all into this," Patrick said quietly. "It seems like—" He stopped and rearranged his thoughts. He wasn't sure really what he wanted to say, but there was something pressing at his chest. "It feels like ever since Izzy—um, that's my daughter—"

"We know," Babs said.

"Oh." He glanced at Ben, who just gave him a small nod. "Right. Um…well, since she—I mean, since M-Day, I keep doing this thing where I charge ahead with even the dumbest ideas, figuring it'll all be fine. And I guess 'fine' is a relative term, because here I am…but also, it's never 'fine.' I'm not 'fine.' There's always such a price. And I—I keep not factoring that into the calculation." He found a smudge of mud on the floor that caught his attention. Something inside of him felt a desperate urge to clean that spot. He dug at it with his fingernails, scraping up the dried crust. "If I stop to think about it too long, sometimes I think maybe I do it hoping one day, one of these things will be the end. For me. But I don't like that, so I don't think about it much. I just charge in. And I bring everyone else with me." He turned and looked at each of the Baby Caps, his eyes misting over. "I'm sorry," he said, choking out the words. "I shouldn't have put you all into—"

"Is this a thing you're going to do a lot?" Alice interrupted.

Patrick blinked at her. "Is…*what* a thing I'm going to do a lot?"

"This sort of sad, guilty monologue," Babs explained. "Who is this for? Is it for you?"

"Is this part of your 'process'?" Alice asked, rolling her eyes.

Patrick was confused. "What's happening right now?"

"We're not here for you," Babs said. "It's practically not even your idea. It's just, like, where the path led."

"We're here because this is how we save Ben," Alice said. "We'd have done this even if you weren't here."

"Look, Patrick," Babs said, leaning back against the wall. She suddenly seemed like a tired elder who had resigned herself to explaining the fundamentals of existence to a curious toddler. "No one knows Ben like you do; no one is closer to Ben than you are. But we've been with him for a pretty long time now, and it's not the same as what you guys have, but Ben is our family. This is a world with no families. And we are so fucking lucky, we *do* have a family, it's each other. It's Ben."

"I feel like I should leave," Ben said, struggling to push himself up from the cot. "This is getting awkward. For me." He teetered off into the next car and shut the door behind him.

"He's not comfortable with his emotions," Patrick explained. "That's always been true. Anyway, please continue."

Babs sighed. "All I'm saying is, Ben is my family. Everyone on this train is my family. These people. These are my *family*. Do you know what I mean?"

Patrick snuffled out a laugh. "Babs…you have no idea how much I know what you mean."

"I mean, even you, now. You're part of this family."

"Oh. Well, I mean, I'm on this train, so it sort of feels like I was included already…and then you added that last little, 'and also, you!' Which I'm—you know what? I'm not going to take that as a slight. I'm sorry. It's not about me." He waved his hands in an *it's fine* kind of motion. "We're a family, families argue—please continue."

"I used to be the most neurotic person on this train," Alice said pointedly.

Babs looked heavenward, as if she were praying for strength. "All we're saying is you don't have to feel the burden of some great guilt. We're not here because you asked us to save Ben. We're here to save Ben."

"But look at you," Patrick said, the corners of his mouth drawn down. "Babs, your arm is fully broken in half."

"And it hurts like a motherfucker," she grimaced. "But this is for Ben."

"He is literally falling apart," Alice reminded him. "Stab wounds and broken bones can heal. There's no coming back from what Ben has. Unless *we* bring him back from it."

Patrick stopped scraping the mud. He sat on the floor, staring in awe at the survivors around him. Something cold rippled up through his gut, prickling across his chest and coursing down his spine. Some hot, awful mess inside of him was drowned in the coolness of it and sizzled out of existence. For the first time in years—for the first time since the alert about the bombs had come across his iPhone, since he'd watched his neighbors choke and swell and liquify from the dust, since he'd punched a hole in his wall because he couldn't get through to Izzy's school, since he'd picked up the phone and heard Annie scream and sputter and bubble out blood to the end of her life—for the first time since that cold, horrible, black-hole day, he felt the weight of always having to know what to do lift from his shoulders, the way a dental technician used to lift the X-ray vest from his chest when they'd finished with all their imaging. He could breathe again, at last. He thought maybe he'd even be able to rest again, when this was all over. Maybe not for good, maybe not for long, but for a moment, and that was a thing he hadn't known that he didn't think he would ever get to have again.

"All right," he said, wiping tears from his eyes. "What can I do to help?"

"You can start by answering the walkie," Babs said. "Horace has been buzzing you for, like, fifteen seconds."

40.

"Horace, what?"

"We're about to die," Horace crackled through the radio, "in case anybody cares."

"I was *just* saying that!" Patrick said proudly. He scrambled up the ladder and popped up through the porthole. They were on a straight stretch of track, which gave them pretty good visibility when the fog cooperated. Through the green cloud, he could see the shadow of a *something* blocking the tracks ahead.

"What am I looking at?" he asked the walkie-talkie.

"Best guess, that's a full-size bur oak tree," Horace responded.

And the people who hauled it there won't be too far off, Patrick thought. He pushed the button on the radio. "Can the ramrod handle it?"

"Negative," Horace said. "Way too heavy."

"Okay. Stand by."

Patrick dropped down into the car. "Anyone who can walk, grab every explosive thing you can find and follow me!" he shouted. He ran up toward the engine car, grabbing up incendiaries along the way—two pipe bombs, a Molotov, and one leftover matchbox cartridge that was almost certainly useless in this particular situation.

Alice set the cold cloth on Lex's chest and followed Patrick. Babs did the best she could, breathing through the pain of her broken elbow and grabbing an oil bomb on her way.

They all passed Ben, who had decided to stare forlornly out the window of the dining car. As they passed, he started to wonder if he should maybe try to help. But he felt so weak, and his skin was so wet, and he was pretty sure his organs were beginning to swell. So he lowered himself down onto a bench seat instead, lying back and sending good vibes for a job well done.

They met Rogers coming out of the engine with his flask. He held it up for Babs. "Maybe after, huh?" She nodded, and he dropped the flask into his pocket.

"There's no roof hatch in the engine, right?" Patrick asked.

"Correct," Rogers said.

"Can we get out there?"

"You can lean out the door."

"Let's go."

They entered the engine car. "I'm stopping her," Horace declared.

"Don't you dare," Patrick replied. "That's what they want. Slow us down, but do *not* stop." He stuffed a pipe bomb into each of his back pockets and made sure he had a lighter there, too. Then he ran over to the side door and pulled it open. He stuck his head out and looked up at the top of the train. "Rogers, give me a boost," he said. Rogers made a net with his fingers, and Patrick planted his shoe in Rogers' palms. The assistant conductor hauled him up, and Patrick scrambled over the top of the train. "Oh, I don't like this," he decided as the wind whipped around him. The force of it was brutal; it was all he could do to keep himself from blowing off the side.

There were metal brackets bolted into the roof, handles for mechanical hatches that hadn't been opened in years. He gripped one with his left hand and reached down toward the door with his right. "Start passing bombs!" he shouted over the wind.

Rogers handed him a Molotov. The train hit a bump in the track, and Patrick flew up and then slammed down on the roof. He dropped the bottle over the side. "Goddammit," he hissed. "Another!"

This time, he held on tight. He worked himself up to his knees and lowered his head against the powerful wind. With a shaking hand, he drew the lighter from his pocket. He lit the rag. The flame fizzled in the wind, but not all the way down. He reared back best he could and hurled the bomb at the tree.

It fell short by ten feet.

The tree was coming up fast.

"More!" Patrick shouted. Rogers passed him another bomb. He lit the rag and threw the bottle as hard as he could. This one smashed against the trunk and started to burn. "More! Fast!"

Rogers passed him more bombs. The next one hit; the one after missed. "Last one," Rogers said.

Patrick hurled the oil-filled jar at the tree. It smashed against the wood and added to the blaze.

The tree was covered in flames, but Horace was right, it was a *big* tree. The fire might be weakening the integrity, but not enough to blast through it with the hydraulic ram.

Time for the last resort.

Please, God, let me not blow up the track.

"Get ready to ram through!" he yelled.

"Umm…" said Rogers.

Patrick pulled both pipe bombs from his pockets. He held them in one hand and lit them with the other. The fuses sparked, and the countdown started. The tree was hurtling toward them. Patrick threw the bombs.

They exploded against the trunk half an instant before the train smashed into the tree. Patrick fell down flat, ducked his head, and held on for his life. Horace pushed the plow. The train blasted through the blown-apart tree, right through the flames. The impact rocked the train. It tilted and groaned, but it stayed on the tracks.

"Woooo!" Patrick cheered. "Holy hell! That was *way* too close and definitely should *not* have worked!"

Down inside the train, Horace held a hand against his thumping chest. "That boy's gonna give me a heart attack," he gasped, breathing hard. "I am *way* too old for this shit."

41.

Douglas felt good. He felt powerful. He felt like a god who had found a higher level of godding and had godded up to mega-god. He spread his hands wide before the New Mexico desert. "I am become Douglas, destroyer of worlds."

"You didn't come up with that," Marcy pointed out. "That's not original."

Douglas let his hands drop to his sides. "I know that, Marcy. That's precisely why I said it."

"Oh, okay," Marcy said, bobbing her head enthusiastically. "I thought maybe you were trying to say something meaningful. For the history book."

Douglas closed his eyes and counted to three. "It *was* meaningful, and it *was* for the history book," he said, trying to keep his voice even. God, Marcy could be so annoying. "It doesn't have to be original to be meaningful."

"I guess that's true," Marcy mused, tapping her chin. "I used to like Taylor Swift, and that's the same sort of thing."

Douglas decided to stop talking to Marcy. This was his big moment, and he wouldn't let her ruin it. "Don't put any of that last part in the book," he said to Franklin, the Recorder of Words. Franklin paused. He sucked on his pencil. He frowned at the paper. He scratched through the last few lines of dialogue. "Good," Douglas nodded. "Now, where was I?"

"Eater of death," Marcy said helpfully.

"I did not say 'eater of death'—eater of death is nothing!" Douglas screamed.

"Oh." Marcy frowned. "You didn't say that?"

"No!"

Marcy looked relieved. "Phew! I was going to say, Death Eaters aren't very original either, but I didn't want to make you angry."

"*Franklin, please strike that conversation from the record and tell me where we left off!*" Douglas screamed.

Franklin scratched out more lines and then consulted the top of the page. "You are become Douglas, destroyer of worlds."

"Yes, yes, of course. Continue from there," Douglas said, annoyed. He cleared his throat and tried to reset. "We enter now into the final stages of the Astoria Project, and with the successful test of our great weapon, I shall become a post-world Oppenheimer."

Marcy raised her hand meekly. Douglas sighed. "Yes, Marcy?"

"Your last name is Baumeister," she said helpfully, if quietly.

Douglas pinched the bridge of his nose. "Marcy. Will you do me a favor?"

"Yes, of course, Douglas!" she said brightly. Marcy secretly loved Douglas, and she would have done anything for him.

"Would you be a dear and go look for my glasses in the prototype shed?"

"Oh," Marcy said. She frowned again. She didn't like the prototype shed. That's where they stored all the old, smaller versions of the bomb. She didn't like to be in there with them. "You think you left your glasses in the prototype shed?" she asked.

"Yes, please go to the prototype shed," Douglas said.

"Oh." Marcy took a deep breath. For Douglas, she would do it. "All right," she said. She trotted off toward the prototype shed, which was far away, on the other end of the compound.

Douglas took the walkie-talkie from his hip. "Lucille, are you there?"

"Yes, Douglas," crackled Lucille.

"Marcy is coming to the prototype shed. Be a dear and detonate all the bombs when she's inside, will you?"

There was a gap of silence from the other end of the line. "You...want me to blow up the building with Marcy inside?" Lucille asked.

"Yes, Lucille. Be a dear, won't you?"

"I...yes, Douglas. Okay." Lucille was in love with Douglas, and she would do anything for him. Douglas only brought on women who were in love with him, in case he needed them to do senseless things.

"Good girl. See you at the afterparty!" He clicked off the walkie and clipped it back onto his hip. He looked down at Franklin's notebook. "Good God, Franklin, don't write any of *that* down!" he said.

Franklin scratched out everything he'd just written. Being the Recorder of Words was a real challenge sometimes.

Douglas sauntered out into the desert, carrying his glass of gin with him. Calling it "gin" was actually pretty egregious; it was a big jar of moonshine poured over a smashed heap of sage and agave. Douglas almost always had a jar of his gin nearby. There was never any ice, so it wasn't a pleasant drinking experience, but his throat had become accustomed to that, and he really quite enjoyed it now.

As he strode across the hardpan, he gestured grandly at the tower he'd directed his people to build. It was sixty feet high, a mishmash of scrap metal and wood, all shored up and fastened together to make a sturdy skeleton, within which was about to beat the horrible heart of Douglas' beautiful brainchild.

"What a wonder!" he crowed. "The perfect support for my perfect creation—the world's first post-apocalyptic atomic bomb!"

"I've been wondering about the tower," Franklin said, scratching his head with the pencil. "Why not just detonate it on the ground?"

Douglas scoffed so hard he choked. "Did Oppenheimer detonate *his* bomb on the ground?!" he demanded. Franklin shrugged. He didn't know. "No! In this brave new world, we replicate with what precision we are able! The bomb will drop, and the world will know a man-god again!"

"Oh. But why did they build it over train tracks?" Franklin asked. And indeed, the base of the tower straddled a set of parallel tracks, so that any train would be forced to run beneath it, like a roller coaster in some deadwood Disneyland.

"Ah! Excellent question," Douglas said. "You see, where Oppenheimer hid his experiment in the lonely desert, our bomb is meant to be a—"

BOOM! The prototype shed exploded, sending a shockwave over the compound. Franklin cried out and hit the dust, but Douglass barely flinched. He only bristled.

He hated being interrupted.

"As I was saying," he continued curtly, while Franklin stood up and brushed himself off, "*our* bomb is meant to be a signal to the world. We have achieved nuclear capability, and we will take our place as emperors of this land!"

Franklin held up a finger, as if to raise a point. "Often, there's only *one* emperor," he said.

"Yes, well. If you insist, then I accept," Douglas said, rubbing his hands together greedily. He watched with anxious glee as a number of his proteges carefully rolled the atomic bomb into place between the tracks. The project manager, a man named Gifford, grabbed the carabiner that hung down from the nylon climbing rope that served as a winch cable for the tower. He pulled it down and tried to clip the carabiner to the bomb, but his hands were shaky, and he slipped. It took him three tries to finally secure the line to the hook on the top of the bomb.

Douglas wasn't angry. This was their first real trial. Everyone was nervous. Shaky hands were expected. They were about to detonate an absolute killer of a bomb; it made sense that the hands on deck would be experiencing some nerves. "All right," he said, laughing in a way he hoped was disarming. "No problem, Gifford! Steady as she goes, man!"

It was all very showy, and meant to be so, since Gifford and the bomb were several hundred feet away, and Douglas hadn't raised his voice.

"This is excellent material for the history book," Franklin mused. "Well done, Douglas."

"Yes it is, and thank you," Douglas smiled. Everything was just so very right with the world.

The walkie-talkie buzzed. It was Lucille. "Douglas? Apparently there's a train coming."

Douglas froze. His entire body became perfectly rigid, as if it had been encased in ice. If he'd moved his thumb, it would have cracked and broke off of his hand. He dared to move his lips ever so slightly when he said, "What?" out loud, though it was barely audible.

"Sorry?" Franklin said politely, wanting to make sure that he captured every word. He prodded Douglas with a finger. Douglas swayed like a punching bag.

Then he snapped out of it. "Hoist it! Hoist it now!" he shouted into the radio. "Stop what you're doing and get it ready to drop!"

Lucille's voice crackled back with a question, but Douglas didn't have time to hear it. He switched the walkie back to a different channel. "You have eyes on this train?" he asked.

"Yessir," a voice crackled back.

"How much longer until they reach target?"

The lookout on the other end of the line hesitated. "Um...they're going very fast, sir."

"How fast?" he demanded. "Fast for the Run? Or fast for a rail?"

The voice hesitated again. "Um...both? I don't understand the question," the voice admitted. That voice belonged to a woman named Miriam, who had very good eyesight, but who didn't score highly on any leadership exams.

"How soon until they get here?" Douglas exploded.

"Oh! Um...really soon, I'd think."

Douglas threw the walkie-talkie onto the ground. "Go, go, go!" he screamed at the team down by the tracks. He was so far away that he couldn't be sure if they could hear him. He sprinted down the slope, waving his arms and screaming about going, going, going.

And, miracle upon miracle, the crew actually seemed to be doing his bidding. As he ran down toward the tracks, he was immensely relieved to see the spherical bomb lift into the air and begin its gradual ascent to the top of the tower. "Excellent! Excellent!" Douglas cried, clapping his hands and skipping a bit as he ran down the hill. He was close enough now that he could scream at the project manager and be heard. "Go, Gifford, go! The train is coming!"

Gifford's face turned pale. His fingers went all tingly, and his legs began to wobble. "We're doing a live test?" he shouted back.

"Yes! Yes! This is what we've been waiting for!" Douglas said cheerfully. Now that he had successfully communicated with Gifford, Douglas skidded to a stop. He turned around and started trotting back up the hill. He wanted to be sure he was well outside of the blast radius when they dropped the world's first post-apocalyptic nuclear bomb.

"Oh, no," Gifford frowned. But it was obvious that Douglas wasn't interested in his concerns, and that he wouldn't even hear them. In order to keep up a good front for the men and women under his command, Gifford twirled his finger in a *keep going and don't stop* kind of motion. They continued to wrench the bomb higher up into the tower. And while they did that, Gifford snuck away, walking slowly at first, then escalating to a jog, then ramping up to an all-out sprint, because he didn't actually know the radius of this bomb, but he knew that, like Douglas, he wanted to be outside of it.

"We're ready!" one of the grunts chirped happily into her walkie once the bomb had been secured to its highest point in the tower. No one had told the grunts how dropping the bomb meant sudden death to anyone within at least a football field's distance from the blast, and now didn't seem like the right time to share that information.

"Great. Don't move. Make sure it drops. Don't leave," Gifford said, while leaving the area very quickly.

Franklin caught up to Douglas on his way past the manager's cabin and hurried to keep pace. "Why the rush?" he panted, trying to scribble notes for the history book while walking at a very, very quick pace. "Why not test it before blowing up a train?"

"Well, now, you see, it's very important that we blow up a train," Douglas said.

"Yes, I understand that," Franklin nodded. He was desperately out of breath. "But for the history book, can you remind me why?"

"Unlike Oppenheimer, who hid his experiment in the desert, I have fashioned *our* experiment specifically here, along these tracks. Oppenheimer—Robert, I should call him, now that we are equals—Robert created his bomb, then did everything he could to try to hide it from the world. But *I* will use *my* atom bomb to exert absolute domination over the surviving world! And there is no better place to assert dominance than on the Slaughterhouse Run, where death is the coin of the realm. The most ruthless man among all ruthless men is a god-king among ants. Please write that down exactly. 'The most ruthless man among all the most ruthless men is a god-king among ants.'"

"I think you just said, 'The most ruthless man among all ruthless men is a god-king among ants.'"

"I would never say something so insipid," Douglas sniped. "Take better notes, Franklin."

"Yes, Douglas." Franklin scribbled as they ran. He hoped he would be able to read his pencil scratches later. "So that's why you want to bomb the train, to show the rest of the cutthroats along the Slaughterhouse Run that you're the most callous and deadly by far. I understand that. But why *this* train? Why not some other train, later, after we've tested your design?"

"Because my design is perfect," Douglas said smugly. "And because word of the Run is spreading. The danger is becoming well known, and there are fewer and fewer trains on the tracks now. It may be months before we see another. By God, situated here, as we are, near the center of the service, surrounded on either side by hundreds of miles of dangerous track, it's possible we may *never* see another train! No, it must be now, and it must be gratuitous!" he said, rubbing his hands together greedily. "Here, this should be far enough now."

They stopped and turned back toward the tracks. They were very far away and only a hair-thin line of black against the yellow-green fog. The bomb itself wasn't even visible at this distance. Douglas felt safe...which was why he felt a bit of concern when he saw Gifford running off along a different vector, much farther even then he and Franklin had gone. "I wonder where he's off to," Douglas mused.

"Hm," Franklin said. "I think I'll move back another few hundred feet."

"Yes, I think I'll join you," Douglas decided.

***

Horace peered through the windshield. "What the hell?"

163

He clicked the walkie-talkie and asked Patrick to send Rogers to the engine. A few moments later, the assistant conductor arrived. "What's happening?"

"Take a look at that," Horace said, pointing up the tracks with the walkie-talkie antenna. "What is that?"

Rogers stared at the strange, rickety tower rising above the tracks ahead. The legs of the tower straddled the tracks so that the train had to pass beneath it. "Is that a water tower?" he asked.

Horace shook his head. "Don't think so. There's *something* up top, but I can't make it out. Not big enough for a water tower. Where's those binoculars?"

"Patrick has them."

Horace radioed back, and soon Patrick came trotting into the engine, holding the glasses. "You rang?"

"Take a look at that, will you?" Horace said. "Can you tell what it is?"

Patrick squinted up the tracks. "Looks like a tower," he decided.

"Yes, thank you," Horace sighed. "What's that up top, there?"

Patrick raised the binoculars to his eyes and focused in on the top of the tower. "Hm," he said, frowning. "I don't know. Is that—is it, like, a medicine ball? I know that sounds like a crazy thing to hoist up to the top of a tower you built over a set of train tracks, but is it, like, a medicine ball?" He handed the binoculars to Rogers. He dialed in on the thing at the top of the tower.

"Hm," he said. "It does look like a medicine ball."

"I think we can safely assume it's *not* a medicine ball," Horace said.

"You don't know that. People get weird about their fitness."

"People do get weird about their fitness," Rogers agreed.

"It's not a medicine ball!" Horace snapped. He had double bags under each eye. He looked like Tommy Lee Jones, but shorter, and with a mustache, and more portly, and more alive, if only marginally. "I think we have to assume it's something bad."

"Feels like a safe bet," Patrick nodded. "So whatever it is, if they're gonna drop it on us, you know what *I* think we should do?"

"Let me guess," Horace grumped. "Go really, really fast?"

Patrick broke out into a big, broad smile. "Horace," he said, "let's go really, *really* fast."

Horace sighed.

He pushed the train into full throttle.

***

"Wow, that train is going fast," Douglas observed. "Is the distance playing tricks on our perspective? Or is that train going *really* fast?"

Franklin consulted his notes. "They told us it was going really fast," he reminded Douglas.

"They said no such thing," Douglas said. "If they had, I might have rethought this strategy. That train might be going *too* fast."

Franklin sighed. He scratched out more words on the page.

Douglas' radio crackled. "They're coming in hot. I'm not sure we're ready," Lucille said.

"Of course we're ready," Douglas replied. "Let's make history! Drop the bomb on my count."

Gifford also had a walkie-talkie that was tuned to the same frequency. He cut in: "Um, maybe I should do the count? As project manager."

"How could you do the count?" Douglas asked, in the snidest voice he could muster. "You're practically standing in Wyoming!"

The radio crackled. "You're standing fifty feet from me," Gifford reminded him. Douglas looked to his right. There was Gifford. Gifford waved.

Douglas glowered. "I am base commander, it is my duty to stand where I can observe all of my people," he said into the radio. "You should be down there at the tower."

"I like to give praise from afar," Gifford said, which is a sentence that didn't make any sense. "Besides, can't we control the release remotely? Shouldn't we get everyone else out of there?"

"Of course not!" Douglas cried. "What if something goes wrong? We need people there to fix it."

"They'll die horribly," Gifford reminded him.

"That didn't stop you from abandoning them, did it?" Douglas snapped.

Gifford didn't reply. It was a pretty fair point.

"Instructions?" Lucille asked. She sounded impatient.

"Drop on my mark," Douglas said.

The radio crackled for a few moments. "Douglas…" Lucille finally started.

"No second-guessing, goodbye!" Douglas clicked off the walkie. He stood there for several long moments, tapping his foot and being generally irritated.

"You need to turn it on to give the order," Franklin reminded him gently.

"I know that!" Douglas snapped. "I remembered it as soon as I turned it off!" He turned the walkie back on and screamed, "Is everything ready?!"

"Yes," Lucille said, but she sounded nervous. "Should we pull back the team?"

"It's too late for all that now," Douglas said. "Here they come. On my mark!"

He watched as the train barreled closer to the tower. It was going so fast. He'd never seen a train go that fast on the Slaughterhouse Run before. Not even close. In some ways, he admired the conductor of that train. Brazen disregard for the train's safety might have otherwise been the thing that brought that train safely to its destination. But they hadn't counted on Douglas Baumeister and his post-apocalyptic bomb. He found himself overcome by a feeling of respect for the people on that train. He held his hand to his forehead in a formal salute. With his other hand, he pressed the button on the walkie. "Drop in three…two…one…"

***

Patrick, Horace, and Rogers all huddled up against the windshield, watching the thing in the tower intently. They were close enough now to see that there were people up in that tower, men and women in white lab coats scurrying around and looking busy, busy, busy. "Is it, like, a one-hundred-pound weight from a 1950s cartoon?" Patrick asked. "I don't understand."

"Maybe it's nothing," Rogers suggested. "Maybe it's just a permanent part of the structure."

"Maybe they worship the sphere," Patrick said, rubbing his chin. "Maybe they have some *extremely* esoteric train-related sphere-worship religion."

"I don't like it," Horace said. "Be ready for anything. We're under it in three…two…one…"

***

The bomb dropped. As it fell through the air, Douglas clenched every muscle in his body. Franklin held his pencil poised above the paper, ready to write. Gifford held his hands up over his head to protect himself from the blast.

Down in the engine car, Patrick winced. Horace winced. Rogers winced. They were going fast, but not fast enough.

The bomb slammed down onto the back end of the very last car.

***

"Wait," Douglas said, his face falling. "What happened?"

"I believe," Franklin began weakly. He cleared his throat and started again. "I believe the bomb...did not go off."

Douglas had watched with great joy and excitement as his nuclear pod had slammed down onto the top of the train. But he had watched with decidedly less enthusiasm as the bomb rolled off the top of the train car, fell to the ground, slid down the gravel siding, and came to a stop a few feet into the grass.

His lack of enthusiasm quickly became fury. "It just bounced off the train! What did you do wrong?!" he shrieked into the walkie-talkie.

Lucille did not respond. It seemed like perhaps she had turned her radio off.

"Goddammit!" Douglas screamed, throwing the walkie onto the ground and stomping it to absolute death. "Of all the useless dick-a-bricks!" He stalked down the hill, back toward the train tracks, ready to tear several new assholes into several of the aforementioned dick-a-bricks. They all saw him coming, and many of them had the good sense to scramble down from the tower and just run away, off into the desert, presumably to start new lives in some non-Douglassed part of the country. A handful of them were too scared to move, though. They just clung to the tower or to their schematics and quaked with fear. It was a rather long quaking, because Douglas had run so very far away from the tower, and it took him the better part of twenty minutes to stomp back down the hill. But his anger had not lessened by the time he arrived. In fact, if anything, he was angrier.

"What the hell is this?!" he demanded, gesturing at the bomb. It just lay there in the dirt, a little scraped up from the collision, but mostly okay. "This is the thing that's supposed to go BOOM!"

A junior engineer stepped forward and cleared her throat. "I, ahm...I think that this *particular* bomb is not yet, ahm, ready for, ahm, primetime. Ahm...as they say."

Douglas gawked at her. "Not ready for primetime?" he said.

The engineer nodded.

"Okay. Okay." Douglas wagged a finger at her. "Don't move. Okay? I don't want you going anywhere. I'm going to figure out what happened, and then I'm going to beat you to death with a hammer. Okay?"

"Oh." The woman's face fell. She turned pale. "Ahm. Okay."

Douglas was so mad he didn't notice as she slowly inched away from the test site and very slowly crept toward one of the operational vehicles.

"Gifford! Where's Gifford?"

"He's run off, sir," said another junior engineer.

"Goddammit!" Douglas screamed. "Where is Lucille?"

The crowd parted to reveal a rather frightened Lucille. She had been crouched behind the entire crew, and she glared at them for giving her up. "Assholes," she muttered.

"Lucille. Why didn't this bomb explode?" Douglas cried. He kicked the bomb for emphasis. Everyone shrieked and threw up their arms. But the bomb didn't go off.

"I don't know, Douglas," Lucille replied, shrugging her shoulders. "I'm not even on the development team. I'm just the property manager."

"You have failed to manage *this* piece of my property!" Douglas shrieked, kicking the bomb again. Everyone screamed again. But still, the bomb did not explode.

"Someone tell me what happened to cause this bomb to fail! You have five seconds, or else I'll pick it up and brain Lucille to death with it in front of your stupid, useless faces!"

"That thing's, like, five hundred pounds," one young man in the back piped up. "I don't think you could—"

"Then I'll bring her face to the bomb!" Douglas shrieked. "*You are missing the point*! Someone tell me why my atomic bomb is a *dud*!"

The rest of the crew sort of hemmed and hawed. They exchanged uncomfortable glances. Lucille pleaded for some engineer, *any* engineer, to step up and help. Finally, one younger woman, who had always sort of liked Lucille, figured this might be a good opportunity to break the ice with her crush. Plus, she was the assistant bomb technician, and she had a pretty good idea why the bomb hadn't exploded.

She approached the bomb. "I think it's this," she said, pointing down at a wire that hung freely from the metal sphere.

Douglas frowned down at the wire. "Oh," he said. His anger had been pretty blinding. He hadn't noticed it hanging disconnected like that.

"It just fell out of that port," she said, pointing at another spot on the bomb. "The one that says DETONATE over it." She crouched down and plugged the loose wire into the DETONATE port. The bomb went *whirrrr-whirrrr-click-click-beeeeeep*. The young woman stood up and nodded. "Now it's ready."

Lucille ran up and threw her arms around the woman. "Oh, God, thank you!" she sobbed. The young woman hugged her back and kissed her ear. Lucille pulled back rather violently—she was shocked by this turn of events; it had not been what she expected. But she looked at the young woman and her plain prettiness, and it lit a fire in her, and soon the two were making out in the dirt, rolling over each other and causing quite a scene.

Douglas grumped. *He* had wanted to make out with Lucille, and with the other young woman, too. Nothing ever worked out for him the way it should. He got mad and kicked the bomb one final time.

***

"Hey. You need to see this," Babs said. She beckoned Patrick away from the engine and pointed up at the porthole. Patrick climbed up and stuck his head through the opening.

"Oh," he said, blinking in surprise at the mushroom cloud that had blossomed in the air behind them. "Um." He reached for his walkie and clicked it to life. "Hey. Horace? Do me a favor. Go *real* fuckin' fast, *right* now, okay?" He put the walkie back on his hip and slowly climbed down from the shelves.

"That's...bad. Right?" Babs asked.

"It's definitely bad for *someone*," Patrick agreed. "Probably not us. It looks sort of small, and we're pretty far away. But...um...nuclear weapons aren't really my area, so...I'm just gonna go make sure Horace goes *real* fuckin' fast for the next thirty minutes, okay?" He patted Babs on the shoulder, then he sprinted up to the front of the train.

"Good news," he said, bursting into the engine. "I know what the thing in the tower was!"

42.

"They made an *atomic bomb?*" Horace said.

"I think it's fairly safe to say they Nagasakied all over themselves," Patrick nodded.

Horace shook his head and whistled. "Wow," he said, amazed. "And we were almost done in by that."

"It would have made a pretty cool obituary," Patrick said. "Death by post-apocalyptic nuke give off some real Terry Pratchett vibes."

The sun had gone down a few minutes earlier and nighttime was closing in fast. The Chihuahuan Desert began to disappear as the light faded, the scrub brush and cacti swallowed up by darkness and mist. A chill rippled along Patrick's spine. The inability to see the threats made the threats just that much worse.

"Survived the first full day," Rogers said, maybe reading Patrick's thoughts. "Making it to darkness is a good thing."

"Yeah," Patrick agreed, though a little reluctantly. "Sort of wish we'd thought to strap some spotlights to the top of the train, though."

"In hindsight…"

"Yeah," Patrick sighed. "Here's hoping we see another morning."

"Babs has my flask, or else I'd drink to that."

"Chin chin," Patrick said.

He wandered out of the engine and headed back through the dining car. Ben had propped himself up at a table. He was alone, picking at a bag of stale chips.

"Eating is good!" Patrick said encouragingly. "Are you feeling any better?"

"No, but Alice said she'd cut my hands off if I didn't eat something."

"She's very persuasive."

"Mm-hmm." Ben raised a chip to his cracked and oozing lips with a shaking hand. He bit into it and tried to chew, but chewing hurt. Everything hurt. So instead, he just swallowed it, and that hurt too. "I hate this," he said quietly.

Patrick joined him at the table. He pounded the bag with his fist, pulverizing what remained of the chips. "Open your mouth," he instructed.

"You're not going to baby bird me," Ben griped. He swiped the bag away from Patrick and tipped some of its contents into his mouth.

"Just let them melt into a slurry. A beautiful Lay's saliva slurry. No chewing, barely any swallowing."

"Lay's saliva slurry," Ben repeated, groaning. "Now I've *really* lost my appetite."

"But you still have both your hands."

"That's true."

Patrick laid the back of his hand against Ben's forehead. "Yikes. We should grab the next cow we pass. We could grill steaks on your face."

"They'd get all green," Ben pointed out. He picked up the ooze-soaked rag he kept with him now and wiped away the green fluid from his cheeks and his arms. "This is the grossest feeling."

"It's the grossest looking, too," Patrick confirmed with a frown. "But good news, I think we're in New Mexico now. Which is good on two fronts! One, it means we're about halfway to your cure. And two, it means we never—and I mean *never*—have to go to Texas again."

"Both good things," Ben agreed. He looked sadly down at the half-empty bag of chips. "I think I'm done," he decided.

"Want some help back to your bunk?"

But Ben had already fallen asleep in the booth.

Patrick found a blanket and draped it over him. He carefully eased Ben onto his side so at least he was lying down on the stiff and uncomfortable bench instead of sitting up at a stiff and uncomfortable table. "Hang in there, Benny Boy," he said sadly. He rubbed Ben's back. "Closer and closer every second."

The door slid open and Alice poked her head in. "We got company," she said.

Patrick closed his eyes. It took everything he had to not burst into tears.

Nighttime was the worst.

43.

The new batch of raiders appeared as tongues of flame speeding toward them from the south. The train was careening into high desert territory, and the fires picked up speed as they zoomed down the foothills of the Guadalupe Mountains. "Torches?" Patrick asked.

"Yep," Alice said, looking through the binoculars.

"Four-wheelers?" he guessed.

"Nope."

"Trucks?"

"Bikes."

"Okay. Dirt bikes or, like, Harleys?"

"No," Alice snorted. "They're riding BMXes."

There were seven of them in all, pedaling down the hill. Judging by their movement, they were aiming to intercept the train a few hundred yards ahead. They looked like they'd picked up enough speed that the timing might work out. But Patrick couldn't help but scratch his head. "They're going to attack the train with…bicycles?"

He stuck his head out the door, and together he and Alice watched with extraordinary interest as the gap between the bikes and the train closed. To their credit, it looked like they had timed their end of things rather well, especially considering how fast the train was going. But it was the question of how seven raiders on BMX bikes were hoping to actually make the transition from bike to train that fascinated Patrick the most.

He clicked the walkie. "Got the Goonies coming in on our port side. If they try to block the train, you have my permission to run them over."

"Ain't got a choice at this point anyway," Horace replied. "Can't slow it down fast enough to not kill them. I might just use the plow to make it more humane."

The riders neared contact. Patrick was actually wiggling with excitement. He couldn't wait to see what happened next.

The lights from the train caught something long and curved resting along the siding ahead. "Oh my God," Patrick said, his voice positively giddy. "They made a ramp!"

It looked like some sort of stoner art project. They had buried a few rows of landscaping blocks into the gravel siding, and perched on top of those blocks was what appeared to be an eight-by-four sheet of plywood that they'd somehow curved, probably with steam. "I have so many questions," Patrick whispered aloud.

The first rider hit the ramp. The plywood buckled under the weight, but it held. The rider arced into the air but hadn't been pedaling fast enough; his bike slammed into the side of the dining car, and both the rider and the bike bounced off the train.

The second rider pulled the exact same play, except something cracked when they hit the train, probably their neck, because when they tumbled back to the ground, it didn't look like they were in any hurry to get back up.

The third bike fared a little better; it hit the ramp at a good speed and launched up over the train. The bike actually landed on the roof of the Baby Caps' car, but the rider couldn't stop the momentum, and both bike and rider went flying off the far side of the train. The fourth rider hit the roof, too, and managed to stick the landing, but the fifth rider was following too closely and plowed right into them, taking them both over the side.

The sixth rider hit the roof and managed to roll off the bike before it skidded over the edge. They just narrowly avoided getting their head taken off by the seventh rider, who had overshot the whole thing altogether and sailed about two feet over the train, crashing headfirst into the scrub on the far side of the track.

'My biggest regret in life is that I won't get to see all of that happen the exact same way ever again," Patrick said in total awe.

He grabbed Bleakachu and climbed up the ladder in Ben's car. He peeked up over the edge of the porthole and saw the lone rider who had landed on the train holding on with all their strength. The train sped around a curve and inertia took the rider's legs away, sliding them over the edge of the train. "Help me!" the rider cried, his feet kicking uselessly against the windows.

"No way!" Patrick said. "You're trying to board our train!"

"In a non-violent manner!" the man insisted. "This is an attempt at non-violent engagement!"

"No thank you," Patrick said, and he began to head back down the ladder.

"Wait! I'm unarmed! Please! I'm not here to do you harm! I came here to say something! A message of peace!"

Patrick hesitated. He poked back up over the edge. "Okay. So say it."

The man frowned. "Can I say it inside?" he pleaded.

"No."

"Come on, brother! I'm one unarmed man against everything you've got in that train! Please, help me!"

Patrick sighed. He looked down into the car. The Baby Caps had all joined him. "What do you think?"

"Let him in," said Alice. "I have some aggression I'd like to work out."

"Umm," said Patrick.

"Is he cute?" asked Babs, who had finished most of Rogers' moonshine. "Let him in if he's cute."

"Umm," Patrick said again.

"If he's really unarmed, we shouldn't just let him fall. He could get caught under the train. I don't think we should treat innocent people like that," Lex said.

"But what if he's not innocent?" Patrick asked. "What if he's extremely armed?"

"Well. Then we have Alice."

"*So* much aggression," she said, testing the sharpness of her current knife with her thumb.

Patrick shrugged. "Okay. If this goes badly, I just want to go on record that it was *not* my idea," he said. He made grabby hands for the makeshift torch that was anchored to the wall, and Lex handed it up. Patrick held onto the oil-soaked end and reached the stick out so the man could grab it. Patrick pulled him over to the porthole…but he pulled a little too hard, and the man came tumbling down inside, hitting the ladder a few times on his way to the floor.

"Ow!" he hollered.

"Oops," Patrick said, though he wasn't particularly sorry.

They got a good look at the cyclist for the first time. He had pale skin and long blond-brown hair that was coiled into filthy dreadlocks. He wore an oversized t-shirt and flowy pants that had been patched so many times with so many handkerchiefs that they almost looked quilted. He was barefoot, despite the chilly night, and his feet were caked with mud and grease. He wore a beaded belt wound around his wrist like a cuff; the stiff leather tassels poked out at odd angles like the horns of a baby demon. He held up two fingers in a V and said, "I come in peace."

"Oh no," Patrick said, his heart sinking. "We let a hippie onto the train."

***

"What's a hippie?" Alice asked, wrinkling her nose.

"That's a hippie," Patrick said, pointing at the man on the floor.

"You say it like a pejorative, man. But I'm about love and harmony, brother," said the hippie.

Patrick felt the urge to throw up. "I'm just glad Ben didn't live to see this," he said, holding his vomit back with extraordinary will power.

"Ben's *dead*?!" Babs exclaimed.

Patrick shook his head. "Not yet, but if he knows we have a hippie, he'll throw himself under the train. Do *not* wake him up!" he said seriously.

"What's all this hostility, man? This is a non-violent sit-in!" the hippie insisted.

"I'm sorry, did you say 'sit-in'?" Patrick asked.

"Well? I'm sitting," the hippie said. He gestured to the confines of the train around him. "In."

"Okay, we have to throw him off the train," Patrick told the Baby Caps.

"But he's not doing anything," Babs said.

"And he *does* seem unarmed," Lex added.

Patrick planted his hands on his hips. "You don't understand. Once they start a sit-in, they don't *stop* sitting in! I never thought I'd say this, but I think it's time to embrace an aggressive police state. On this train. Right now."

"Whoa, man," the hippie said, looking disgusted. "This sort of aural blockage is exactly why people like me need to engage in peaceful protest. Otherwise, you'll never get it."

Patrick rubbed his forehead. "Okay. Fine. *I'll* throw myself under the train."

"What are you protesting?" Babs asked the hippie.

"Showers," Patrick said.

"Environmental injustice," the hippie corrected him. "Listen. My name is Shawn—"

"Of *course* your name is Shawn," Patrick rolled his eyes.

"...and I'm here to protest the burning of coal to make these trains run."

175

"Oh my God," Patrick said. "I am going to find something to break his head with." He walked out of the car and started rummaging through the weapons further up the train.

"Listen, young ones," the hippie said, "you may not know this, because environmental protection has taken a deep backseat since the day of reckoning. But burning coal isn't just bad for your lungs. It's also bad for the Earth's lungs. It's bad for Mother Earth."

"Trains don't burn coal!" Patrick shouted from the next car up.

"Hear that?" the hippie asked the Baby Caps. "That's the sound of willful ignorance. He turns a blind eye to the murder he's committing—that's right, I said *murder*—because it helps him achieve his goals. That's why *I'm* here, to peacefully and patiently make sure he sees the error of his way." Shawn produced a pair of handcuffs from his pocket. He secured one bracelet around his own wrist, then he snapped the other around the bookshelf that was bolted into the floor. "I'm going to sit right here until you turn off this train and remove its engine."

The Baby Caps exchanged glances. "Is this some kind of joke?" Babs asked.

"Hey—I'm not doing this for me, young ones. You think this feels good?" He rattled the handcuffs. "It does not. I'm not doing this for me. I'm doing this for *all of us*."

Patrick reemerged holding Alice's cutting torch. "Stand back, I'm going to cut his hand off."

"Dude. That thing runs on gas. *So* harmful to the planet. And the fact that you're willing to take it this far to keep your pollution project going just shows me how far down the coal hole you really are."

"Please, God, just stop talking before I put this torch up *your* coal hole," Patrick said. "Trains haven't run on coal power for, like, fifty years. This train, *this train* that you are sitting in, has never—and I want to be clear about this, *never*—operated on coal."

The hippie blinked. He tossed his hair. "What is it, like, nuclear or something? 'Cause, like, that's pretty clean energy…"

"Nuclear?" Patrick asked, floored. "You're asking me if this train runs on *nuclear energy*? Have you taken the time to learn *anything* about *anything*?"

"I've changed my mind," Babs said. "We should throw him back."

Shawn jangled his handcuffs to remind her that he was locked in. He winked at her. She rolled her eyes.

"This train runs on cooking oil!" Patrick exclaimed. "Not coal. Not nuclear. Fucking Crisco!"

"Oh, man," the hippie said, clucking his tongue. He looked at Patrick with such disappointment. "Burning oil is so bad for the environment."

"It's recycled cooking oil!" Patrick cried. "We're not going to the grocery store and buying a gallon at a time! This is used, recycled cooking oil!"

The hippie's eyes grew wide. "Oh, wow," he breathed. "You guys run on *recycled* oil?"

"Yes!" Patrick exploded.

"Wow. I was really wrong about you." He laid his free hand on his heart. "*Mea culpa, mijo. Mea culpa.*"

"Those are two different languages!" Patrick snapped. "Go be a *culpa* somewhere else! Or so help me, I will cut you out of there, and I am *not* good with this torch."

"Whoa-whoa-whoa! No can do, my brother! It is so great that I was able to open your eyes to the power of recycled fuel—"

"We converted it *years* ago!"

"—but now I need your help spreading the good word far and wide! I've made a huge difference here, and I am so proud of that." Once again, he touched his heart. "But as long as this train rides the rails, I must ride it as well, to spread the joy of a clean Earth to the furthest reaches of the tracks."

"We have a strict 'no hobos' policy, Weary Willy. Now hold still while I torch your hand off." Patrick fired up the cutting torch and turned up the flame.

The door to the gangway slid open. Ben stumbled into the car.

Everyone turned to look at him. "Oh no," Patrick gasped. "Now you're gonna *wish* you'd been torched."

Ben looked at the man handcuffed to the shelves. He looked at the Baby Caps. He looked back at the hippie. There was pitch-black fire in his eyes. "I'm only gonna ask this once," he said, his voice wobbly and weak. "Why is there a goddamn hippie on my train?"

"Whoa! My man! We're cool!" said the hippie. "We're all on Team Planet here! We are brethren! I am here because your kind colleagues want to help me spread the word of clean energy through a ravaged land."

"That is *not* why he's here," Patrick clarified.

"He's here because Lex felt bad," Alice glowered.

Lex frowned. It *was* pretty much his fault. "I thought he was an innocent man! I didn't know he'd be like…*this*."

"Thank you, little brother," Shawn beamed.

Ben held the edge of the doorway for support. "Listen to me, you flea-bag rat nest," he said, glaring at the hippie. "I have to go grab something from another car. You've got until I get back here to get your patchouli-poisoned, patched-pants pagan ass off of my train, or else I'm cutting off your filthy goddamn dreads and shoving them so far down your throat

177

you'll have to pull them out through your dick hole just to eat straight." He turned and stormed off into the next car, leaving Patrick and the Red Caps in wide-eyed surprise.

"That's *way* more words than he's said at once since I got here," Patrick said.

Babs breathed in awe. "He hates hippies so hard it's bringing him back to life."

"I don't like that look of that guy," the hippie frowned. "He looks like he might actually kill me."

"We're all getting close," Alice assured him.

Patrick cleared the air with his hands. "Look, weirdo, we don't have time for this. Do you have a key for those cuffs?"

"Of course I have a key," the hippie said, producing a small key from his oversized pocket.

"Great. Do us all a favor and use it to—oh, *come on!*"

The hippie had flung the key up and through the porthole. It hit the top of the train and clinked its way over the side, into the desert sand. "You want me out of here, you'll have to torch me!" the hippie cried.

"Are all hippies like this?" Lex asked, disgusted.

"Yes," said Patrick.

"Yes!" said the hippie.

"Awful."

The door slid open again, and Ben reappeared dragging a pool noodle behind him. "Get off my train!" he hollered, smacking the hippie on the head with the foam noodle. "Go back to your yurt! Take your headlice with you!"

"Is that a pool noodle?" the hippie asked, unfazed by the barrage of conks.

"The bat is too heavy for me to lift!" Ben cried. He was already out of breath. He took a few more swings, gently battering the hippie's ears, and then he had to sit down. His chest was heaving, and his arms would no longer respond. He dropped the wet, slimy pool noodle from his wet, slimy hands and sank down to the floor. "You'd better be gone when I wake up," he said, and then he began to snore.

"I think your friend is sick," the hippie observed.

"All right," Patrick fumed, "someone hold him down, I'm torching the cuffs."

"No! You can't!" the hippie cried. He clung to the bookshelf with both hands, wedging his body in between the handcuffs and the blowtorch. Lex and Alice hurried forward and grabbed his free arm. They wrenched it back so that the hippie had no choice but to turn away from the shelves, sobbing and pleading for them to let him stay. "My friends died so I could spread this message!" he wailed. "Don't let their sacrifices be in vain!"

"Your friends are fine," Patrick pointed out. "They just...missed."

"One of them broke his neck," Alice reminded him. "He's probably dead."

"Oh, right," Patrick nodded. "One of your friends is probably dead, but everyone else is fine."

"His last wish was that we work together to heal Mother Earth!" the hippie cried.

"His last wish was probably to take a header into the broad side of a train so he wouldn't have to talk to you anymore." Patrick lowered the torch to the cuff chain.

"Karma will punish you for this!" hollered the hippie.

"Hold still!" Patrick hissed.

"Karma always wins in the end!"

THUMP.

Something landed on the roof of the train.

Patrick closed his eyes and exhaled. "Come on, not now..." he groaned.

The hippie grinned. "See?" he said. "Karma!"

Patrick killed the torch and tossed it aside, grabbing up his machete instead. "Babs, go get Rogers," he said quietly. "Have him station at the next skylight, in case we need help from above."

Babs nodded and left the car.

Alice picked up her crossbow and held it to her shoulder, ready to fire. Lex looked around and picked up the first weapon he saw: a hammer. He gave it a few practice swings. He was still feeling a little lightheaded, but he figured if he swung it hard enough, it probably wouldn't matter how bad his aim was.

They heard the sounds of someone crawling toward the porthole. Everyone tensed.

A man popped his head into the opening. "Hello!" he beamed. He had a broad face with red cheeks, framed by a wild mop of curly blond hair. He was probably in his forties, but he had a babyish sort of shine that made him look like a doll come to life. "Permission to come aboard?"

"No," Patrick said.

"Too bad!" The man swung around and leapt down onto the train. He was wearing torn-up jeans and a white hooded sweatshirt with a yellow sun emblazoned on the front. It looked like he had painted it with his fingers. He wore a yellow sash tied around his waist, and his ratty sneakers were painted with yellow lines that were probably meant to be rays of sun-shine but that really looked more like urine stains.

He also held a pistol in his hand, which was pointed at Patrick's belly.

The man looked around the train and noted with special interest the hippie who was handcuffed to the bookshelf. "Seems I'm interrupting something. Would be fascinated to hear the story here, but no time! We have exactly ninety seconds, so I'll just dive in, all right?"

"Ninety seconds?" Lex asked.

The man in the sunshine shirt ignored the question and barreled straight to the point. "My name is Lucas. I am a high priest of the sun god Solrahbi, the first and most blessed of his name. In approximately one minute, this train will enter onto a bridge. That bridge spans a chasm. That chasm is the temple of Solrahbi. Solrahbi demands a sacrifice when crossing over his temple. One of you will be that sacrifice. If you do not choose one of your number to sacrifice, the people of Solrahbi's church, who are watching us closely, will blow the bridge before you reach the end, thus sending you all to your deaths. If you attempt to destroy me, I will use this firearm, which I assure you is fully loaded, and I will kill as many of you as I can. If you manage to overpower me, I will then not give my signal, and the people of Solrahbi's church will blow the bridge. You must choose one of your number to die as sacrifice to Solrahbi. Otherwise, you all will die. You now have thirty-nine seconds to determine which one of you will die. Begin."

They didn't even need to look at each other. All of them pointed im-mediately to the hippie. "Him," they said in unison.

"Hey!" the hippie cried.

The high priest suddenly looked uneasy. "Umm…just like that? You don't want to…deliberate?"

"No," Patrick said. "Take him."

"No, don't!" the hippie pleaded.

The high priest frowned. "Oh," he said. He cleared his throat. He rubbed his cheek. "It's just that, normally people go into sort of a…I don't know, a terror frenzy, a whole morality spiral, and they argue, and some people offer themselves up, and other people tell them they won't let them do that…you know, that sort of thing."

"Okay," Patrick said. "But you're here now, and you can take him."

"Take him," Alice agreed.

"Take him," Lex nodded.

The high priest pursed his lips and looked around hesitantly. "Is there someone else I should talk to, or…?"

"Talk to me!" the hippie begged. "Don't listen to them—are you insane?!"

"Hm...okay, yes, this is more in line with expectations," the high priest said, rubbing his chin. He looked up at the crew. "And you're all *sure* you choose this man? You don't want to, like, deliberate? Or...?"

"Down to thirty seconds by your count, champ," Patrick said, patting the high priest on the shoulder. "Less talky, more cutty these handcuffs from the shelvy." He handed Lucas the cutting torch and made some encouraging gestures with his hands. The high priest frowned down at the torch. He looked over at the hippie. He looked back at the torch. He shrugged. He fired it up and went to work.

"Wait, stop!" the hippie screamed. "You can't do this! Come on! Peace and love, man! Don't you know about peace and love?!"

But the high priest didn't answer. He had a job to do, and he was on the clock. He lodged himself between the hippie's torso and his handcuffed arm. Using his body as a block, he quickly cut through the chain. The hippie fell free.

"Seventeen seconds," the high priest said, sounding a little disappointed. "Come with me, little goat."

"Do you mean greatest of all time?" the hippie sobbed hopefully.

"Pretty sure he means like a sacrificial goat," Patrick said.

"I mean a sacrificial goat," the high priest confirmed. He grabbed the hippie's wrists and dragged him out into the gangway and over to the door. "Solrahbi smiles upon your sacrifice," he said, trying to offer some comfort. But his heart wasn't really into it. Then he leaned in and said more confidentially, "But I would have worked harder in choosing my friends, if I were you."

"They're not my friends!" the hippie yelled. "I don't even know them!"

"Oh," said the high priest. His jaw relaxed. "Then that makes all of this a little bit easier, actually." The train crossed over onto the bridge, and the narrow maw of the chasm opened up below them. The high priest put his sneaker to the small of the hippie's back. "A bright new life awaits you in Solrahbi's glow," he assured the hippie. Then he gave him a kick, and the hippie went flying out the door, and down into the canyon, flailing and screaming, "Not cool, maaaannnnnn!"

The high priest whipped the yellow sash from his waist. He held it out the door and waved it in huge arcs. This apparently was the signal of success, because the bridge remained unexploded and the train barreled on through the desert night.

"Solrahbi thanks you for your sacrifice," the high priest sighed, sounding pretty disappointed. "This was...less exciting than most." He turned and poked his head out of the train. He gave himself an internal count, then he leapt from the car and landed on a king-sized air mattress that was waiting for him next to the tracks. It wasn't even close to big enough to actually give him a safe landing from a train going that speed, but he hit it squarely, and it provided a good enough bounce onto the desert hardpan that he surely would survive.

With both the hippie and the high priest suddenly removed from the train, Rogers came jogging back to the car. "Everyone okay?"

"A hippie in the hand is worth two birds in a stone," Patrick confirmed.

"That's not even close to a saying," Rogers pointed out.

"And yet, here we are," Patrick mused, tapping his chin. "Free and clear of both threats at once."

The walkie-talkie buzzed and Horace said, "We've got a problem."

Patrick took a deep breath. Once again, he decided to cry.

44.

"Hey. Are you okay?" Horace asked.

"I'm at the top of my game," Patrick said, wiping tears from his eyes. "Why do you ask?"

"You're crying."

"No, I'm not," he sniffled.

"I'm watching you cry right now."

"Oh. Well, that's nothing. My prefrontal cortex is just taking a little break while my amygdala takes over for a while. It's been a long couple of days...and that's just in the last few hours. But it should all even out once I get twenty straight hours of sleep."

"I wish I could tell you to go lie down, son. But we've got a problem."

"So I've heard. What's up?"

"We've got dusters."

"Okay. That's fine. Right?" Patrick asked. "We've got the plow, we've got speed, and we've got Zom-Be-Gone in case they try to board. We're ready for that. Right?"

"No, Patrick," Horace frowned. He grabbed Patrick by the shoulders and turned his body so he could look through the window of the side door. "I mean, we have *dusters.*"

Patrick's mouth fell open. He stepped closer to the door. He put his forehead against the window and gaped out at the silvery desert. "That," he breathed, "is a *lot* of dusters."

They were streaming down from a low mesa in the distance, barely lit by the moon, running shoulder-to-shoulder in a horde so vast that it looked as if the desert were a dam, and it had just broken open. A flood of zombies spilled down into the plain, snarling and slavering and snapping their teeth. They filled the horizon from end to end, like one fluid, solid mass, and as the duster vanguard hit the bottom of the mesa, there were still more pouring over the top. And it wasn't just humans; duster animals ran with the pack, too—coyotes and rabbits and foxes and bobcats, sprinting their way through the horde.

Tens of thousands of raving, hungry dusters tearing across the desert, and they were heading straight for the train.

"There's a tunnel up ahead, maybe two, three miles. We could lose 'em there. But they'll be on us before that," Horace said. "I need you to buy us the time to get there."

Patrick didn't respond. He was already running back through the train.

***

"Alice! Get your crossbow!"

"I already have my crossbow," Alice said.

"Great. Where are the arrows?" She pointed at a makeshift quiver on the bookshelf. There were six bolts left. Patrick frowned. "Not a lot. Okay. Let me think."

Babs had just noticed the swarm of dusters out the window. "Oh my God," she said, pressing her good hand against the glass. "Is that a *horde* of zombies?"

"Technically no, but now's not the time to get into it. All right. We need to keep them away from the train. We get hit with a wave like that, they'll take us off the tracks."

"Pour zombie repellant on the train?" Lex suggested.

"Yeah, I don't think that'll be enough. The ones in the back won't smell it, and they'll push the others forward like a battering ram. We need a buffer zone." He grabbed up a towel, one that Ben had been using to soak up his green ooze. Patrick yanked at it, groaning and straining to rip it in half. He twisted the ends around his knuckles and tried again, pulling as hard as he could until veins popped out in his neck and beads of sweat appeared across his forehead. He let go, panting heavily. He looked up. Alice held out her hand. Patrick handed her the towel. She flipped out her knife and cut the rag into strips. "Thanks," he panted. "Tie those to the bolts, one each, near the back." He ran to his bag while the Lex and Alice got to work on the knots. He dug out a vial of Zom-Be-Gone and poured an equal measure on each of the fabric strips, until the vial was empty and

184

the towels were lightly soaked with purple fluid. "Alice, shoot these things as far in front of us as you can without getting off target."

"What's the target?" she asked.

"The ground. Stick them in like fenceposts. Five to ten feet off the tracks."

Alice frowned. "You don't want me to shoot the zombies?"

"You don't have eight million bolts. And anyway, depending on how far gone they are, arrows will probably just bounce off them anyway. Put them in the ground so the rags stick up in the air. This much should be good for maybe a twenty-five foot radius. Let's say twenty, to be safe. That means we need an arrow every forty feet."

"I only have six arrows."

"It's not ideal. But it'll buy us some time."

"How much is forty feet? I'm bad with distance."

Patrick peered out the window. "Fast as we're going, I'd guess we move about eighty or ninety feet every second."

Alice stared at him. "You want me to shoot two bolts a second?"

"Do your best. It won't be a solid wall, but at least they'll have to funnel through the gaps. That'll slow them down, and it buys us time. Ready?"

"I guess."

"Great. We're out of time."

She climbed up the bookshelf with the crossbow, and Patrick scurried up after her, holding the quiver. The zombies were already closer than he'd like. "There," he shouted over the wind, pointing at a boulder about fifty yards in front of the train. "Can you get close to that rock?"

Alice held the crossbow to her shoulder and looked down the sights. "Yeah," she decided.

"Start there. Then unload," he shouted.

Alice took a breath. She squeezed the trigger.

The bolt sank into the hardpan about six feet from the boulder.

"Nice shot."

She held out a hand. "Bolt."

He handed her another arrow, and she nocked it and fired, hitting maybe twenty feet in front of the first. "Further is better than closer!" Patrick said. He handed her another arrow. This one, she sank about thirty feet beyond the second.

In quick succession, she fired the next three arrows. Patrick could just barely see the opening of the tunnel a few dozen yards in front of the farthest arrow. If the arrow fence kept the zombies out, they'd still have about fifteen seconds of total exposure. As long as the horde didn't break and split to the west and go around the arrows, they'd be fine.

"Good," Patrick said, giving her a nod.

"Now what?"

Patrick shrugged. "Now we watch."

The train caught up to the first arrow just as the dusters crossed onto the siding. It was like watching a tidal wave of teeth and bone crashing down on their ship. The first dozen or so runners smashed into the train, clawing at the steel walls and screaming. But then the horde caught up to the arrows, and the front few lines skidded to a stop. The zombies behind them slammed forward and shoved them through, but the repellant did its job, and though some of the dusters broke across the line, the second they plunged into the Zom-Be-Gone smell zone, they devolved into piles of hissing, writhing snakes on the desert floor, clawing at their noses and trying to scratch their way back away from the train.

The screams were deafening. Patrick held his hands over his ears.

Some dusters did get funneled into the gaps between the arrows, but as Patrick predicted, they'd been slowed down enough to be pretty ineffective against the train. They collided with the side, and the train cars rocked, but not enough to cause any damage.

"It's working!" Patrick called out, relieved, as they zipped past the third and fourth arrows. "We're almost clear!"

He felt something tug at his sleeve. He whirled around. It was Alice. She was yelling something. He lowered his hands from his ears. "What?"

Alice grabbed his head and turned it toward the tunnel. "*Look!*"

Patrick's heart sank. "Oh shit," he sighed.

Most of the dusters had stayed on their path—almost all of them, in fact. There were only a few stragglers that had broken wide and were running around the end of the arrow line. The plow could handle them easily.

But there was something else charging across the desert, skirting around the arrows: a huge, hulking creature with sharp horns and fiery eyes. Its hooves pounded the hardpan, sending shockwaves through the earth. Its thick hide was torn open near its shoulders and along its rib cage, where broken bones had stabbed through the skin and now stuck out with their jagged edges like armor spikes along the creature's flanks. Green and red bubbles of blood frothed from the beast's mouth. It trampled the zombies running ahead of it, mowing them down and clearing the way to charge the train.

"What *is* that thing?" Alice asked.

"That," he said, "is Dark Ponch."

***

186

"You guys, I think it's a buffalo," Babs called from her perch at the window.

Patrick dropped down and ran through the car. "Lex—with me!" He sprinted into Ben's bunk, Lex trailing behind. Ben was still snoring on the floor. "Get him to the front, *now!*" Patrick ordered. Lex knelt down and worked his hands beneath Ben's limp, wet body.

Patrick looked out the window. *Shit, this is gonna be close.* "Move, move, move!" he cried. Lex struggled with Ben's unconscious body and finally managed to cradle him like a huge baby.

"He's heavy and slippery," Lex complained.

"Lex! *Now!*"

Dark Ponch was hurtling toward the train with incredible speed. The tunnel was only a few yards away. The engine would make it in fine, and maybe the dining car too, but two thousand pounds of reinforced zombie bison was about to spear them right in the middle. Lex shuffled through the door and into the Baby Caps' car. "All the way up!" Patrick yelled. "All of you! Go!" He grabbed the makeshift torch from the wall and tried to light it, but his BIC wouldn't catch. "Goddammit, come on," he mumbled. He looked back up through the window. Dark Ponch was too close. There was no time.

He'd have to blow the coupler from this side.

"Don't stop, no matter what!" he yelled up at the Baby Caps. They disappeared into the dining car. Patrick cursed at the lighter. He flicked it and flicked it, but the spark wouldn't catch. "*Come on!*" he screamed.

He looked up just in time to see Dark Ponch hit a prairie dog hole. The creature's hoof went down, and he stumbled. The bison didn't fall, but the tumble had cut half a second off his trajectory, and it had changed his angle just enough that he'd miss the Baby Caps' car.

"Thank Christ," Patrick mumbled. "Now come on, you goddamn lighter, come on…"

Then Dark Ponch was on them.

Patrick clicked the lighter. The flame caught.

The torch went up in flames. Patrick smashed it down on the coupler bombs. They exploded with enough force to knock Patrick onto his back. The car broke free just as Dark Ponch slammed into its broadside. The steel of the car crumpled inward like a tin can. It lifted off its wheels and crashed onto the siding, tumbling end over end with the agonizing shriek of twisting metal and screaming bison.

Patrick sat up. His feet dangled just over the edge of the car, hanging out over the tracks through nothing but empty air. The snarling of the zombies became fainter and fainter, and then the world went dark as the train was swallowed up by the safety of the tunnel.

Patrick collapsed back onto the floor, breathing hard. "Not today, Dark Ponch."

45.

The Run was quiet for the rest of the night. After an hour without incident, the crew decided to take turns closing their eyes for a bit. Patrick sent the Baby Caps off to bed first while he and Rogers kept watch from the dining car. Every now and then, a fox or an owl would perk up its head and watch the train rumble by, but the night was otherwise still.

"I don't suppose we're in California yet," Patrick said.

Rogers shook his head. "Still in New Mexico, I think."

Patrick sighed. "Still a long way to go."

"Mm," Rogers agreed.

After about an hour, Babs appeared in the doorway. She couldn't sleep, on account of her elbow. She'd finished Rogers' moonshine and it hadn't really helped all that much. But she'd been able to rest well enough, and she told Patrick to head back and take a shift on a cot. He wanted her to take more time, but she wouldn't hear of it and said she was done. Pretty soon after, Alice joined them, too. She'd slept deeply for a short while and woke up feeling alert and "ready to stab people." Even Horace eventually came back and asked Rogers to take the helm for a while so he could get a few winks. "You wake me as soon as you see *anything*," he instructed, and Rogers promised he would. "I don't want to wake up to another car gone," he huffed.

Patrick finally relented. He went back and made himself a nest on the floor next to Ben's cot. Lex was snoring softly, completely lost to the world. Ben was out, too, breathing hard with wet breaths. It sounded like the Monkey fluid was getting into his lungs. That meant the organ walls were probably breaking down. Once they filled and swelled, that was it. It wouldn't be much longer now.

Patrick tried not to let himself think about what that might mean for their timeline. They just had to keep going. Keep pushing ahead, fast as they can. No stopping. No slowing. A shotgun blast to the end, whatever that ended up being.

Patrick closed his eyes and laid down.

He was asleep before his head hit the floor.

***

He woke to sunlight filtering in through the windows.

"*Snnzrk?*" he said, snoring himself awake. He bolted upright. For a few seconds, he couldn't remember where he was. He'd been dreaming of his old apartment in Chicago. In the dream, Annie had been there with him. Izzy had not.

It was always hard to wake up after having an Izzy dream. But sometimes it was a lot harder to wake up from one without her.

He looked around and found himself alone in the car. He stood up off the floor, his back stiff, his muscles tight. He stretched like a cat. The car was chilly. They must be up in the mountains now, because goosebumps prickled up over Patrick's arms, and he thought he could see just a hint of his own breath.

"Oh," he said, blinking out at the world through the windows. "Snow."

Having grown up in St. Louis, spending almost a decade in Chicago, and now wandering around the Appalachians for the better part of the last three years, Patrick was no stranger to snow. But he'd never seen it in a desert before. Snow-covered cacti were a brand new thing to cross off his list.

He shuffled drowsily into the dining car. "He wakes!" Rogers announced. Lex gave a small round of applause. Alice said, very unconvincingly, "Woo."

"Sorry I was out so long," Patrick yawned, stretching again. "No trouble?"

"Not really. Some white collar boardroom guys high on something stood along the tracks and hit the train with palm fronds. But that's about it."

"I've never understood teambuilding exercises," Patrick admitted. He crossed through the dining car and poked his head in the engine. "Morning, Horace."

"It is morning," Horace confirmed.

"How far to the next station? Any idea?"

"Matter of fact, we're coming up on it soon. Maybe fifteen minutes? Why? You want to stretch your legs?"

"I decidedly do not," Patrick nodded. "But—and this is the only time I'm going to ask this—do you think you can ease off the gas a little on approach?"

Horace raised an eyebrow. "You're asking me to stop the train?"

"I am *not* asking you to stop the train, and in fact I am pleading with you to very specifically keep the train going. But if you can slow it down a bit, I could use an extra few seconds through the station."

Horace shrugged. "Sure. Okay. Why?"

"I'm going to play doctor."

***

Horace eased off the throttle about half a mile before the Benson, AZ station. The train approached the platform at a relatively mild forty miles per hour. To his surprise, he felt nervous slowing the train down to what only two days ago was the fastest he was willing to go. But Patrick had been right: Going fast had given them an advantage. A train you can't catch is a train you can't board. Who knew how many other Slaughterhouse gangs had just let them pass unmolested, deciding not to even bother trying for a train at full speed?

He kept his eyes busy as the speedometer notched downward. He scanned the station and the sleepy buildings behind it, watching for any sign of an ambush. Without taking his eyes off the scene, he picked up the walkie-talkie and said, "Coming up on the station now."

Patrick picked up a cardboard box and tossed it to Lex. "You want up or down?"

"I'm afraid of heights," Lex said.

"Down it is."

Patrick grabbed an empty duffel bag and climbed up the bookshelf. He threw the duffel's shoulder strap over his head, securing the bag across his chest. Then he carefully hauled himself up onto the roof of the train and began crawling toward the edge.

The steel sheeting was covered in a thin dusting of snow, making it impossibly slick. Patrick eased himself slowly toward the edge, lodging his fingers and toes in the shallow grooves in the train's roof as he went. The station ahead was exactly as Patrick had hoped—a classic, narrow, mid-century brick building with a roof that sloped down just enough to cover the platform. As they rolled into the station, Patrick opened the bag up wide, and when they got to the platform, he reached forward and dragged the duffel along the top of the roof. The angle was clumsy, but it helped to be able to put some weight on the station roof, and eventually he managed to keep the bag level enough to scoop up a solid mound of snow as the train passed.

Down below, Lex was doing a version of the same thing, leaning out of the train and trying to catch any clumps Patrick knocked off in his cardboard box. By the time they pulled out of the station, they had gathered up a pretty good pile. Patrick zipped his duffel bag shut and crawled back to the porthole. He dropped down into the train with a look of triumph on his cold, wet face.

"That went off with *way* fewer hitches than expected!" he said proudly.

He took out a few handfuls of snow and portioned them onto the rags that were waiting. Lex tied them up into makeshift ice packs. "They won't last long," Patrick said, "but hopefully they'll help the swelling a bit."

Lex put one to his forehead and sighed pleasantly at the chill of relief. Babs picked one up and held it gingerly to her elbow.

Patrick handed the third to Alice. "For your face," he explained. "The cuts are looking okay, but your cheek's pretty swollen."

Patrick consolidated the snow from the box with the snow in the bag, and then he followed Rogers to the engine. The assistant conductor produced a metal coffee can from one of the overhead bins. "You don't want to know what's been in here," he warned. "But it's probably the best thing we have."

Patrick nodded and carefully dumped the snow into the can. Rogers pulled open the window. He used a length of twine to tie the coffee can to the door handle on the outside of the train. It wasn't a perfect solution, but they hoped the cold air would keep the snow solid long enough to fill a second round of packs.

Patrick headed back to check on the Baby Caps. Alice had already put her ice pack aside, but Lex and Babs were still holding theirs against their skin. There wasn't a whole lot of visible change in their wounds, but they all seemed to be feeling some measure of relief. That, at least, was something.

Then they heard the sound of glass shattering against the train.

Patrick ducked next to the window and peered outside. There were people running alongside the train, lined up on both sides, hurling glass bottles as they passed. Most of them broke against the walls or windows, shattering and spraying some syrupy, clear liquid across the exterior. Some of the jars landed in the gangways and smashed open on the metal floor. Two jars sailed in through the broken window. One of them nearly hit

Alice in the head. She ducked just in time; that jar and the next smashed against the luggage rack behind her.

"What's happening?" asked Lex. "What are they—?" But he stopped in mid-sentence, because suddenly his eyes started to burn, and his skin started to prickle, and the hairs inside his nostrils felt like they were catching fire.

"What is this?!" Babs cried, tears streaming from her burning eyes. "What did they do?!"

Patrick choked on the fumes. His eyes burned like he'd smeared them with ghost pepper oil. He felt the sting of ten thousand fire ants sinking their fangs into his skin. "Everyone out!" he shouted. "Get on top of the train!"

The air itself became suffocating. Each breath was like inhaling a gallon of wet cement that was on fire. Alice scrambled up the bookshelf and burst through the hole like a drowning woman breaking through the water. Patrick and Lex fumbled with Ben, who was just starting to wake up from the new kind of pain on his skin and eyes. Lex hauled him up the bookshelf, with Patrick pushing up from below, helping Lex stay steady. Babs started crying. The pain in her arm was unbearable; there was no way she could climb. Rogers threw an arm around her and led her out the back of the train, onto the half platform that used to be a vestibule between cars. He picked up one of the steel shields on their way.

When they got to the platform, he helped guide Babs out onto the ledge, showing her the metal handle set into the side of the train car and wrapping the shield around her back to keep her safe from gas bombs and from falling off the train. A Mason jar full of clear liquid smashed against the shield, and the noxious gas filled the air, but out in the open on a fast-moving train, it dissipated quickly enough. "Hold tight," Rogers instructed as they clung to the back of the car. "Don't fall."

Patrick scrambled up onto the roof. He pulled the walkie and said, "Horace, how's the engine?"

"No problems. What's going on back there?"

"Do *not* open the door to the dining car! We've been gassed."

"Oh, Lord!" Horace wailed before clicking off the walkie.

The four of them clung desperately to the slippery roof of the train. Ben was barely conscious, murmuring something about palm trees. Lex had his arm hooked around Ben's waist; he was the only thing keeping the invalid from sliding off into the desert mob. Alice was perched on the roof like a cat, surveying the situation. The tracks were lined with dozens of people holding jars. "Incoming!" she shouted. Another Mason jar flew at them from below. Patrick ducked behind his arms, but Alice caught the jar with two hands like she was catching an egg, then hurled it back at the person who'd thrown it. The attacker screeched as the jar smashed at her feet. The raiders around her scattered.

"What is this stuff?" Lex asked, blinking away the tears in his eyes.

"Some sort of gas. Maybe chlorine. We're up here until it clears," Patrick said, squinting against the burn in his eyes.

Alice caught another jar and sent it back down to the ground. There were more screams and more scattering. "Where's Babs?" she shouted.

"Rogers took her out the back!" Lex called.

"They're exposed back there! We need to give them cover," Alice bellowed over the wind.

Patrick nodded. He slapped his pockets and found them empty. He tried to lower his head into the porthole to see if there were any weapons close, but the gas was still too powerful. As soon as he got near the vent, his eyes began to water again, and his skin prickled and became itchy. "Alice, you got anything?" he said.

Alice slipped a thin chamois cloth bundle from her back pocket. She let the chamois fall open, and inside glittered eight polished throwing knives.

"Where does you *get* all these things?" Patrick asked.

She didn't answer. She stepped lithely over Lex and Ben, and she prowled across the top of the train until she reached the end of the car. "You all right?" she called down to the two Red Caps.

"Could use some help," Rogers admitted, blocking another chlorine bomb with the shield. "This thing is heavy as hell...I can't hold it much longer."

Alice dodged a jar that sailed over the train and hit the raiders on the other side. She drew a throwing knife and hunted for a target. She saw a man to her left rearing back to throw a jar. Alice flung the knife at him; it stuck straight into his heart. The man collapsed and the chlorine bomb broke on the hardpan. The raiders around him scattered as the train left them in a whorl of dust.

Another woman on the right cocked a jar over her shoulder, ready to throw. Alice's knife sailed through the air and caught her in the throat. The woman tried to throw the bomb as she gasped and gurgled her own blood, but it only bounced a few feet forward, smashing on the siding and sending more raiders running back into the desert.

Two more knives and they finally got the message. "Fall back!" one of the raiders yelled, and the order made its way up the chain. The bombs stopped flying, and aggressors dispersed, scurrying away to whatever holes they'd crawled out of.

After fifteen minutes of clinging to the roof, Patrick stuck his head into the porthole. "I think we're good," he said after a few deep breaths. He lowered himself cautiously into the train. Between the open gangways and the broken windows, the air whipping through had dissipated the gas enough to breath comfortably.

He helped Lex lower Ben onto the bookshelf. "I can climb down myself," Ben insisted. He stepped down and slipped on the first shelf. Patrick caught him at the bottom.

"You nailed it," he said.

"Shut up," Ben replied. "What was that all about? Why were we on top of the train?"

"Some jags tried to gas us out."

"They did a good job."

"Yeah. They probably thought we'd stop the train. The engine is closed off, though, so Horace wasn't affected—at least not enough to stop."

"Good old Horace."

"Good old crabby Horace."

"If you don't want him to be crabby, stop destroying his train," Ben suggested.

"I will not," Patrick shook his head. "Destroying his train is my passion."

46.

They were rolling through suburban Tucson when Patrick's walk-ie-talkie crackled to life. "Help," a woman's voice said. "Can you help me?"

Patrick stared down at the walkie. "Uhh...did Horace take up voice work?"

"I sure did not," Horace said, stomping into the car. He held up his radio. "Who the heck is that?"

"Please...if you can hear me, please," the voice crackled through both speakers. "You're on the train. Right?"

Patrick stared at his walkie. "This feels pretty not-good," he decided. He raised the walkie to his lips.

"Don't answer it!" Horace whispered.

"I *am* going to answer it! Someone needs our help," Patrick whispered back.

"We can't help her!"

"We don't know that. Also, why are we whispering?"

"I don't know!" Horace whispered.

"Please," the voice in the walkie pleaded. "Is anyone there?"

Patrick pressed the button. "Hi. Who is this?"

Hi, who is this? Ben mouthed. *What?* Patrick mouthed back. Ben shook his head.

"My name's Annie. I need help."

Ben's eyes grew wide. *Annie?* he mouthed.

"I'm sure it's a different Annie," Patrick assured him. Ben rolled his eyes. Patrick went back to the radio. "How are you coming through?"

"I hijacked your signal. You're on the train, right? I can see you. I'm on the top of the Pioneer Hotel."

"Um. I don't know these buildings," Patrick said.

"Ahead and to your left. Close to the train station. I'm trapped up here. Please. Can you help me?"

Patrick exhaled. He pressed the antenna of the walkie into his forehead, hard enough to hurt. He pressed the button. "No," he said. "We can't stop."

There was a long pause on the other end of the line. Patrick looked around at the rest of the crew. They all wore the same look of helplessness.

The radio crackled. "This isn't a trap. I know you can't, like, take my word for it, but I swear to you, this isn't a trap. I'm all alone. Tucson's been quiet for weeks. You can stop here, it's safe. I promise." The woman on the other end burst into tears. "I know this is what someone would say if this were a trap, but I swear to God, it's not a trap! I need your help!"

"Annie…" Patrick said. Then he took his thumb off the button because he didn't really know what to say after that.

"Zombies came. I don't even live here. Zombies came while I was scavenging, I ran into the hotel and climbed the stairs to the roof. I thought they'd move on,but they're still at the door. I can hear them. I've been sitting on this roof for six days. I haven't had any food or water. Please. I'll die here."

"How did she hijack our signal from the roof of a hotel?" Rogers asked.

Patrick considered this. He nodded. "Annie, how'd you hack our frequency?"

"I worked in comms. I was military, retired. I know radios, I have all this equipment…I packed it all, I was going to trade it for food. I haven't gotten anyone on the radio in months. I have all the equipment…I don't have any food or water. I've been scanning frequencies since I got up here. You're the first. You're the only one. Please. I'll die up here."

"Annie. We can't stop."

Annie let him listen to the sound of her sobbing. "It gets so cold at night," she said. "It's getting colder."

Patrick felt like someone had wrapped his guts around their hand and twisted. "Annie. Is there a fire escape? Or another building to jump to?"

"I can't jump. Too far. There was a fire escape, but it's gone now. I'm trapped." She cried more, her breaths coming in wet, ragged gasps. "Please. There won't be anyone else."

"Annie, you don't understand. We can't stop. We have a sick man. We're getting him to a doctor. He's…" Patrick looked at Ben. Ben nodded.

Go ahead, the nod said. *I already know.* Patrick pinched the bridge of his nose. "He's dying, Annie, and we are running out of time."

Annie was quiet for another few moments. The train rumbled into downtown. They saw the tracks spread. They sped into the station, and the train blasted through. Patrick peered out the window at the buildings on the left. He saw a speck of a silhouette on top of one of the buildings.

"I'm sorry," he said, his voice cracking.

The walkie crackled. "You didn't stop," she said, sounding numb.

"I'm sorry, Annie."

The crackling resumed. Annie was holding down her button, but she didn't say anything. The static pops filled the air for a long time, long enough for the train to make it past downtown and for the building to thin. Finally, she said, "Is it the Green Fever?"

"Yeah," Patrick replied.

Bzzrt. "You can slow it with peaches. I don't know how. I don't know why. Some sort of enzyme in peaches. It won't do much, but it'll give you more time. If you have peaches."

The radio started to crackle in and out. She was losing the frequency.

The frequency, Ben thought. Then he bolted upright. "Oh, shit! Patrick, bemme walkie!"

Patrick winkled his brow. "What?"

Ben collapsed against Patrick's shoulder and shouted weakly at the walkie. "Annie! Listen to me. There's a frequency the dusters can't hear. I don't know what it is. It's high. But if you sound it, they'll run away. They can't stand it. Can you do that with your equipment?"

"Breaking up—" Annie replied. "You—high frequency? The—handle—?"

"Play the frequency!" Ben shouted into the walkie. "They'll go away! Try them all! Fuck, I don't even know how that works!" he cried.

The walkie was dead. They were out of range.

"Do you think she heard me?" Ben asked.

Patrick mopped his face with his hand. "Yeah, Benny Boy," he decided, taking a huge breath. "I think probably she did."

Ben handed over the walkie. "I don't know why I didn't remember," he said quietly.

"You did. She heard it," Rogers assured him.

"She did," Horace agreed. "Hopefully you just saved her life."

They all sat quietly for a while, rumbling through the Tucson suburbs.

"Shouldn't someone be driving this train?" Alice finally asked.

"On it," Rogers said, giving them a salute and disappearing into the engine.

Babs cleared her throat. "Do you think it's real? What she said about peaches?" she asked. "Because, um, we have, like, a thousand cans."

47.

"We don't have a thousand of anything," Horace pointed out.

"Okay, not a thousand," Babs said, rolling her eyes. "It's probably actually, like, ten cans. But we do have some. Lex is allergic and no one else likes them, so we've been sort of saving them for desperate times."

"That's great!" Patrick said. "Bemme cans! Load this boy up! Peaches for days!"

"Yech," Ben said, making a sour face. "I hate peaches."

"Ben, you are going to eat so many peaches right now," Patrick informed him.

"I don't like them!" Ben insisted. "They're too sweet."

"Okay, princess, your objections have been noted. Lex, can you please fetch forth all the peaches?"

Lex hemmed and hawed. "It's just…I'm allergic," he said.

"They're in cans."

Lex shrugged. "I need to be careful."

"I don't understand, do you die if you touch peaches?" Patrick asked, genuinely interested.

"I'll go get the peaches," Alice said, annoyed. She stomped off into the dining car and returned a minute later with an armload of cans. She dumped them at Ben's feet.

"I think I'd rather die," Ben decided.

"No such luck!" Patrick beamed. "You're going to eat so many cans of these gross babies that we're going to call you Princess Peach."

"I hate everything about this," Ben said.

"Except the living part. You like living."

"One rando on one roof in one weird town tells you that peaches cure the fever, and now you're the Presidents of the United States of America?"

The Baby Caps furrowed their brows, confused. "The band," Rogers told them, "not the actual people."

This did nothing to clarify the issue.

"Just eat the dumb peaches," Patrick said, stabbing into the can with a knife and wrenching back the lid. "Worst case scenario, you don't get better but you get a good excuse to do your favorite Nicolas Cage impression."

"My favorite Nicolas Cage impression is from *Moonstruck*," Ben glowered, "*not* from *Face/Off*. You should know that."

"Well, if your hand explodes from the fever, you can have *Moonstruck* too. Now eat the fucking peach."

"That's what she said," Rogers and Ben said in unison.

"What do *any* parts of this conversation mean?" Babs sighed.

Patrick stabbed the knife through a syrupy peach slice and held it in front of Ben's mouth. "Don't make me Slaughterhouse Run you," he warned. Ben bristled at the sight of the sickly sweet fruit, but he swiped the knife out of Patrick's hand and stuffed the peach slice into his mouth.

"Oh my God, it tastes like grade school and vomit," he groaned.

"Grade school vomit smells like polypropylene absorbent, everyone knows that," Patrick countered.

"I never know the words he uses," Lex whispered to Babs.

"I'm not sure he does either," Babs reassured him.

They sat there and watched Patrick force feed Ben old canned peaches until the tin was empty. It was pretty uncomfortable to watch, but there just weren't many other places to go on the train anymore.

48.

Alice climbed up to the roof and watched the desert slip past. They were hoping to make one last snow grab, but the next station was Marico-pa, halfway across the state, and the snow had pretty much dried up after Tucson. The air was still cold, though, and Alice enjoyed the stabbing chill of it. It kept her awake. It made her sharp.

"See anything up there?" Patrick asked.

"Nope. Just a bunch of dead earth."

"Yes, we call that 'Arizona.'" Patrick rapped on the shelf with his knuckles. "Welp, on that note, just use the secret word if you see anything life-threatening coming our way."

"What's the secret word?" Alice asked.

"Parsimonious."

"Parsimonious."

"Yes."

"No. I mean, parsimonious."

"You got it right the first time."

"No. Patrick." Alice pointed up the tracks. "Parsimonious."

Patrick popped his head up through the porthole. An overpass loomed above the tracks ahead, and behind it, on the north side of the tracks, lay a huge wreck of twisted steel boxes. The wreck took sharper shape as they closed in, and by the time they reached the overpass, Patrick's fears had been confirmed.

"It's a train," Alice said.

"It *was* a train," Patrick corrected her. "Something forced it off the tracks. Hard."

The demolished Amtrak had five cars, all of them thrown together against the embankment like matchsticks. Most had come uncoupled in the crash, and two of them were fully upside-down, their wheels pointing up toward the sky. One of the cars had a huge gash in its side, a hole big enough for a person to walk through easily. And perhaps strangest of all, there were deep skid marks carved into the earth, as if the train had been dragged off the rails.

"Patrick?" Horace said over the walkie-talkie.

"I see it," Patrick replied. "Any ideas?"

"I don't got the first clue on what could do that to a train."

"I'm thinking mythological giants, but it's just a working theory right now. I'll let you know if it evolves. In the meantime, stay sharp up there. And—"

"And go faster, yeah, yeah, yeah…" Horace clicked off the walkie.

"You ever see anything like that before?" Patrick asked. Alice shook her head.

A few miles further down, through the next overpass, they passed a second wreck, a short freight train this time, done in just like the first. Patrick made his way to the engine car. "Someone's using these bridges to derail trains," he said.

"Yeah," Rogers replied, "but *how*?"

"I haven't come up with anything better than a Greek titan," Patrick shrugged. "How many more overpasses like this do we have on this stretch?"

Horace looked at him as if he were an absolute idiot. "What am I, Mapquest?"

"I don't know, you're a train guy, you know train stuff," Patrick grumbled.

"Overpasses are car stuff," Rogers pointed out.

"All right, well, if anyone sees Jay Leno, be sure to ask him," Patrick said, waving them away and skulking back to the Baby Caps' car.

They passed another wreck a few miles later, and after another twenty minutes, they saw a fourth. "This is bad," Patrick mumbled, flexing his fingers to try to dispel his anxiety. "Bad, bad, bad, bad, bad."

"Maybe it's the Angel of Death," Ben rasped.

Patrick whirled around, surprised. He didn't know Ben was awake. "What?"

"Overpass. Passover. The Angel of Death comes for any train not marked with sacrificial blood."

"We've shed plenty of sacrificial blood," Patrick pointed out.

"Oh," said Ben. "Then we'll probably be fine."

"Since when are you a spiritual advisor?"

"Since I've been knee deep in a bright-light tunnel for a week."

"I didn't know dying made you good at Bible," Patrick said.

"It was the one thing I wasn't good at. Now I am complete."

"At least we know where to look, right?" Babs asked. "All these wrecks are right after overpasses. I mean, we don't know what it is, but we know it's *something*, so if we watch the overpasses from here on out, we can at least be prepared. Right?"

"I don't know," Patrick said. "Maybe."

"Persimmons," Alice called down.

"What about them?" Patrick said.

"Persimmons!" she yelled.

"Honestly, I don't know if I've ever had one," Ben said.

"You know, I can't swear that I have, either," Patrick realized.

"No! Idiots! We've got trouble, starboard side!"

"Oh!" Patrick said brightly. "The word was 'parsimonious.' But I see how you got there." He leaned back and looked out the window. A trio of pickups roared toward them through the desert, kicking up a wall of dust. Patrick frowned. "They didn't even wait for an overpass."

The trucks had big natural gas tanks loaded into their beds, and behind those crouched a handful of whooping, hollering raiders holding hydraulic spear guns. The drivers had their pedals to the floor; the trucks were on them in seconds, keeping pace easily once they pulled up alongside.

"Weapons!" Patrick cried. Every able-bodied crewmate picked up the nearest lethal thing. "What do you want?" Patrick called up to Alice.

"Pipe bombs," she decided.

Patrick scooped up four and shoveled them up through the porthole. "Fire at will," he said.

Alice lit the first bomb and hurled it at the lead truck. The bomb exploded against the driver's side door, ripping the surface metal to shreds and blasting a concave crater in the side. The driver was slammed from his left, and he jerked the truck right, but the blast wasn't enough to debilitate the vehicle, and the driver quickly regained control and jammed the truck back over alongside the train. The riders in that truck were knocked down, but none of them fell out, and they were back up on their feet in a flash.

Meanwhile, riders in the backs of the other two trucks took aim with their guns and fired harpoons into the side of the train. The reinforced spears pierced the steel side easily, blasting all the way through and exploding through the interior wall. The hooked points lodged there, and the train was caught like a Nantucket whale. Each spear was tethered by a long nylon rope that disappeared into a tall and broad coil in the center of the truck bed.

The riders in the first truck had fired off their shots too, before Alice had lit the second bomb. But she did light it, and she tossed it into the bed of the truck. One of the raiders caught it in midair and flung it back at the train. Alice ducked, and the pipe bomb exploded just to her right, about two feet above the train roof. The force of the blast pushed her back, but her foot was pressed firmly against the inside ledge of the porthole, and she didn't go sliding back. But the sound of the explosion set her eardrums ringing, and the world wavered a bit when she opened her eyes.

The sound of more spears piercing metal sounded from the Baby Caps' car. Eleven lines streamed from the side of the train into the backs of the trucks. One of the riders twirled his finger in the air, some unspoken signal to the rest of the crew. They dropped their guns and set straight to work, expertly sorting the ends of their rope lines and tying them all to each other in one big knot.

"What's happening?" Ben asked.

"Nothing good," Patrick said miserably. He climbed up and gripped Alice by the knee. He gave her a gentle shake. She turned her head and looked at him, dazed. "You okay?" he asked. She just stared at him.

Patrick gently pulled her leg toward him and slid her down into the porthole. She slipped through the opening like a ragdoll. Patrick caught her in both arms and carefully brought her back down into the car. He laid her down on her cot. Then he turned to the others. "Alice is out. I'm going up."

"They're moving *fast*," Babs said, her voice twinged with awe. The riders had finished tying their knots, and the three trucks had converged in a well-rehearsed bit of vehicular synchronization. The riders on the outside handed their knotted lines to their comrades in the center truck, and *those* bandits knitted the whole thing together into one huge knot, so that suddenly the train was tethered by eleven ropes to one souped-up Honda, tearing ass through the desert like some insane Roger Corman version of *James and the Giant Peach*. By the time Patrick had reached the roof, the other two trucks had peeled off, leaving just the one. Patrick lit a pipe bomb and threw it at the truck, but the driver saw it coming and turned the wheel to dodge it easily. The nylon ropes had plenty of slack, and the truck wove freely in and out alongside the train. The bomb hit the ground and blew some ancient cactus to shit.

"What is this?" Rogers yelled, running into the car.

"I don't know!" Patrick yelled back in frustration. What the hell did they hope to accomplish? That little Ridgeline may have had 250 horsepower, but it wasn't going to pull the train off the tracks. In fact, if it tried, the opposite would happen; the train would drag the truck along behind it, grinding it through the hardpan until the ropes frayed and snapped.

"Come on, come on, come on," he muttered, "what are you up to?" The truck was just keeping pace, and at a healthy distance. The rope line was incredibly long; the truck was probably twenty yards out, and Patrick could still see plenty of slack spooled in the bed. He turned and looked down the tracks. The fog was thick and visibility was bad. But soon, the unmistakable silhouette of an overpass appeared in the mist. The truck driver saw it as soon as Patrick did; he slammed down on the gas, and the pick-up roared past the train. "Shit!" Patrick cried. He called down for the binoculars and Rogers passed them up. He focused in on the overpass. "Oh my God," he whispered.

Patrick leapt down into the train car. "We've got to cut those lines, *now!*" he ordered. Rogers strode across the car and grabbed the red emergency handle set into the window trim. He pulled down hard, and decades' worth of grime slowly peeled away as he pulled the seal from the window. He and Patrick tilted the glass and let it slide out of the window. It shattered on the desert earth, and in an instant, they were past it, hurtling toward the overpass.

Patrick grabbed his machete from its sheath and stuck it awkwardly out the window, sawing at one of the ropes. Rogers pulled the knife from his belt and started to work on a second. The fibers frayed, but the blades wouldn't cut through.

"What the hell kind of rope *is* that?" Babs asked.

"Kevlar fibers," Patrick guessed. "They'll cut! Keep going!"

Lex joined them, hacking away at a third line. The ropes weren't breaking; the threads were holding. They sawed away, slowly peeling back the fibers, way, way too slowly.

Alice grabbed her head, trying to slow down the spinning. She snapped her fingers next to her ear. Her hearing was coming back, at least a little.

"What'd you see?" she asked Patrick.

"They reinforced the struts. *Seriously* reinforced them. And they cut a horizontal notch in the center pier."

"What does that mean?" Alice asked, frustrated.

Patrick slammed Bleakachu down on the cord. He wasn't even halfway through one yet. "It means they're going to feed the rope into it. Like they're catching that pier Red Rover-style. Got it? The huge Kevlar knot will be on one side of the very, very strong concrete pillar, and we'll be on the other side. The bridge will hold; the train won't. As soon as we pass it, the knot catches, the rope pulls tight, we slingshot off the tracks—game over. Get your eighty-three knives and help us cut these lines!" Patrick yelled.

Alice stood there, in the center of the car, solid on her feet and scowling. She stared into the middle space, not moving, not blinking, just scowling.

"Alice! Move!" Patrick yelled.

"She's thinking," Lex told him. "Let her think."

Patrick's palms were slick with sweat. The machete slipped in his hand. He just barely caught it before it tumbled out into the desert. He cursed and went back to sawing at the rope. He was almost through one. Rogers was, too. Lex was making decent progress.

Once they each got through, it'd be three down. Eight to go.

Patrick wasn't even sure they had enough time for the first three.

"Alice! Think about cutting these lines!" Patrick cried.

Alice broke from her trance. She snatched up the rag Ben was using to wipe off his slime. "Hey," he protested weakly. Alice held him down and mopped the rag over every exposed inch of his body, arms, neck, face, head—until the rag was soggy with Monkey goo. Alice picked up a pipe bomb and a lighter, and she climbed the bookshelf up to the roof. She crouched low, riding the train and waiting for the right moment. They were screaming toward the overpass. The truck reached it first, and just as Patrick had predicted, the rider fed the line through the channel in the concrete, and the trap was set. Alice turned her back to the wind to protect the lighter, and she clicked it to life. She held the flame against the bomb's makeshift wick, an old line of yarn they'd smeared with candle wax and sprinkled with black powder. The bomb lit, and the fuse hissed. Alice wrapped the bomb in the wet, goopy rag, careful not to wrap up the fuse. The train reached the overpass. Alice tossed the wrapped bomb at the pier. It hit the cement with a wet *SMACK*. The sticky wetness of the rag caused the whole package to stick to the surface, inching down slowly while the flame ate up the fuse.

The train passed under the bridge. The Kevlar ropes tightened. The bomb slid down. When it got as far as the channel in the concrete pier, the flame ran out.

The bomb exploded, blowing half the cement pilon with it.

The train yanked the damaged knot through the now sizably widened hole. It dragged behind the train, alongside the tracks, bumping over the hardpan. The raider in the cab tried to start the truck, but the explosion had shattered his window, and his face had been cut to shreds by the shards of glass. Blood was in his eyes and on his fingers. He fumbled with the key, screaming for help. The man in the bed had been knocked down from the blast and had smashed his head against the side wall of the truck. He drowsily pushed himself to his feet and stumbled over the side of the truck, falling onto the ground.

The bridge collapsed before either of them could get out, crushing them under 5,000 tons of concrete and steel.

Patrick exhaled. He fell back into a seat, his chest heaving, covered in sweat.

"What happened?" Ben asked.

Alice jumped down from the roof. "I made a sticky bomb using your gross body," she said. "Smushed two bad guys to juice, too."

Ben wretched. He turned and puked into his bag.

"Pretty brilliant," Patrick said, smiling and shaking his head. "Pretty disgusting, but pretty brilliant."

"And now we have some new harpoons to play with," Alice said happily. She reached through the window and finished sawing through the cord Patrick had started, then she wrenched the harpoon from the side of the train and hauled it inside. She admired it in the weak light. "Looks sharp," she said approvingly.

"Let's get the rest of these free before that knot catches on something else," Rogers said.

"Yep," Patrick nodded, getting back to work. The crew sawed at the Kevlar ropes, and Ben laid back on his cot, letting his arms and legs sink into the mattress. "Happy Passover," he murmured, but no one heard what he said.

49.

Horace ambled into the Baby Caps' car. "I have good news," he announced.

"I'm withholding my excitement until I hear said news," Patrick decided.

"Ditto," Babs frowned.

"We are officially in California."

Patrick brightened up. "Oh!" he said. "That *is* good news!" He looked over at Ben, who was muttering to himself about aliens and an ice bath. "Benny Boy! You hear that? We're in California!"

Ben loved California. He always had. Not the Napa-Sonoma, San Francisco, Silicon Valley circle jerk billionaires used to shit all over before mining gold from the manure. He loved the old California, the desert California, the Hunter S. Thompson fever dream, Clint Eastwood cracked-lip, Palm Spring flare-out, John Steinbeck Dust Bowl, Tijuana turnstile, high-mountain lonely version of California; the California where dreams hadn't even had the chance to wash out in Los Angeles because they'd never even made it past the swallow-up of Barstow or the bake-plain of Joshua Tree.

About two years after college, Ben had just wandered away. All of a sudden, Patrick couldn't reach him; Ben's mom couldn't reach him. His apartment was dark, his car was gone, and no one knew where he'd disappeared to. He'd been working at Blockbuster Video, a job he loved almost as much as he loved to complain about working there, but he hadn't even told his manager he was leaving. One night, he closed up the store; the next morning, he missed his shift, and no one knew where he was.

It turned out he'd gone to California. He'd packed up his old Chevrolet Celebrity and had driven it across the heartsick prairies of Kansas and Oklahoma, over the end-times wall of the Rocky Mountains, down into the hot-dirt desert of New Mexico, to Arizona, and on into California, where his car rolled to a stop just south of Joshua Tree Park, not far from the Salton Sea. He'd just stayed there, for months, living off of thin rations that he'd pick up from reluctant drives into Indio, or sometimes Desert Palm, and he'd squirrel himself out just as soon as he could, back to his tent, back to the deadlands, where he squatted in some middle place between Coachella and Painted Canyon, hiding away from the world...not because something had gone wrong, not because his life had been anything but stable, but because as far as he could tell, working as a video clerk with an English degree in a young person's town in an old rancher's state, life was too stable. Suffocating and stable. So he broke out his copy of *On the Road*, read a few chapters for courage, then packed up a bag and drove out west until he was as far west as he ever wanted to go.

People talk about finding themselves, in all sorts of places, but that wasn't what happened to Ben. He didn't find himself out in the desert; he'd found himself much earlier on, drifting away into ash in the mid-Missouri college town. He knew himself fully already, and he knew what he had to find was not himself, but the place where his self would draw in the world and make it right at home.

He camped in the desert for seventeen weeks. Everyone thought he was dead.

Patrick thought he was dead.

But one day, a postcard arrived. Patrick didn't know how Ben had found his and Annie's new address, in the apartment they told people was in River North, though it was really on the other side of Goose Island, technically in Noble Square. But somehow, the postcard had arrived, four months after Ben had disappeared. It was from Palm Springs, in the old-school style, "Greetings from Palm Springs," the town's letters huge and blocky, with palm trees filling their lines. On the back of the postcard, Ben had written only, "Get bent." Annie had framed it in a cheap plastic frame from Goodwill and hung it near the kitchen, over the old corded telephone that was bolted to the wall but which hadn't even had a working line running to it since at least 2004.

Eventually, he changed camps, moving west, moving south, but Ben stayed in California, broke and alone, for almost three years. They'd written him off as not dead but gone, and then Ben showed up at Patrick and

Annie's doorstep. He rang the bell like he was any other visitor. Annie opened the door. "I guess I'm ready to be here," Ben said with a shrug. Annie stepped out onto the sidewalk and hugged him. Ben didn't hug her back. He didn't remember how. But he did let himself be led into their apartment, and a few years later, the Monkey bombs fell.

"Ben," Patrick said again, shaking his friend gently. "Did you hear me? We're in California."

"The Angel of the East," Ben murmured. His forehead was so heavy with fever that Patrick could feel the heat radiating off of him from ten inches away.

Patrick looked around for his bag and found it kicked against the far wall, between two of the seat rows. He pulled out a can of peaches and wrenched it open. "Ben, you have to eat this," he said, gently stuffing a syrupy peach slice between Ben's teeth.

"Too gooey," he muttered back.

"The peaches or you?" Patrick asked.

"Yeah," Ben replied. He turned over in his cot and tried to hide.

"Ben. You have to eat this." Patrick gripped his shoulder and pulled him gently back over. Ben fought against it, but he was too weak.

"We don't even know if it works!" he protested.

"But we don't know that it doesn't, and it's literally the one and only thing that we know we can do that might help slow any of this down," Patrick said, his temper rising. "And in case you haven't noticed, we've got a whole train here full of people who are giving everything they have to try to save your life, they have scarred faces and broken bones and swollen brains, none of which existed before they voted to put their lives on the line to take a massive risk on a small shot. We have been smashed, banged, bruised, and broken, we have killed people to get this far, we have charged our way through this slaughterhouse, all because we want you to live, and Benny Boy, I am telling you, in the face of all that, if you cannot find the courage to eat one goddamn slice of one goddamn peach, I swear to absolute Christ that I will stab you in the heart with one of our new harpoons and hoist you up above the train like a dead, flapping flag until the flies eat your eyes from your skull and their maggots chew your face to the bone. Eat. The fucking. Peach!"

Ben gaped at Patrick. The corner of his eyelids cracked with the strain of surprise. He raised his head and chomped on the peach slice Patrick held between his fingers. He chewed it. He swallowed it. "Do—do you want me to eat more?" he asked, scared.

"Yes, Ben," Patrick sighed, fishing another peach slice from the can, "I would like you to eat more."

Ben ate almost the entire can. He might have finished the last two slices if Horace hadn't crackled into the walkie and said, "Hey Patrick. Come take a look at this."

50.

"I was force-feeding stone fruit to a grown adult man…this had better be important," Patrick muttered.

"Got something up ahead," Horace replied. "Doesn't look like anything serious, but wanted to get your eyes on it."

"Okay," Patrick sighed into the walkie. "I'll take a look."

He grabbed the binoculars and hauled himself up through the porthole. Up ahead, he could just make out what appeared to be two human silhouettes standing a dozen or so feet away from the tracks. They were holding large rectangular signs over their heads.

Patrick raised the binoculars to his eyes. He turned the dial and focused in on the shapes.

"Absolutely not!" he cried into the walkie-talkie. "Horace, do not stop, and if at all possible, swerve this train twelve feet to the right and run them over when we pass!"

"Umm," Horace replied, sounding confused, "they're just holding signs."

"One minute they're holding signs, the next minute they're barbecuing your best friend!" Patrick hollered. "Don't look at them! Maybe throw something at them? And whatever you do…"

"I know, I know," Horace interrupted, "don't stop this train."

Back down in the car, Babs gave Ben a confused look. "Who tried to barbecue you?" she asked.

"I don't know, I…ohhh shit," Ben grinned, choking out a laugh that dissolved into a small fit of coughs. "I think you guys are about to meet the monks."

***

Brother Toldus hopped excitedly from one foot to the other. "Brother Spyndthrift! Brother Spyndthrift!" he shouted excitedly. "A train approaches!"

"I see it, I see it!" Brother Spyndthrift confirmed just as excitedly. "After all these many days of waiting!"

"I would say many *weeks*!" Brother Toldus countered

"I would not deign to be so generous with my calendar beneath the eye of the Great Centralizer," Brother Spyndthrift chided Brother Toldus, clucking his tongue. "Surely it has not been many *weeks*."

"But it *has* been many weeks!" Brother Toldus insisted. "By the moon's count, we've been standing here for more than a fortnight, and only once in that time have we seen a train!"

"More than a fortnight?!" Brother Spyndthrift asked, astonished. "It cannot be true!"

"But it *is* true!" Brother Toldus said. "I have kept careful watch of the Book of Temporal Indignity!"

"You have many failings, Brother Toldus, but an inability to properly keep the Book of Temporal Indignity is not one of them," Brother Spyndthrift begrudgingly admitted. "We have converted far fewer souls than I had hoped we would on this journey."

"We have converted precisely no souls," Brother Toldus pointed out.

"That is indeed fewer than I had hoped. And with the infrequency of trains on this track, let us therefore hold up our signs harder than we have ever held them up before!"

"My arms ache at the thrill of it!" Brother Toldus beamed.

They hoisted their signs into the air and held them up as hard as they could.

***

"What are they even *doing* out here?!" Patrick demanded. His blood was steaming on high heat. "Their dumb brown robes with their stupid fucking hoods and their insatiable hunger for friends!" Running into Dark Ponch had dredged up all those old loving feelings of his sweet bison war-

214

rior, and the very sight of two members of the Post-Alignment Brother-hood sent him straight over the edge.

"They spread out," Ben said. He didn't know if it was the peaches or the general glee he received from Patrick's cartoonish suffering, but he was suddenly feeling a little better. "I saw two of them out near the zombie lab. They had a pet tiger."

Patrick narrowed his eyes. "I hope that tiger ate them so fucking hard," he said.

Ben nodded. "Wish granted," he said.

"Good," he decided, though he didn't say it with quite as much heart. His fury at the Brotherhood was more badlucklust than bloodlust. "I hope you *all* get eaten by tigers," he shouted at the monks ahead, but the words felt half-hearted, and they were still too far away to hear anyway.

Ben fished out another peach slice and popped it into his mouth. He wanted to be as healthy as possible so he could properly witness Patrick's meltdown.

"Who are these people?" Babs asked, holding her injured arm close.

"A frog-blood cult of real weirdos," Ben replied through a mouthful of peach. "Nice enough, but absolutely insane."

"Look at them!" Patrick shouted from above, to nobody in particular. He was staring through his binoculars. "'ASK ME ABOUT THE GREAT CENTRALIZER.' We're going fifty miles an hour, we're not going to stop to ask them about the Great Centralizer!"

"But we already know about the Great Centralizer," Ben reminded him. "Maybe we'd stop if we didn't."

"The other sign isn't even in English!" Patrick continued. "'DOO-BLAY OH-SEE NO-MOR-NAY.' What *is* that?"

"Latsish," Ben said.

"*I know it's Latsish!*" Patrick exploded. "It is a fully made-up, nonsense language! Who is that sign for?!"

***

"I'm really glad we went with the Latsish sign," Brother Toldus said happily. "It really gives a flavor of who the Order is!"

"That is true," Brother Spyndthrift admitted, "though I do worry about the message not landing, presented in this way."

"Brother Spyndthrift!" gasped Brother Toldus, aghast. "The message is clear as the sun! 'The path of the future is ovarian!' Surely our mission can't be written any more concisely than that!"

"I suppose that's true," mused Brother Spyndthrift. "Do you think the language barrier is an issue?"

"Oh, no," Brother Toldus replied, shaking his head vehemently. "If anything, it works in our favor, for any man who can read the sacred language of the ancient Muroos is certain to be a brother-in-mammaries!"

"Hm. Yes, I see your point," Brother Spyndthrift said.

"Are you all right, Brother Spyndthrift? You seem suddenly distracted."

Brother Spyndthrift frowned. "Well, Brother Toldus, it's just that as the train comes closer, I can see a man standing astride it. Just there, on the roof. Do you see?"

"I do see," Brother Toldus enthusiastically agreed.

"I know it can't be so, but as he comes closer and closer, I can swear that I know this man."

Brother Toldus clucked his tongue. "Surely not, Brother Spyndthrift, as we are so very far from home."

"It is unlikely," Brother Spyndthrift agreed. "Yet I feel a twinge of familiarity..."

The train approached. The monks held up their signs even harder. The Amtrak blasted past them. The man poking out through the roof threw an empty Del Monte can at them, splattering their heads with peach juice. "For Ponch!" he screamed as the train whisked him away.

Brother Spyndthrift gasped. Brother Toldus gaped.

"Great Centralizer!" they both cried in unison. "That was Brother Patrick!"

They dropped their signs, hitched up their robes and hurried after the train.

51.

"I think they're running after us," Lex observed, glancing out through the back of the train.

"Maybe if we hit reverse we can go back and run them over," Patrick grumped, plopping back down into the car. He mumbled to himself, "Post-Alignment Brotherhood. Unbelievable."

He checked in on Babs, who was in pretty bad shape. Her arm was swollen to more than twice its normal size, and when Patrick hovered his hand a few inches above her skin, he could feel the heat radiating off it. There was a huge patch of purple bruising at the elbow; it wrapped all the way around her arm like a cuff. Any hope of finding more snow was long gone. Babs shook her head when he asked her how badly it hurt, but she hadn't stopped quietly crying in over an hour, and by the way she was positioning herself against the seat, he guessed the pain had spread beyond her arm and into her chest. "We're going to find someone who can help you," he promised. "Dr. Gustheed might know how to set an arm. If she can't do it, she'll know someone who can." Babs nodded through her tears, and she tried to smile. Patrick felt his heart twist and crack. He gave her his best smile in return, then spun away before she could see that he was about to start crying, too.

"How about you? How's the crown?" he asked Lex, pointing at his head.

"The headache's not as bad now. And everything stopped spinning. I think I'm good."

Patrick squeezed his arm gently. "Takes a licking and keeps on ticking," he said. "Good. Alice, your face looks…like it's still on. Mostly."

"I've had worse this *month*," she scowled.

"Does anyone want to know how *I'm* doing?" Ben fussed.

"We know how you're doing, Slimer. You're dying," Patrick said.

"Yeah," Ben nodded, "but not as bad as I was dying yesterday."

Patrick raised a suspicious eyebrow. "At the risk of sounding right, can I assume the peaches are helping?"

"I think seeing you get so mad at the monks has given me life," Ben decided. He coughed into his elbow, and yellow-green mucous globbed out onto his skin. He wiped it on his ooze towel. "But it's possible it might be the peaches."

"You don't look better," Alice pointed out.

"Thanks," Ben grumbled.

"Your skin is still leaking."

"But your stomach's not filling up like a water balloon," Patrick pointed out. "And somehow we find ourselves in a world where that's a huge and surprising relief."

"I don't feel *much* better. I just feel *some* better," Ben said, suddenly feeling grumpier. "I can sit up for more than ten minutes, and I don't feel like throwing up every time I think of drinking water."

"You still have a fever," Patrick confirmed, pressing the back of his hand against Ben's forehead.

"I know! I'm still fucking sick!" Ben said, slapping Patrick's hand away. "I'm just trying to say I feel eight percent better, leave me the fuck alone!"

"It's hard to know if you're extra grumpy because you're feeling sick or if you're extra grumpy because you're feeling better."

"Shut up! How about you just be happy that the peaches are working at least well enough to make me want to punch you in the throat!"

Patrick turned to the Baby Caps. He held one hand up to the side of his mouth to shield his words from Ben and whispered, "He's an angry elf."

Alice snorted. "Yeah. We know."

"Screw you guys," Ben said. He struggled up from the cot and stood on shaky legs. "I'm going to go tell someone who cares how much better I feel." He lost his balance and almost fell back onto the cot. He was shivering so much he looked like a marionette being yanked up by its strings. He grabbed his sticky, goo-stained blanket and wrapped it around himself. "Good day," he grumped, and he headed toward the engine.

"Ben, you shouldn't be up here," Horace protested when he came through the door. "Go back there and rest. You're not well."

"What a joy, to be alive," Ben glowered. "How much longer to LA?"

"If we can keep up this clip, we're looking at about three hours," Rogers said. He let himself crack a smile. "I'm starting to think we might actually save your life."

"Don't jinx it!" Horace snapped, shaking his head like a dog shedding water. "The last thing we need now is a jinx!"

"All right, all right, don't get your cootie catcher in a twist," Ben said, rolling his eyes. He tightened the blanket around his shoulders and shuffled back toward the door. "Someday you'll graduate high school, and then you'll realize: There's no such thing as a jinx."

52.

Up in the mountains, overlooking the railroad tracks, Rascal plucked a stick of dynamite from the stack. He carefully threaded it down into the narrow cylinder he'd cut into the stone. The TNT was old as hell and sweating more than a little; just one wrong move would blow both him and the mountain to bits.

"Done yet?" Lainey asked over his shoulder.

"Jesus Christ!" Rascal screamed, nearly dropping the dynamite. "What the hell are you doin' sneakin' up on a man like that?!" he demanded. "Don't you know how sensitive this shit is?!"

"No," Lainey shrugged. "That's why *you're* doing it."

"Jesus Christ," he said again, muttering under his breath. He gently set the dynamite down so it touched the bottom of the hole in the rock. "There," he said, sweating bullets. "Five done. I think one more ought to do it."

They had ten sticks of dynamite in all, found inside some old crate that asshole Meatball had dug up in the mountain somewhere. Meatball was always lucking out, finding the most interesting things. A few months back, he'd stumbled on an old, half-drunk bottle of some rancid moonshine that looked like it'd been left in the bottle for a hundred years or more. It tasted like shit, but they all drank it anyway. And just last week, ol' Meatball had fetched a whole pig skeleton out of the river, not a single bone missing. But he'd really hit the jackpot when he dug up the box full of dynamite.

Rascal was the only one with any sort of notion of how dangerous TNT could be, on account of his great-uncle's appetite for old spaghetti westerns like *The Dirty Outlaws* and *The Forgotten Pistolero*. Rascal had watched those movies with Uncle Norman when he was a kid and dumb idiots were always getting blown up by sweating dynamite sticks in those things. He didn't know what made TNT sweat, but he knew it was a bad sign, and he also knew the older the stick, the more volatile it was, so he'd treated the crate of explosives like it was a swaddled and sleeping babe.

There were lots of fun ideas on how to use the dynamite, everything from fishing to excavation to some pretty devastating pranks most of the gang wanted to play on young Marty while he slept. No one much cared for young Marty, in no small part because he was always saying things like, "I got some dinner for you!" while gesturing crudely at his crotch. There was a sizeable consensus that agreed the most fun thing to do with the dynamite would be to try to jam one of the sticks right up Marty's urethra, but despite the enthusiasm, the plan presented insurmountable logistical concerns, so in the end, they decided to blow the hell out of the mountain instead.

They weren't just doing it to do it, either. It was part of a larger plan that had the benefit of being both strategically smart *and* terrifically exciting. The train tracks of the Slaughterhouse Run ran around the base of their mountain, which was not far south of Joshua Tree Park. Usually, to hold up their end of the Slaughterhouse bargain, Lainey and her gang would barricade the track with great piles of sagebrush that they set on fire, much in the same way Blackbeard the pirate used to put candles in his beard when he rolled up on a raid so that the victims would swear there was something supernatural afoot. "Ain't much that'll shake a man to his knees like a burning bush," Lainey sometimes said, and her daddy had been a Baptist preacher, so she would know. She wasn't wrong, either—the burning bush trick almost always worked.

Or sometimes they would hole up under the railroad bridge that passed over the arroyo that cut through the landscape like a deep, dead scar. A handful of them would wait down there, beneath the trestles, with rattlesnake jars in hand. That's what they called their version of Molotov cocktails, because they didn't know what sort of Italian or Norwegian or whoever had named them Molotovs, but they knew damn was it wasn't a proper Christian American name, so they called them rattlesnake jars instead. They were small bombs built of handkerchiefs slicked with creosote and stuffed into old bottles full of nail polish remover, or some variation on that theme. They'd hide out beneath the tracks with those rattlesnake jars in hand, and when the train passed overhead, they'd just light and lob. This worked particularly well on the Amtraks, which had wide open vestibules between the cars. Toss in a couple dozen rattlers, then sit back and wait while the train goes boom big enough to scare everyone off it, and the rest of the gang would be waiting on the other side of the gulley to take control of the train.

But the dynamite had opened up a whole avenue of new possibilities. The specific option they ended up settling on was a plan to blow up the mountain and flood the tracks with an avalanche of granite. It was just the sort of fear-inspiring "fuck you" to those dumb enough to take their chances on the Slaughterhouse Run that would draw admiration from the other gangs along the way. It was post-apocalyptic P.R., using century-old dynamite to rain run-ending hell on a train.

And because of Rascal's familiarity with fictional TNT, he was put in charge of placement and detonation. Which was how he'd ended up at the top of one of the San Jacinto mountains, drilling holes into the rock with a battery-powered driver and a diamond-tipped bit, stopping twenty minutes after he started drilling in order to let the battery charge in a solar device that took two hours to get it to full. It had been a long and mostly boring two days he'd spent on the work, but the parts that weren't boring were *extremely* not boring, given the volatility of the dynamite, so it all shook out in the end, really.

Rascal was reluctant to admit it, but he had something of an artist's soul. His daddy had squashed those creative instincts under his boot when Rascal was a small boy, and some weeds have a hard time regrowing in harsh conditions. But his interest in making one thing into something other and more interesting never truly left him, despite the bruises and the breaks, and now, with Daddy and all the world dead, he let himself take artistic liberties from time to time. Take the dynamite placement, for example; he'd scratched out a perfect pentagram in his mind, thinking with a wry giddiness that he could give a whole new meaning to "blowing the mountain to hell." He'd dabbled in Satanic culture on the internet during college, up until the bombs fell, and he thought now that if he was going to drill holes in the rock and stuff them with TNT, he might as well make a whole pageant out of it, even if it was only a pageant for one.

That interest in Satanic symbology was probably also a direct result of his daddy's bootheel. It was also something Lainey wouldn't abide, being so staunch and righteous and all.

He'd set the five sticks so far in the points of the star, but he really needed one more hole, right in the center of the star, to make it make sense. If there was a central pin of dynamite, he could tie together long fuses that would crisscross the stone, using the center stick as a pulley point, and make a really nice-looking pentagram. "Yep," he confirmed, nodding enthusiastically, "one more hole will really bring the whole boomscape together."

"Boomscape?" Lainey asked, spitting out the word like she might spit out a mouthful of sour milk.

"Landscape that goes boom. Just something I thought up," Rascal said proudly.

Lainey shook her head with annoyance. "Whatever, Rascal. We don't have time to drill another hole. Five sticks is plenty."

Rascal frowned. His mental canvas started to shrivel up at the edges, and it caused him to flinch in psychic pain. "Yeah, Lainey, but I gotta tell you, as the dynamite expert here, I think a sixth will *really* seal the deal on this bad boy."

"There's no time for a sixth," she snapped, clearly losing patience. "A train's coming. Right now."

"Right now?" Rascal asked, his eyes wide with disappointment. The mind-canvas flaked into a million dry, dusty pieces and scattered from his consciousness. "Oh no."

"What do you mean, 'oh no'? What is wrong with you, Rascal? This is great news! We haven't seen a train take the Run in almost two months and now we've got one right at a time when we're ready to make our big splash! This timing is straight from the Holy Spirit, and I won't explain to you how deep you must be in with the devil if you can't see this is part of God's plan!"

If you only knew, Rascal thought miserably.

"Plus!" Lainey said excitedly. She hit him on the shoulder. Her face was making some goofy smile, and her eyebrows were wagging up and down. It was weird. "*Plus,* this train—this train that's coming right now, will be here any minute—*this* train, Rascal, is coming from the *east!*"

Rascal's spine stiffened, and he said, "Oh!" Now that *was* surprising news! "They've made it through the Run?"

"They've *almost* made it through the Run," Lainey corrected him. "They beat everyone else out there. Every single one of them serpent-sucking sons of Satan 'tween here and New Orleans, this train beat every one of them. This is an opportunity for incredible glory. Do you understand that, Rascal?"

"I do," Rascal said, nodding. And he meant it.

"Good. Then I want you to forget about this nonsense bullshit about a sixth hole, and I want you to set the charges."

"How much time we got?" Rascal asked.

Lainey turned and peered out over the desert valley. Right on cue, the Amtrak came barreling over the horizon, not more than three miles away.

"They're moving fast," she observed with a nervous frown. "Faster than normal."

"I can get this ready in three minutes," Rascal said, scurrying around the top of the mountain and gathering the long strips of creosote-soaked twine he'd prepared as fuses.

"They'll be gone in three minutes," Lainey snapped. "I want this mountain to blow in two."

Rascal nodded as he set to work, tying twine to wicks and gathering up the bunch to make one long fuse that he could light from a safe enough distance. The fact that he had to give up his perfect pentagram was disappointing, but Lainey was right: It was much better to take down a train coming from the east than to agonize over some perfect artistic ideal.

Satisfied that Rascal was properly motivated, Lainey retreated back down the mountain, on the northern side, where she'd be clear of the blast zone and any debris. The rest of the gang was down there, waiting anxiously at the base of the mountain, fiddling with their weapons and squirming with anticipation.

Rascal hurried through the final steps of his preparation, double checking the new fuses to make sure they all connected. Once satisfied, he picked up the end of the twine and hurried over the peak of the rock, just as the Amtrak approached from below. He brought out his lighter and clicked it to life.

The fuse lit. The fire hissed like a snake. Rascal ran for cover and dove behind an outcropping on the north side of the mountain before the whole thing blew itself to shit.

***

"Three hours!" Patrick cried, actually leaping with joy. "That's almost like *no* hours!"

"It's several hours," Alice said.

"It's a *few* hours," Patrick corrected her, "and compared to *many* hours, a *few* hours is like no hours at all!"

"Does—does that mean we're through the Slaughterhouse?" Lex asked, so hopeful that he sounded sad.

"If we're not now, we will be soon!" Patrick replied. He clapped his hands and gave a "Woo!"

"I've never heard you say 'Woo!'," Ben said suspiciously.

"I've never survived so hard on so few hours of sleep," Patrick said. He clapped his hands against Ben's cheeks, cradling his face in his hands. "Benny Boy, we are *actually* going to get you that cure," he promised.

The gut-shaking rumble of a massive explosion tumbled through the train. Patrick dropped Ben's face and climbed up through the porthole to take a look. A cloud of gray smoke rose from the top of a mountain a few hundred yards ahead of them, up to the right.

"What is it?" Babs asked, clenching her teeth through the pain.

"I don't know," Patrick replied, squinting at the smoke. "There are no volcanoes in California...are there?"

Alice scurried up the bookshelf and pushed past Patrick, climbing all the way out onto the roof. "Anything?" Patrick asked her.

Alice's jaw tightened. "Explosion," she said. "Someone set charges."

Patrick felt his stomach drop into his knees. A familiar cold chill prickled up his spine and spread across his shoulders. "What kind of charges?" he asked.

Alice didn't respond. She didn't have to. Their eyes were glued to the mountain, and as the smoke rose, the air cleared, and they saw a huge chunk of the San Jacinto peak crack away from its mooring and start the deep-rumble slide down the face of the cliff.

"Horace!" Patrick screamed, forgetting that he wasn't speaking into the walkie-talkie. "*Go!*"

Down below, Lex found the radio. He snatched it up and fumbled with the button. When he finally managed to hold it down, he said, "Horace, Patrick says we gotta move." His breath was coming hard and fast, though he wasn't sure why. He couldn't see what was up ahead, but something about Patrick's tone was different. New.

Alarming.

"Avalanche!" Patrick screamed down. He jumped back into the car and sprinted up to the engine. "Horace!" he yelled, bursting through the door. "*Avalanche!*"

"I see it!" Horace yelled back. "They're pulling the whole damn mountain down on top of us!"

"Faster!" Patrick cried. "Push your buttons! Make us faster!"

"I'm doing it, I'm doing it!" Horace screamed. "I've got her at full throttle, but she's not a McLaren! She takes time to build!"

"Cut the weight," Rogers suddenly said. He looked at Patrick. "Get everyone up here. Blow the cars."

Patrick snapped his fingers. "Yep," he said. "Okay." He ran back out through the dining car shouting, "Code Stuff! Code Stuff! Everyone in the engine, *now!*"

Horace gritted his teeth as he peered out the windshield at the avalanche that was building speed toward the tracks. It looked like five hundred metric tons of granite was cascading down the mountain. The sound of it was ear-crushing. It sent jolts through Horace's jaw, as if he were grinding pebbles between his molars. "Those rocks are moving too fast." His whole face was pinched down into a pinpoint of frustration. His hands felt heavy on the controls. His bones felt heavy in his skin. "It's too late to lose the cars," he said. "We're not gonna make it."

Rogers set his mouth into a straight line. "I know," he said, watching the rockslide. "And we're going too fast to stop." He reached out and laid his hand on Horace's shoulder, his own eyes filmed over with tears of exhaustion. "But at least this gives him something to do."

***

"Code Stuff!" Patrick yelled, barreling through the train. "Code Stuff! Get to the engine! *Now!*"

Alice sprang into action. She sprinted into the dining car and yanked open a storage locker in the corner. Piled inside were three identical blue nylon bags, each with a white Amtrak logo embroidered on the side. She pulled out all three bags. She slid one back into the other car; Lex picked it up and threw it over his shoulder. Alice slung the other two over her arm and hurried to the engine, reaching beneath tables on her way, sliding out knives she'd secreted there and slipping them easily into her waistband, like some magician pulling her final trick.

The scraping of the boulders sliding down the mountain was louder now. It sounded like the old stone gods were waking, standing up tall and grinding their joints. Any second now, they'd bring their fists down on top of the train. Patrick skidded to a stop in front of Ben. "Still feeling good? We gotta go." He threw Ben's arm over his own shoulder and lifted him to his feet.

"Do the Baby Caps have go bags?" Ben asked, confused, watching Lex situate his duffel. "How come they have go bags? Why don't I have a go bag? I want a go bag!"

"You're an adult—figure out your own go bag," Babs sniped, draping her good arm around Lex's shoulder and leaning on him as they hurried out of the car.

"Go. Now," Patrick instructed. Ben grumbled but let himself be led through the dining car. Patrick snatched up anything useful he passed along the way—the walkie-talkie, a B-tier machete, the black plastic shopping bag that Alice kept the cherry bombs in. Bleakachu was nowhere to be found, but he didn't have time to mourn her. There would be time for that agony later. He stuck the blade of the lesser machete between his teeth so he could grab up an armful of snacks that were lying on the dining car counter. "Go," he urged Ben, his voice muffled by steel. They pushed through into the engine. It was a tight fit with all of them inside. Patrick dumped his haul onto the floor, then he reached back into the dining car and pulled the torch from the wall.

They were pulling up level with the mountain now. The boulders were hurtling toward them like meteors. "Hurry!" Babs cried.

"I need a lighter!" Patrick screamed.

"Patrick," Horace said, but his voice was so quiet.

"Lighter!" Patrick repeated, holding out a hand.

"I've got one," Lex said.

"Hurry!" Babs sobbed.

"We're not going to make it," Alice realized.

"Lighter!" Patrick screamed.

Lex fumbled with the lighter. It clattered to the ground.

It didn't matter.

The avalanche was on them.

The boulders slammed into the engine first.

The other cars were lost, too, but it was the engine that took the first wave.

"Hold on!" Horace screamed.

Ten thousand pounds of huge granite chunks moving faster than Mack trucks on an interstate smashed into the engine. The train car was tossed off the tracks as easily as a Rottweiler might toss a rag doll. The engine car spun like a cyclone as it flew down the mountain, chased by a tidal wave of stones. It crashed into the hardpan earth ten yards from the tracks. The boulders landed on top of it, in front of it, behind it, around it, smashing the steel and shattering the glass and flinging the car. The couplers broke on impact, and the rest of the train trailed them down the foot of the mountain, all three cars rolling like dice and smashing themselves into unintelligible shapes against the stone.

The engine slid to a stop about fifty yards from the tracks. A few errant boulders slammed into the side of the car, which was now the top of the car, and they bounced off and tumbled down the rest of the slope. Inside the train, the crew were splayed like the boards of a shipwreck that had washed up onto a cramped and grimy shore.

Patrick raised his head. The whole world spun. He was numbly aware of some sort of burn in his right leg. His ears were ringing. He couldn't see straight over the sound of the silence. He blinked and cast his eyes around. Ben lay on his side, huddled against the roof, which was now pointed out toward the valley. Babs lay on the earthen side of the car, her face smashed into the broken window, trickles of blood dripping down her face. Her broken arm had loosed itself from its sling, and it pointed out awkwardly to the side, a position that would have had her screaming in agony if she hadn't been knocked completely unconscious. The spinning and tumbling of the car had thrown Alice around like a paperweight in a cyclone; most of the knives in her belt had stabbed themselves into her hips and thighs, and scarlet creeks of blood streamed out from the holes in her jeans and puddled on the train's new floor. Lex had crashed to a stop on his shoulder blades, his legs propped up against the proper floor, his head bleeding against a set of lockers.

Patrick turned his head, looking for Horace and Rogers. He saw their silhouettes, motionless in the cab. He blinked again, trying to clear out the blood and the sweat, trying to focus his eyes, but the harder he worked, the more the world went blurry. He reached back to the base of his skull, and his fingers came away hot and sticky with blood. Dark sparkles fizzled in front of his eyes, and the train car swirled, and Patrick lost consciousness as the air cracked with the cheers of the raiders, who were sprinting down the hill toward the train.

53.

Patrick was in a bright white space.

There was no light source. Or, rather, the entire world was a light source. The glare was invisible spears slicing into his retinas. He tried to shield his eyes, but the blinding light was omnipresent, and even when he squeezed his eyes shut, the brightness shone through his lids. His head throbbed.

He sensed a presence. He cracked open his eyes and peered out through the slits. His eyes watered, staring into the space like that. He could just make out three figures—human, or at least humanoid. Two tall ones, each holding the hand of a smaller one in the middle. The every-where-light shot through them like X-rays. Their edges were thin, and from so far away, their bodies looked like black cellophane molded over black steel rods. They stepped closer to Patrick. But no, that wasn't quite right. They didn't step, they *moved*, sort of floated, sort of just appeared to be closer, then closer again, then closer still. As the gap between them closed, their bodies took solid shape, until at last Patrick exhaled with a sigh of relief. He knew these three forms.

Annie. Izzy. Carla.

Patrick. Wake up.

Their mouths didn't move, but their voices were clear as gunshot in his head. The sound of their sadness pulled down at his heart, stretching it like taffy, until it was too thin to beat.

Patrick. Wake up.

"Why?" Patrick asked. Hot tears spilled down his cheeks. "Shouldn't I stay?"

Daddy. The dark ones are coming.

The sound of Izzy's voice, so young and sweet, just as it had been the day she died, but now also pressed down by a desperate weariness that tore his chest. He would have given every breath he had to keep that sort of sadness from her in life, and he couldn't bear the thought of her experiencing it in eternity. "Oh, pudding cup," he whispered, sinking to his knees. "I want to stay here with you."

Patrick. Wake up, Annie said.

Patrick! Wake up! Carla shouted.

There's no more time, Daddy. The dark ones are here.

The dazzling light began to dim quickly. The world was suddenly like a halogen light bulb that was turned off and drawing down. From somewhere in the center, back behind the women, the world began to char. The fabric of this strange world crackled into flaky black charcoal and exhaled ash. The darkness spread from the center and enveloped the light around them. Soon, they would all be swallowed up by the burned and blackened space.

"Annie? What's happening? Carla! Can you stop this?" Patrick buried his face in his hands. "Izzy," he wept. "God…Izzy…"

The lights were flickering all the way out.

Patrick. WAKE UP!

Patrick opened his eyes. Rogers was shaking him by the shoulders, hissing, "Wake up. Wake up!"

Patrick blinked into the dim light of the train. Everything was on its side. They were lying on the wall. The world through the windshield was ninety degrees wrong. "What happened?" he asked. His mind was a bright glare of cotton gauze.

"We derailed. You have to get the kids out of here."

Patrick turned his head like he was moving through a pool of Jell-O. The whole crew was there, in the sideways engine car, some of them awake, some of them not. It was so hard to see. His eyes hadn't adjusted to the darkness.

"We're leaving," Patrick said. It wasn't a question—he was coming to understand that it was true as the words rolled thick and heavy from his mouth.

"Yes. Take the kids. Get them safe. Go." Rogers jammed something into Patrick's lap. It was a nylon duffel bag. Patrick looked down at it, confused.

"You're coming," he said.

Rogers shook his head. "No. You. The kids. Ben. Get them safe. Go find help. Get the cure. You have to go. Now."

The world was starting to pull itself together inside Patrick's brain. He shook his head. There were still a few pieces that didn't make sense. "Not without you. Horace. We all go."

"No," Rogers said again. "We'll stay here. Hold them off best we can. They're already at the train. Patrick. You *have* to go. *Now.*"

Lex took Patrick's arm. "I think we should go," he whispered through a creek bed of tears. Patrick could hear some other sound, some other voices, hollering out in the night. They were the voices of discovery. The mountain raiders, the ones who'd blown up the rock...they'd already made it down to the nearest car.

The engine had been hit hardest, and it had somersaulted a few dozen yards further down the ravine than any of the other cars. The other there were scattered out behind it like a star trail. But it wouldn't take long for the raiders to clear them.

Rogers grabbed Patrick by the chin. He pulled his face to center and bore down on him with his sharp, dark eyes. "Go now. You can get to the ravine. It curves around toward the mountain. Go that way. They won't expect you to circle up, and the canyon will keep you hidden. But only if you go now. Do you understand?"

"No," Patrick answered honestly.

The dark ones are coming...

Alice hobbled over, her jeans streaked with blood, her wounds still spurting red. "Come on," she demanded. She gripped Patrick's wrist with an iron claw and pulled him to his feet.

"Come with us," Patrick told Rogers. "Get Horace. Let's go."

"Not an option," Rogers said, in that same even tone.

"We go together!" Patrick insisted.

"Patrick. Go," Horace said, his voice clotted with phlegm. "A conductor goes down with his train."

"That's a captain and a ship," Patrick said. "Conductors clock out and live their lives on the land."

Horace chuckled. "Not this conductor," he said. That was when Patrick noticed a dark sort of glistening at Horace's gut. He looked down. The steel shaft that the conductor had fallen upon had impaled him through the center of his back, shattering his spine and nicking an artery before bursting out the front end, the sanded edge of it still dripping with Horace's dark blood.

"Oh God," Patrick said, scrambling forward and pressing his hands against the wound. "Stay calm. Okay? We'll stop the bleeding." He yelled back at Rogers, "Get me a towel!" But Rogers didn't move. "Get me a fucking towel!" he screamed.

Horace grabbed Patrick's hands. "Patrick. Stop," he whispered as his heart slowly bled out. "I'm too gone, and there's no time."

"I am not leaving you here to die," Patrick said, tears pouring down, sliding across his lip, wetting his clenched teeth.

Horace looked down at Patrick through his half-moon spectacles. "Son. It has been a great honor to know you. Ben has become family to me. True family. I think you understand that. There ain't no cure for me, but there might be one for him. You get him to it. Make this worth it." He patted Patrick's clenched fists. "This is okay," he said. "If you make it worth it."

Patrick squeezed his eyes closed. He screamed through his clenched teeth. His whole body shook with helplessness and rage.

Of course, Horace was right. The only path was the one straight ahead, with whomever could still make the trek.

"Let's go," he sobbed, motioning to Lex and Alice. Lex picked up the unconscious Babs, groaning as he struggled her onto his shoulder in a fireman's carry. He peeked out the doorway, out into the space where there used to be another train car but now was just chapparal and dust. The raiders were still uphill of the engine, swarming on the second car, and they only had a few seconds left before they were seen. Lex jumped down and hurried into the ravine, disappearing around the curve, holding Babs tight.

Alice followed him, limping on both legs but moving with the determination of a mountain lion. She slipped into the shadows, and then it was just Horace and Rogers and Patrick and Ben, and also a whole host of voices that would be on them any second.

"You don't have to do this," Patrick told Rogers.

Rogers snorted. "He can't buy you time on his own. I can do that for you." He held out his hand, and Patrick saw that it held the plastic bag filled with cherry bombs. "We'll distract them. Give you as much time as we can."

Patrick shook his head. "I—" he whispered.

"No," Rogers said sharply. "Remember. We're all small parts of a much bigger story. You and Ben...you're the story. This is my part. You understand?"

Patrick's heart had broken so many times in the last ten years, he couldn't believe there was any morsel still left whole enough to crack. But it did, just then, and he squeezed Rogers' hand with his own blood-soaked hand, and he said, "Yeah. I understand."

"Good," Rogers said, nodding once. "Save the kids. Find the cure. We'll give you as much time as we can."

Patrick wanted to say something meaningful, something heartfelt and important that would adequately express to Rogers, and to Horace, what their sacrifice meant, what their lives had meant, what their friendship had meant. But the voices of the raiders were close enough to hear whispers now, so instead, Patrick turned away, pulled Ben to his feet, dragged him to the door, tumbled out into the dirt, and slipped down the ravine without saying another word.

Rogers exhaled. "Well, old man," he said, grabbing Horace's hand and squeezing it tightly. "It's sure been a hell of a run."

Horace didn't answer. Horace was dead.

54.

What was left of the crew regrouped in the ravine, hidden from the raiders' view by the dip in the earth that formed the arroyo. But when they got as far as the engine car, they'd have been able to see over the rim, so the crew had to move. They scraped and hobbled and dragged themselves around the bend, circling back up near the mountain as Rogers had recommended. The canyon was steeper there and they were better hidden.

They hurried up the arroyo as best they could, dragging along their injuries and their more unconscious members. They'd made it maybe thirty yards when they heard the first cherry bomb pop.

The small explosion was followed by a chorus of confusion and alarm as the raiders scattered for cover. The bombs continued to crack through the near-dusk air, reverberating across the canyon. The raiders shouted orders at each other, and eventually they must have found a way into the engine car; Rogers had maybe thirteen firecrackers, but he'd only managed to set off six. Then the desert was quiet and still, and Patrick's small crew was on its own.

Nighttime was coming on fast, and he was grateful for the added cover of darkness. But one of the raiders must have found their tracks, because after twenty minutes of dragging themselves through the canyon, they heard the excited hollering of a man whose words they couldn't quite make out, but soon they could hear quite a few men, and it sounded like they were getting closer, fast. "Shit," Patrick spat. "We have to move."

Babs was still unconscious and slung over Lex's shoulder. He was sweating from the exertion of carrying her, but he hefted her up a bit higher near his neck and puffed ahead, picking up the pace. Alice moved like a panther, despite her injured legs, which hadn't stopped bleeding. Ben was mostly awake now and Patrick pulled him along. "Where's Horace?" Ben asked, looking around, confused. "Rogers?"

"They said to go on," Patrick mumbled. "We gotta go faster."

They snaked their way through the canyon. It broke away from the mountain after a time, leading them west. It was difficult to see the ground in front of them and they kept stumbling every few steps over loose sagebrush and exposed granite. The voices were getting closer, and they sounded sporting, like they were in on some sort of game. It couldn't have been more opposite of the wrenching grip in Patrick's gut. They couldn't keep running through the arroyo. Now that they were found out, they were like rats in a maze down inside the canyon.

As they ran, the canyon grew shallower, gradually rising up to meet the dirt. They broke free of the arroyo and spilled out into the open Sonoran Desert.

They skidded to a stop.

There, at the mouth of the canyon, they had run straight into a small camp, with two older folks, a man and a woman, sitting on sun-bleached tree trunks around a crackling campfire. Behind them loomed a huge RV with a retrofitted natural gas tank strapped onto its roof with metal braces. Before them was a meager meal of jerky laid out atop a colorful but faded Saltillo serape. Resting across the man's lap was the longest double-barrel shotgun Patrick had ever seen.

"Well," said the old man, shifting his weight and bringing the barrel of the shotgun around. "Hello."

They held up their hands. "We don't mean any trouble," Patrick said, slowly stepping forward, putting himself between the gun and the Caps. "We didn't know you were up here."

The man let his eyes slide over the newcomers. "Y'all look injured," he observed. "You shouldn't be on the move like that."

"Believe me, we'd prefer not to be," Patrick said, his hands still high in the air.

Now the old woman leaned forward, her eyes sharp and narrow. "What're y'all doin' out here?" she asked.

"Right now? Running," Patrick said. He indicated the arroyo with a tip of his head. "We've got raiders coming up on our tail. They'll be here any second." And indeed, the sound of whooping and hollering from the canyon was growing louder and louder.

"I mean, what're y'all doin' *out here*?" the woman said. "Not many people in this desert except for bad'uns."

"We sure seen a lot of bad'uns," the old man agreed, cocking one of the barrels.

"We shot the Slaughterhouse Run," Patrick said. "The men chasing us derailed our train with a rockslide. I'm sorry we led them to you. We're just trying to get away."

The old man nodded at Alice's thighs, at the dark, wet stains spreading across her jeans there. "You miscarry?" he asked.

"The fuck?" Alice spat.

The old man raised a hand in apology, though he still kept the shotgun pointed in their direction. "Forgive me, young lady, I mean it to be helpful. We've been on our own out here so long now, my ability to converse in an acceptable manner is in need of some practice. Signs of wound like that, I'm concerned you may have suffered a traumatic event that, if not attended to, could result in the loss of more blood than you have to spare. I'm a doctor, see, or I was, before the bombs fell. Not an obstetrician, but an ER doc, so I've seen plenty." He rested his apology hand back on the stock of the shotgun. "I'm just doin' triage, is all."

Patrick's heart was knocking against his bones. The voices behind them were close now. "Please," he said, not knowing what else to say. "They're coming."

"She's got knife wounds in her thighs," the woman said, pointing at Alice's bloody legs as if Patrick hadn't spoken at all. "That one's got a broken arm," she said, pointing at Babs' limp body, slung over Lex's shoulder. "Might be the elbow, even." She moved her eyes over the Ben, took in the slimy green texture to his skin, and a dark shadow passed across her eyes. "And we know what's wrong with that one, don't we?" she said.

"Yes, Mother, I believe we do," the old man agreed.

"Please," Patrick whispered. They were out of time. The raiders were on them.

But the old man continued on with his slow drawl, as if time were a netherworld force that couldn't penetrate this campfire realm. "Listen, honey, I know them legs must be on fire, but do me a favor and scooch maybe ten, twelve feet that way, wouldja?" he said to Alice, nudging his head to the right.

"Alice…" Patrick said, preempting whatever dark and righteous fury was burning inside the lethal girl's chest.

She gritted her teeth and bit back her tongue. Grudgingly, she trudged off to her left, as she had been instructed.

The raiders rounded the last bend in the canyon and sprinted up the arroyo, up toward the desert floor. Alice's departure from her original spot had left open a clear alley between the canyon and the campfire.

"I'm obliged," the old doctor said to Alice. Then he squeezed the trigger and shot the first raider dead-set in the chest with a blast from the left barrel. The raider's head snapped back, and his feet kept moving forward. The back of his head slammed against the earth and was dragged forward by his body's momentum.

The rest of the raiders skidded to a stop. There were eight more of them, each with a knife or a sword or a machete raised high, breathing hard and looking confused in the face of this unexpected turn.

"Y'all turn around now, y'hear?" the doctor said. He cocked the other barrel.

The raiders exchanged glances. No one seemed to be in charge. No one seemed to know what to do.

"I'd listen to him," the old woman tutted. "He's never been a man with patience."

The raiders elbowed each other. "What do we do?" one hissed under his breath. "They fuckin' shot Bobby."

"You wanna go back to Lainey empty-handed?" another one whispered harshly. "She ain't gonna like that!"

"Is Bobby dead?" a third raider asked.

"Just kill the old fool," snarled a fourth.

"*You* kill the old fool."

"Kill all of 'em!"

"He has a gun!"

"He's got one barrel left."

"Okay, you take that one, then we'll gut the rest."

"*You* take that one. I'm supposed to be on watch tonight."

The bickering continued for a few moments longer, and it gave the old doctor a chance to crack open his shotgun, pull out the spent casing, pop in a new one, and snap the gun back together. "Okay, time's up," he said. He raised the shotgun and blasted a round into another raider's shoulder. The man blew backward and screamed in agony.

"Rock salt," the old man explained to Patrick's crew. "Not usually lethal. Hurts like a sumbitch, though." He cocked the second barrel and fired again. This next shot ripped into a man who had been sneaking up on the group, using the chaos as his cover. The rock salt peppered his chest and he fell to the ground, writhing and shrieking in pain.

The rest of the raiders were in full-on panic. They bumped into each other, trying to scramble away. The old man took advantage of the mishegoss and popped out the two spent shells, reloading them easily and snapping the gun back together. But he didn't get a chance to fire another round; the raiders ran off, leaving their wounded to fend for themselves. The two men who were awake enough to feel the pain clawed their way back into the arroyo, bawling and screaming for help. The first man who had come through—the one who'd taken the shot to the chest—was still unconscious, and he lay there in the hardpan like an oversized and stamped-out rag doll.

"Reckon that's handled," the woman said.

"Reckon so," the old man agreed. He set the butt of the shotgun down on the ground and stood it up against the camper. "Y'all come on. Have some jerky if you want. Let's get them wounds seen to, then we can get you on your way."

55.

The old man introduced himself as Dr. Byron T. Huckabee, but he said everyone just called him Doc. His wife was Aggie, and they didn't seem too bent on learning the names of their visitors. "You won't be here long enough for it to matter," Doc said as he set out his medical supplies. He had a good number of them, too: bandages and scalpels and peroxide and a surgical saw and catgut sutures and clamps and slings and all sorts of useful things. He set to work on Babs first. He carefully removed the make- shift sling Rogers had tied and inspected her broken elbow, a piece of jerky hanging out between his teeth. He gnawed on it while he worked, the way some men might chew on a toothpick. It was a little unsettling, and almost certainly not hygienic, but it wasn't like the RV was a sterilized space. "I used to be a smoker," Doc said, noticing Patrick's squeamish frown. "Bad thing for a doctor to be, I know it, but once it has its hooks in you, it can be damn hard to shake. Can't find Marlboros anymore, of course, so I find it helps to keep my teeth busy. Keeps the cravings a little bit at bay."

He apologized to Babs for the pain that his examination was going to cause, then he gave her elbow gentle squeezes in a few places, trying to feel for the specific location of the break in the bone. Babs closed her eyes and cried through her lids, bearing down with her teeth and trying not to cry out. After a few tries, Doc seemed to find what he was looking for. He nod- ded and held her arm steady while he reached for a fresh roll of bandages. He wrapped her arm, tightly, forming as close to a solid cast as he could with just a few long strips of fabric. Then he fetched a contraption of his own design, a piece of six-inch PVC pipe that was halved down the middle lengthwise. Fabric straps had been fed through drilled holes on both ends. He laid Babs' forearm into the PVC channel, then tied the fabric together over her shoulder, behind her neck. "It's not ideal," he said, chewing on his jerky, "but it'll help you keep it immobile."

He pulled open a drawer next to his workstation and rummaged through it until he found the bottle of pills he was looking for. He shook out two tablets and gave them to Babs. "Penicillin," he explained. "May or may not help, may not even be effective anymore, but sure won't hurt. Unless you're allergic. Are you allergic?" Babs didn't know. She'd never heard of penicillin. Doc frowned. "Well. Guess we'll find out."

He let her chase the antibiotic with some prescription strength pain-killers, and for that, she was incredibly grateful.

He turned his attention to Alice next. She let him clean up the wounds on her face, but she dug her nails into his wrist when he asked her to take down her jeans. "Strictly professional, young lady," the old doctor assured her, but Alice wouldn't have it. She gathered up the alcohol pads and the bandages and stormed off into the back of the RV, slamming the accordion door behind her

Doc glanced nervously at the rest of the group. "It wasn't anything untoward," he swore. "The cuts on her legs are bleeding bad. She may need sutures."

"If she does, she'll know it," Lex told him. "And she'll stitch herself up, too."

Doc raised an eyebrow. "Interesting girl."

"I like her," Aggie decided.

The old man checked out the rest of them. He gave Lex some pain killers, too, and he even found an old chemical cold pack that he wasn't sure would work, but he cracked it and mixed it, and it immediately turned icy, and he rested it on top of Babs' exposed elbow.

There wasn't anything he could do for Ben, of course. He said as much, and no one was surprised to hear it. Patrick had only minor injuries, and he waved off the notion of painkillers. "All right," Doc said, nodding. "Mother, how about some tea, then?"

Aggie set to work in the RV's tiny kitchen, heating up water in an electric kettle and mashing a collection of herbs and weeds with a mortar and pestle.

Doc led Patrick, Ben, and Lex back outside, where they built up the fire and warmed themselves before its blaze. Babs stayed inside with Aggie, but Alice soon joined them, white bandage strips peeking through the holes in her jeans. "Where y'all headed?" Doc asked.

"To the coast," Patrick said. "Long Beach."

"You got people out there?" Doc asked. Patrick nodded. Doc seemed content with that response. "I wonder if it's whale season," he mused. "Aggie and I used to go see whales there, years and years back. Keep an eye out for 'em," he said with a smile. He stuck a new piece of jerky between his lips. He fanned out a small collection of handmade meat strips and said, "Anyone?"

They all declined. Something about the way he was chewing them until they were soddened and soft made the whole idea of beef jerky feel upsetting.

Doc shrugged and slipped the jerky strips into his shirt pocket. "We ain't been to Long Beach in years, like I said," he continued. "I wouldn't mind seeing whales again. Y'all looking for a ride?"

"We're looking to get there as fast as we can," Patrick said.

"Or at least before I die," Ben put in.

"Last wishes," Patrick hurriedly explained, giving Lex a look that made it clear he didn't think they should share their real intentions with a stranger.

"Yeah," Lex nodded, taking the cue. "It's all he wants. To see Long Beach."

Doc sighed. He stabbed at the fire with a dead, dry branch. "Plenty of worse places to pass," he said. "Well, I'll tell you what, Aggie and I just been talkin' about how we's feelin' ready to move on. It's getting' late, but no time like the present. Let's let her make that tea, we'll enjoy a cup, and then if you want, we'll load up and drive you out. Shouldn't be more than three or four hours."

Patrick exhaled. His exhaustion filled the chilly night air, and the release of it made his shoulders just a little lighter. "We'd be grateful," he said. "We've had a hard trip."

"I reckon you have," the doctor said, looking at Patrick thoughtfully. He slid his eyes across the log so that they locked onto Ben. "You must *really* want to see Long Beach, son."

Ben shrugged. "I heard their aquarium is to die for. Figured we should put it to the test."

The doctor bust out laughing. "To die for," he said, shaking his head and giggling. "That's a good one." Patrick and Ben exchanged uneasy glances.

"There's someone he needs to say goodbye to," Lex blurted out. Everyone looked at him, and his ears twinged red. "Um…someone worth the trouble," he added, looking down at his shoes.

"Ah," Doc said, nodding slowly. "Now *that*, I do understand." He raised his piece of jerky in a salute to Ben, then went back to work, chomping on the wet and ragged end.

Just then, Aggie kicked open the door from the inside and stepped out carrying a tray of mismatched cups. Her homebrew tonic sloshed around inside, and she distributed the tea to their guests, and gave a cup to Doc, too. "What's this?" Alice asked, sniffing the concoction.

"Just a little home-blend tea to help y'all relax," Aggie assured her. "Dandelion root, passionflower, valerian root, some mushrooms, lemongrass, lavender, a few other things. Sometimes I add sage, if I have it. Matter of fact, that's why we're down here. Picked some this morning, but it's still drying and won't be ready for a time yet."

"You get the girl inside set up with a cup?" Doc asked.

"You know I did," Aggie replied, handing him the last mug on the tray. Doc sipped with a loud slurp. A smile spread across his face like ice melt.

"That does do wonders," he nodded.

Alice sniffed at the tea. It smelled all right.

Patrick blew on his to cool it, enjoying the time around the fire, but anxious to keep moving. "You're sure you don't mind driving us out there tonight?" he asked, just to keep their priorities up front and center.

"I told our new friends we'd drive them the rest of their way to Long Beach tonight. That all right with you, mother?"

Aggie frowned. "You know I don't like driving at night," she fretted.

"You don't have to do nothin' of the sort," Doc assured her. "I'll do all the drivin'."

"Well," Aggie said, coming around to the idea. "I suppose it would be nice to see the whales again."

"That's what I was just sayin'!" Doc hooted, slapping his thigh. "Settled, then." He took another drink of his tea. Patrick raised his own cup to his lips and took a sip. It tasted a lot like the sleepytime blend Annie used to keep in the cupboard. His shoulders relaxed, and he let himself enjoy the campfire and the sounds of the small desert creatures skittering out there in the dust.

They chatted for the next half hour or so, neither Patrick's group nor the doctor and his wife giving away much about their present lives. But they took turns telling stories of their lives before M-Day. The Baby Caps couldn't remember much—Lex was pretty sure he'd grown up in Wisconsin, and Alice knew the names of the other kids in her foster family, but she couldn't remember the names of the parents, even though they'd treated her nicely enough. Mostly, Patrick talked about growing up outside of St. Louis and what it was like to be in college at Mizzou on Sept. 11, 2001, and how strangely the idea of that particular day had changed in light of the Monkey bombs. Ben didn't have the energy for stories, but he did summon up the strength to correct Patrick when he went wrong on the details. Doc talked about growing up in the sticks of Alabama, and how his earliest medical training had taken place outside his daddy's barn, where they'd butchered pigs and chickens, and sometimes cattle, when the farmer down the road needed a hand. Once he was older and got to medical school, he was surprised in equal measure by both the similarities and the differences between humans and livestock, when you took a look inside them both. He was just starting in on a particularly amusing story about his mama's chickens when Babs kicked open the RV door from inside and stumbled out into the dirt.

"I don't feel right," she said. Her brow was shiny with sweat, and her feet seemed unable to hold her firmly in one place. She favored her injured arm but actually fell backward and slammed her good shoulder into the side of the RV. It must have sent a shockwave of pain down her broken elbow, to be jostled like that, but she didn't make a sound. She just slid down the RV and plopped quietly onto the ground.

Patrick set his mug on the ground and leapt up to help her…but when he stood, the ground tilted around, and the campfire suddenly looked like he was watching it tumble around in a clothes dryer. He lost sense of which way was up, and he fell what seemed like sideways, but when his shoulder slammed into a hard surface, he was sure it was the ground, because some of the dust got into his mouth, and he had to cough it away.

Something hit the ground next to him and shook the earth with its weight. It was Lex, moaning softly and trying to speak, but his words wouldn't come. Patrick noticed that this own tongue was thick in his mouth, and he couldn't talk if he wanted to, either.

From his sideways vantage point, he saw that Alice was fully slumped back over the log she'd been leaning against, her back arcing over the wood like a fairy tale bridge. Ben managed to stand up, but as soon as he did, his legs shuffled him sideways, and he hit the side of the RV before crumpling down in a pile next to Babs.

"Good tea, mother," Doc told his wife, setting his own cup down.

"Got about a good twenty minutes, I'd guess," Aggie said. "Didn't want to use too much, after what happened last time."

"That's all right," Doc assured her. "I still got some of that vecuronium we found up north. Go fetch it, will ya? That'll keep them immobile at least."

Patrick's head felt thick and slow. He could hear the words they were saying, but he was having trouble processing them. Every part of his body felt like it was made of solid lead; each finger felt as if it weighed thirty pounds. This was bad, and he knew it, but his brain couldn't quite figure out just how bad it really was.

Aggie crept inside the RV and reemerged about a minute later holding a small glass vial and a syringe that, as best Patrick could tell from his limited vantage point, was pretty well-used. "What's the order here?" she asked, nodding at their doped-up guests and speaking as freely as if they'd not been there at all.

"Well, the big boy is obviously the prize," Doc said, pointing a thumb at Lex, "but he's gonna take some time, and I'm not sure the winch would hold him anyway. We'll have to take him back to the barn."

"And the girl with the elbow has some infection running through her," Aggie added. "You'll want to see if that penicillin can break it."

"Right. The green one's no good; don't waste nothin' on him—not even time, I'd say. Throw him in the gully, and that's a problem solved for him *and* us."

Aggie looked at Patrick and licked her lips. "You wanna do him up tonight?"

"Yeah," Doc nodded. "He's skinny, but there's something to work with there."

"More so than the girl," Aggie said, frowning at Alice.

"More so than her," Doc agreed. "You wanna string him up, or you want to administer the medicine, darlin'?"

Somewhere in the back of Patrick's brain, alarm bells were blaring. He could hear them like distant fog horns in a faraway ocean. But he couldn't quite make sense of what they meant, or who they were for. The doctor's words still weren't making much sense, though he could swear he knew each and every one of them by definition.

He closed his eyes. Maybe it would be better to sleep.

But that was not to be. A few seconds after his eyes went dark, he felt something pulling at his ankles. He couldn't move his head to look down and see what was happening, but he felt something like pressure drawing his feet together. Then suddenly he was being dragged across the desert floor, moving away from the fire, sliding past Lex, who just stared as he passed, his eyes all quiet and blank. The RV came into Patrick's periphery, and then he was hoisted upward, feet first, pulled up into the air so that he dangled above the hardpan. His body spun on a brand new axis, and out of the bottom of his vision he could see that his ankles were bound by a strap, and that he was hanging from a winch that peeked over the roof of the RV, with the benefit of a rope that was secured to its pullies and terminated in a hook that pulled the strap around Patrick's ankles. The winch churned until Patrick's feet were nearly pressed against the metal arm. His head hung maybe three feet off the ground. The rope stopped, and he swung there, just slightly, spinning in a slow and lazy pirouette.

He couldn't make his mind work out what was happening.

"Ready to drain!" Doc shouted happily, hopping out from behind the winch controls in the RV cab.

"Movin' faster than me," Aggie grumbled. The night was dark, and her eyes were long since shot. She was having trouble sticking the needle into the tiny bullseye in the center of the glass vial's cap. "Can't find my damn glasses," she muttered, knowing full well she'd broken them four days earlier but hadn't found the courage to tell Doc about it. He got mad sometimes, and it wasn't worth it to get his ire up.

"We got time," Doc reassured her, chomping on a new piece of jerky. He appreciated having something to do with his mouth while he worked. He stepped into the back of the RV, rummaged through his equipment, and came back out holding a neat and tidy scalpel. The sharp metal glinted in the firelight. Patrick couldn't help but feel a sense of awe at the sleekness of the instrument. It wasn't every day he saw something that clean, not for years now.

Doc carefully situated the scalpel so that the blade rested in his palm, and he presented the handle to Aggie. "You want to do the honors, mother?" he asked.

"Oh, I don't know," she said, still annoyed about the vecuronium. "It always makes such a mess."

"Darlin', I keep tellin' you, you just need to stand off to the side," Doc said, in a voice that made it clear they'd had this discussion many times before.

He's right, Patrick wanted to say, *the blood will spurt straight out, you'll be fine if you slit my throat from the side*, but of course he couldn't talk, and even if he could, he had the strangest feeling that saying something like that might be somehow inappropriate in this moment, though he only wanted to help.

"You do it," Aggie continued. She pushed his hand away, though gently, knowing full well how sharp the blade of that scalpel was. "I'll go set up the dehydrator. See if we can get this one ready for morning breakfast."

"I do love fresh jerky for breakfast," the old doctor beamed, giving his wife a kiss on her forehead. He held out the scalpel and placed it against Patrick's throat. "You got any more of that dried garlic, get it set out. We've got such an abundance of riches now, might as well plan on grease-fried liver, too, and the garlic jerky is best with that, I think."

I wonder if we'll be joining for breakfast, Patrick wondered dully.

Aggie hugged her husband and looked up at him with eyes that were dry, and wrinkled, and content. "Who's got it better than us?" she said.

"No one," he replied. He gave her another peck on the top of her head. "Now go on, get yourself inside. I'll set this one drainin', then I'll administer the injections to the rest."

"Thank you, baby," she said.

"You're welcome, sugar."

Doc let Aggie loose and returned his attention to the scalpel in his hand. *Oh, no*, Patrick thought, though he didn't really understand what was wrong.

Doc put a light pressure on the blade, and it sliced into Patrick's throat. The steel was so fine, and so sharp.

Something moved in the corner of Patrick's vision. He couldn't make sense of it, but it seemed to surprise the doctor; the old man lifted the scalpel from Patrick's bleeding neck and cried out in surprise. The gentle disruption of that simple withdrawal was just enough to set Patrick's suspended body spinning, ever so slightly, and just enough so that the whole bloody scene fell right into his field of vision.

It was Alice he'd seen moving, one small, shiny skinning knife held tightly in each hand. She leapt into the space behind Doc and Aggie as quick as a rattlesnake bite. That was what had sent Doc turning over his shoulder, pulling back the scalpel. But he and Aggie were old and slow, and Alice was angry and fast. The knife in her right hand she plunged into Aggie's neck, slicing through a carotid artery. Aggie coughed out a surprised groan, and Alice released her grip on the knife, leaving it lodged in the old woman's throat. Doc spun around, slashing out at Alice with his scalpel, but she dropped to one knee and made three quick cuts in his upper thigh, near the groin, slicing his femoral artery wide open with each flick of her blade.

Doc looked down at his crotch in horror. 'You fucking bitch," he managed to say before his legs gave out and he collapsed to the desert floor. Blood shot out of his wounds like a Las Vegas fountain show. He pressed his hands down on the wound to try to slow the bleeding. Alice took the opportunity to finish the job. She picked up her knife and, with both hands, drove the blade deep into his chest, through his sternum and into his ascending aorta. Doc's eyes bulged, and then his body went soft. Alice wrenched the skinning knife from his chest. A spurt of blood arced up behind it. She spun and grabbed the hilt of her other knife, still jutting out from Aggie's neck. She yanked it free of the old woman's meat, and another stream of blood burst out behind it. Alice took both knives and drove them into the backs of Aggie's knees. The old woman fell down onto her knees, then toppled over, hitting the dust hard with her face and exhaling one last breath into the dust.

Doc bled out behind her, the lights in his eyes going dark as the night that draped itself over the campsite.

Alice wiped the blood from her blades on the sides of her jeans. She slipped the knives back into their respective places at her hip. She walked up to Patrick and examined the small cut on his neck. "You okay?" she asked.

Patrick stared at her with confused wonder. "What?" he said.

Alice frowned. "You drank their tea."

"Did they...eat me?" he wondered.

"Almost."

Alice untied the strap around his ankles. His legs came free, and he crashed onto the crown of his head. "Ow?" he guessed, though he didn't really feel anything.

Alice shook her head, annoyed. She grabbed Doc's shotgun, found the stash of rock salt rounds, reloaded the barrels, and sat next to the fire, waiting for either the desert or her friends to come back to life.

56.

The whole group sat around the fire as the first colors of the morning sun began to twinge the sky in the east. "I've learned an important lesson here today," Patrick announced. "And it is to never drink anything that has mushrooms inside."

"I did mushrooms once," Ben groaned. "They didn't do anything like that."

"I was there watching you do those mushrooms," Patrick noted, "and I recall that they did something *exactly* like that."

"Is that guy dead?" Babs asked, looking at the raider who had been shot at pretty close range with a shotgun blast of rock salt. He hadn't moved all night long and sandflies were starting to seem interested.

"I have to guess yes," Patrick decided.

Babs composed herself. She was in so much pain. But she wanted to present her case in a way that was level and rational. "I know we've needed time to get whatever the hell they gave us out of our systems," she began.

"Not me," Alice said, reminding all of them, not for the first time, that she had been the only one canny enough not to actually drink the potion that had been distributed to them by weird strangers.

Babs rolled her eyes toward the sky and took a breath. "*Most* of us have needed time," she corrected herself, "but the effects seem to be mostly passed, and I don't like just sitting around in the desert with three dead bodies."

"You've never sat around with three dead bodies before?" Alice asked, raising an eyebrow.

"Not with deaths I've been *involved* in!" Babs replied.

"We need to move anyway," Patrick said, frowning at the corpses that littered the campsite. "If things had gone better..." He drifted off, thinking about the things that had not gone better the last five or six hours. In the end, he'd actually let himself expect that they'd make it through the Slaughterhouse Run. They would have made it to the Queen Mary hours ago. He'd allowed himself to want that.

But it wasn't what the desert had allowed. Now Horace was dead. Rogers was dead. They'd been drugged and almost butchered by strangers for jerky, and now those strangers were dead, and they were no nearer the coast.

They were so close. But the Queen Mary had never felt farther away.

"How's everyone feeling?" Patrick asked, glancing around. "Lex? Babs?"

Lex was sitting back against a log and slowly unfolding himself back to a recognizable state. "Okay, I think," he said, flexing his fingers.

"I hate this and want it to be done," Babs said curtly, huddled up against the wall of the RV, hunching over her injured arm.

Patrick lowered his eyes. "Yeah," he said sadly. He chanced a look over at Ben. "You?"

"I think I need more peaches," he rasped. The greenish sweat had returned to his skin.

"I feel great," Alice offered.

"We know," Patrick groaned, nursing a throbbing headache that pulsed through the back of his skull. "Which is why we've decided you'll be the one to drive us to L.A."

"Good," Alice said. She climbed around to the driver's seat and looked down at the wheel. She slammed her hand down in the center of it and the RV's horn blared across the desert.

Patrick frowned. "Have you ever driven a car before?" he asked.

"No," Alice said. She slammed her hand down on the horn three more times. The sound reverberated across the Sonoran. "Why isn't it going?" she asked, annoyed.

Patrick took a few deep and frustrated breaths. "Just...hang tight," he sighed. "I'll be there in a minute to help." He helped Ben up to his feet. Ben curled his arm around Patrick's shoulder. He hadn't been kidding when he said he needed more peaches; Patrick could feel in the weight of his friend just how much weaker Ben's legs were, and he didn't think it was just the effect of the tea. The heat of fever radiated off of his body, making Patrick's skin hot and uncomfortable even through their clothes. "Hang in there, Benny Boy. Not much longer now." He patted Ben's belly, meaning it to be playful, but the skin there felt distended beneath Ben's shirt. And they heard something slosh inside. Patrick met Ben's eyes. They pleaded like twin moons. "Aw, Ben, no…"

He was pushing into the final stage of the Green Sickness. The cure could be only a few hours away…but he might not have a few hours left.

"Don't tell the kids," Ben muttered, urging Patrick forward.

Patrick helped him the rest of the way to the RV and guided him up the stairs. When Ben was inside, Patrick shut the door, then went up and climbed into the cab. He reached over and turned the key in the ignition. The RV fired right up. "Press down on the left pedal," he instructed. Alice stepped on the brake with her left foot, and Patrick shoved the RV into drive. "Great. Now take your foot off that one and don't touch it again. Press the other pedal to the floor, and don't let up 'til we smash into the ocean."

Alice stomped down on the gas. The engine whined, the tires kicked dust, and then the RV lurched forward into the dark and quiet desert.

57.

They found pavement easily enough, some old backcountry farm road that had probably been desolate even before the end of the world. They caught up with State Highway 86 right before a small town called Thermal. As instructed, Alice hadn't taken her foot off the gas once, bouncing them straight through potholes and over apocalyptic detritus at nearly ninety miles an hour. The shocks on the RV were stiff as hell, and every bump rattled their bones, but Alice kept her foot down and didn't apologize for it. "I'm sorry!" Patrick called back to Babs from time to time. He knew the impacts must be tearing through her broken elbow. He could hear her whimpering, and he could see Lex's look of concern every time he turned around. But they didn't have a choice. They had to get to Long Beach.

They barreled through Coachella, and Patrick was too tired to make any jokes about hippies. They connected with the 10 in Indio, and the road opened up, giving Alice wider space to weave. This far out of L.A. County, the interstate wasn't too bad, though the closer they got to the Santa Anas, the more congested the highway would become with wrecked and abandoned vehicles. "It's going to get tough to navigate the further we go," Patrick warned Alice. "Do your best to find a way through."

"We'll get through," she said, gritting her teeth and gripping the wheel. "Just tell me where to go."

Patrick found an old Rand McNally in the glove compartment. It was well-used and well-worn, thick with creases and darkened in places with coffee stains that were decades old. The age marks made navigation a bit of a challenge, but he found their general location on the 10 and charted a path through Riverside, then west on Highway 91 through Corona and Anaheim Then they could jump south on Highway 710 right near Compton and take that down to Long Beach, if the road stayed clear enough. He didn't know where exactly the Queen Mary was docked, but once they got to the coast, it should be easy enough to find a three-stack ocean liner in the water. "Stay on this for a while," Patrick told Alice. "I'll tell you when to take the ramp."

"I don't know what that means," Alice told him.

Patrick sighed. "Great."

The number of dead cars littering the road increased with every mile, as they'd expected. Soon, Alice was swerving across the highway, dodging stalled pick-ups and hybrid sedans. She clipped more than a few mirrors as she tore across the highway like a recreational hellion, but Patrick insisted she was doing fine and told her to keep going and to not let her foot off the gas.

Every few minutes, he turned around to see how Ben was doing. There was no mistaking it: His belly was swollen, and so was his left side. The ribs there were starting to push up through his skin, forced outward by a lung that was filling with fluid. Not that he needed to see Ben's ribs to know his lungs were in trouble; the wet, sucking sounds of Ben's breath were plenty on their own.

"He's hotter than I've ever felt him," Lex said as they neared the exchange at Riverside. His eyes were wide and frightened. "Patrick...I don't think..."

"We'll make it," Patrick said, holding Lex's eyes. "Okay? We'll make it in time."

Lex nodded. "O-okay," he said. But the paleness of his face and the stammer in his voice made it pretty clear that he didn't really believe it.

Patrick pointed at the exit, which was choked with cars. Alice cursed under her breath, but she didn't let up on the pedal. She jerked the wheel and skidded the RV into the shoulder. It slammed up against the safety wall, and Patrick tried not to look down at the drop on the other side down to the surface road. The shoulder served them well enough, except there was an old Volkswagen Beetle that had its whole front end out of the lane, blocking their way. "Shit," Alice cursed, plenty loud this time.

"Hit it," Patrick said. "The engine's in the trunk. The front is light enough. Hold onto something!" he shouted over his shoulder.

Babs looked around helplessly at the interior of the RV. "Like what?"

Patrick didn't have any advice, but it didn't matter, because he didn't have any time, either. Before he could open his mouth, Alice plowed into the front of the Beetle, knocking it around. It jammed up against the Dodge Ram in front of it, and as Alice kept the RV barreling forward, the hood of the Volkswagen crumpled like tin foil. The RV took a hard hit, and Patrick nearly fell out of his chair, even with the seatbelt on. But the airbags didn't deploy, and the RV blasted through, curving around the exchange ramp and emptying out onto 91 West.

"Good," Patrick said, nodding his approval. "Now buckle up. This is where it gets hard."

"I *am* buckled up," Alice said through gritted teeth. Her adrenaline was pumping like an oil derrick gone wild.

"It was a figure of speech," Patrick groaned. "Just be careful with all the…"

He was going to say "traffic," but what he saw on 91 made him stop short. There were cars, yes—a *lot* of cars. More cars than he'd ever seen in one place since the bombs fell, or at least since leaving Chicago for Disney World. But someone—no, some*thing*, Patrick corrected himself—had plowed a lane through the cars. It looked as if some heavy duty monstrosity of a truck had smashed through the traffic with a heavy V-plow, knocking cars left and right with enough force to send them up and over other cars in the other lanes, leaving behind a perfectly clear driving path as far down the highway as they could see.

"That's bad," Alice said.

"Almost certainly," Patrick agreed.

"You think it's a trap?"

"Well. It could be that someone just needed a path cleared five years ago, got it done, used it, never thought about it again, and now is living out retirement up in Napa," Patrick shrugged.

Alice scoffed. "Or…"

"Or," Patrick sighed, "we just funneled ourselves right into a trap."

"Want to know which one I think?"

"I know which one you think. I think so too. But."

Alice gripped the wheel so tightly, the fake leather squeaked. "But the only way out is through. Yeah."

Patrick turned back to the rest of the crew. "What's our weapons situation?" he asked. "I've got my machete. Alice has a thousand knives."

"Fifteen knives," she corrected him.

Patrick started. "Wait, seriously? You have *fifteen knives*?!" He looked over her tiny frame, and at the tight black tank top she wore over her equally tight jeans. He counted four knives. "Where on earth are you hiding fifteen knives?"

"Keep looking at me like a pervert and you're gonna find out," she growled.

"I'm not—!" Patrick protested. "I wasn't—! It's not—! I was looking for knives!"

"Not much back here," Lex interrupted, his cheeks burning crimson. "A few pipe bombs and two Molotovs. They kind of spilled over, though…"

"I have a hammer," Babs offered.

"I have a machete," Lex added.

"And we have the cannibal's shotgun," Patrick said. "Probably more rounds of rock salt in here somewhere. That's not nothing."

"I have a spoon," Ben said weakly, murmuring mid-fever-dream.

"There's a tank of natural gas on the roof of the RV," Patrick remembered, "powering this whole thing. Worse comes to worse, if we have to stop, we can try to blow it up."

"It's not much," Alice frowned.

"No," Patrick agreed. "It's not."

The night was fully dark, nothing but the headlights of the RV lighting the way forward. The cars on either side of the clear path appeared like ghosts before the halogen halo, then whipped past and disappeared back into the ethereal blackness behind. They caught flashes here and there of the desert mountains that loomed to their left. The hillside was covered in tufts of small and unimpressive scrub, and a lot of it seemed to have been burned black by a wildfire that had scorched the mountain in recent days. This theory was given credence after a couple dozen miles by a light-orange glow that broke through from above the hilltops to the south. The flames were still burning out there, on their way down to Temecula, with all its dead and dry grapevines thirsty for the fire. The glow did nothing to illuminate their path, but it was somehow heartening to see it in the distance all the same. It was a good reminder that the world hadn't slipped away into the night. It was still out there, burning and waiting, like it always had been.

The cleared-out lane stretched much farther than they imagined it would. Whatever trap was waiting for them at the end was tight-lipped on the details but heavy on the anticipation. It was a strange feeling, as they cruised down 91 West, to be so grateful for something that you were so certain was going to try to claim your life any second. They drove like that for nearly an hour, their skin prickling on high alert as they wound around the base of the mountains at Corona and climbed the pass through Chino Hills Park, all the way until they started to see signs for Anaheim. Long Beach wasn't much farther past that. But as they neared the exit for Yorba Linda, Patrick's heart sank.

The cleared aisle veered off the road, leading down the exit ramp to Highway 90. Down to the surface road, where it was even darker, except for the barrel fires burning at this late hour along the street, and where it was even quieter, except for the human screams that pierced the air every few seconds like banshee wails before being abruptly lost to the night.

"We can't go down there," Alice said.

But they didn't have many options. The road in front of them was blocked with cars, yes. But it was even worse than that: The highway had been blown apart, not by big charges, but by explosions powerful enough to fully separate the highway into two halves, a short chasm of ten or so feet between them.

"What do we do?"

Patrick's mind clicked and whirred. He did some quick calculations. "Hoo boy," he said, exhaling in an uncertain whistle, "you're not gonna like it."

"I figured."

The explosion that tore apart the freeway had happened right beneath a double-trailer semi. From the look of things, the chasm had opened up right beneath her rear wheels, and the back end had crashed down to the surface road below, dragging the rest of the truck with it. But the front trailer had gotten lodged against the edge of the chasm closest to the RV, and the cab had jack-knifed beneath it, so while the rear trailer was dangling or touching ground beneath the freeway, the front trailer was sticking up from the broken road at a forty-five or fifty-degree angle, and it was stuck tight. Or it looked to be, anyway.

"Ram the semi," Patrick said.

"Are you serious?" Alice hissed.

"Dead serious."

"Don't say it like that."

"Sorry." Patrick turned around. "Hey. Put your seatbelts on."

"There are no seatbelts back here," Babs said. "I feel like you never listen to me."

"Find something. Now. This one's gonna hurt." He turned back to Alice. "Hit the gas. Hard."

Alice took a deep breath. "This is the dumbest shit…" she muttered.

"Oh my God," Lex said, putting together the pieces of Patrick's plan. "We're going to drive up the semi?!"

"Yes. Hold on."

They sped toward the lodged truck.

"Is it even wide enough?!" Lex squeaked.

"I don't know! Hold on!"

They ran out of cleared space and crashed through a pair of cars that blocked the way to the truck.

"What are we even going to land on?!" Babs cried.

"I don't know!" Patrick hollered. "*Hold! On!*"

Babs slipped down from her seat and squeezed herself beneath the small table, her broad shoulder blades pinching back against her spine as she wedged herself in. She bumped her cast on the table's single leg and screamed in pain. Lex grabbed Ben and gave him a bear hug, careful not to squeeze his organs while pinning the sick man's body against his own bulk. He ducked his head. He shut his eyes. Patrick held onto the ceiling handle with both hands. He closed his eyes and winced. "This is gonna hurt."

They hit the angled-up semi going eighty-two. The RV lurched up as the front wheels screamed up the incline. It turned out their wheels *were* wider than the trailer, or at least wide enough that all four couldn't find solid purchase at once. They tilted upward, fast and hard, the RV slamming them into their seats then pulling them up against their restraints. Alice fought the wheel for control of the tires as they skidded and slipped off the squared edges of the trailer. The back right tire slid fully off the truck beneath them and the RV started to spin. Alice gunned it harder, spinning the remaining three tires diagonally up the smooth metal surface. Momentum carried them as much as anything, and the RV shot up the ramp like a lit two-ton firework in a Wile E. Coyote cartoon. They launched off the end of the incline, and time seemed to freeze as the RV's wheels left solid purchase and the entire vehicle sailed through the air. They had been skidding around to the left as they sailed off the ramp, and the RV continued its slow pirouette as it arced over a knot of rusty, dead cars. Patrick watched the world spin outside the windshield. The RV had nearly come to face fully the wrong direction when it slammed down onto the pavement and all hell broke loose.

Or at least the RV did.

The entire undercarriage of the vehicle squealed as it ground against the pavement. The sharp snaps of breaking metal popped off like fireworks beneath them as the chassis was shredded by the impact. The front passenger tire exploded with a *BANG!* that sent Patrick's ears ringing. The hood latch broke loose and the hood itself flew open, flying so hard that it smashed into the windshield, leaving a spiderweb of broken glass in the center. Then the hood snapped off its hinges and went sailing to the side, knifing into the burned-out husk of a Scion a few yards away. The muffler broke off, and the engine—which miraculously was still running—roared into the night like a furious beast. Every single cabinet and draw inside

256

the RV flew open; plates, glasses, pots, pans, and every manner of kitchen thing rained down on the table over Babs' head. An Instant Pot smashed directly onto the seat where her head had been twenty seconds earlier. A carving knife flew blade-first into the Formica tabletop over her neck with a *thunk*. Small glass vials and plastic pill bottles showered Lex and Ben. The sharper medical instruments had been kept in the back room, thank God, where none of them had dared yet venture. The airbags finally popped; Alice's nose crunched against the driver's bag, and blood pooled out of her nostril. Patrick's neck twisted on impact, but not hard enough to do any long-term damage.

It hurt like hell, though.

Something up on the roof went *CHUNK*, and at first, Patrick couldn't figure out why that sound, more than all the others, set his brain screaming alarm bells in his ears.

It took a few seconds for him to remember. *The gas tank,* he realized, a cold feeling spreading through his gut. *The gas tank just came loose.*

He braced for an explosion, but after a few moments of still being alive, he allowed his shoulders to unclench, just a little. The tank hadn't come all the way loose, because it hadn't rolled off the roof; it was probably just one latch that had popped. The tank may have been breached or the hose maybe ripped out. If so, there wasn't anything causing a spark up there, and that was good, at least.

But there probably *was* a hole, either in the tank or the line. Which meant they were hemorrhaging fuel. Fuel they couldn't afford to waste.

Patrick turned his screaming neck, surveying the damage. "Everyone okay?" he asked them, ridiculously.

"No, you asshole!" Babs cried.

"Babs is okay," Patrick said, making a mental note. "Lex? Ben?"

Lex groaned as he unfolded himself from around Ben, who was so still he seemed comatose. Or straight-up dead. Lex carefully checked over Ben's torso, looking for ruptures but finding only the normal amount of green slime and grotesque swelling. "I think we're okay," he said, though he was moving so stiffly and slowly Patrick knew that couldn't be completely true.

Patrick turned to Alice.

"I'm fine," she said, spitting a glob of blood onto the floor between them.

Patrick nodded. "Okay. You good to keep driving?"

"Are you serious?"

"We have to move."

"We blew a tire."

"We blew the whole RV!" Babs corrected her.

"I can take over," Patrick offered.

"The hell you will," Alice snarled. She wiped her bloody nose on her forearm and threw the RV back into gear.

"It may not get us far, but we have to move," Patrick repeated. "Whoever wanted us down that ramp is likely coming for us. And we may be leaking gas. We have to get as far as we can before it runs out, or until the whole 'only have three wheels' thing does us in."

"Yep," Alice said. She pushed her foot down on the pedal. The tires groaned back to life, or at least the ones that had any life to groan back to did. Alice nudged the RV through a gap in the abandoned cars and managed to turn them around. The front passenger wheel ground against the asphalt and the whole RV slumped *very* noticeably in that direction. But the axles had held, and the tires did their job, pushing them forward. The shattered vehicle shuddered its way forward. Alice wove in and out of cars, moving slowly, but moving.

Patrick glanced back at Ben. It was dark inside the RV, and all he could see was a shadow huddled up on a seat, a head pressed against a window. The shadow's shoulders rose and fell, just a bit, with every ragged breath. There was still time. They could still save him.

They crept through the night, into the gathering fog.

58.

They made it about twenty miles before someone started hitting them with bombs.

They were fairly small explosions, but strong enough to rock the RV as it hobbled past. "How does everyone have bombs?!" Patrick demanded, ducking away from the window.

"They're easy to make," Alice said, leaning away from her own window as a fireball exploded on the road three feet from her door.

It was still too dark outside to see more than a foot or two outside the high beams, and whoever was lobbing the bombs at them was cloaked in the darkness. They were coming from the left, but whether they were being tossed from the surface road below or the embankment ahead or from the other lane of the highway they were on, Patrick couldn't tell. He watched as a lit fuse arced through the air and landed directly on top of the RV. Patrick screamed as it exploded, and if he hadn't been so goddamn dehydrated, he would have wet his pants waiting for the leaking fuel tank to catch fire and blow them all to hell. "Jesus shit!" he gasped when the explosion didn't happen. He slumped back in his seat and clutched at his racing heart. "Guess the fuel tank's still good."

A second something on the roof went *CHUNK*. Then there was a low rumble that slowly picked up speed and volume as it barreled toward the front of the RV. Alice slowed, trying to peer up through the windshield at whatever was on top of them.

"Oh, no," Patrick groaned.

The fuel tank was *not* good. It rolled off the roof and down the cracked windshield, a cylinder of steel half-full of highly explosive gas tumbling down the front of the RV. And it was on fire. What had coated the tank to make it so flammable, Patrick couldn't say—some accelerant or other added to the bomb. It had coated the outside of the tank, and the bomb had blown loose the second strap, and now the flaming natural gas tank was bounding off the exposed engine, igniting small, oily grease stains and rumbling toward the grille.

A gunshot cracked the night in half.

"Fuck," Patrick said.

He reached over and grabbed Alice by the shoulders. He yanked her out of the driver's seat, pulling her with him as he threw himself into the back of the RV. The bullet hit the gas tank, and the cylinder exploded in a ten-foot fireball.

Every window shattered. The force of the blast slammed down on the exposed engine, driving the entire front end of the RV down into the asphalt. The back end kicked up, and the floor rose to meet Patrick and Alice; they smashed face-first into the floor and skidded on their heads. The RV spun as it flipped upward, and for the second time they soared through the air. The vehicle came down hard on its side. The passengers flew down and crashed into the cabinets. Babs' PVC cast smacked Lex across the teeth, causing them both to howl in pain. Patrick cracked his skull on an open cabinet door; blood filled his ear canal and spilled down his chin. Alice hit the wall hard with her shoulder and heard something go *crunch*. Ben had already been lying on a bench seat on that side of the RV, so he didn't have far to fall.

Cabinets dislodged from the wall that was now the ceiling and crashed down on them. The hot water heater, a hefty cube of porcelain, broke free of its pipes and smashed down somewhere near Lex, or maybe on top of him. There was a TV in the cabin, an older 28-inch kind with tubes, and it crashed down from above, too. More plates and silverware rained down. A small cascade of water spilled down and soaked them. Wires sparked. Metal squealed.

The truck skidded on its side, throwing a trail of twisted, steaming metal in its wake. It hit a deep rut in the highway, and the dip and the momentum were enough for the RV to tilt itself back up on four tires—or three tires and a ground-out wheel well, at least. It came down with a *WHUMP*, and the crew were thrown to the floor.

Patrick swam at the edge of consciousness. Blood pooled beneath his neck, sticky and warm on the cold vinyl floor. Everything was still and dark. The RV was finished.

He tried to turn his head to see if the others were still with him, but when he tilted his neck, his brain spun like a whirlpool, and he had to lay his head back and close his eyes to make it stop. When he opened them again, he saw the beams of two flashlights flooding into the cab. He reached his hands out blindly, looking for something, *anything*, to defend himself with, but all he found were cotton balls and tiny shards of glass, way too small to be useful.

"Hey," Patrick groaned to the rest of the crew. "Anyone all right?"

No one said anything.

The RV was as silent as death.

Whatever was left of the driver's door was pulled open from the outside. A figure hopped into the seat, turning the flashlight onto the broken passengers in the back. Patrick squeezed his eyes shut when the light swept over his face. The person with the flashlight climbed over the seat and crept toward them, crunching over the shards of broken windshield glass. Patrick tried to pry open his eyes, but the light was excruciating.

"Don't move," the person said. It was a man's voice, gruff and curt. Patrick considered pointing out that he was way too injured to move even if he wanted to but decided to save his strength.

The light from the second flashlight shone in through the main cabin door on the passenger side. It wasn't really a door anymore, actually, more of an accordion-shaped hole that had once held a door, back when it was rectangular in shape. The second beam swung through the cabin and lit on the face of the first man. He had a rifle slung over his shoulder. He was wearing a black sweatshirt with the hood up. Beneath the hood, tangles of dark hair poked out from behind what Patrick could only describe as a vintage Mickey Mouse mask. It was made of burlap or cheesecloth, and it hung loosely in strange pouches near his chin and his temples. The fabric had probably once been white, but it had been yellowed and browned with time and spills. The mouth was painted on, a red oval surrounded by thick black lips. The nose was a smudge of black, and the eyes had been drawn on as simple circles that someone had cut by hand, and badly. They were different sizes, those holes. The one on the left almost filled the entire drawn circle, showing the man's eye and his eyebrow. The one on the right was much smaller, so small the man could hardly see out of it. It was much smaller than the circle that had been drawn for it. The ears were loops of wire over which more of the old fabric had been stretched, but because of the nature of time, the fabric there was badly worn through, and the exposed wire beneath the black-painted burlap or cheesecloth or whatever it was glinted in the light of the torch.

"Get that out of my face!" Mickey grumbled.

"Sorry," said the second person, a woman, by the sound of it. She stepped into the RV, and in the glow of the lights, Patrick could see that she was wearing a similar mask, except hers had a tattered red bow with white polka dots glued to the top of the head. "You get anything?"

Mickey shined his light in the corner of the cabin. "Duffels there. Some machetes and knives scattered around. Watch out for the glass."

"I know to watch out for glass," Minnie grumbled. "They dead?"

"Yeah, I think so. Not this one, though." He pointed his light at Patrick. Patrick shut his eyes and squirmed against the glare.

Minnie crept through the cabin and snatched up their bags. She found a couple of Alice's knives on the floor, and she pocketed those too. "You gonna kill him?" She asked it in the same way she might ask if he wanted cream in his coffee.

"Thinkin' 'about it," Mickey said.

"The real Mickey would never do that," Patrick rasped.

"The real Mickey was a cartoon, you dumb fuck," nightmare Mickey said.

"Yeah, and Walt's gonna sue the shit out of you when they unfreeze his head."

Nightmare Mickey tilted his head. The effect was chilling. "You talk a lot for a man who's bleedin' to death."

"I know a lot of words and I want to say them all before I go," Patrick said. He coughed up a glob of blood and spat it out the side of his mouth. "Meconium."

"Huh?" Nightmare Mickey said.

"It's a word I know," Patrick explained, his voice barely higher than a gasp. "I don't think I ever said it out loud. I can cross it off the list."

Minnie joined her partner and grabbed him by the arm. "Hey. Leave him be."

Mickey snorted. "Why? You listenin' to this shit? His brain's all smashed to hell."

"I don't wanna kill a...you know. A *slow* person," Minnie said. "It don't feel right."

"Hey," Patrick protested weakly.

Mickey sighed. "Yeah. You're right. Quick sweep and let's get outta here."

"Yeah," Minnie said, sounding relieved. "This highway gives me the heebies. Three different nights since we been here, I seen zombies running up along here."

"Yeah, yeah," Mickey grumbled. "Let's get the shit and go."

They ripped through the RV, yanking up anything that looked valuable and stuffing it into the stolen packs. "You guys are in trouble," Patrick sighed as they ransacked the ruined cabin. "This is the part where Alice jumps you and uses your own intestines as a garrote wire."

But Alice didn't jump. Alice didn't move. Alice lay still and crumpled in the corner like a wadded-up napkin that had missed the trash can.

The nightmare mice finished their sweep. They cinched the bags shut, threw them over their shoulders, and without so much as a second look over their shoulder, they slipped out of the RV and ran away into the darkness.

Patrick lay there for another few minutes, his body unwilling to cooperate with his commands, his mind racing in the quiet darkness. Why wasn't anyone else making noise? Why wasn't anyone else moving? He turned his head, biting back the urge to throw up as the world spun between his ears. But he made himself turn, made himself look. All he saw were canyons and valleys, lumps of people and fallen things, all jumbled together on the floor. He pushed his will down into his legs and, groaning against the strain, managed to bend one leg and plant that sneaker flat on the floor. He pushed off his heel and rolled into a kneeling crouch, which was about as much as he could do for three or four minutes, until he caught his breath. Then, slowly, he made his way across the RV, toward the still pile of his friends.

He found Ben's shoes sticking out from beneath the water heater. It had lodged against the wall, catching him underneath, but it didn't seem to have broken any bones inside. Patrick struggled with the small box and rolled it away. He crawled closer, inspecting Ben's stomach. It was swollen, but his shirt wasn't soaked through with the dark green goo that would indicate a rupture. His skin was still slick with the normal amount of sickly slime. Patrick gently pressed on Ben's abdomen, just to make sure. His fingers squished into the swollen sack of fluids that was Ben's belly. Everything was still intact.

"Stop touching me," Ben grumbled.

Patrick looked up, surprised. "I don't know if I'm more surprised that you're awake or that you're alive."

"I'm not, I'm dead. Go away."

"No such luck," Patrick said, shaking his head. "We gotta get you out of here." He patted Ben's leg. Now that he was safe, it was on to the dreaded task of checking on the kids.

Lex was closest. He lay on his back. His eyes were closed. He wasn't moving. By the look of it, the TV had smashed over his head; the thick glass tube was cracked in a decidedly skull-sized web, and the tendrils of jagged glass were clogged with Lex's hair and mottled with his blood. Patrick leaned his ear down to Lex's chest. He exhaled with relief when he heard the heartbeat.

"He got clocked. Hard. But he's alive."

"The others?" Ben croaked.

Patrick frowned. He shuffled over next to Babs. She was breathing—he could see her shoulder rising and falling. Her PVC sling had come loose, and her broken elbow was twisted behind her back and pinned beneath her waist. He gently rolled her forward onto her stomach, clearing away debris so she could lie more or less comfortably flat on the floor, taking the pressure off of her broken arm. He reset the sling as best he could and hoped it would at least give the injury some stability until she regained consciousness.

He turned toward Alice. She lay huddled against the back of the driver's chair, looking in the darkness more like a broken bird than a warrior. He half-walked, half-crawled to her, and his sneaker slipped out from under him when it hit the trail of her blood. He fell into a sticky red stain that was puddling down from her body.

The RV wall helped tell the story. Even in the darkness, he could make out a shiny spray of Alice's blood spattered against the paneling, about a third of the way up the wall. She had cracked her head in the fall when the truck flipped over on its side, hard enough to leave a smear of blood on the wall. Hard enough to trickle out into a pool on the floor. "Oh, God..." Patrick groaned, his stomach sick.

Ben perked up at that. "What? Is she okay?"

Patrick didn't answer. He scraped his way to her body. He placed one hand on her shoulder, and with the other, he gently cradled her head. Her black hair was matted and shiny with blood. He carefully rolled her over onto her back so that she came to a rest lying in his lap. Her eyes were open a little and staring.

"Patrick," Ben said, his voice twinged with panic. "Is she okay?"

Patrick closed his eyes. He shook his head. "Ben..." he said quietly. He took a deep breath. He turned over his shoulder. "She's gone," he finally whispered.

"Fuck you 'I'm gone,'" Alice sneered. Her voice was a desert wind through animal bones, dusty and dry. But it was there, and it was hers.

Patrick squeaked in surprise and nearly dropped her back onto her head. "*Actual* zombie!" he cried.

"Stop holding me like a baby," Alice said.

Patrick frowned. "Sorry." He laid her gently back on the floor. "I thought you were dead."

"It's a necrophilia thing," Ben piped up from behind them.

"It is not!" Patrick yelled.

Alice closed her eyes and took a few deep breaths. Her nose was broken, and her inhales were staggered. Patrick found a pair of pants in the rubble and held them against the wound in her head. She pushed him off and held the pants there herself, sopping up the blood. "We good?" she asked.

"Are *we* good?" Patrick asked, surprised. "Kid, *you're* not good, and no, we're not good."

"Who's dead?"

"Oh," Patrick said. "Well…no one. Technically."

"Then we're good."

"I don't think *I* would categorize it that way."

"We're good," came Babs' voice from the darkness. She pushed through the detritus and slowly raised herself up to her knees. She refitted the sling to make it taut. They couldn't see much of her face through the gloom, but the ridges of her brow were wrinkled, and her jaw was set. She must have been in incredible pain. "Good to keep moving," she said, though the way her breath carried her words, it was like someone had just punched her in the gut.

"You are not good to keep moving. None of us are good to keep moving." He caught himself, and he held up his hands, trying to grab back some of that last sentence. "Well…I am. I think."

"You look like shit," Ben told him.

"You can't even see me. It's pitch black in here."

"Yeah, and I still know you look like shit," he replied, coughing up a lump of green phlegm. "That's how much like shit you look."

"I can go," he said, ignoring Ben. "I can get Ben to the boat."

"Ship," Alice corrected him.

"I swear to God…" Patrick muttered, rubbing his forehead.

"Wait," said Babs, "so you're going to take Ben to the doctor and leave us all here to die?"

"No!" Patrick exclaimed. "And—boy, I sure wish you hadn't put it like that."

"That's what you're doing."

"Look. Eight seconds ago, all three of you were in blood-soaked comas. Lex is *still* in a coma!"

"No I'm not," Lex said, rousing.

"Oh, for fuck's sake, what is this, a Hallmark movie?!" Patrick cried. "Will you all pass back out and fucking *rest*?!"

265

"What's happening?" Lex groaned. He touched the top of his head gently and winced.

"You're all in severe medical crisis and you need to lie still while I go get a doctor."

"He's trying to ditch us," Alice translated.

"I am not!"

Lex tilted his head. "After all that, you would just…leave Ben behind?"

"Oh, no, he's bringing Ben," Babs said, and Patrick couldn't see it, but he could practically *hear* her rolling her eyes.

"I am the chosen one," Ben whispered. The fever was taking him again.

"I'm not—" Patrick began, his words fighting for dominance over his frustration. He closed his eyes and bit his fist. He tried again. "Listen. What I'm saying is Ben needs help *now*. You all need help *very soon*. I need help not long after. The person in the best shape can take the person in the worst shape and get help that he then brings back to the people in middle shape."

"This sounds like an SAT problem," Babs soured.

"How do you even know what an SAT is?!" Patrick exploded.

"How much farther is it?" Lex said, his voice quiet and thoughtful and totally at odds with Patrick's.

Patrick blustered through his lips. "I don't know. Ten miles? Fifteen?"

"Fifteen miles?" Babs asked, incredulous. She snorted. "Yeah, okay, we're not stopping now."

"Your arm is the size of a ham!" Patrick said. "Stay here and rest it!"

"Not a chance," Babs replied.

Patrick took a deep breath. He counted to five. It did not calm him down. "You guys. Look. This place is safe. There's no one else out here."

"Except for the people who blew up our gas tank and robbed us," Lex pointed out.

"Okay. Yes. They were here, now they're gone. Now this is just a junked RV on a junked-up highway full of junked-out cars in a junked-out world. It is perfect camouflage. And if anyone *does* come, just play dead. Just act like you look!"

"Stop," Alice said, and she spoke with such finality that everyone froze. She was still lying on her back with her eyes closed, but she held a finger in the air and said, "Listen." She tilted her finger slowly toward the passenger side of the RV until it was pointing directly at the door.

And at the sounds coming from the other side.

They were quiet—so quiet that Patrick couldn't understand how she had heard them, and he had to admit that maybe she really was in a lot better shape than he thought. They strained their ears to hear the noise that sounded like a tin can full of rattlesnakes being piped across the desert by a loudspeaker. But the sound got louder as the sound got closer, and it was only a few seconds before everyone knew what was hurtling toward them.

"Runners," Babs breathed.

Patrick held up his hands for calm. "It's okay," he assured them. "You've all got the Zom-Be-Gone. Now, it sounds like a big horde, and it's going to be scary as hell to watch them rush us, but trust me, they won't get within ten feet. We're safe."

The RV filled with uncomfortable silence. "Um," Lex said.

"Uh," Babs put in.

Patrick cocked an eyebrow. "What? What's wrong?"

"We...umm..." Babs started.

· "We cut off the wristbands," Alice finished for her. "They weren't comfortable."

"You cut off the wristbands?!" Patrick hollered, throwing up his hands. "The life-saving, miracle-of-science wristbands that made you zombie-proof?! You *cut* them *off*?!"

"It was uncomfortable!" Babs echoed. "Mine gave me a rash!"

"Well what do you think fucking *zombie teeth* are going to give you, Babs?!"

"We were on a train!" she wailed. "And you had more!"

"I *did* have more, and now I *don't* have more, because Mickey fucking Kruger took it all!" Patrick's heart was skipping beats. A clamp tightened around his chest. Hot prickles crept along the wrinkles of his brain. "Great, now I'm having a panic attack," he complained.

Lex looked nervously toward the RV door. "What do we do?" he asked.

"We fly," Ben said dreamily.

Patrick pushed the air out of his lungs in a low, resigned groan. "Well, Lex, I guess the RV is no longer the safe haven it once was."

"Never was," Alice corrected him.

"So, yeah," Patrick said, ignoring her, "I guess Ben's right. We all better fly." He slid into the front seat and kicked open the twisted door. "The good thing about being robbed is, now we travel super light."

He hopped out of the RV, then he helped the others down, one after the other, and herded them down the highway. He held a finger to his lips, signaling for quiet as they took off through the dead cars. They were a bloody and broken crew, more stumble than hustle, and Patrick winced as Lex took a bad step and glanced off the fender of a Buick. "Almost there," he reminded himself. "Almost there."

The moaning buzz of the duster horde was rising. Patrick chanced a peek around the back end of the RV. He couldn't make out the runners, not really—just a shadow of movement against the darkness of the night. Best he could tell, they were streaming up the nearest on-ramp, about fifty yards away, and they were moving fast, for a crowd of mindless hungry things ping-ponging off a minefield of abandoned trucks.

Patrick felt weirdly off-balance without the weight of a knapsack keeping him grounded. His shoulders felt like they were filled with helium. He wriggled his neck and tried not to think about the things they'd lost. "Just you and me, little friend," he said, looking down at Izzy's princess watch. "Time to finish the run."

59.

"Where are we going?" Babs shouted over her shoulder, huffing and puffing as she weaved through the cars.

"Away from the zombies," Lex called back, narrowly dodging a Stratus.

"Helpful," Babs said. She looked back and saw Patrick hobbling along with Ben at the back of the pack. "We're not fast enough."

"No kidding," Alice said, sprinting ahead.

The dusters were nearly on them. The cars and trucks behind them rocked and swayed as iron-skulled zombies stumbled into them, fell down, picked themselves up, and sprinted on. It was impossible to tell how many were on their tail, but their moaning had become a deafening roar, and it was safe to say the crew was outnumbered by at least a factor of one hundred.

Patrick swore as he pulled Ben along. "Benny Boy, I know you're mostly dead, but would it kill you to put some weight on your legs?"

"It's gummy," Ben replied, resting his head on Patrick's shoulder.

Patrick grunted. "Great."

A duster at the front of the pack leapt over the hood of an old Sebring and lunged at them. Patrick didn't even flinch; the duster hit the scent of the Zom-Be-Gone on his wrist like it had slammed into an invisible wall. The creature screeched and clawed its way back into the horde, where it was trampled by the mob of dusters with a series of loud crunches.

"We have to go south!" Patrick bellowed at the Baby Caps, who were pulling ahead. "Get down to the surface road!" Another two dusters leapt at him and Ben, only to meet the same fate as the first.

The princess watch would keep the vanguard at bay for a minute or two. But it wouldn't hold against the horde.

Babs peeked over the edge of the highway rail. The road below was a good thirty-foot drop. "Cool, we're supposed to jump onto asphalt?"

"Aim for a car," Lex suggested.

"Breaking bones either way," Babs glowered.

"Move." Alice ran over to a fire truck that was laid over on its side. She gripped the water hose and yanked it loose. The spool was stiff with rust, but she got it moving. She dragged the hose over to the railing and threw it over the side. Together, the Baby Caps pulled at the hose, grabbing enough slack for the nozzle end to touch the highway surface below. With the hose the right length, Alice found a pipe wrench in the fire truck's storage closet and jammed it into the spool, jamming it in place so it wouldn't unravel when they put their weight on the line. She looked back down the highway. She could see the zombies now, or some of them anyway. They were crashing through the cars like a river. The first line of them were nipping at Patrick's heels, but the repellent was doing its work. She cursed herself silently for cutting off her wristband. Stupid, stupid, stupid.

She wouldn't be that stupid again.

"Go," she told the others.

Babs' face was drawn down with helplessness. "But Patrick…"

"He's fine," Alice said. And as they watched, the pack of zombies broke around him, giving him a wide berth. They sprinted up along the edges of the highway, struggling with the scent, then finally making it past the invisible barrier and closing back together, leaving Patrick and Ben alone in a fifteen-foot bubble that was bobbing slowly down the duster river.

"Go!" Alice said again, sharply. "Now!"

Lex went first, throwing a leg over the side of the railing and easing himself over the edge. He motioned for Babs to grab the rope just above him. She did so with her good hand, and she carefully laced her broken arm around his neck. Straining at the weight of the two of them, Lex started lowering them down the hose. They made it about ten feet before he lost his grip, and they slid down the rest of the way. Lex screamed, his hands burned raw by the filthy nylon. They hit the asphalt hard. Babs unhooked her bad arm just in time to avoid having it crushed by Lex's shoulders. They landed in a heap, their breath knocked out, Lex's shoulder blades shooting with pain.

"Run!" Alice said. She leapt on top of the railing and gripped the fire hose. She moved with an easy grace, passing hand over hand down the line until she landed lightly on the highway.

"Show-off," Babs muttered.

"Okay, don't run," Alice said, annoyed. She looked up at the overpass. A wave of zombies crashed against the railing, knocking it off its brackets and smashing right through the metal. They fell over the side, snarling and snapping their jaws. Their stiff, jagged arms wheeled as they plummeted through the air. Hard as their arteries were, they were no match for gravity, and the *CRACK-CRACK-CRACK* of crunching bones echoed across the highway retaining walls as the zombies fell to their deaths.

Or at least to their immobilizations, Alice corrected herself, staring down with interest at a mangled duster whose neck was broken at a ninety-degree angle. Its teeth were still snapping at her foot.

The wave of falling zombies thinned, and Patrick and Ben poked their heads over the edge of the overpass. "Well, this looks safe," Patrick decided.

He looked out over the road below, at the abandoned Hyundai crossovers and the scattered bodies of fallen dusters. The road stretched to the south, all the way to Long Beach, if he remembered the map correctly. On either side of the road were the hulking husks of department stores and gas stations, their windows smashed out, their roofs burned off or caving in. It was a familiar tableau of post-apocalyptic suburbia.

But just as he leaned down to grab the hose, something not-so-familiar caught his eye, over near the sidewalk next to a shattered, busted-up bus stop. He squinted into the gloom, doing a quick count in his head as the tidal wave of runners broke around him, filling the overpass and raining down on the road below like sparks from a welder.

In the middle of that hungry, slavering madness, a smile spread slowly across Patrick's face.

***

"What the hell is this?" Alice asked.

"This," Patrick said happily, patting a pair of black rubber handlebars, "is an e-scooter."

Alice blinked. "A what?"

"An e-scooter! You stand on it and it scoots you! Electronically. And not only are *these* little babies outfitted with solar," he added fondly, admiring the beat-up Lime scooter, "but if that mangled NFC receiver is any indication, they're also wonderfully jailbroken." He pressed down on the throttle and pushed. The Lime scooter hummed to life.

"I don't understand anything you just said," Babs sighed.

Alice frowned. "They're green," she said.

"*Lime* green!" Patrick beamed. "Get it?"

Alice shook her head in annoyance. "Just begging for someone to notice you and pick you off."

"Lucky for us it's nighttime," Patrick agreed. "Hop on!"

The roar of the dusters on the overpass was deafening. They were still falling, and most were breaking their bones badly enough to render themselves immobile, but a handful of them were pulling themselves out from the wreckage and stalking toward them on shaky limbs. Some of the runners were sprinting off to the west, and sooner or later they'd come to an embankment they use to escape the highway and double back. Between the groaning and the snarling and the cracking of bones, it was no wonder that Patrick didn't hear Ben the first few times he spoke up.

"Patrick," he said again, tugging at Patrick's leg this time. Patrick whirled around and looked down at Ben, who was sitting on the curb and listing forward, as if he might tumble head-first into the gutter.

"Oh, Ben! I almost forgot about you in my excitement about ecologically responsible pedestrian transit." He crouched down and laid his hand on Ben's wet, sticky back. "You okay?"

Ben shook his head. He leaned back, exposing his belly to the sky. A dark green stain the size of a grapefruit soaked through his shirt.

Patrick's heart froze and cracked. "Oh no," he whispered.

He lifted up the hem of Ben's shirt. The gaping wound beneath his ribcage was mottled with blood, pus, and a dark green fluid. The crater went down so deep, Patrick could see a sliver of ivory that was the edge of Ben's ribcage. The skin had broken and folded outward like a sunflower. It looked as if a small bomb had gone off in Ben's gut. Whatever properties of the Monkey dust that hardened the veins and clogged the organs seemed to have dammed the wound and eased the loss of blood. The hole just *existed*, open and hollow like a mine drilled deep into Ben's core.

"Patrick…" he said again. His eyes rolled up to meet his friend's. The whites around his iris were now fully jaundiced and green. His eyelids slowly sank down.

Patrick grabbed Ben's face. "No!" he shouted. He gave Ben's head a firm shake. "Wake up! Wake *up!* Goddammit, Benny Boy, not like this! Not here, not so close! *Wake up!"*

Ben didn't respond. His chest rose and fell slowly. And then it stopped. It didn't rise again.

Patrick's sobs shook the earth. He cradled Ben to his chest and rocked him back and forth, bellowing his tears and screaming with all the force of his heart.

Alice elbowed Patrick away. He pushed back against her, reaching out for Ben, but she planted a boot on his ribcage and gently but firmly pushed him away. Patrick wailed as his wet, slimy hands slipped from Ben's form. He fell back onto the sidewalk, his chest heaving, his world breaking. Alice laid Ben down and tilted up his chin. She breathed into his mouth and then pushed the heels of her hands down on his diaphragm. It took three tries before Ben coughed back to life, his breath wet, sucking, and shallow. But it was breath.

"Ben! Jesus!" Patrick sobbed, scrambling over. He watched as Ben's chest rose and fell once more. This time, he was making a habit of it.

"Holy fuck," Patrick wheezed, wiping away tears and gasping for air, "I cannot handle this."

"No kidding," Alice replied dryly. She caught his eyes and held them with her own. "We have to go."

Patrick nodded. "We're out of time." Alice helped him to his feet. Lex hurried over and picked up Ben like a sack of flour and threw him over his shoulder. He stepped onto a scooter, Ben's feet dangling over the handlebars. Alice hopped onto a second scooter, and Babs climbed on behind her, wrapping her good arm around Alice's waist and holding on tight. Patrick mounted the third scooter, and without another word, they were off, rolling down the sidewalk of Long Beach Boulevard, making one last desperate push into the dying night.

60.

The sky was pale with pre-dawn light when they finally reached the Queen Mary. The horizon was nothing but overgrown palms and sickly fog, and Patrick's stomach began tying itself into knots, and a voice in his head wouldn't stop whispering, *You're not even close, Ben is going to die.* But then, suddenly, there they were, three huge cylinders rising up behind the trees, and Ben's shoulders were still rising and falling with breath, and relief broke over Patrick like sunshine. They were going to make it.

They sped around a convention center and arced past an old aquarium, which itself looked like the long-abandoned shell of an angry elder god that had crawled up from the ocean to swallow the world whole. As they rounded the aquarium, the HMS Queen Mary slid fully into view, its towering black hull and bright white cabins gleaming in the early light.

They raced across the bridge and dumped their scooters at the pier. The ship was huge and dark and silent. "Doesn't *look* like a lab," Babs said.

"Positivity, Babs," Patrick said, running his eyes over the Queen Mary, scanning for signs of life. "We need positivity right now."

There were three gangways connecting the ship to the pier, and they had stopped their scooters at the base of the nearest one. The door on the ship side was closed up tight. Seams of rust streaked the hull. The whole ship looked like it hadn't been boarded in years. "Please," Patrick whispered. "Please, please, please."

He led them across the gangway and reached for the handle of the door.

"Stop there." The voice came from the ship deck above. A man appeared at the rail, pointing a paintball gun at Patrick's chest. Judging by the metallic clacking that emanated from the hopper, the gun had been modified to fire steel ball bearings. Patrick froze. "Wherever you think you are," the man continued, "you're not. Turn yourselves around and go back the way you came."

Patrick's spine tensed. He glanced up, his eyes tracking over the length of the ship. The man with the warning wasn't the only sentry standing watch. Figures in black had appeared every ten or fifteen feet, all of them with similarly modified guns pointing at Patrick and his friends.

"We're here to see Dr. Gustheed," Patrick said loudly enough to be heard all the way down the ship. "We don't want any trouble. We just need to see the doctor."

"Back off," the man above them warned again. "Leave now or I put you down."

Patrick raised his hands high in the air, showing them that he held no weapons. "We can't do that," he said. "We've got a dying man. He won't make it to sunrise."

"Lots of people don't. This is your final warning."

Patrick gritted his teeth. Babs had started easing her way back toward the pier. Alice was holding firm, but Lex glanced nervously at Patrick, his eyes huge and wet with worry. "I'm friends with Regina Philbin," Patrick said, his voice tight with desperation now. "Regina said—" *CRACK!* The gun went off. A half-inch steel ball hit the gangway two inches in front of Patrick's feet, blasting a hole through the wood. Patrick jolted, but he stood his ground. His arms trembled, but he kept his hands raised high. "Regina said Dr. Gustheed had a cure for Monkey fever, we can't leave without—"

CRACK!

Patrick's whole body clenched. His luck, if that was what it could be called, had finally run out.

"Put your guns down, you G.I. Momos," a woman's voice sneered from above. Patrick opened his eyes. Dr. Regina Philbin stood on the deck of the ship, lowering the gun she'd just fired into the air. "Can't you see they need help?"

The man standing above them growled, but he reluctantly lowered his gun. The other sentries followed his lead. One by one, they lowered their guns, slipped away, and disappeared from the rail.

Philbin leaned out over the railing. "Patrick! Is that you?"

Patrick patted his crotch to see if it was wet. "Hey, Reeg," he said weakly.

"What the heck are you doing here?" she chirped brightly. Then she noticed the limp body slung over Lex's shoulder, and her face dropped. "Oh. Never mind."

"Green fever," Patrick said, his voice cracking. "Final stage."

Philbin frowned. "Is that—is that your Ben?" Patrick nodded. "Oh, wow. Bring him in." She leaned out over the railing and slapped her hand against the steel hull three times. "Open up!" she shouted down at the door. Someone inside the ship threw back a series of bolts and turned the handle. The door fell open and a warm flood of electric light spilled out onto the gangway. "Show him to the table," Regina called down to the guard at the door. "And get Susannah! I'll meet you down there."

The armed woman at the door beckoned them in. Patrick went first, stepping cautiously through into the ship. Lex came after, ducking low and squeezing through the small door, careful not to bump Ben's body against the frame. Alice and Babs hurried in after them, and then the guard closed and locked the door.

They found themselves in a brightly-lit corridor with cream-colored walls and burgundy carpet. The electric sconces along the wall bathed the hallway in steady orange-yellow light, the first fully functioning electricity Patrick had seen in years.

The guard pushed through them and muttered a gruff, "Follow me." She marched quickly down the hall, and the gang had to hurry to keep pace.

The hallway was so narrow that they had to walk single file. Patrick kept throwing nervous glances back at Ben, who no longer sounded like he was breathing. The wet, sucking gasp from his lungs that had been ever-present now drew down to a whisper of breath through a pinhole. As unsettling as the wheezing had been, the silence was infinitely worse. Out in the open air, Patrick hadn't noticed the stench of fetid skin and death that pulsed from Ben's failing body like waves in the ocean, but here, in the close confines of the ship, the smell was unimaginable. It stung his eyes and singed the hairs in his nostrils, and he fought back the urge to gag.

Their gracious host sighed audibly as she engaged in the indignity of leading them around a corner. They twisted through the labyrinthine hallways until they came to a swinging door with a round window set into its center. The guard pushed through and led them into a large room with tile floors and bare white walls. A trio of flush mount ceiling fixtures washed the room in brilliant white light. A glass-front cabinet stood against one wall, boxes of latex gloves and alcohol wipes visible through the doors. A medium-height wine fridge was plugged into the opposite corner; it had been retrofitted with flat shelves that held an army of small vials. In the center of the room rested a tall surgical cot, fitted with what appeared to be fairly clean sheets, minus a few stains in the center that Patrick found it best not to spend too much time considering. A vital signs monitor stood behind the bed, and in front of that sat a squat rolling tray table, its contents covered with a blue towel.

Patrick couldn't hide his astonishment at the sheer otherworldliness of the room. He let out an impressed whistle. He hadn't seen anything close to this room, in terms of overall organization and illumination, since the Before Times. He sure as hell hadn't expected to find it on a boat.

The guard motioned impatiently at the bed, and Patrick helped Lex gently lower Ben onto his back. The sight of him laid out under the lights like this chased Patrick's breath back into his lungs. The darkness of the world had obscured the worst truths about Ben's state. He had been soggy and pale, mottled with green, yes, but here beneath the lights, he was a living dead thing with dark, closed, sunken hollows for eyes and cracked, bleeding lips. His skin was the pale green of an unripe apple, but he was so chalky from the sheen of sickness and fever that it was as if he had rubbed pistachio flour all over his skin. The hole in his gut was a horror; the wound was the sort of thing that might result from sewing a small, lit bomb into his belly just to watch it blow. The skin that had erupted outward was dry and crusted with green flakes, and deeper inside, nudging up against the white of his ribs was red, wet, angry tissue that pulsed slowly, struggling desperately to retain its life. There was blood too, but it had pooled at the bottom of the gaping well; the Monkey dust was doing its work and sealing the blood vessels closed.

"What seems to be the trouble?" The door slammed open, and in strode a statuesque woman with copper-colored hair and the most impressive set of cheekbones Patrick had ever seen. She looked like a Roman goddess come to Earth, and she carried herself like one, too. Her hair was stretched back into an obscenely tight ponytail. She wore dark pants and a black turtleneck beneath a long, white lab coat mottled with faded pink stains. She pulled a pair of latex gloves from her coat pocket and snapped them over her long, steely fingers. She walked directly up to the gurney and smiled down at Ben. "I'm kidding, of course. His spleen exploded."

Patrick was off his axis. He looked up at the woman, who was a good two inches taller than he was, and he blinked. "Exploded?" he asked.

"Burst. Ruptured. Popped." She pointed down at the hole in Ben's gut. "Boom." She turned and waved everyone away, herding them toward the door. "Out. I need to work."

The Baby Caps stumbled backward, caught off guard by the level of self-assured command that the woman exuded. They bumbled toward the door and let themselves be swept out by the guard with the gun, but Patrick dug in his heels and refused to move. "I'm not going anywhere," he said.

The woman in the lab coat arched an eyebrow. "Are you family?" Patrick nodded. "No, you're not," she decided.

Patrick glowered. "Not blood. But family."

The woman considered this. "Don't get in the way, all right?"

"Dr. Gustheed, I presume?" Patrick said, finally finding his footing.

"Pronunciation needs work, but you're approximately correct," she said. She grabbed a pair of surgical scissors from the cabinet and used them to slice Ben's t-shirt in half. It was so thin and ratty from wear that it practically fell away on its own as soon as the scissors got close. Dr. Gustheed peeled back the flimsy layers of cotton and exposed Ben's sunken chest and ruined belly. She turned and fiddled with the vital signs monitor before connecting a series of wires to Ben's chest. They immediately picked up his heartbeat, and the monitor made short blips every few seconds.

BEEP...

BEEP...

BEEP...

The beats were far too spaced out to be considered "normal." Patrick was no doctor, but even he knew his friend was hanging by a thread, dangling over the dark abyss.

Gustheed situated a few other clips and pads on Ben's clammy body, then she bent over the gaping wound in his gut. She produced a small pen light from her pocket and shined it inside the hole. "Lovely!" she declared.

"Lovely? He's dying," Patrick countered, narrowing his eyes. He suddenly understood why Regina had crossed the country for her. They were out of their minds in the same vicious way.

And so are you, a voice gnawed its way into his head. He stuffed it down and tried to focus.

"Yes, clearly he is dying," Gustheed replied. She clicked off her light. "The good news is, you can live without your spleen. The bad news is, you can still die if you *don't* have it. All in all, I'd call this wound a draw."

"He's dying from the Fever," Patrick said.

Susannah turned to him and sighed. "Your name's Patrick, right? Listen, Patrick. I'm a doctor. I'm quite a good doctor. As such, I was able to deduce immediately that your friend is dying from the Fever. My explaining this to you is causing us to waste time we don't really have. Are there any additional pearls of medical wisdom you'd like to impart?"

Patrick set his mouth into a hard line. "Regina said you were working on a cure. Do you have it?"

Susannah grinned. "It's quite extraordinary, isn't it? A monumental accomplishment. I'd win every award imaginable, if there were still honor committees, don't you think?" She reached for the tray table and whipped back the blue towel dramatically. A syringe filled with pink fluid gleamed in the brilliant light.

"Haven't seen that color yet," Patrick muttered.

"What's that?"

"Nothing." He glanced down at Ben. His chest wasn't moving. A cold shade of blue had begun creeping into his cheeks. Patrick fell forward and cupped one hand around Ben's cheek. "Ben? Ben!" he cried, panicked. He gave the cold, clammy shoulders a shake. "Do not die on me, goddammit, not after all this." Patrick looked up at Susannah, his eyes frantic. "He's not breathing!"

"Oh, yes, that happens," Susannah agreed. She casually placed one hand on Ben's chest and gave it a good, solid push. Ben's back arched and he gasped to life, ragged and choking and wet.

"Can you save him or not?!" Patrick demanded.

"Yes, yes, calm down," Susannah sighed.

The door swung open again, and this time Regina Philbin popped her head in. "Don't jostle him, Suze. He's fragile."

"So I see."

"I'm not fragile!" Patrick cried. "The only family I have left is on death's literal fucking doorstep after three bullshit, breakneck, blood-soaked days on the Slaughterhouse Run where those kids out there got beat to shit and we lost two good men who didn't deserve to die, and you're making jokes and telling me to calm down while he has a hole the size of a baseball in his gut, his stomach is swollen to burst, and he's already stopped breathing twice! I will *calm down* when you stop acting like a fucking Muppet and decide to finally, at *so* long last, save Ben's goddamn life!"

The room was still except for the intermittent beep of Ben's weakening vitals. Gustheed looked down at Patrick with wide, shocked eyes. She hadn't been spoken to like that in years. Maybe ever. Her surprise turned to gall, and her eyelids narrowed into slits. She bared her teeth at him, and without looking away, she reached out with her right hand, plucked the syringe from the table, pushed out the air, and jammed the needle into Ben's arm...all without looking away, all without blinking. She emptied the pink formula into his flesh, then she yanked the needle out and slammed the syringe down on the tray. "Fine. Happy?" she glowered.

Patrick broke away from her stare and turned his full attention on Ben. "How long does it take?" he asked, his voice cracking.

"The change begins immediately," Gustheed said, a smug smirk splitting her face. "The active components of the Monkey dust in your friend's system, to put it in words you will understand, are currently being 'turned off.' His skin will regain its color in about one minute. He'll be fully conscious in two. His vital organs have already begun to drain, and his heartbeat should pick up to normal right about…" She checked her watch which, unlike Patrick's, still kept perfect time. With her other hand, she pointed at the monitor. "Now."

Ben's heartbeat flatlined.

Patrick's spine stiffened. "What is that? Why is that happening?"

"Just…hold on," Gustheed said, but the look on her face had gone from smug to confused in an instant. Her mask had slipped away, and there was a spark of panic in her eyes. "Give it a second."

The steady squeal from the monitor pierced the room, echoing off the walls, filling Patrick's brain with its high-pitched whine. "Why did his heart stop?! Fix it!"

"Give me a minute," Gustheed said, placing a hand on Ben's chest. He wasn't breathing. His pulse was at zero. His heart wasn't beating. He was dead.

"Do something!" Patrick cried.

Regina stood in the doorway, her fingers now gripping the edge of the door so tightly that her knuckles were as white as the bright, glaring lights overhead. "Susannah…"

"Give me a minute!" Gustheed said again.

"This hasn't happened before," Regina said, biting her lip.

"*Just give me a minute!*" Gustheed screamed. She planted both palms on Ben's chest and began to pump his heart. She scooted around the bed, knocking over the tray table. She cursed and kicked the fallen metal thing away. She bent down and put her mouth on Ben's and blew air into his lungs. She went back to work on his heart, pulsing down on his chest. The monitor continued to squeal. "Goddammit!"

"Ben!" Patrick cried, tears spilling down his cheek. "No, no, no, no, Ben!" He took Ben's face between his hands and gently patted his cheeks, trying to coax him out of whatever blackness he'd fallen into. "Come back, come back. Please. Ben. God, no. Ben! Ben!" He was shrieking now, his tears so thick he couldn't see. Snot flowed out of his nose, mucous clogged his throat. "Ben! Goddammit, Ben, wake up!" He slapped Ben's cheeks harder. They were cold and clammy.

"Move!" Gustheed shouted. She flung Patrick's hands out of the way and breathed into Ben's mouth again.

"Susannah," Regina said from the edge of the room, her voice shaky.

"Not now!" Gustheed screeched. She hammered Ben's chest with her fist. "Come on, goddammit," she growled.

"Susannah," Regina tried again.

"Oh God, Ben…" Patrick whispered through his sobs. He cradled his dead friend's head in his arms and rocked with him there, holding him close, pressing Ben's cheek to his heart. "No…" was all he could muster as thick sobs wracked his chest and burst out through his throat in blubbering, gut-wrenching wails.

"Susannah!" Regina shouted over the sounds of the screams and the sobs.

"What?!" Gustheed shouted, throwing up her hands and glaring fire down at Ben's corpse.

"Move!" Regina elbowed past Gustheed, putting her shoulder into the taller woman's ribcage. Surprised, Gustheed backed away, nearly tripping over the fallen tray table. Regina stepped up and uncapped the syringe she had grabbed from the cabinet across the room. She flicked the barrel, put her thumb on the plunger, lifted her arm above her head, and drove the needle down into Ben's chest as hard as she could.

Breath exploded from Ben's chest. His eyes flew open, and his whole body spasmed. The heartbeat monitor went silent.

Dumbfounded, Patrick stared at the small green dot on the monitor screen.

BEEP…

BEEP…

BEEP…BEEP…BEEP… The green dot jumped to life, marking out a steady, healthy heartbeat that didn't stutter or slow.

"Ben!" Patrick cried, his shoulders heaving with sobs, this time tears of relief. He squeezed Ben's poor head harder and planted a kiss on his green, slimy forehead.

"Don't like that," Ben rasped, trying to squirm away. Patrick laughed and relaxed his grip, but he could not and would not let go.

Gustheed stared at her partner in amazement. "Regina…?"

Regina held up the empty syringe between two fingers like it was a cigarette from which she'd just taken a *very* satisfactory drag. "Adrenaline," she explained, her whole face positively beaming. "Duh."

Gustheed exhaled. Her coppery hair had come loose from its tie and hung in flustered ringlets around her flushed cheeks. She pushed the flyaway strands out of her eyes and stumbled her way out of the wreckage of the tray table. "I'd have thought of it eventually," she decided, squeezing Regina's shoulder as she passed. She planted a kiss on the top of the woman's head. "Please never say 'duh' again." She ambled like a sleepwalker to the other side of the room and pushed her way out through the door.

Regina smirked as she watched her go. "Not every day you get to upstage the great Susannah Gustheed," she teased, though she said it quietly, out of her partner's earshot. Regina turned to share some self-congratulatory plaudits with Patrick, but she stopped when she saw the two friends locked in their embrace. Or, to be more accurate, when she saw Ben locked in Patrick's unrelenting grip.

"Get off me, you gross weirdo," Ben said, screwing up his face in disgust. But he didn't really sound like he meant it.

Tears of joy welled up in Regina's eyes. "Oh, I love a happy ending," she said quietly. She dabbed her eyes and backed away from the gurney, aiming to give the two friends space. When she got to the door, though, it flew open, knocking Regina off her feet with a yelp. Gustheed strode back into the room, her hairs all back in place, her jaw once again set and determined. "Forgot his spleen exploded! He still needs a *lot* of medical attention," she announced. She marched over to the cabinet and began pulling out gauze pads and towels. "His arteries are going to soften right up, and that hole's going to start gushing blood any sec—ope, there it goes!"

She rushed over and began the long work of stemming the flow of blood. More people hurried into the room, pulling on face masks and dousing their hands in sanitizer. Regina picked herself up from the floor and gently put her arm around Patrick. "Come with me," she said, patting his shoulder. "Let Susannah work. She's an extraordinary surgeon." She turned Patrick around, and he reluctantly let himself be led out of the room. He cast a last look back at Ben, whose face was screwed up in pain—a difficult thing to see, but one that, Patrick assumed, was a very, very good sign.

"It's hard, I know. But let's go find your friends, yeah? We'll get you all settled, you can stay as long as you want," Regina said, leading him out the door. "You've made it out of the Slaughterhouse, Patrick. Ben is going to be fine."

For the first time in a long time, Patrick sighed and felt real, genuine relief.

61.

Three hard knocks, two soft knocks, one long knock, three short knocks, two and a quarter rapid-fire knocks, one flat palm slap, four knuckle taps, two palm slaps, seven knuckle taps, one long knock—

"Wait. Shit," Ben head Patrick curse from the other side of the door.

Three hard knocks, two soft knocks, one long knock, three short knocks, two and a quarter rapid-fire knocks, one flat palm slap, four knuckle taps—

"Dammit!" The door rattled in its jamb when Patrick punched it. "Can I just come in?!"

"No, that's not the password," Ben called out from his bed.

"Why are we even *using* a password, this whole ship is protected by more than twenty command-bros with semi-automatic ball bearing weapons. You know for a *fact* that the only people on this ship are people who *don't* want to kill you!"

"I've seen *Under Siege 2*," Ben insisted. "I know people can still get on heavily guarded ships."

"If Steven Segal came here to kill you, I'd let him!" Patrick cried. He hit the door again, for dramatic emphasis. "Unfortunately for us all, I'm pretty sure he died on M-Day."

"It's not *that* unfortunate," Ben pointed out.

"Well, no, he was a real sex monster, I'm glad he's gone."

"We're all glad he's gone," Ben said, "but you're stalling. The *real* Patrick would have remembered the Knock Code."

"Oh, for—" Patrick swore. Then, grumbling to himself, he added, "I don't know why we're even having this conversation, I have the stupid key to this door…"

There was a fumbling at the lock while Patrick worked the key. He finally pushed the door open hard enough that it slammed against the wall. "Good morning!"

"Oh, it's you," Ben said, relieved.

Patrick rubbed his forehead with the thumb and forefinger of his left hand. "I swear to God, I should have thrown you to the alligators," he said.

"You can't be too careful."

"Do you make Gustheed do the Knock Code?"

"Of course not," Ben rolled his eyes, "she's my doctor; she would never hurt me. She took an oath."

"And you think I would hurt you," Patrick said, narrowing his eyes.

"You haven't taken an oath saying you wouldn't," Ben pointed out. "And based on the way your eyebrow is twitching right now, yes, I do think it's possible you might wish me some harm."

"Oh, buddy, you have no idea." Patrick crossed the room and slid open the curtain that hung over the cabin's lone window. The late-morning glare made Ben squirm back under his blanket. "Don't hide from the day!" Patrick called, suddenly buoyant despite the fact that every bit of the sky was hidden by a particularly thick green fog. "Don't you know what that is out there?"

"An uncaring ocean filling a vast canyon of darkness that would just as soon feed you to the sharp-toothed alien horrors in its depths as kill you with the slow death of hypothermia in June?"

"Today is not the day for your weird and gloomy opinions about the ocean," Patrick reminded him. "In fact, don't even think about the ocean. I'm not talking about the ocean. I'm talking about the great, wide world!"

"All I can see is the ocean," Ben pointed out. "And Monkey fog."

Patrick waved his hands through the air, clearing the gloom away. "Okay, okay, listen, pretend your room is on the *other* side of the boat and you just looked out the window and saw Long Beach. Okay?"

"Los Angeles is similarly soul-sucking," Ben pointed out.

"Okay, look, Jesus, what I'm saying is, out there is the *world*! Today's the day you get to go experience it!"

"I have experienced it," Ben sighed. "It's not very good anymore."

"But it's better today than it was yesterday!" Patrick beamed. "Because you get to go into it for the first time in three months!"

Ben winced. "It's really been three months?"

"To the day." Patrick plopped down on the edge of the bed. Ben flinched out of habit, but his gut no longer seared with pain when he was jostled. He hadn't felt that particular discomfort for a couple weeks now. By all accounts, his spleen explosion was healing nicely. Gustheed had explained that he'd be at much higher risk of "incredibly messy death," as she put it, from infections now, but otherwise he'd be normal and fine. And the Green Fever symptoms had all vanished by the third day after the injection. He felt stiff and weak from all the bed rest, but otherwise, Ben hadn't actually felt this good in years.

"Doc says we can let you out today," Patrick continued. "You are confined to short, depressing walks through the Queen Mary halls no longer! Today is an *outdoor* recess day!"

"Good," Ben said. "They keep taking me past the room with the old empty pool, and I swear to God there are kids laughing in there."

"Wrong," Patrick said, shaking his head. "Rest assured, there are no wee ones on the ship!"

"Yeah, I know, which is exactly the problem," Ben said.

A look of sudden realization dawned across Patrick's face. "Oh, you think it's haunted! That is so adorable."

"I know what I heard," Ben grumped, crossing his arms.

"I'm sure you do," Patrick cooed as he ruffled Ben's non-existent hair. "Look, the only ghosts on this ship are you and me. We've been wandering the earth like dying dead men, and for extremely good reason. But I for one am ready to rejoin the living." He reached out his hand. "What do you say, you old spook? Wanna go feel the sunshine of life?"

Ben frowned at Patrick's outstretched hand. "Only if you stop talking like that," he said. He slapped his hand inside of Patrick's, and together they hauled Ben up to a standing position. Ben motioned at the cane Regina had found for him in the wreckage of a nearby Rite Aid. Patrick fetched it for him, and they headed slowly toward the cabin door.

"You know this thing has a peephole," Patrick said, tapping the small glass circle as they passed. "You *could* just get off your happy ass and look."

"Someone might hide off to the side," Ben said, shaking his head. "The Knock Code is safer."

They eased their way down the hall, back the way they'd first come, all those weeks earlier. They nodded familiarly to members of the Queen Mary's crew as they passed. They hadn't gotten particularly close with any of them over the last three months, but they were all friendly enough. As far as they could tell, there were three types of lodgers at the RMS Queen Mary. First, there were the Docs, led by Gustheed herself, of course. There were seven medical professionals on board, not counting Gustheed, and they weren't all really doctors; only two of them were, in fact. Three of them were nurses, and the last two were physician's assistants. And even though Philbin wasn't a medical doctor, they counted her as one of the Docs anyway. For the most part, the Docs kept pretty busy tending to the care of the second type of guest, the Injured Masses. These were sick or injured people who either found their way to the ship or were found by people *from* the ship. There were about three dozen IMs on the ship at any given time. Patrick, Ben, and the Baby Caps were counted in that number, which made Patrick bristle a bit, since he was not injured, nor was he one of the masses; he was a genuine acquaintance of Dr. Regina Philbin, which he felt earned him more of a Doc role. But when he mentioned this to Philbin one morning at breakfast, she had laughed so hard she choked on her powdered eggs and probably would have died with Patrick looking on in horror if not for the quick actions of one of the *actual* Docs, so he hadn't brought it up again. Then, of course, there were the Guards, a couple dozen men and women who took themselves way too seriously and all looked like extras from the *Predator* franchise.

All in all, the Queen Mary wasn't exactly a who's who of post-apocalyptic social butterflies. Patrick was glad that Ben was back on his feet.

"How are the Baby Caps?" Ben asked. He asked this question probably twice a day.

"Thriving, Benny Boy. They are absolutely thriving," Patrick assured him. "Babs is finally out of her cast, and I think Lex's head has just about stopped spinning from all the concussions! I think they're out fishing, we'll go find them. Maybe push Alice in the ocean. Like for a joke."

"The only thing scarier than the ocean is Alice," Ben said with a shudder. "I want no part of this plan."

"I'm telling her it was all your idea," Patrick beamed.

They reached the door. Patrick said, "Hi, Jessica!" to the Guard keeping watch. She ignored him and made him open the door himself. "This is part of our fun routine," Patrick explained. "Really, Jessica and I get along so well. We're thinking about getting a canasta game going."

"I would rather strip my own skin off with a steak knife than spend one minute of my leisure time with you," the guard said seriously.

Patrick winked and shook his head playfully at Ben. "Classic Jessica. She's joking."

"I'm not," the guard replied.

"Is her name even Jessica?" Ben whispered. He had caught most of the guards' names from conversations with Gustheed and Philbin, and he didn't remember there being a Jessica.

"I don't know, she won't tell me," Patrick said happily. They scooted out onto the gangway. "See you soon!" Patrick called back to the guard. She slammed the door shut before he could finish the sentence. "She's so nice once you get to know her."

"I'm not sure *she's* the problem here," Ben pointed out.

They slowly made their way to the dock. The Baby Caps weren't down at the end in their usual fishing spot after all. Patrick frowned. "That's weird," he said quietly. Then he shrugged. "Well, they're out here somewhere." They turned and made their way back toward land, Ben leaning heavily on his cane and already panting from the exertion.

"I've never felt so goddamn old," he complained, wiping sweat from his furrowed brow.

"You've never *been* so goddamn old," Patrick reminded him. "So that all lines up."

The world was quiet as they walked. The only sounds were the thump of Ben's cane on the dock and the slow creak of the ropes that moored the ship to the shore. Mornings were always the worst for the Monkey fog, and this morning was particularly bad. The greenish haze seemed to hang in the air, and Patrick couldn't help but thinking they were more swimming than walking as they pushed their way toward the beach. Halfway down the dock, they couldn't see either end, and now they'd lost sight of the gangway, too. There was nothing before them and nothing behind them. Just a dock beneath their feet and a haunted ship lost to the fog.

Not haunted, Patrick reminded himself. But the cold prickles of condensation on his shoulder blades felt like spindly fingers crawling up his back, and his heart suddenly started to quicken its pace. There was something off about the world, something suddenly uncomfortable and wrong. The quiet was too quiet; the fog drowned out the world like a heavy curtain, it was too quiet, and Patrick suddenly felt claustrophobic. Beads of sweat mixed with the dots of condensation on his forehead. It was difficult to breathe. His scalp itched.

"Are you feeling that?" Ben asked. Patrick looked at his friend. Ben's eyes were wide, and his arms were covered in goosebumps.

A wave of relief crashed over Patrick's shoulders. "So it's not just me," he exhaled. "Something's not right. Right? Something's wrong."

Ben peered around at the fog. "Call for the Baby Caps," he said. There was a tightness to his words, a pitch in his voice, *something* that Patrick recognized intimately as fear.

Patrick nodded. Ben's diaphragm was too weak to penetrate the gauzy walls around them. He held his hands to his mouth and shouted, "Babs! Alice? You out there?"

The fog seemed to swallow his words. They waited and listened.

"Patrick," came a voice dripping with honey. It was the voice of a panther that had just cornered a rabbit. It cut through the curtain of clouds and sliced into his chest. "After all this time, is that finally you?"

Ben turned to look at Patrick, whose face had flushed fully white. What blood ran through him ran cold. Patrick's hands began to shake.

"Patrick?" Ben asked. "Who is that?"

Patrick heard the question like he was listening through a pool of water. It floated toward him, into him, caught up in the same spinning whorls as the rest of the world. The dock turned beneath his feet, the clouds threatening to swallow him whole. His stomach was a frozen cave; icicles cracked and broke in his chest. Somewhere beyond him, outside the cold and spinning world, the trade winds blew, their timing impeccable. They whipped through the fog, swirling it away, brushing it off the dock and pushing it into the coast. A line of silhouettes emerged through the yellow-green gloom. Patrick recognized the shapes of the three Baby Caps. Alice lay on the ground, quiet and still, a dark, wet puddle pooling around her head. Lex had been forced to his knees, the thick end of a baseball bat held against his cheekbone, his shoulders quivering from the force of his sobs. Only Babs was still on her feet, her wrists held behind her, a hunting knife pressed to her throat. Behind the Baby Caps stood the shapes of six men, spread out in a line across the dock.

"Patrick," Ben whispered again, digging his nails into his friend's arm. "Who is that?"

The ghosts of Patrick's past flickered into his vision.

Annie. Izzy. Carla.

The dark ones are coming.

The dark ones are here.

"It's him, Ben," Patrick whispered. "He found me."

Roman Marwood and his blood-hungry Red Caps had tracked them to the end of the world.

ACKNOWLEDGEMENTS

Steven Luna did what he always does, and he took this manuscript and with a handful of incredibly deft suggestions took it from a good story to a great story. Thank you, Luna, for consistently being the best editor a guy could ask for.

I also owe a huge debt of gratitude to Dave Bloom, who read an early version of this manuscript and then traveled across several states so we could sit around a campfire and he could tell me how to make the story shine. Dave is an incredibly talented storyteller, and I'm so grateful he has taken this series under his wing.

And thank you to Erin for always offering incredible support of my unhinged need to squirrel myself away and write stories about people hitting each other with hammers. I couldn't carve out the time or the space without your help and sacrifice, and I am grateful for you forever.

ABOUT THE AUTHOR

photo by Emily Rose Studios

Clayton Smith is an award-winning writer who once erroneously referred to himself as "a national treasure." He is the author of several novels, short story collections, and plays, and his short fiction has been featured in national literary journals, including Canyon Voices and Write City Magazine.

He is also rather tall.

Find him online at www.StateOfClayton.com and on social media as @Claytonsaurus.

Made in the USA
Columbia, SC
08 July 2025

60414121R00181